Born and raised on the Wirral Peninsula in England, **Charlotte Hawkes** is mum to two intrepid boys who love her to play building block games with them, and who object loudly to the amount of time she spends on the computer. When she isn't writing—or building with blocks—she is company director for a small Anglo/French construction firm. Charlotte loves to hear from readers, and you can contact her at her website: charlotte-hawkes.com.

Married to the man she met at eighteen, **Susanne Hampton** is the mother of two adult daughters, Orianthi and Tina. She has enjoyed a varied career path, but finally found her way to her favourite role of all: Medical Romance author. Susanne has always read romance novels and says, 'I love a happy-ever-after, so writing for Mills & Boon is a dream come true.'

Also by Charlotte Hawkes

Reunited on the Front Line miniseries

Second Chance with His Army Doc
Reawakened by Her Army Major

Royal Christmas at Seattle General collection

Falling for the Secret Prince by Alison Roberts
Neurosurgeon's Christmas to Remember by Traci Douglass
The Bodyguard's Christmas Proposal
The Princess's Christmas Baby by Louisa George

Also by Susanne Hampton

A Baby to Bind Them
A Mummy to Make Christmas
Twin Surprise for the Single Doc
White Christmas for the Single Mum
The Doctor's Cinderella
Mending the Single Dad's Heart

Discover more at millsandboon.co.uk.

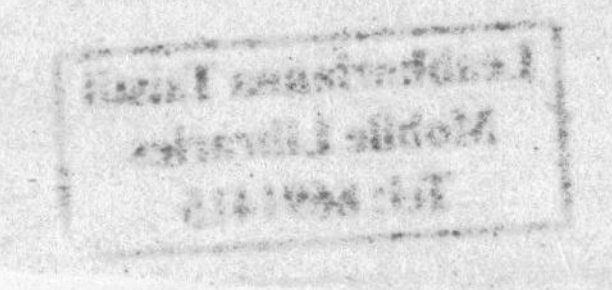

THE DOCTOR'S ONE NIGHT TO REMEMBER

CHARLOTTE HAWKES

REUNITED WITH HER SECRET PRINCE

SUSANNE HAMPTON

MILLS & BOON

First Published in Great Britain 2021
by Mills & Boon, an imprint of HarperCollins*Publishers*
1 London Bridge Street, London, SE1 9GF

ISBN: 978-0-263-29752-2

MIX
Paper from
responsible sources
FSC™ C007454

This book is produced from independently certified FSC™ paper
to ensure responsible forest management.
For more information visit www.harpercollins.co.uk/green.

Printed and bound in Spain
by CPI, Barcelona

THE DOCTOR'S ONE NIGHT TO REMEMBER

CHARLOTTE HAWKES

MILLS & BOON

To Helen.
For the walks, the giggles, and the odd jogs…
though our boat experiences were never quite like Isla's! xx

CHAPTER ONE

'WHICH ONE OF them is faking it, do you think?' Isla Sinclair wondered breezily, as she eyed the honeymooning couple frolicking together on the Chilean beach.

Her stepsister Leonora—former stepsister, if Isla was going to be strictly accurate—put down her summer cocktail and turned gracefully to look.

'Don't let what Brad-the-Cad did turn you into some hardened cynic, Isla.' Leo smiled softly. 'Maybe they're actually in love?'

'And you're such a hopeless romantic.' Isla grinned, making a conscious effort to thrust any unwelcome memories of her ex-fiancé out of her head. 'You know as well as I do that someone is always faking it. If they're really lucky, then they're enjoying a mutually advantageous marriage, like my mother and your father had.'

Or at least it had been mutually advantageous for a blissful five years, ending perfectly amicably thirteen years ago, when Isla and Leo had been nineteen.

Onwards and upwards. Certainly that was a lesson Isla had learned at the knee of her beautiful, charming mother who had bounced her, cooed to her and whispered to her just what had to be done in order to negotiate for her next, richer, even more well-connected husband.

Marianna Sinclair-Raleigh-Burton had always seen

marriage more like a business negotiation, with each party agreeing in advance what the other would bring to the table.

'I can just hear your mother now.' Leo shook her head affectionately. *'Why complicate things by pretending to be in love, girls? Far better to be up-front. That way, there are no nasty surprises.'*

'Ugh!' Isla mimicked one of her mother's comical, yet simultaneously elegant shudders. 'Perish the thought.'

Leo laughed, a tinkly kind of sound that Isla had always thought was the prettiest laugh she'd ever heard.

'You sound just like her, Isla.'

'I can live with that. Where is my mother anyway?'

'She said she was going to have a lie-down.' Leo pulled a wry face. 'But what are the chances she's found herself a new suitor?'

'Well, firstly, she's a new divorcee, *again.*' Isla ticked the points off on her fingers. 'Secondly, she insisted on coming out here and turning it into a holiday, even though I told her that I had come out early for some quiet, to get my head around my new role as ship's doctor in two days. And thirdly, she booked us into the most expensive hotel in this part of the region—possibly in the whole of Chile. So if she hasn't already eyed up a new husband for herself then I'd be surprised.'

'Better her looking for herself than trying to set one of us two up,' Leo groaned, though there was no rancour in her tone.

Both girls knew that, for all her faults, Marianna was the closest thing Leo had ever had to a mother, even all these years after their respective parents' divorce. And in Isla's eyes too, Marianna was the most loving, generous mother she thought a girl could ever have.

Still, that didn't stop her from rolling her eyes good-naturedly now. 'Quite. But I won't hold my breath.'

'Me neither.' Leo turned to eye the honeymoon couple again. 'Maybe they really are in love.'

'Maybe.'

With a sigh, Isla let her eyes drift back to them. They certainly looked like they were loving life.

It just wasn't the life that Isla had ever wanted for herself.

'Anyway, I fancy checking out a few little stores I saw on the walk down here.' Leo finished her drink and pushed it to the side. 'Do you want to come?'

Isla hesitated for a moment. 'No, actually, if you don't mind I think I'd like to go for a walk along the beach. Once I'm on board, it might be a while before I get a chance to set foot on land again.'

'Makes sense.' Leo slipped off the stool and hooked her summery purse over her head. 'See you back at the hotel?'

'Yeah, about an hour?'

'An hour.' Leo nodded, heading daintily out of the bar and, unsurprisingly, in the direction of the honeymooners.

Typically romantic Leo. Isla smiled to herself.

But she definitely wasn't here for love, or even for a holiday romance—the idea of either was enough to make her shudder—she was here for work. Better than that, she was here for the job of her life, the job she'd dreamed of doing ever since she'd been a kid—junior doctor on a cruise ship.

The *Jewel of Hestia.*

Perhaps not the incredible *Queen Cassiopeia*, the flagship of the Port-Star Cruise Line fleet that was anchored out at sea right now, but a good one all the same. One that would allow her to do the work she loved combined with travelling around the world.

What could be more perfect?

And if it also got her away from the humiliation of Bradley, and away from her mother's next shenanigans, then wasn't that a bonus?

Downing the last of her drink, Isla stood up and made herself smile. This wasn't about the past; this was about the future. Or, until her ship sailed into port in a couple of days' time, this was about living in the present and exploring as much as she could of what this part of Chile had to offer.

The sudden commotion behind her made Isla spin around to where an argument between two young men was going on in the next bar. Two six-foot, muscle-bound lads squaring—rather drunkenly—up to each other, both of whom might have looked at home in a boxing ring.

Clearly, the crowd seemed to think so. As much as they were entertained, they were evidently keeping their distance, not wanting to get caught in the middle.

That's my cue.

Weaving through the tables, the occupants of which were mostly focused on the fact that the argument was turning into a brawl, Isla made her way to the strip of walkway between the bars and the beach and turned in the opposite direction from the fight. And the loud crash that ensued.

It wasn't her business, and she didn't care. She kept her head down and picked up her pace, right up to the moment when a deafening crash split the air.

Isla's heart jolted and she whirled around despite herself—just in time to see a ship's officer vaulting over the barrier to the sand and racing to haul one of the drunken young men—still flailing and punching—off the one who was now lying unconscious on the ground, as though the lad weighed little more than a sack of potatoes.

With one word, the newcomer had the crowd flipping

from ghoulish spectators to concerned citizens, grouping around the injured party and checking him over, whilst the officer pinned the still-agitated second lad to a concrete pillar to stop him from reaching his quarry to rain down yet more punches.

The officer was at least as tall as the would-be boxer and, even though he wasn't as obviously bulked up, there was no doubt that he was strong and skilled enough to control the bigger man, apparently quietly and smoothly talking him down before pressing a couple of the other stronger locals into taking the lad further away until he calmed down completely. Then he pulled a walkie-talkie from his waist and issued more instructions into that.

It was mesmerising how smoothly and efficiently the man had seemed to take charge of a situation which could have escalated far too easily. Her heart jolted again, and she told herself it was nothing more than an adrenalin rush due to the situation. Or perhaps it was because it highlighted, so aptly, all of her ex's failings. Brad had liked to pretend that he was that kind of bark-a-command-and-everyone-jumps alpha male, but the truth was that he'd been more of a make-the-bullets-for-someone-else-to-fire kind of a man.

So what did it say about her that it had taken her so long to see the truth?

Enough! Isla chastised silently, shaking the guilt and shame from her thoughts. This was why she was here in Chile, waiting for the *Jewel of Hestia* to arrive. The ship's junior doctor wasn't just a new career; it was to be a new start.

Isla turned to leave, when suddenly she heard a series of shouts, mostly for emergency services, and then one shout which she couldn't ignore.

'Médico? Es alguien médico?'

Swinging back, her stomach lurching slightly, she surveyed the severity of the scene for a moment. Almost hoping someone else might step forward.

Nobody did.

'Soy médica,' she muttered at length, stumbled forward and pushed her way through the tight throng, her eyes taking in each detail as it came into focus.

Close up, she could now see that the man who had fallen had crashed through a glass-laden table and was now lying on his back on the ground, the table and shards of glass beneath him. Blood pooled somewhere around his lower back.

'You.' Isla pointed to some random gawking bystanders as she quickly and efficiently picked her way through the debris. 'Can you move the tables? *Mover las mesas?*'

She crouched down beside the casualty, but until the glass was swept away she didn't dare kneel.

'And you…a sweeping brush…*un cepillo para…*' her brain scrabbled for the words *'...para barrer los...fragmentos de vidrio.'*

She only paused long enough to see the bartender acknowledge her before she turned her focus to the patient. Not unconscious after all, but certainly groggy.

'Hello, can you tell me your name? *Cómo se llama?*'

He groaned and weakly tried to push her hand away, possibly hearing her but not processing her words. Another observation to file away for the ambulance crew.

'Okay—you're okay. I'm a doctor. *Soy médica.*'

A quick check of his pulse suggested an erratic beat, hardly surprising after a bar fight and then demolishing a glass table. But there were no shards on his front, which meant the blood had to be coming from an injury on his back.

'Someone has called for an ambulance? *Ambulancia?*'

'Sí, sí,' several people relayed at once, flowing into a

torrent of Chilean Spanish that Isla wasn't entirely sure she understood.

At least the barman had now swept away the worst of the broken glass and she could tend to the patient, although the guy was big and muscular and moving him was proving harder than she'd expected.

'Help me roll him onto his front,' she instructed anyone who was listening. *'Ayudar me...rodar...'*

'Leave him, please.'

Isla jerked her head up at the commanding voice, unprepared for the man who was bearing down on her. The cruise ship officer from before—as if her body hadn't already prickled in awareness. She told herself it was just the heat—the downdraught that his body created as he moved closer—and nothing more.

Her eyes seemed intent on drinking in every inch of him, not least the epaulettes on his shoulders. A senior officer, at that. A first officer—practically the Captain's right-hand man.

'I take it he's one of yours?' she bit out, furious with herself. 'Good—you can tell me his name?'

'He is one of mine,' First Officer McHotty growled. 'And he clearly needs a doctor.'

'I *am* a doctor.'

'Is that so?' He barely paused a fraction of a beat. 'What I mean is that we have our own doctors to deal with our crew.'

'Right, but they aren't here, are they?' Isla kept her eyes on the patient, her hands finding a good purchase. 'However, I *am* here, and he's bleeding out. So I suggest you help me roll him. And tell me his name. Oh, and what language does he speak?'

She sensed rather than saw the moment of hesitation as

McHotty took in the scene for himself, but she was having enough trouble focusing.

Impressive enough from a distance, up close he was also possibly the most breathtaking specimen of a male that Isla thought she'd ever seen, as galling as that was to admit. He wasn't classically handsome; that would have been too banal for the man. Instead there was an arresting quality about him, from the sharp, square jaw to the blade of a nose. His eyes were the richest, deepest caramel she'd ever seen, with a smokiness to match that raw masculine voice. And his body? Her brain refused to go there—she didn't even want to start *thinking* about his body.

It was unfortunate then that her brain didn't appear to be in control of anything right now. Despite all her silent cerebral protestations, her eyes slid—seemingly of their own volition—to the body crouched down beside her.

The powerful thighs brushing hers, and unwittingly sending little bolts of electricity through her. His pristine uniform clung like a lover to hewn muscle, from strong thighs, to contoured torso, to wide shoulders—no wonder he'd had little trouble besting the brawny would-be fighter.

If the world had stopped spinning, Isla wouldn't have been all that surprised, and yet the entire interaction took less than a couple of seconds. Nonetheless, it galled her beyond all measure that her mouth felt parched as her eyes drank it all in. As if she'd never seen a man before in her life.

Only, if she were to be honest, she'd certainly never seen a man like *this* before. Surely the hottest male specimen to have ever walked the planet? And, judging by the doe-eyed females in the crowd, she definitely wasn't the only one to think it.

Isla thrust the traitorous thought aside and forced her attention back to her unexpected patient.

'What language, please?' she repeated, as firmly as she could.

'His name is Philippe. He can speak English.'

'Okay, Philippe, I'm Isla, I'm a doctor, I'm here to help you. We're going to roll you onto your stomach, okay?' she warned, as McHotty crouched down beside her—so close that it made her feel altogether too many sensations in too many places, the heat seeping from his body into hers playing havoc with her insides.

Then he took the patient, rolling the muscle-bound hulk as if he weighed nothing.

The crowd collectively sucked in a breath.

A long, sharp shard of glass was protruding from the man's left buttock, blood surrounding the area. There was no doubt that it had severed his superior gluteal artery.

As her new, unwelcome companion grabbed his walkie and issued another irate command for the ship's doctor, Isla looked around for some material, eventually settling on her own chiffony scarf. Wrapping it around her hand, she prepared to grab the shard.

'What are you doing now?' McHotty demanded abruptly, dropping back next to her.

'I need to remove the glass.'

'If you remove it, won't he just bleed all the more? Or can you tourniquet it?'

'I can't tourniquet his backside.' She shook her head, drawing the shard out carefully. 'And yes, the artery will need occluding.'

'I suggest you would do better to leave it in place,' he continued in a voice which bore little resemblance to a suggestion and entirely too much like a command. 'Certainly until my ship's doctor arrives.'

This last comment was clearly a slight. She'd heard

them before; there was no reason this should rankle more just because it was coming from this stranger.

She forced herself to keep her tone even. 'Your ship's doctor is taking their time. Time this patient may not have.'

She could tell that he was caught between wanting to make another call and not leaving her alone with his crewman. What did it say about her that she got a tiny kick out of unsettling this man, who was clearly acutely accustomed to being the one in control?

'Not when he's unconscious and his heartbeat is so erratic. What if he suddenly needs CPR? Also, it's best to remove glass immediately to reduce the risk of infection, and to prevent any allergic response. I need to remove the foreign body and clean the wound.'

'Not just a patient. *My* crewman. You will wait.'

'I'm afraid not. You might be second in command on that floating city out at sea, but right here, right now, this is a medical emergency and *I'm* the only doctor on scene. So you need to wind your neck in; we're doing it my way.'

Had she really just told a man who was senior enough to be her boss to *wind his neck in?*

When was the last time anyone had got under her skin the way that he seemed to have done?

She could practically feel the castigation in his glower; it *zinged* through her.

'You misunderstand...' he growled, and a lesser woman might have quaked at the warning tone in his voice.

After Bradley, Isla had certainly had enough of being the *lesser woman.*

'There,' she cut in, holding aloft the long shard and smiling sweetly. 'All out.'

The giant of a man glanced down, and she could swear, just for a fraction of a moment, that he blanched. So fleeting that she thought she might have imagined it.

'He's still bleeding,' McHotty rasped. 'How are you going to stop that now?'

'Like this,' she said grimly, quickly cleaning up the wound and plugging it with her finger.

As though it was every day that she stared at the hottest man she'd ever seen in her life whilst her finger was plugging some other guy's arse cheek. Worse, she was almost sure she saw amusement flicker over his impossibly arresting features.

'See?' She glowered. 'Now where's that damned ambulance?'

Nikhil Dara listened as the doctor—*Isla*, she'd said her name was—wound up her handover to the emergency services, and instructed himself to concentrate on how efficiently she performed her job, rather than how particularly ravishing she was. It was surprisingly difficult—certainly for him.

He knew his reputation for being single-minded, and exacting—as well as several less polite terms his crew used, particularly when they were exhausted and he was making them run a scenario one more time to ensure that it was *right*. Rather than balk at such nicknames, however, he had always prided himself on them. Yet now, for the first time in memory, he found himself struggling to focus purely on the task in hand without letting his gaze slide to the arresting doctor.

As if being at sea meant he'd somehow been deprived of female company when the truth was that his life as First Officer on a cruise liner often entailed women—crew and passengers—offering themselves up to him daily on a silver platter. On one occasion, quite literally.

He never bit.

Certainly never on board and, if on shore, then never

with anyone he would see again. It was a measure of control on which he prided himself. Which made it all the more aggravating that he seemed to have to fight his own body to keep his distance from the young doctor, as he concentrated on instructing his recently arrived junior officer to accompany Philippe in the ambulance and then for said officer to keep him informed of the hospital's progress.

Helping the crew to close the doors, he watched the vehicle speed off and finally turned to the doctor and bobbed his head in acknowledgement.

'Thank you for your help. Philippe is fortunate that you were there.'

'No problem.' She shrugged, hauling out her phone for a moment and frowning as she read some message.

There was no reason on earth for him to wonder what it was that had irritated her. Or why he should notice quite how her blue eyes looked almost silvery-grey when she nodded back and swung away from him. Or how her golden-brown hair skimmed her shoulders from the ponytail high on the back of her head.

Ridiculously fanciful, he berated himself, with a rough shake of his head. As if he could dislodge the ball of pressure that had been squatting on his brain for days, pressing up against his skull, creating a dull throb. One that no amount of headache medication could hope to touch.

He wasn't himself.

He hadn't been since he'd received the birthday card from Daksh yesterday.

Daksh. The brother he hadn't heard from in over two decades but who now, out of the blue, apparently wanted to meet. Right here, in Chile.

How the hell Daksh had even tracked him down was beyond him. But, worse than that, the man who was his brother in nothing but name was stirring up old ghosts that should be left buried. Preferably as deep as possible.

Better yet, left to burn in some hell at the centre of the earth.

Nikhil cursed silently. No wonder his head was all over the place. No wonder he was letting the attraction for this woman, this stranger, get under his skin. If he'd been himself, he would have dismissed it as simple physical attraction—pleasant enough but best left unexplored in the middle of a cruise.

He tried to clear his head.

'Okay,' offered the young doctor when the silence stretched out an uncomfortable touch too long. 'Well, I guess I should be going.'

Without warning, something twisted and darted within Nikhil's veins. The sudden realisation that a few more steps and she would be gone. Inexplicably, he found that he didn't want her to leave.

'Wait.' The command was out before he even realised he was going to issue it.

She stopped, then turned back slowly. As if she didn't really want to, but felt compelled.

As compelled as he did? The notion was fascinating.

'Let me buy you a drink.'

She stared at him, not blinking.

'No,' she managed at last, and he had the oddest notion that it was harder for her than she thought it should have been.

'Why not?' He grinned, liking the way her eyes darted to his mouth, and then she flushed.

As if her thoughts weren't entirely proper.

'Because I don't even know your name,' she blurted out, and then squeezed her eyes shut, suggesting that she hadn't intended to say that.

'Nikhil.' He inclined his head. 'And you're Isla.'

She looked surprised, and Nikhil shrugged. 'You told Philippe your name, even though he was unconscious.'

'Right.' She bobbed her head. 'Well, you can never be sure how much a person can hear, even then.'

'So I've heard,' he acknowledged.

It was a topic that had long interested him, yet right now he couldn't think of anything less fascinating.

'Now introductions have been made, how about that drink?'

'I…' She pulled a rueful face, tailing off into a telling silence.

'As a thank you.'

Why was he pushing this? He should just return to the ship, finish up his shift and get ready for his rare evening onshore. Alone. Instead, he heard himself speaking again.

'The company will want to take your details—for their report. I can guide you through filling it out.'

It was true, but it hadn't been the thought at the forefront of his mind. Odd, since it ought to have been.

'It's okay. I can provide a report of my own if necessary.'

There was something in his tone that he couldn't quite place. He found that he didn't care for the way it unbalanced him. He'd spent years ensuring nothing, and no one, ever rattled him. Yet this woman affected him like no one else ever had.

It had to be that damned birthday card he'd received yesterday from his brother. If 'brother' was what you could call the stranger Nikhil hadn't heard anything from in practically two decades.

'The forms are unnecessarily convoluted,' he warned, shutting down the other, errant thought.

'I just had my finger in your crewman's arse cheek. A ship's form doesn't faze me.'

A ghost of a smile played at her mouth, and it seemed to jolt through his entire body. Somehow, it was more than just attraction. He was well-versed in sexual chemistry, and equally skilled at controlling it, not giving in to it. But this was…different. She—*Isla*—got to him. And he didn't care for such a realisation.

'Is that so?'

'It is.' She bobbed her head. 'I may not be one of the doctors on *your* ship, but I am actually Port-Star Cruise's newest doctor.'

'Say again?'

She laughed unexpectedly and her face lit up so stunningly, so vibrantly, that for a moment he was sure she'd eclipsed the hot Chilean sun.

Suddenly he realised he wanted more of that smile. More of that joy. As if he'd taken a shot of something earth-shaking. And now he needed more.

'You work for Port-Star?'

'I do. The *Jewel of Hestia* will come into this port in two days' time, and it will be my first assignment.'

'A new career move then?' he mused. 'All the more reason to celebrate, surely.'

And although it should have been a question, Nikhil realised that it hadn't been.

'Dinner, I think. I'll collect you around seven-thirty. Where are you staying?'

'What if I have a boyfriend?' she asked, but he could tell it was more curiosity than refusal.

'You don't,' he answered simply. 'You have a line where you have recently removed a ring. Judging by the width of it, I'd say an engagement ring, not a wedding ring. And, as you just said, your assignment on the *Hestia* will be your first. So, a fresh start.'

And if the fact that he'd noticed so much about her in so short a time worried him, he was determined to ignore it.

She stared at him for a long moment, those expressive eyes of hers threatening to draw him in with every sweep of her gaze.

What the hell was he doing?

'Fine,' she answered after what seemed like for ever. 'I don't have a boyfriend, but I have…friends here, with me. I can't just ditch them.'

'You've ditched them now,' he pointed out. 'Or they've ditched you. Either way, you clearly don't live in each other's pockets. You have your last night with them tomorrow, and presumably that's the big farewell meal, so you're free to meet me tonight.'

She opened her mouth but then closed it again.

She was tempted…and that gave him more of a kick than it had any right to.

'Plus it's my birthday—are you really going to leave me to celebrate it alone?'

Why the hell had he told her that?

Fury shot through him. It had to be Daksh's letter and imperious command to meet that had rattled him.

He never told anyone when his birthday was.

If he were honest, Nikhil didn't know why it was such a secret, or how it had come to be this big thing. Nor did he know quite why he got such a kick out of the fact that no one on board knew. Perhaps it was because, in these close-quarter confines, everybody knew everything about everyone else's business and this was one little nugget he could keep to himself—save for the Captain and HR, both of whom would have been in breach for divulging it.

Yet now he'd just announced it to the newest member of

Port-Star. It should have been his cue to turn around and walk. Instead, he heard himself speaking again.

'Which hotel then, Isla?'

Her blue-grey eyes sparked, and yet still she didn't shut him down.

'Okay,' she answered suddenly, biting out the name quickly.

His eyebrows shot up; too late, he wished he hadn't reacted. But that hotel was well-known to be a playground for the rich and famous. Certainly not somewhere the average ship's officer might stay, not even a doctor, and the last thing he wanted to do was get involved with the monied crowd.

They, apparently, were more his brother's crowd than his.

'A farewell gift from my…friends,' Isla said suddenly, as if reading his thoughts. Though he could tell she was holding something back. 'We thought we'd push the boat out, if you'll pardon the pun.'

He could understand that. Didn't he do the same thing each year, when he booked twelve months ahead just to eat in Chile's world-renowned Te Tinca restaurant?

Alone.

'Ah. And they can't spare you for an evening?'

So why was he now insisting on the stunning doctor accompanying him?

It had to be his way of avoiding Daksh.

'I… They… I suppose they could,' she hazarded after a moment. 'Not a date, of course.'

'Of course not,' he demurred. 'Well, Little Doc, shall we say seven-thirty? In this lobby.'

And then, before anything else could be said—or any more damage done—Nikhil turned around and strode away.

CHAPTER TWO

ISLA DIDN'T KNOW what had possessed her to agree to dinner with Nikhil.

Or at least that was what she tried to tell herself.

She could pretend that it was because of the text she'd received from her mother moments before Nikhil had asked her for that drink. Even as she'd been walking away from him, she'd seen the message demanding to know where she was. More than that, she'd been able to practically hear her mother's excitement in every word, as Marianna had crowed about finding the most perfect new man for her to meet.

Isla shuddered, just as she had back then. The last thing she wanted was a blind date, or any date, really. Which was why her head had been calmly telling her to politely decline Nikhil's offer, even whilst her skin had been on fire and her insides had been jostling as if her organs were playing a game of musical chairs.

But then, instead of a refusal, she'd listened to that devilish voice in her head telling her that the best way to avoid being pressed into a blind date by her mother would be to tell her that she already had a date—with a First Officer, no less.

It was a logical solution. But, deep down, Isla suspected that her motives weren't quite so logical. If she was honest, she might suspect that they had less to do with practicality and more to do with the way that Nikhil had made her body feel…alive.

Just by looking at her. There had been more chemistry between her and this relative stranger than she thought she'd ever felt with Brad.

And wasn't that rather sad?

Certainly it explained why she was now standing in front of the mirror, trying to quash some unwanted thrill as she critically assessed her sixth outfit choice so far, like the kind of teenager she had never really been.

She might have spoken to Leo, but her former stepsister didn't seem to have got back to the hotel either. Isla tried not to take that as *fate* giving her a naughty little push.

Staring at her outfit again, she heaved a sigh. She *never* dithered over her clothing choices. And her room had certainly never looked as though she'd emptied the contents of the closet onto her bed. That was for other girls. Just as the rich lipstick was, purchased barely two hours ago from the hotel's extortionately priced boutique.

Ridiculous.

There was taking the opportunity to avoid a blind date set up by her mother, and then there was dressing up as though this dinner with Nikhil was a date in itself.

Well, it wasn't happening.

Marching into the bathroom, she wiped the lipstick off her mouth and threw the tube into the bin and marched back out into the bedroom. Then she proceeded to quickly and neatly put all the clothes back onto the hangers and away, as though she could restore some order into her suddenly uncharacteristically topsy-turvy world.

And if her hands were shaking slightly, and her eyes kept flying to the clock to see that the digits had barely changed from the last time she'd checked, then at least no one else but her would ever know.

Finally, her room was clear again. Pristine. Ordered. The way she liked it. Isla checked the clock again. Five minutes had passed.

This was ridiculous.

She was acting like an adolescent, wound up for her first date. The worst of it was that she'd never acted this way even when she *had* been an adolescent. Snatching up her purse and sliding her room key card inside, Isla stepped out of her room and strode down the hall to the elevators.

He was just a man, like any other, she reminded herself as she jabbed irritably at the buttons. And if her traitorous brain was having trouble remembering that simple fact, then a walk around the town for half an hour should be enough to clear her head and get things in order.

The elevator bounced slightly as it stopped at the ground floor, the doors opening with an efficient *swish* as the sounds of an Argentine tango, and plenty of chatter, filled her ears.

The distraction was so much better than the quiet of her room. She even felt empowered by the way her heels clicked on the marble floor.

This was just a *thank you* dinner, from the First Officer of the ship whose crewman she'd just helped. Nothing more.

Then she lifted her eyes, only for them to slam into Nikhil's as he sat in the lobby, barely fifteen metres away, his powerful frame making the large wingback look almost fragile as he lounged. One ankle was balanced casually on the knee of his other leg, a large broadsheet in his hands, yet he looked even more arcane and forbidding than he had a few hours earlier. Her entire body seemed to turn to liquid. Boiling hot liquid that bubbled through her veins and smouldered in her chest, leaving her almost feverish.

And that was before he unfolded his legs with a casualness she didn't know why she thought was deceptive, and stood up. Her breath caught in a hard ball in her chest.

His body—which had looked hewn enough in his officer's uniform—somehow appeared even more dangerous clad in his own clothes. Even more lethal. She thought she might even have swayed slightly, feeling momentarily light-headed, as if she'd had several drinks too many, when the truth was that she hadn't touched a drop.

It isn't a real date, she said desperately to herself. *It's just dinner, and it's just to avoid Marianna's latest blind date set-up.*

Isla wasn't sure her brain was listening. The guy was positively intoxicating and now she'd started drinking him in she seemed wholly incapable of dragging her gaze away. Even as he approached, it was all Isla could do not to lift her hands, though to ward him off or pull him closer she was afraid she couldn't be certain.

'You're early,' she managed instead, barely recognising the husky quality of her voice.

'As are you,' Nikhil countered dryly. 'It's a welcome surprise.'

Any other time she might have had a quick retort on the tip of her tongue about inherent sexism, especially as she believed he was deliberately baiting her, but then he turned to stand beside her with his large hand pressed to the small of her back. The unexpected contact scorched her skin and stirred her very soul, and it was all she could do to remember how to walk, let alone speak.

'You look stunning, Little Doc.'

'I don't think I care for that term,' she lied, because something told her she *ought* not like it.

He waved his hand negligently. 'Apologies. You look quite lovely, *Isla*.'

She thought she preferred the previous compliment; it somehow sounded more…off-guard. And she liked the idea of unbalancing this man who was clearly accustomed to being so in-control.

'I… Thank you.' Electricity jolted through her as Nikhil lifted his hand to the small of her back again and began to usher her smoothly to the doors. 'But this isn't a date.'

She wasn't sure whether she'd intended it as a reminder to him, or to her. But, either way, she felt the first hint of disappointment when he dipped his head instantly.

'Of course not.'

It was wholly, utterly insane, the way he affected her. Surely this couldn't be normal? It certainly wasn't normal for her.

With hindsight, it was now all the more evident to Isla that she really ought to have declined his invitation to dinner. So, what did it say about her that something inside was practically elated that it was too late to back out now?

Touching her had been a mistake, Nikhil realised the moment his fingers touched her skin and a fresh bolt of awareness crackled through his entire body.

Another mistake. On top of the fact that he'd asked her to dinner in the first place.

All because he'd been thrown off-kilter by a goddamned birthday card, and it provided the escape that he needed to avoid meeting the man who he had once looked up to as his hero brother.

Back when he'd been naïve, he thought angrily, before Daksh had betrayed him so comprehensively.

It was that which had made him so edgy today. So unlike his usual unruffled self that he'd ended up inviting this woman—this stranger—to join him at his annual pilgrimage to Te Tinca. All because of a bout of plain old sexual attraction.

Except that there was nothing *plain*, or *old*, about the attraction he felt for the unexpected doctor, was there? After all, from the moment he'd heard her shoes echoing on the marble floor and looked up to see her striding so confidently, sexily, towards him, in heels that make her calves look all the more shapely, and her backside that little bit perter, he'd felt something kick hard, low in his abdomen.

And lower still.

Sexual attraction was one thing, but he had no words for the intensity of what had arced between the two of them ever since he'd crouched down next to her, beside Philippe. And he could read women well enough to know that she felt it too.

Even tonight he'd paced his suite like some sort of caged beast, unable to stay on the ship and finding himself in the lobby of her hotel, still battling to tame this uninvited thing which roared through him.

He could put it down to the long months at sea—unlike a significant proportion of the ship, he had never indulged in the bed-hopping for which cruises were renowned. He'd prided himself that he'd always kept his career life clearly distinct from his sex life. Yet it had never left him feeling as restless, and jumpy, as he did now.

The backstreets to the restaurant were dark and quiet, allowing the sound of her heels to click that little bit longer. His skull hurt from shutting down all the X-rated images that it kept throwing up in his mind. It felt all too intimate. As if the warm night had cleared everywhere out just for them.

He didn't want a meal, or a conversation. He just wanted to kiss her, to scratch this impossible itch that she'd caused—all over his skin. The kind of deep, unreachable, visceral itch that he didn't think he'd ever experienced before.

Nikhil locked his jaw tight and propelled them on. Desire was closing around him, as terrifyingly vast and deep as the ocean itself. Every moment he spent with this woman felt like sinking beneath the waves that little bit further. And there was nothing he could do to save himself.

Worse, there was nothing he *wanted* to do to save himself.

'You will be glad to know that Philippe is doing well,' he ground out.

As if a scrap of banal conversation could diminish the swell of need. As if it were a pinpoint of light and he was swimming back up to meet it.

'Oh. That's great.' But her voice was too thick, as if she, too, was fighting to resurface.

'Thanks, in no small part, to you.'

The silence swirled around them again. Heavy. Bewitching.

'What about your doctor? I presume you found out why he wasn't on shore where you expected him to be.'

They both pretended there wasn't desperation in her voice. That she, like him, wasn't trying to fill the silence in order to stave off this animal lust that seemed to flow through them both.

'Appendicitis,' he told her grimly. 'He'll be out for a couple of weeks, so they're flying another doctor in tomorrow.'

'How does the crew feel about having a new doctor mid-cruise?' she asked suddenly.

And, against all expectation, the tension seemed to have cranked down a notch.

Nikhil shrugged, though she wasn't looking at him, her attention focused ahead of her.

'It depends on the doctor. Fortunately, I know the guy they're flying in; I worked with him in the past, before I joined the *Queen Cassiopeia*.'

'Right,' she stated flatly. 'Makes things easier.'

'Ah, you're worried about how easy your own move will be, onto the *Jewel of Hestia*.'

She pulled a rueful face and he told himself that it didn't mean anything that he could read her so easily. It was a skill he'd acquired after years of being an officer and reading his colleagues. Or being a kid and reading his father's temper. It had nothing to do with *her* per se.

He wasn't entirely sure he believed that.

'You'll be fine. The *Cassiopeia* is out for months at a time; many of the crew have been working together for years. The *Jewel* runs shorter cruises, and the staff and crew turnover is higher. It's a good ship but it's a stepping stone for promotion to bigger and better liners, so they're well accustomed to new faces.'

'You think so?'

'Keep performing like you did today with Philippe and they'll be only too glad to have you as one of their doctors.'

'That's a relief.' She blew out a breath and, that easily, the tension eased down another notch.

Maybe dinner wouldn't be so fraught, after all.

He stopped her outside a nondescript door which no one would ever have realised was the entrance to the restaurant of a world-renowned chef if they hadn't known it was there, and tried not to think about the fact that 'Little Doc Isla' was the only woman he'd ever brought here, in all these years.

It meant nothing, he told himself as he opened the door

and waited for her to step in ahead of him. *And if he believed that, well...he was in more trouble than he'd realised.*

'Nikhil!' A man, clearly the maître d', even though he was dressed far more casually than Isla might have expected, made his way across the tightly packed room to embrace Nikhil in a back-slapping hug, the moment they entered. His accent was so strong that Isla could only just understand the words spoken in Chilean Spanish.

'Is good to see you back, my friend.'

'It's good to be back,' Nikhil responded in Spanish, slightly clearer to Isla, but still so full of Chilean slang that she couldn't follow as they plunged into conversation.

And then, suddenly, the chef turned to her with an unexpectedly assessing look, his English almost as heavily accented as his native language.

'You are bringing company, Nikhil?'

'Isla, this is Hernandez. Hernandez, this is Isla. A... colleague.'

'Encantada de conocerte.'

'Encantado.' He took her hand and kissed it, but Isla didn't miss the unfathomable look that passed between the two men. 'Come, I sit you both here. Best table in the housing.'

As Isla followed Hernandez, all too aware of Nikhil right behind her, she took in some of the people at the tables. And then, as she glanced into the open kitchen beyond the pass, she startled.

'That's Chef Miguel.'

'It is,' Nikhil confirmed, with a casualness that she couldn't quite have said why she didn't believe.

'I heard his restaurants are always booked up months in advance?'

Nikhil watched her for a moment before answering.

'Six months in advance, yes. I've been coming here for seven years, every time I'm in port. So maybe two or three times a year.'

'And the Captain gives you shore leave each time?'

'In the beginning, when I was more junior, it was the only one I ever actually asked for. Otherwise, I'd take any others people didn't want.'

'Then you became First Officer and got the prime choices?'

There was something about her tone that made him pause, just for a fraction of a moment. As though she was expecting the worst. As though she expected people to be selfish.

It was the way he'd felt almost his entire life but somehow, on her, it didn't seem to fit.

'I get more choice now, it's true, but I still try to play fair.'

And what did it say about her that she believed him?

'Impressive place to bring all your dates.' She tried to keep her tone light, but it was still an attempt to counter any gullibility on her part.

'I thought we weren't on a date?'

She flushed prettily, and he liked it rather too much.

'We aren't…of course not… I meant…'

'Relax.' He grinned. 'You're the first date-but-not-a-date I've ever brought here.'

Cobalt-blue eyes slid away, narrowed, then slid back to his.

'Really? You expect me to believe that?'

'I don't expect you to do anything. But you asked, and I answered. I've never brought any date here. Save for the Captain once, a year ago, I've never brought anyone here.'

Nikhil bit down on his tongue, but it was too late. The

admission was out there, although, judging by the look of disbelief on Isla's face, she didn't believe him anyway.

And that was a good thing, he told himself.

He had no idea what the heck it was about this woman that was so compelling, but he needed to work it out as soon as possible. She was like a puzzle, and he hated puzzles.

No, more accurately, he *enjoyed* puzzles; he just hated an unsolved one. And the brain-teaser that was Doc Isla was taking up far too much of his time.

So, as far as Nikhil was concerned, the sooner he solved it—*her*—the sooner normal life could resume.

CHAPTER THREE

ISLA SWALLOWED AGAIN. She wanted to show him that she didn't believe that he hadn't brought any other date here. More to the point, that it didn't matter to her even if he had.

The problem was that it *did* matter to her.

Rather too much.

An uninvited thrill rippled through her as she thought back to the look of surprise on Hernandez' face when he'd realised Nikhil had brought her as a date. That unspoken communication that had travelled between the two of them supported Nikhil's claim, and therefore made her feel all the more special.

Just like Bradley had.

Pretending that he'd cared for her, and that her money, her connections, her social standing, didn't enter into it. Briefly, she wondered if Nikhil was as straight-talking as he appeared, or if he was also the kind of man to lie, and pretend he loved a woman.

She shook the thoughts from her head irritably. Why did everything have to lead back to Bradley? Even now, months and months later, she was still giving him the power to dominate her thoughts, her actions. And she was furious with herself for doing so.

He was in her past.

Gone.

She didn't want to think about him any more.

'You said the *Hestia* was to be your first cruise?'

Isla blinked and looked up to realise that they'd been sitting in silence for so long she'd finished her course without even realising it.

'I've been a doctor for ten years, but this will be the first time I've been a doctor for a cruise ship,' she offered eventually.

'Ten years?' He didn't look convinced. 'Doctors are qualifying in their teens now, Little Doc?'

'I'm thirty-two.' She fought to keep her voice even.

She'd faced bigger slights than that. There was no reason for it to cut any deeper simply because it came from this man.

'I didn't realise.' His expression changed. 'Still, you must have worked hard to graduate at twenty-two.'

She had—not least because people had wanted to doubt her. Because of her age. And because of who her previous stepfather had been.

But although Stefan Claybourne had been one of the best stepfathers she'd ever known, and he'd certainly encouraged her dream to become a doctor, his kindness and support hadn't been a substitute for her own hard work.

'Being a doctor is all I've ever wanted to do.' She shrugged instead. 'Even as a child, I dreamed of it when other kids were dreaming of being princesses or pirates.'

'Doesn't make the work any easier.'

'No,' she conceded, 'it doesn't. But it does mean that the hard work has always been worth it. Then again, you must know that. You don't get to First Officer on a line like the *Queen Cassiopeia* without being equally dedicated to what you do.'

'For me it was a way out. It was never a dream.'

Isla turned her head sharply to look at him. She wasn't sure which of them was more surprised at the revelation.

'A way out?'

He didn't answer for a long time.

'Where I came from there weren't many choices in life. Maritime was one of them, and so I decided if I was going to go into that, then I wasn't going to be in some hot, stinking job in the bowels of a ship.'

'I think that makes what you've achieved all the more impressive.' She swallowed.

It was impossible to shake the hunch that he wasn't the kind of man who was usually this open with people. Then again, what did she know? Bradley had been a terrible liar, and yet she'd never thought to question him. Because she'd believed—contrary to everything her mother's carefully negotiated marriages had taught her—that true love really did exist.

Nikhil could just be incredibly skilled at making people—*women*—believe that he was revealing some hitherto unknown facet of himself. At making a woman feel special.

But she wasn't that stupid. What did they say about fooling a person once…?

So then, what are you doing here? a silent voice taunted her.

Isla stifled it quickly. She didn't want to hear what it had to say.

'What about your parents? They must be proud.'

'My parents are both dead.'

There was nothing emotional about the admission; a casual observer would have thought it factual, with an even and calm delivery. Yet Isla thought that something altogether bleaker flashed through his eyes for a fraction of a moment.

Then it was gone, leaving her wondering if she'd merely imagined it.

'Oh—' she scrambled for the appropriate response '—I'm sorry.'

'It happened a long time ago.'

Nikhil shrugged, but she didn't know if that made it better or worse. But then Hernandez came with another course from the tasting menu, and Isla found herself fascinated by the dish. Such a precise, delicate-looking creation that should surely have been more at home in an art gallery but which, when tasted, exploded in her mouth like the most perfect taste she'd ever known.

'Impressive, isn't it?' Nikhil asked.

'Incredible,' she breathed. 'Is this always what you have? I can see why you come back every time you can.'

'No, it's always a different tasting menu for me. And every time I think it can't possibly get any better. Yet it does.'

For several more minutes they tasted and praised, and Isla didn't know how it had happened but the last of her disquiet seemed to have eased.

'So the *Hestia* is to be your new start?'

He jerked his head down and she was once again reminded of her now bare ring finger, giving her away without her even speaking a word. She pasted a bright smile onto her lips.

'Yes, it's a good career move. A chance for me to concentrate on being a doctor, with no distractions.'

His deep bark of laughter, rich and full-bodied, filled her with something new.

'You're not serious?'

'I am.' She frowned. 'What's wrong with that?'

'This is a cruise ship you're going on.' He laughed

again, and suddenly she wished she could bottle it up and take it with her.

She didn't know why.

'I know it's a cruise ship. And I'm a doctor.'

'You're a stunning, educated, newly single doctor,' he corrected. 'And you must know the reputation cruise ships have for bed-hopping. Among staff just as much as among the passengers. Sometimes even more so.'

It was insane how his words instantly threw out a series of images of Nikhil bed-hopping. And even more insane how her body balked against them. As if it actually mattered to her.

'I thought you said you didn't bed-hop.' She tried not to sound so prim, but failed.

'I never mentioned my private life on board.' He arched his eyebrows, giving her the oddest impression that he could read her every naughty thought. 'I merely said I'd never brought a date to this restaurant.'

Fire scorched through her cheeks. 'Oh.'

'But, for what it's worth, I don't.' She didn't know why he'd suddenly relented. 'I try to keep my private life quite distinct from my role as ship's officer.'

It said rather too much, in Isla's mind, that they were the words she'd wanted to hear. She straightened her shoulders. 'As I intend to do.'

He laughed again. 'The difference is, Little Doc, that you're already inviting speculation the moment they see that faded mark around your finger.'

'Well, I won't answer it.'

'You'll have to; they won't let it go because it's too juicy a story. The heartbroken new doc.'

'I don't want to be a juicy story, and I'm not heartbroken.'

'Aren't you?' He sounded genuinely curious. 'Your engagement has broken down and suddenly you're a doctor on a cruise ship heading around the world. Like you're running away.'

Indignation fired up her spine. 'I'm not running away.'

Was she?

'Is that so?' he asked, then lifted his shoulders. 'Well, ships are such odd environments. Some might say we're tight-knit cities, others would say we're just living in each other's pockets. Either way, there are never really any secrets, and people are always in everyone else's business.'

'Meaning?'

'Meaning that I can already see some well-meaning colleagues trying to set you up with all and sundry, just to get you over your heartbreak.'

'I told you...'

'You're not heartbroken,' he finished. 'Yes, I heard. But I don't imagine that will stop them.'

'God, that's just like my mother.' Isla rolled her eyes. 'She's equally well-intentioned, but it doesn't make it any less irritating. She's always on about me having a rebound fling. If I hadn't told her that I was on a date with a First Officer, then she already had a blind date set up for me.'

If he was surprised that she'd suddenly mentioned her mother when she'd told him that afternoon that she was with friends then he didn't show it.

'So you're only with me to dodge your mother? I'm flattered,' he drawled, not looking in the least concerned. 'Anyway, I thought this wasn't a date?'

'Is isn't.' She stumbled over her words.

Why did she keep making that mistake?

'Shame—' another wicked smile played on his lips, toying with them and simultaneously pulling at something low in her belly '—I don't think I'd have minded you using me to get over whoever he was.'

Desire seeped through her. At this point she wasn't entirely sure she'd have minded that either.

'Anyway…' she began, trying to change the subject before her mind went blank.

She was almost relieved when Hernandez came with the next course of the tasting menu.

'Wow, this smells incredible.'

'Doesn't it?' he agreed. 'But be aware that Chef Miguel likes to play with the senses. Whatever you think you're getting, be prepared for it to catch you out.'

Nodding slowly, Isla loaded a careful amount onto her fork and lifted it to her mouth. Taste and sensation exploded in her mouth and, just as Nikhil had predicted, it challenged her expectations of what she'd thought she'd smelled.

'That's amazing. He's really brilliant.'

'He is. And, like I said, he's always evolving and inventing.'

'I guess I'm going to have to come back and see for myself.' She grinned, and then felt a jolt. 'I mean…by myself. I'm not… That wasn't…'

'Relax, I understand what you meant,' Nikhil cut in. 'I take it your mother would rather have you be a private practice doctor than travelling around the world on a cruise ship?'

'My mother would rather I not be a doctor at all,' Isla admitted before thinking twice, as Nikhil pulled his brows together.

'Really? She isn't proud of you?'

Was it just her imagination, or did she detect a note of… *something* in his tone?

'Sorry, that isn't fair.' She wrinkled her nose. 'My mother is always proud. Although she doesn't really understand why it's my dream.'

'Why not?'

She paused; this wasn't usually a conversation she had with strangers. Or many people, in fact. But, rather than push her, Nikhil waited, his eyes never leaving hers. So different from the way Bradley had always been far more interested in who he could see, who could see him, what was on his phone.

It was potent to have Nikhil's attention so assuredly on her. As if nothing else mattered to him but whatever she was saying. It almost had her telling him things that she rarely told anyone.

Isla just about caught herself in time and moderated what she'd been about to say.

'My mother can't see the appeal of actually working in the trenches with blood, and vomit, and sick people. Her philosophy is that she can contribute more by marrying well, playing her role, organising fundraisers and raising millions, which she then gives to hospitals and charities.'

'And your father?'

'My father died when I was two. I have photos though I don't remember him. But I had a surgeon stepfather, Stefan, when I was fourteen.' No need to tell him she'd had five stepfathers so far. 'He encouraged me to follow my dream and go into medicine.'

'He was kind?' asked Nikhil, too sharply and too quickly.

Had he had his own, less fortunate experiences with a stepfather? Stepmother?

'He was very kind. I was lucky.' Isla smiled softly.

None of her stepfathers had ever been unkind; her mother would never have married them otherwise. But Stefan had been like the father she'd never known.

'He even had a daughter, Leonora, who was about the same age as me. She didn't want to go into medicine. In fact she wanted to be an artist and she could paint the most stunning paintings, and he always encouraged her too. There was never any favour to either of us. He treated us both like we were his daughters.'

'You speak of it in the past,' Nikhil pointed out.

'Yeah, their marriage—business agreement—ended when I was nineteen, though Stefan came to see me a couple of times at the hospital where I did my first few rotations. But Leo and I are still best friends. We're each the sister the other never had.'

'It sounds very…civilised,' Nikhil commented.

She might have said *through gritted teeth* if she hadn't thought better of it. Instead, she laughed quietly.

'Civility is my mother's mantra. What about you? You don't have any siblings?'

It took him a beat too long to answer and, when he did, it struck Isla as an incredibly telling and personal statement.

'I have a brother. But I lost him a long time ago.'

'I'm sorry to hear that,' she offered genuinely. The thought of losing Leo wasn't one she wanted to even consider. 'You must miss him.'

'Not really,' Nikhil replied instantly.

But, despite his attempt at a casual tone, Isla couldn't help thinking she saw something deeper, more genuine, usually hidden. Something profoundly sad. Though perhaps she was just being fanciful.

As if he was going to show her a side of himself that no one else ever saw.

'My brother wasn't what you might call the dependable sort. Most people aren't, which is why I can understand why your mother doesn't believe in love.'

Guilt lanced through Isla.

'My mother might not believe in *love* as some deep, romantic concept, but she definitely believes in love for me as her daughter,' she said, almost apologetically. 'And for Leo, come to that. Even now, she still treats Leo like another daughter. If she phones me to see how I am, she will have either called, or be about to call Leo too. If she buys me something, she buys something for Leo.'

'You don't resent that?'

'It makes me feel as though we're still family. In fact, when I told you before that I was here with friends, I wasn't being entirely truthful. My mother flew herself and Leo out yesterday as a surprise. And, as you surmised, we're going for dinner together tomorrow night. Though she'll be furious she didn't book here. That's her idea of love.'

'Indeed.' Nikhil offered a half-smile but didn't elaborate. Instead, he turned his questions back on her. 'And what about you? Do you believe in love?'

Isla hesitated. She had done. Once upon a time.

For all her mother's wisdom and lessons, she'd believed that true love—soulmates—had to exist, somewhere. A thousand blockbuster romantic films couldn't be wrong. And when she'd fallen for Bradley she'd understood what every single one of them meant.

Or she'd *thought* she'd understood.

'Not any more,' she told Nikhil simply, quashing the traitorous part of her that tried to argue. 'You?'

'Never,' he answered.

And she thought it was the fact that it was said so certainly, with no emotion or heat, that made it all the more… *lamentable.*

'Are you always so controlled? Don't you ever feel passionate about anything?'

It was a foolish question. She realised it at exactly the same moment that his eyes darkened, his expression walloping her like a punch to the solar plexus—only far, far more exhilarating.

'I might only be able to offer one night, Little Doc, but I can show plenty of passion, if that's what you want.'

The heat, the intensity, that she'd felt earlier now felt more like a wall. And she was racing straight for it.

'Not a date,' she managed weakly.

'Of course not,' he agreed with a smile that she could swear she could actually feel against her sex. 'But if you feel yourself wavering, just let me know.'

'Right,' she murmured. Unable to even deny it.

The wall was approaching faster now.

If she wasn't careful, she was going to crash—and that could only hurt.

It was several hours before they left the restaurant. The last to leave, after being served one incredible dish after another, and even Chef Miguel had left the kitchen to come and sit with them for after-dinner drinks, chatting with Nikhil as though they were old friends.

Clearly they were.

But whilst Brad would have preened and peacocked, making her cringe a little at his sycophantism—the way that he always had when Isla had taken him to one of her mother's high-society events—Nikhil kept it all comfortable and easy.

It told her a lot more about him. And she liked what she saw.

But now it was just the two of them. Her and Nikhil, in the quiet, narrow back streets, which were glowing faintly from the warm yellow-orange lights spilling out from the buildings on either side.

His arm was around her, almost protectively, and she was wholly conscious of fitting far too well to the shape of his body. *As if they were designed to fit together.* He moved with such grace, propelling them on, with every step taking them closer and closer to her hotel.

To end the night? Or to begin it?

Her head was warring with the rest of her body, as everything started to pull gradually tighter and tighter. It pooled in her chest, her belly, and lower. She ought to speak. To stop this. One-night stands weren't her thing, but lord, the temptation to stay silent and simply indulge in the moment made her mouth dry up completely.

In the end, it was her legs that stopped her. Slowing her down, as though against her will.

'What if I've changed my mind?'

'Changed your mind?' he asked, stopping beside her, his arm still around her waist.

Still making her blood fizz and her head spin.

'This,' Isla managed. 'Us. You said it yourself. When I go onto the *Hestia* I'll be the heartbroken girl with a broken engagement who needs fixing. They'll all be telling me I need a rebound…unless I can tell them I've already had my rebound.'

Isla ignored the voice whispering that if she felt that was a solution then she could still pretend that she'd had a rebound without actually having one. She prayed that Nikhil wouldn't point it out either.

She wanted this one night. It would put what had happened with Bradley firmly in the past. Drawing a line between that life and this new one on the *Hestia.* Perhaps she really did need it.

Although she didn't care to analyse the fact that no other man had made her want to do something so uncharacteristic—only Nikhil.

'I don't have anything else to offer,' he said quietly, as she wondered if she imagined that tinge of regret.

'I know.'

'Be sure, Little Doc, because I'm not in the habit of talking a woman into a situation she might later regret.'

'The perfect officer and gentleman,' she quipped, wondering why he wasn't kissing her already.

He was trying to make sure she had really considered it and, as gentlemanly as that was, it left her with a faint afternote of disappointment rather than relief.

And then his voice grew edgier. Raw. 'I'm an officer but I've never been a gentleman.'

'Good, then maybe you can start by being a little less gentlemanly now.' She didn't know what had got into her, but her mouth seemed to run away with itself, egged on by more carnal parts of her body.

His eyes gleamed in the faint yellow-orange light and a kind of reckless desire poured through her, making her stomach clench—in a good way. Impulsively, she stepped forward, reached up and pressed her lips to his—finally, *finally* kissing him.

And in that incredible moment it felt as though her whole life was turning on its axis.

CHAPTER FOUR

NIKHIL COULDN'T HELP himself any longer. Or, more aptly, he didn't want to, not now Isla had initiated their kiss. It was perhaps the hottest thing he could recall experiencing.

He pressed her into the wall until every last inch of her delectable body, with all the delicious heat spilling out of it, was pressed against every last inch of his. And he lowered his mouth to her neck, and indulged. As if he couldn't help himself.

Perhaps he couldn't.

Never, in all his years, had Nikhil ever felt so hollow, and needy, and raw. As if he'd die if he didn't have her. If he didn't bury himself inside her. Right here. Right now. He, who prided himself on never losing control.

Not since that bleak, black night less than some twenty-odd years ago when, his body black and blue, his ribs cracked, his face bleeding, he'd finally stopped cowering to that monster who'd had no right to ever call himself a father. He'd unfolded himself from a heap on the floor and he'd shown that demon what it really felt like to be a punchbag.

Not that he could remember a moment of it.

To this day, Nikhil still didn't remember the moment when he'd actually killed his pathetic excuse for a father. He had, of course, because there was no other explanation. Yet he couldn't remember it. He remembered his father raging, and he remembered wresting the knife from his father's hands…but then it all went hazy, and the only thing he could remember was being led out of the apartment by a sympathetic policeman whilst they'd put his father in a body bag.

So what other explanation could there be?

And now he had that damned birthday card to deal with. Nikhil shook the unwelcome memories from his brain.

Tonight wasn't about revisiting his grubby past. Instead, tonight was about indulging in the unexpected seduction of this moment. And the temptation that was Isla. He intended to learn every millimetre of her oh-so-sensuous body. With his hands, his mouth, his tongue. He didn't care which.

Though preferably all three.

He wanted to touch her and taste her. *Lord, how he wanted to taste her.* He wanted to drink her in as though he were a parched man and she was his oasis.

'One night, Little Doc,' he heard himself grind out, scarcely able to lift his head from her neck. So hot, so smooth, with the faintest tang of salt in the still-hot night.

'Yes,' she muttered, arching her body into him and letting her head tip back as if to grant him better access. As if half-afraid he was going to move away.

'That means no recriminations once the morning comes,' he repeated, only he wasn't sure who he was reminding. Her? Or himself?

'I'm well aware of what it means.' She yanked her head up abruptly and scowled at him. 'I'm not a gullible teenage girl. But I can't control your morning tantrums.'

'No, I meant you…' It took him a moment to realise that she was teasing him. Playing him at his own game. He rather liked that. It was like a fresh kick of desire in his gut. Lower, if he was going to be honest.

'Don't say I didn't warn you,' he growled, lowering his head back to that sensitive hollow at the base of her neck—where she seemed to like him the most.

So far.

'You should learn to stop talking,' gasped Isla, slicking her fingers through his hair just rough enough. 'One might think you're overcompensating.'

'Say again?'

He lifted his head again, though he still kept her pinned to the wall with his body.

'You're building yourself up to be God's gift,' she continued, though he noted with some satisfaction that she couldn't keep the desire from thickening her voice. 'It would be a terrible disappointment to discover your mouth is making promises that your body can't deliver.'

Was she seriously questioning his prowess?

'Oh, believe me, my body can deliver.'

'So your mouth keeps saying—' she heaved a deliberate sigh, and the shakiness of it shot through him all the more '—but your body…'

'Trust me, Little Doc, my mouth can deliver too.'

'Sorry?' This time it was her turn to question.

Just as he'd intended. He shot a smile that felt infinitely wolfish.

'My body can deliver. And so can my mouth.'

She stared at him for a moment, and then a deep stain spread over her cheeks and down the elegant line of her neck.

'Oh…you mean…'

'I intend to eat you alive, Little Doc. Until you sob my name.'

'I won't sob your name.'

He wasn't sure if that was meant to be a promise or a challenge. He found he didn't care.

'You will,' he assured her with conviction. 'And you won't only sob it, but you'll shout it, and you'll scream it. Right before you beg me for more. And more again. I intend to make absolutely sure of that.'

She made a delicious half-strangled sound, and he asked himself what it said about him that he wondered if that was the kind of sound he would hear again and again, as she broke apart in his arms.

He was so hard that he ached. Barely able to resist the wicked urge to drop to his knees right here, lift that flimsy dress of hers and prove his point once and for all.

If he wasn't careful, he risked losing the last of his grip on some semblance of self-control. With a supreme effort, Nikhil peeled his body from Isla's, took her hand and began to walk them down the street.

'Come,' he gritted out. 'I suggest we get back to your hotel now, before we indulge in the middle of the street and embarrass both of us.'

Although, for the very first time in his incredibly discreet professional life, Nikhil found he wouldn't have cared if the whole city knew that Little Doc was his.

Even if only for this one night.

Isla felt crazy. Wild. Out of control. Totally unlike herself.

And it was so freeing.

She'd spent her life trying to be different from her mother—as much as she loved her—trying to concentrate on her career rather than simply making a series of strategic marriages.

She'd become known as Isla, the sensible one. And she'd prided herself on such a moniker.

But now she didn't feel sensible at all. She felt excited, and charged, and feverish. Her heart slammed madly in her chest. Her legs trembled like a newborn foal. And, far from terrifying her, as she suspected they ought to, they instead felt like truly joyous sensations. Every last one of them.

She hurried along beside him, trying not to be so aware of the way his large hand enveloped her small one. Or how the *click-clack* of her heels seemed to echo with such titillating rudeness as she raced to keep up with his long strides. As though he could barely wait any longer than she could.

Did he feel as though he was about to burst from the inside out, the way that she did?

They moved swiftly through the narrow streets, with Nikhil weaving a path that kept them away from the melee of tourists, sparing them from being seen. Given that she suspected her desire was stamped blatantly on her face, Isla was eternally grateful. And then they were walking through the hotel doors.

And upstairs was her bedroom.

'Key card?' he demanded, his voice low.

'In my purse.' She licked her suddenly parched lips.

With a nod, he changed course slightly and made straight for the elevators on the far side where one was, mercifully, already there.

An elderly couple were already stepping inside and Nikhil slowed his pace.

'Which floor?'

To her embarrassment, her mind went blank. Nikhil's voice was hoarser than before, and she found herself too busy savouring the way it revealed more than she suspected he would have liked.

'What floor, Isla?' he repeated, with more urgency.

Snapping back to the present, she shook her head before fumbling with the clasp of her clutch and fishing out her key card. She handed it to him discreetly, not trusting herself, and let him lead her forward for what felt the longest elevator-ride of her life.

How did he manage, so easily, to respond as the elderly couple made pleasant conversation, when her own tongue felt as though it was glued to the roof of her mouth? Her body might as well have been on fire, and her brain could barely process their questions let alone formulate suitable responses. Yet Nikhil seemed more than comfortable engaging in small talk and suggesting some of the more tucked-away places to visit when they asked for his advice.

It was only as they stood outside her tiny suite, the doors pinging behind them as it finally separated them from the elderly couple, that Nikhil handed her key card back to her. Without unlocking her door.

She stared at the tiny rectangle of plastic without taking it, and frowned up at him. 'You've changed your mind?'

Coal-black eyes bored into her, making everything tingle all over again. 'I have not.' His voice was a low rumble. Full of promise. And barely contained restraint. 'But I'm giving you one more chance to change yours.'

Something like panic shot through her. 'Why?'

He lifted his shoulders. Not quite a shrug, but close enough. 'You went so quiet in the lift. I thought you were having second thoughts.'

A wave of relief crashed over her, and the panic was swept away in an instant. She struggled to contain the grin as it tugged at the corners of her mouth. And with it came a welcome boost of confidence.

Extending her fingers, Isla plucked the key card from his hand and slid it home, stepping over the threshold and turning to face him. Her hands lifting up until her palms were pressed against the warm, impossibly sculpted ridges of his chest.

Moving over them.

Acquainting herself with them.

'I wasn't,' she murmured, raising herself on tiptoe and letting her lips graze his. 'I didn't change my mind for a moment. And I don't intend to now.'

Then, before he could answer, she closed her fists around his lapels and tugged him off balance, right over the threshold to her room.

Nikhil fully intended to take his time. To taste, to sample, to tend to Isla's needs before he even began to think about his own. But, uncharacteristically, he found she'd caught him off-guard, his wondrous 'Little Doc', and he found himself fighting his own urgency.

No other woman had ever made him feel so intoxicated. So possessed.

Stumbling inside, he managed to close the door before spinning her around so that her back was against the door, his hands exploring her ravishing body.

And she let him. She more than let him, she actively spurred him on, wrapping her arms around his neck and fitting herself to him. Moulding herself as though she were hand-crafted—*just for him*. The prospect should have been enough to set off warning bells, loud and clear, in his head.

He deliberately didn't stop to consider the fact that it hadn't.

Instead, Nikhil focused his entire thoughts on lowering his head to claim her mouth with his. Hot, demanding, hungry. From the slide of her lips to the slick of his tongue, all of which elicited from her the greediest little moans of approval, and all of which his body lapped up.

He didn't think he'd ever been so hard, so *needy* his entire life. How had this woman slid under his skin? It was ridiculous. He had to slow down.

Setting one hand against the flimsy door beside her

head, Nikhil slid the other down the side of her body, letting it curve around her waist, feeling her heat seep into him. His mouth never leaving hers. Slowly, he moved his fingers, a teasing caress, walking his way across her abdomen, not quite enough to tickle, but feeling her stomach clench sensitively nonetheless.

Anticipation. Usually, he was all about it. All about the build-up. Today, with this woman, it was taking every bit of self-control he had not to simply rip her clothes off and bury himself inside her. The way her rocking body kept urging him on was enough to drive him out of his mind. Enough to make him forget he'd ever wanted any other woman in his life before her.

He'd certainly never wanted them with this ferocity. And still she shifted and rolled her hips. Searing heat against the hardest part of himself.

He made himself ignore it, though he had no idea how he managed it, choosing instead to concentrate on the feel of movement of her diaphragm beneath his hands as she breathed. Heavily, he noted with satisfaction. He took his time walking his fingers a little further, a little higher, and then he was pushing her bra aside and cupping her breast in his hand, testing it, letting his thumb pad rake over her hard, proud nipple.

The urge to lower his head and take it in his mouth was overwhelming. And so he did. Tugging the flimsy material of the dress and the lace of the bra out of the way as he did.

Isla gasped, her fingers raking through his hair and her head dropping back. Nikhil revelled in it. She tasted of pure desire. Ripe and unrestrained, and as Nikhil used his tongue to toy with the taut peak he couldn't resist moving his hand to free her other breast from its fabric constraints and lavish upon it an equal amount of attention.

The world seemed to stop, or maybe it spun faster, but

he refused to be hurried. He might be teetering on the edge of control, but he'd be damned if he gave in to this overwhelming, aching desire for her, until he'd brought her pleasure first.

Brushing his hand over her body, down her belly and to the hem of her skirt, he lifted it with a forced laziness, relishing the way Isla's breath caught, and fractured.

And then, so slowly, he grazed his fingers up the inside of her thigh and skimmed where she was so very hot, so very wet, that it was almost his undoing. He was so hard, so aching, that it was almost like pain, and he had no idea how he managed not to simply bury himself inside her.

Isla was going out of her mind. She was sure of it.

She briefly wondered how Nikhil kept his control when she'd long since lost hers, but then he hooked his finger inside her panties and stroked her core, and she ignited. Over and over he stroked her, and she couldn't speak, couldn't think. It was like nothing that had ever gone before.

Instead, lost between his mouth at her neck and his fingers on her sex, she simply let her body listen to the rhythm that he was setting. Meeting it. Matching it. And surely those needy, visceral noises couldn't possibly be her?

Still, he kept stroking her. Over and over, like the most exquisite kind of torture, driving her onward, and upward, until she realised—almost too late—that she was toppling over the edge.

Isla just about managed to cling to Nikhil's strong shoulders as she fell. Hurtling weightlessly, pleasure fragmenting around her. And she had absolutely no idea how long she fell, she was only vaguely aware of holding him tightly—as if afraid that if she let go he would disappear—as he wrapped her legs around his waist, and carried her to the huge bed in the middle of the room.

She could only watch, spellbound, as he stripped her off. And then again, as he ruthlessly shed his own clothing. Naked, hard, and clearly ready for her. Undoubtedly the most beautiful man she'd ever known in her life.

Isla reached for him.

'What's the rush, Little Doc?' he drawled.

But she heard the tightness in his tone, as though he wasn't quite as restrained as he wanted to appear. It was a thrilling notion and one which she considered exploiting—right up until she watched him lodge himself between her legs, his mouth impossibly close to where she was already molten.

'I don't think I can again…' she whispered shakily.

There was no other way to describe his grin but as decidedly wicked.

'I disagree,' he murmured.

Then, before she could add anything more, he lowered his head and licked his way into her.

She screamed his name. It was impossible not to. And somehow her hands had made their way to his head as she threaded her fingers into his hair as if to give herself better purchase as she bucked her hips beneath him. Towards him.

As if she was utterly incapable of doing anything less.

As if he had completely taken over her. And she couldn't have resisted, even if she'd wanted to.

Was this what she'd been missing? All these years? It made a mockery of everything that had gone before. Had she really been happy to settle for less with Bradley—and not even realised it?

For the first time, Isla felt as though her eyes had been opened. She felt alive. In a rush, she realised that, as transient as tonight would be, she would always remember Nikhil for showing her how much richer her life could be.

And then she couldn't think any more.

She could only feel, as he used his mouth, his fingers, weaving some kind of spell around her, more carnal than she'd ever dreamed possible. With another sweep of his tongue he toppled her straight back into the flames, and she briefly considered that even if she burned alive she wouldn't care.

She bucked, and she let her hips roll. And this time when she gave herself up to him, breaking, splintering, she somehow knew that this was the way she was going to make herself anew.

And for the first time in her life Isla let herself go completely.

By the time she came to, Nikhil had moved his body up to cover hers, carefully and gently, as though to give her time to regain her breath. Nonetheless the evidence of his desire pressed deliciously, like velvety steel, against her belly.

Isla ran her hands over his body, taking it all in. From the knotted muscles of his back, to strong biceps, and then the solid bulk of his shoulders. She frowned slightly at the rough scar that adorned one of them. It was old, but it caught her doctor's eye instantly.

'What was this from?'

She hated the way his eyes shuttered on her.

'Old war wound, as they say.'

'It looks like a knife wound. A deep one at that.'

His eyes held hers. So intently that she almost forgot to breathe. And she didn't know why it was so important to her, but she found herself urging him to talk to her. Not to shut her out again.

'We're not here for story-telling, Little Doc. We don't have to share life stories.'

Disappointment rolled through her, but she pasted on as much of a smile as she could.

'I only asked what the scar was from. I wasn't asking for your life story, Nikhil.'

He watched her a little longer before offering an almost imperceptible dip of his head.

'You're right; it was a knife wound,' he confirmed. 'A kitchen accident with a carving knife. Does that satisfy your curiosity?'

She wanted to say that it didn't. That she hated the way he was pulling away from her. But she didn't. She couldn't. Nikhil was right. They weren't here to share life stories; they were here for sex. Incredible sex. But still sex. She was an idiot for making it so personal. And now she'd broken the moment, and the mood.

She cranked up her smile another notch.

'Completely satisfied,' she lied, wondering how best to extricate herself from such an intimate position without making things all the more awkward.

At least her answer seemed to have eased the tension slightly.

'You're sure?' he asked suddenly. 'Completely satisfied?'

And then he flexed against her and Isla marvelled at how the awkwardness dissipated in an instant. As though there was no room for it when her desire came cannoning back.

'You think you can do better?' she teased after a moment.

His eyebrows shot up, and she liked that she had finally found a way to tease him back.

'A challenge, Little Doc?'

'A gauntlet.' She grinned, only for it to fade into a low gasp as he shifted, pressing her legs apart again and nudging at her entrance.

She slid her hands to his back, almost in readiness as he held himself steady, poised above her.

'Then allow me to defend my honour,' he growled.

And, before she could answer, he thrust inside her. Deep, and big, and perfect. Isla cried out, low and wanton, her back arching up and sensation seeping all around her body. Nikhil slid out slowly, almost teasing her, and she opened her eyes to meet the cocoa-rich depths of his, seeing the same intense, primal expression that echoed inside her. Something walloped inside her chest but she didn't care to examine it any further.

Instead she simply gave herself up to the sensations, letting Nikhil drive the rhythm and matching him stroke for stroke, her fingers biting into the strong cords of muscles at his neck. And then she felt the wave cresting over her. That blissful shiver pouring straight through her.

'Stop fighting it,' he growled.

Low and raw, into that crook of her neck. Making her tremble.

'I'm not fighting,' she countered.

But maybe she was. Maybe she never wanted this moment, this feverish need, to end. What if this was the only time she would ever know something this good?

As if reading her thoughts, Nikhil lifted his head, his eyes boring straight into her.

'We have all night, Little Doc. And I intend to make use of every last minute of it.'

Then, before she could answer, he slid his hand between them. Down. Right to the centre of her need. And he played with her.

It was too much, and it was perfect.

It was as though Isla's entire world was imploding.

She was catapulted into space. Into oblivion. The most glorious ride that anyone had surely ever known. All she could do was hold on tightly, and sob out his name—just as he'd predicted.

She soared for miles. For ever. And when she finally began to return to herself she realised he was waiting for her, his face taut with his own need, lifting her legs to wrap around him, as though it could pull him in deeper.

A shudder tore through him in an instant as he gripped her closer, building that pace back up. Faster now, harder, and more demanding. Grazing her fingers down his back, she cupped his backside, urging him on with such abandon that she barely recognised herself.

A bolder side of herself that she'd never realised had lurked within. She rather thought she liked it.

Then Nikhil thrust into her one last time, deep and true, and she couldn't think any more. She just wanted to *experience* everything that this arresting man had to teach her.

And this time, when Nikhil tossed her back into that glorious abyss, he followed, her name never sounding more beautiful on his lips.

CHAPTER FIVE

'HIS NAME IS JALEEL,' the security officer explained as he hastily led Isla down a rabbit warren of corridors to the ship's laundry room.

And not the *Hestia*, as had been planned, right up until the phone call from Head Office that morning—less than an hour after Nikhil had left her bed, and her hotel—but on the *Cassiopeia* itself.

She could only imagine how furious he would be when he discovered her here—if he hadn't already been advised. Goosebumps prickled over her skin at the mere thought.

But there was no time to think about that now. She'd been in the middle of her orientation tour with her new medical team when the medical call had come in, and now she had *Jaleel* to concentrate on.

Talk about being thrown in at the deep end.

'His colleague said that he stood up when there was an open machine door above him and it cut his face,' the security guard continued.

'My report said that he's unconscious,' Isla stated, adrenalin pumping through her body.

'Yeah, apparently he fell back, and they heard him cry out, and then he hit his head and fell unconscious.'

'Understood. And it's Jaleel?'

'Jaleel, yeah.'

She'd barely stepped on board—she had only just met the first of her colleagues, a stunning American nurse by the name of Jordanna—when the call had come in.

The senior doctor—a Dr Turner, according to her email—had been in his consultation room with a patient when she'd arrived. And though he could probably have taken the emergency call, Isla knew that his priority would be passengers, whilst hers, as junior doctor, would be crew and staff. There would be some crossover, of course, but in broad terms that was how this ship worked, and the sooner she jumped into that, the better she would be likely to fit in.

Finally arriving at the laundry room, Isla ducked inside and quickly took in the scene. The patient, Jaleel, was now conscious and clutching a blood-soaked towel to his face. Even from here, it looked like he was a mess, not helped by the sapping heat of the loud, airless room.

'Hi, Jaleel—' she flashed her brightest, most confident smile '—I'm Isla, the new doctor. Let's have a look at the damage, shall we?'

'He no speak English,' the woman offered, before appearing to translate.

'Thank you.' Isla flashed her a smile as she crouched down beside Jaleel. She carefully helped him to peel the towel away and peered at the wound, then stood up.

'Which machine?'

'This…' A young woman stepped forward. 'This machine.'

Isla inspected it carefully, looking for the likely metal culprit.

'Is this where you caught it, Jaleel?'

She didn't really need to hear them say it; the blood was evidence enough. Still there was a quick exchange between the two colleagues before the woman issued a confirmation.

'Okay, good.' She crouched back down to check his vitals, shining a light into his eyes to check pupil responses.

Ideally a CT would check that he hadn't hit his head when he'd fallen backwards, but that wasn't possible on board. Still, nothing jumped out at her as a cause for alarm, save for the one long, ugly gash running down his cheek.

'It's too deep to simply glue the sides together, so let's get him back to the med centre, where I can stitch him back up,' she told the security guard, before turning back to Jaleel's colleague. 'How long was he out, do you know?'

'Out?'

'Sorry, unconscious.'

'Oh…maybe one minute? Maybe two?'

So, not long. That was good. Nonetheless, it would be safer to transport him on the emergency gurney that they'd brought. Quickly, she set it up next to Jaleel and popped a collar around his neck for stability. She didn't think he'd injured it in the fall, but until they got him back to the medical centre it wouldn't hurt to take precautions.

'Okay, gentlemen—' she lifted her head to the security guys, who were also around the stretcher '—one, two, three, lift. Good. Now, let's get him to the medical centre.'

Jordanna was bustling around quickly and efficiently as Isla arrived in the medical centre, its location in the passenger area of the ship evident as they left behind the cold grey metal and vinyl floor of the crew decks and stepped into the pristine white-walled and plushly carpeted passenger areas.

This time Dr Turner could be seen behind his desk, his consultation door open. He was an older gentleman dressed in an immaculate uniform, and out of the corner of her eye Isla was aware that he'd stood up as soon as she'd entered with Jaleel.

She kept her focus on her patient. No doubt the medical team would all be a little uncertain of her, as a new arrival, but the better she performed here, the quicker she proved herself as a valuable member of the team.

'Jordanna, can you go ahead and ready some gauze swabs to staunch the bleeding once I remove this towel from Jaleel's face, and a suture kit, please?'

'Sure, Dr Sinclair.'

'And some local anaesthetic,' added Isla.

She busied herself checking over Jaleel's neck once more, before she finally removed the collar. Then, as Jordanna laid out all the equipment for her, she glanced at Jaleel's colleague and smiled gently.

'Can you warn him that the needle will need to go as close to the edges of the wound as possible, so it's going to be uncomfortable?'

She waited for Jaleel to nod his confirmation, and then she lifted the syringe.

'Okay, here we go.'

A few moments later, as the anaesthetic began to kick in, she picked up a small probe.

'I just want to check there is no debris in there. No metal from the machine or anything. He might feel his cheek moving elsewhere, but he won't feel any pain.'

As his friend translated, Jaleel gave them both a weak nod. It occurred to Isla that a significant proportion of his—and his friend's—anxiety might have more to do with the fact that he wanted to get back to work. It was widely acknowledged that the laundry was one of the locations on the ship where sickness was least tolerated.

Picking up the needle and sutures, Isla began one tiny stitch after another, working slowly and methodically to draw the edges of the wound together, trying to make it as neat and unobtrusive as possible. With a facial wound this deep, she would have preferred it to have been left to a plastic surgeon—but that wasn't an option out here. All Jaleel had was her, so she would be damned sure she made it as good a job as possible.

By the time she was finished, Jaleel had reluctantly allowed himself to be talked into twelve hours' observation, his colleague had shot off to try to catch up on the mountain of laundry that no doubt awaited her, and the report logged in the computer system, Isla looked up to see Jordanna, Dr Turner and a couple of other medical staff approaching her.

'Nice job, Dr Sinclair.' Jordanna smiled welcomingly.

'Isla,' she corrected instantly, relieved that her first impression had apparently gone down so well.

'Isla,' the nurse echoed happily.

'Yes, very competent,' the senior doctor commended in a cut-glass accent.

She'd assumed he'd been happy enough when he'd left her to it as she'd started cleaning up the wound, but the confirmation was nice all the same.

'And you're also the doctor who stepped in to look after our rather hot-headed crewman yesterday?'

'I just happened to be on scene.' Isla smiled again.

'Well, I'm glad you could change ships and step into our medical team at the last minute. *Hestia's* loss is *Cassiopeia's* gain indeed.'

'Thank you,' Isla replied sincerely. Her fears about being seen as a cuckoo in the previous doctor's nest were appearing unfounded.

At least they were with the medical team. The same wouldn't necessarily be said for Nikhil.

Nikhil.

Isla shut down the unbidden thought and concentrated on her new colleague.

'Welcome to our ship's medical centre, Dr Sinclair,' the older man continued. 'I'm Dr Turner, as I'm sure you've deduced. When appropriate, you can call me Reginald.'

Presumably *appropriate* would be situations like now, when it was just the medical team, or when it was just officers. Nevertheless, Isla decided that the first time she addressed him should also be more official.

'It's lovely to meet you, Dr Turner.' Isla smiled warmly, eying his outstretched hand for a fraction of a moment before shaking it confidently.

Her training had taught her that shaking hands on board was discouraged, but she imagined that Dr Turner was old school and didn't care much for such regulations. It was his way of getting the measure of his colleagues, and Isla felt a punch of triumph when he gave a tacit nod of approval, before turning to one of the other nurses who Isla had yet to meet.

'I'm Lisa,' announced an Australian nurse.

'Gerd.' A German man stepped forward, clearly the senior nurse.

'Shall we all have some tea, and introduce ourselves properly?' Reginald boomed.

'Good idea.' Gerd grinned, and headed out of the room and into the beautiful, exotic-flower-strewn reception.

It felt as though she'd passed his first subtle test and he was genuinely pleased to have her on board. Though Nikhil's reaction to the news would inevitably be an entirely different matter. It was impossible to ignore the thought any longer, though she commended herself for doing so well up until that point. She hadn't thought of him when she'd been treating Jaleel. She certainly hadn't thought of him when Head Office had called a few hours ago and asked her—though she didn't think she had genuinely had much choice in the matter—to transfer to the *Cassiopeia*.

Liar, whispered a voice inside her head. *He was the first thing you thought when you got that call.*

Isla's heart jolted abruptly. He was bound to be furious. He'd made it abundantly clear that he didn't sleep with colleagues, and that he was only interested in her because she was going to be on board a different ship.

And now, here she was, the new stand-in doctor on the *Queen Cassiopeia.*

Well, he wasn't the only one who had been thrown by the sudden turn of events, she told herself defiantly. She hadn't planned this. Sleeping with the boss certainly hadn't been on her cruise ship to-do list. And if he thought that she was going to be angling for a repeat performance, then she would be more than happy to set him straight.

After Bradley, there was no way she wanted anything complicated with anyone. Even someone who looked like Nikhil, who *kissed* like Nikhil and never mind the rest of his incredible arsenal of skills.

Abruptly, her traitorous body gave a delicious shiver at the memory.

Could it only be this morning that he'd left her bed? It felt like a lifetime ago. She'd gone down to breakfast alone, somewhere between floating on air after their night together and fighting the strangest sense of…what she could only describe as *loss,* when her mobile had rung and she'd looked down to see the Port-Star company name—and she'd just *known.*

Isla pretended that the little celebratory dance that had started in her belly was because she was effectively being upgraded from a two-week tour of the South Americas on the *Jewel of Hestia* to a two-month round-the-world tour on the stunning *Queen Cassiopeia.*

The truth, she feared, was far more shameful.

Her body wasn't spinning crazily at the fact that the

cruise liner was the best ship in the fleet—possibly the world; it was spiralling madly at the fact that it was *Nikhil's* ship. And some naïve part of herself appeared to be holding onto the fantasy notion that, on some secret level, Nikhil might be a tiny bit pleased to see her too.

'Have you seen around our little terrain down here?' Reginald asked, hauling her back to the present.

'Yes, I showed Isla the consultation rooms, the crew ward and the private rooms for the passengers before the emergency,' Jordanna announced quickly, clearly not wanting to be seen to be slacking.

'It's more luxurious than any medical centre I've ever worked in before.' Isla laughed.

'Isn't it?' The senior doctor's proud smile said it all. 'Not to mention the fact that we get to see the world. I might not have the private practice that some of my former med school compatriots might have, but how many of them can intersperse their surgeries with visits to the Pyramids in Egypt, the Sydney Opera House or the Norwegian fjords?'

'So we do get to visit these places?' Isla asked.

'Yes.'

'Often.'

'It's an amazing lifestyle,' chorused the three nurses simultaneously.

'They said so on the course, and in the training documents,' Isla admitted. 'But I didn't know if it really worked well in practice.'

'It works,' Reginald assured her. 'Normally, at the start of every cruise, our team gets together and calls dibs on the places they really want to visit. Because you're coming in partway through, you've missed out on that, so you'll have to make do with the sights that Dr Morris—the doctor you've replaced—chose, but I'm sure you'll be happy.'

'I can't recall all of his selections,' Gerd added, 'but

I think some of them included a banana plantation in Ecuador, a high-speed boating afternoon in Mexico and an exclusive restaurant in Los Angeles. Although I think one of those might have been as a shore doctor on duty.'

'Lucky you.' Lisa laughed. 'Ecuador is coming up soon.'

'I have a museum in Peru and the Panama Canal,' Reginald added. 'So, you see, we keep one doctor on duty on-board, and the other can go ashore.'

'And we usually keep one nurse on board, whilst the other two can go ashore.' Lisa grinned. 'It isn't a bad way to see the world.'

'It isn't bad at all,' agreed Isla.

'Lisa and I are going for a break below; shall we show you around?' Jordanna asked suddenly. 'Surgery isn't for another couple of hours, and Gerd is on duty until then.'

'Sure; that would be lovely.' Isla fought to sound even, and calm.

Being invited to join the two nurses was proof that they had begun to like her, which would make the entire transition a lot easier.

'You don't want to join us?' Lisa grinned at Reginald, who grinned back.

'No, thank you, my dear. Very kind, though.'

Isla recalled some of the trainers on her familiarisation course telling her that the hierarchy on a ship was one of the most important anywhere. It dictated whether you were confined to the hot, smelly bowels of the ship, or whether you got to tread the immaculate hallways of the glamorous passenger decks.

She couldn't imagine Dr Reginald Turner frequenting the crew bars or being part of the bed-hopping culture that she'd been assured existed. Although, given the glint in his eye, she imagined he might have had some fun in his free and single youth.

Well, she might be single but she had no intention of being part of any bed-hopping. Last night with Nikhil was the only action she intended to have for the next few months. As a minimum.

'Did you have your interview with the Captain?' Lisa asked as the three of them began to stroll down the passageways.

'Yes.' As necessarily brief as it had been. 'He seems decent enough.'

'Yeah, he's okay.' Jordanna nodded. 'Generally fair and runs a good ship. But wait until you see his right-hand man.'

As both nurses let out a low, appreciative whistle, Isla didn't know how she kept putting one foot in front of the other. There was no question they were talking about Nikhil.

'That is one seriously hot male specimen.' Jordanna swooned as Lisa nodded vigorously.

'*Seriously* hot.'

'Practically every woman on this ship has thrown themselves at him at some point,' the American continued. 'Crew, staff and passengers.'

Isla tried to bite her tongue. She didn't want to get sucked into the gossip and yet she couldn't seem to stop herself. It was a terrible compulsion—the likes of which she'd never suffered before.

'He's a player then?' she heard herself ask.

'You'd have thought so—' Lisa grimaced '—but the guy never bites.'

'Maybe he does, in secret?' She didn't know what made her say it, but both nurses laughed out loud.

'Not a chance,' scoffed Lisa, turning to her colleague to back her up.

'You can't have secrets on a ship. It's impossible; we

all live in each other's pockets. No matter how discreet, someone is always watching.'

'And talking,' Lisa added. 'Fair warning.'

'Heeded.' Isla forced herself to smile, though now her cheeks felt tight with the effort. 'So he has never slept with anyone? Ever?'

'Not on board ship,' Lisa confirmed. 'Though I imagine there have been women. How could there not have been, the way he looks?'

'You'll understand it better when you see him,' Jordanna agreed. 'People like to gossip, of course. And there are always stories of people who know someone, who know someone, who *heard* he'd slept with someone. But in five years on board the same ships as him, I have never known anyone who could actually substantiate it. And, like I said, ship life has no secrets.'

'Plus there are rumours that he once hooked up with a colleague who was leaving the cruising way of life to set up a café in Spain,' added Lisa. 'But as she was leaving, no one knows for sure.'

Jordanna nodded again. 'You can imagine there have been several girls that desperate to get with him over the years they've applied for transfers in the hope that he would then look at them.'

'And has it worked?' Isla couldn't seem to stop herself from asking.

Lisa snorted scornfully. 'No. They were airheads if they thought it would.'

'Right.' Isla shrugged. It really shouldn't matter to her one iota what kind of a reputation Nikhil Dara had. 'Well, as one of the senior officers, I doubt we'll see much of him anyway.'

'Certainly not enough.' Jordanna pulled a rueful face. 'Part of his job includes safety and security so he does come down here now and then to do his rounds, but certainly not enough.'

'We'd all like to see a lot more of him,' quipped Lisa, her insinuating wink driving home her pun. 'If you know what I mean.'

'We know what you mean, Lisa.' Jordanna rolled her eyes good-naturedly. 'The whole of Chile probably knows what you mean.'

'Says the girl who threw herself on him the first night she was ever on board.'

Isla watched, intrigued, as the stunning American flushed slightly.

'Yes, well, he turned me down without even blinking an eye.'

'The only guy who ever has.' Lisa threaded her arm through her friend's in solidarity, before turning to Isla. 'Makes me feel better about the fact that he's never looked twice at me either, though. If he can turn down Miss USA here, then what chance do the rest of us stand? Although you're pretty striking too, Isla. You both make me feel dowdy by comparison.'

'You're beautiful,' Isla and Jordanna chorused instantly, and both nurses turned to look at her approvingly.

'Yeah—' Lisa grinned '—you'll do fine, Doc. Hard worker, knows her medical stuff and nice to boot. We'll definitely keep you over your condescending predecessor any day.'

'Thanks—' she laughed '—I think.'

And though she didn't mention it, she quietly filed away the fact that the previous doctor apparently hadn't been a good fit for the medical team, and they were glad to have her on board. Somehow, that made the idea of having to face Nikhil that much easier.

Although, with any luck, she wouldn't have to.

The smells and sounds of the crew bar reached Isla's senses long before they reached the room itself. Even so, she wasn't prepared for the sights as she rounded the corner and stepped through the doors.

It felt as if there were hundreds of crew in the place already mingling with raucous laughter, although it couldn't even be half of those crew on board. And the place was gargantuan. There were TV screens and arcade games, a bank of computers on one wall and a bowling alley on the other. There were even several pool tables, ice-hockey tables and football tables in there. And still there would be room for more.

'Come on.' Jordanna grabbed her hand as the three of them weaved through the people to the bar. 'It's a bit of a shock to the senses, I know, but Lisa will get the drinks, we'll get the seats and you'll soon start to settle.'

Obediently, Isla followed, circling the room twice before Jordanna spotted a small group getting ready to leave a table and pounced.

'Impressive,' Isla commented.

'Yeah, well, in here you have to be faster than a passenger grabbing the last chocolate éclair off the dessert buffet.'

Isla didn't bother to say that passenger would probably have been her mother.

'So this is your first cruise?' Jordanna asked as they shuffled into the seats.

'Yes, I was supposed to be joining the *Jewel of Hestia* tomorrow but…'

'Thank God you're with us,' Jordanna cut in. 'Do a good job and you could probably put in a request to stay here permanently. If you carry on the way you're going, the rest of us would definitely stand character for you. And Reginald holds a lot of sway.'

'The previous doctor was that bad?'

'Worse.' The nurse squeezed her eyes shut as she shook her head. 'Not with the passengers, of course. He was the epitome of a caring doctor to them. But with the crew, and with us…? No, he was horrid.'

For a moment, Isla hesitated. She was desperate to hear more, but starting the job bad-mouthing a colleague who she'd never met wasn't her style. Instead, she opted to change the conversation.

'So what are the patients like?'

That easily, the conversation flipped to medical scenarios, both the routine and the unusual, and when Lisa made her way over with their drinks they indulged in the inexorable horror scenarios.

It was perhaps a good half hour of free-flowing conversation before the two nurses abruptly fell quiet, leaving Isla to look up from the straw of her drink and see a disapproving Nikhil looming over their table.

'Dr Sinclair, drinking already?'

Isla flashed hot then cold, shock and unwanted excitement coursing through her like petrol, and with the sheer unfairness of his accusation as the match.

She drew in a deep, furious breath. 'I don't think…'

'I'm not asking what you think, Doctor.' He cut her off instantly. 'A word, please. Now.'

CHAPTER SIX

Nikhil barely waited for Isla to join him before striding out of the bar and back along the corridor to the bank of crew-only elevators, trying not to think about where they'd been heading the last time they'd been in an elevator together.

And wasn't that the problem?

Seeing her sitting there in the bar, already so at home with his crew, was like a punch to the gut. Not least because he'd been *glad* to see her there.

What the hell was that about?

He never liked to mix professional and private. Yet, in that moment, the only thing he'd really wanted to do was get her alone and pick back up where they'd left off that morning.

He simply hadn't been able to help himself from heading over to her. The woman was like some kind of opiate, and he seemed hell-bent on getting a high. If he'd walked away, no one would have known any different. Instead, he'd marched up to her in front of half of the rest of the medical staff and made some kind of damned scene.

All because he wanted Isla Sinclair, with a ferocity that he'd never experienced before.

Stepping inside the elevator beside him, she turned

around and folded her arms over her chest, a hint of mulishness about her delicious mouth.

'I didn't ask for this transfer,' she announced.

'Not here, please,' he clipped out swiftly.

'You think someone's going to overhear us?'

'Not here,' he repeated simply. A command, not a request.

And possibly more to keep his own charging, roaring emotions in check than anything else. Still, Nikhil wouldn't have been surprised if she'd made a point of non-compliance. But, even though she exhaled deeply, she didn't try to say anything more, and Nikhil was left to his own thoughts.

The overriding one being that he should feel more aggrieved than he did that she was here, on *his* ship.

He'd received the call from Head Office a few hours ago informing him that, to expedite handovers, they'd opted to transfer a Dr Sinclair to his ship because she happened to be in Chile.

She might never have told him her surname, but his gut had known instantly it was her. If he hadn't been caught up with a safety boat issue on the crew decks he probably would have been the one to conduct her interview in place of the Captain.

He was glad he hadn't. It had taken all this time for him to get his head straight. If he even had it straight now.

Deep in the logical side of his brain he knew it made sense. She was in Chile waiting for the *Hestia* to arrive, once the *Cassiopeia* had left. So assigning her to this ship meant that they wouldn't be late leaving port. Apparently, another doctor who was, even now, airborne and on their way to this port would be better placed to join the *Hestia* instead.

But it wasn't the efficacy of the transfer that concerned

him the most. This thing that was worming its way through him wasn't annoyance or aggravation. It was something far, far more dangerous. More inappropriate.

It was altogether too much like *pleasure.* A sort of *thrill* that she was here—on *his* ship. And as much as Nikhil tried to punch it down, it wouldn't go.

He, who had spent his entire career zealously avoiding blurring the lines between his personal life and his professional one.

He'd known he had a problem last night when they'd had sex—maybe even before that. He'd wanted it—*her*—too much. With a ferocity that he couldn't explain. And when he'd left that morning it had taken all he'd had not to turn around and stay, just that little bit longer.

And longer, again.

So what did it say that the urge to pull her into his arms, right here and now, and take up where they'd left off that morning was so damned strong?

He clenched his fists tightly and thrust them into the pockets of his uniform. He could smell the light hint of coconut in her shampoo from here, pervading his nostrils and conjuring up images he was a desperately trying not to see, his mind echoing with memories of her gasps and cries as he'd licked her to ecstasy.

What would she do if, right now, he pressed her against that wall, slid his fingers into her waistband and indulged in all that soft, wet heat that was, even now, making him hard, aching, in a way that no one else had ever made him feel?

God, how he wanted to.

Clenching his jaw until it was locked so tight that it was actually painful, Nikhil glowered at some abstract point on the metal doors in front of him. He was grateful when the elevator drew to a halt and the doors finally opened, finally releasing him from the temptations of that enclosed space.

Marching down the corridor to his office, he didn't even stop to see if Isla was following. Opening the door, he held it open and wordlessly ushered her inside.

'Like I said,' she began, even before the door had closed behind them or he'd made his way around the other side—the safe side—of his desk, 'I didn't ask for this transfer, but what was I supposed to say when they contacted me? *No, sorry, I can't. I just slept with the ship's First Officer, and he won't like it*?'

'So you did realise that I wouldn't welcome your arrival?' he managed curtly, wondering why the words that were coming out of his mouth sounded so awkward. So hollow.

'No, actually, I didn't consider you at all.'

She met his eyes for a brief moment, then let them slide away. She was lying; they both knew it. Although why it should make him feel so victorious was a different matter.

'Then now is the time to start.'

'I'm not quitting.' Her head snapped up in an instant.

'I'm not asking you to. I'm well aware it was a Head Office decision.'

'Really? Because you're acting like I'm at least partly to blame.' She sighed, raking her hand through her hair.

He remembered too clearly how soft it felt. That vaguely coconut scent. His traitorous body twitched in response, but he quashed it furiously.

Then…what?

'We can't change what happened,' he said grimly, making himself sit down behind the desk, and gesturing for Isla to do the same. 'But I want to establish the rules from here on in.'

For himself, as much as for her. Since the sight of her

standing there, her uniform lovingly fitting her curves—too pristine and perfect—was making him think of all kinds of ways to sully it.

He felt like some sex-crazed kid. Worse, he kind of liked this new sensation.

'I told you that I don't do relationships.' He wasn't sure if he was reminding Isla or himself. He'd never had to remind himself of anything like that before.

'So I hear.' Her eyes narrowed at him, too sharply for Nikhil's liking. 'You like to keep yourself single and available.'

It was about as far from the truth as it was possible to get. And yet, as reasons went, why not go with it? It would be more likely to put her off than anything else, and Lord knew he needed help to stay away from this woman.

There had been no reason for him to speak to her at all, and yet he'd found himself in that bar, having sought her out.

For what, exactly?

'I never promised you exclusivity, Isla,' he bit out, though every word tasted bitter in his mouth.

Did they sound as hollow as they felt?

'No. And I don't recall asking for it, now,' she pointed out evenly.

He might have expected her to appear more manipulative. They usually were, which was why he generally liked to be able to walk away. Only right now he seemed to be the one having the most trouble with that concept. If he'd been a lesser man it might have dented his ego.

What the hell was wrong with him?

'You think you're the only one? That you're somehow special? That we're going to pick up where we left off now we're working on the same ship together?'

He'd intended the words to score a hit, but when she

blanched he actually felt it like a physical blow. He opened his mouth to apologise, but something stopped him.

Wasn't this what he'd intended? Still, he waited, needing to hear whatever it was she was going to say.

'I understand that your one-night stand suddenly being transferred to your ship is a shock.' Isla eyed him contemptuously. 'But trust me, I'm no less thrown by it than you are.'

'Good, so long as you don't have…expectations of us now embarking on some great love affair.'

He was acting like a jerk. It was so unlike him, and yet he couldn't seem to get a grip. Yet another example of how she made him feel like some untried kid.

'I told you, this is a fresh start for me. I certainly don't need to get tangled up with any jackass men,' she added pointedly. 'Talking of love, which never really exists.'

Something he couldn't identify, or didn't want to, caught at him. Whether she'd intended it or not, he found himself hooked, reeled in—wanting to know more. Keen to uncover whatever her opinion of *love* was, in the puzzle that was Dr Isla Sinclair.

But he hadn't brought her here to piece her together in his head. He'd come here to remind them both that there could be no repeat of what had happened between them in Chile.

Only the previous night?

It felt like a lifetime ago—could it really have been that recent? Could it only have been hours ago that they had shared a bed? That he'd held her body against his, and around him?

Despite all his brain's objections, something slammed inside his chest. He might have thought it was his heart picking up pace, if he'd actually *had* a heart. If it hadn't been killed years ago, when he'd plunged that knife into his raging father.

And still he couldn't remember it. Guilt had blocked it out too tightly, clearly. Even now, trying to push that guilt down, Nikhil found himself scrabbling for something else to hold onto. A distraction that would grant him a desperate reprieve.

'Why are we here, Nikhil?' she demanded suddenly. 'Why do we need to clarify anything? Why not just stay away from each other?'

'I'm First Officer on this ship and you—thanks to Head Office's little shuffles—are now my junior doctor. Our working paths will unquestionably cross. Regularly. I've worked hard at my career, and at keeping my private life wholly removed from my professional one.'

'And what?' she snapped, and he found it fascinating the way her eyes sparked when she was angry. He suspected very few people ever got to see this side of the unflappable Dr Sinclair. 'You think I'm here to broadcast our liaison to the entire ship?'

'Some women in your position might.'

She snorted—actually *snorted*—at him. He wasn't sure anyone had ever snorted at him—at least, not in the last decade. It was so…unexpected.

'It might have escaped your notice, in your essentially Nikhil-centric way of thinking, but that's *my* private life that would be on show too. And I value my career as much as you do. Possibly more, given that, despite all the advances we women have made, who I sleep with will come under more scrutiny than who *you* sleep with.'

'I can't say that I remember much sleeping going on,' he quipped, before he could stop himself.

Suddenly, in spite of everything, he found himself grinning at her little cry of frustration. She got under his skin that easily.

'My God, you're unreasonable.'

He didn't realise when he'd moved, or how he came to be standing in front of her, but suddenly he was there, within touching distance of her. That dark thing inside him railing in its cage, howling for things it had no right to crave.

'On the contrary,' he grated out. 'I am the epitome of reason.'

At least he usually was. Before this woman had come along and turned everything upside down.

He took another step closer.

'What are you doing, Nikhil?' Isla asked.

But her voice had changed. Breathy, and fragile, and hesitant, and she watched him with that expression that made him hard and melting all at once.

It was impossible. *She* was impossible. And yet she was right…*here.*

'I don't know what you want from me,' she said, her voice thick, echoing every emotion swirling through his own body.

'You know precisely what I want.' There had to be some kind of remedy for this madness he felt every time she was in the room. But if there was, he feared that right now he wouldn't even take it.

'Because I want it too,' he heard himself growl.

She stirred him up in a way that no other woman had ever done, electrifying him and challenging him in equal measure.

She swallowed. Hard. And her bashfulness was all the more bewitching.

'I…don't know anything of the sort.'

'Then it appears I have no choice but to employ the only means to show you, *pyar*,' he growled.

And then, as if he couldn't make it any worse, he bent his head and kissed her.

Isla felt as though she was falling. Fast, and hard, with no idea what was at the bottom. And she couldn't seem to bring herself to care.

She tried to cling to some last grain of reality, but it was slipping further away with every foot that she fell.

And she was plummeting.

How was it that this kiss was so different from any last night, when she thought that they'd spent the entire night kissing. And touching. And tasting. Yet this was something different again. More intense, somehow. As though neither of them wanted to give into temptation, and at the same time as if there was nowhere else either of them wanted to be.

She knew it was wrong—certainly on an intellectual level. Hadn't they just been asserting—vociferously—their respective career choices? Hadn't they both just agreed that private lives and professional lives were clear and distinct entities which had no business becoming complicated?

And yet here they were, complicating things in the most base, primal way possible. And as wrong as Isla knew it was, she couldn't stop herself from wanting more.

Much more.

It was possibly the most thrilling, terrifying sensation that she had ever experienced. A complete loss of control, and a complete inability to care.

So long as Nikhil never stopped kissing her.

Isla was aware of nothing. And everything. Like his tongue gliding over her lips, parting them so effortlessly, and dipping so wickedly inside. Like his large hand, splayed against her back and holding her close, so deliciously close, to him. Like the way every inch of her body moulded itself, as if instinctively, to every inch of his.

It was like fire. More than that—an inferno, and she was dancing in the flames.

With every twist of his mouth against hers, and every tangle of his tongue, she made a tiny new sound in her throat. Greedy, eager, impatient. She hungered for him more than she'd hungered for anything. Even her job on this ship, it seemed.

But, rather than helping her to stop, the knowledge only made her feel that much more desperate. More daring. He made her feel glorious and proud, as if she could do anything. Even walk on the very water that encircled this ship.

If this was him keeping away from her, then she couldn't say she was complaining. Though some part of her whispered that she should.

And then his hands were moving over her. Leisurely, lazy, yet still they scorched a path as they went, leaving her quivering with heat, and fresh need. Tracing the contours of her sides and the dip of her back he slowly—too slowly—began to pull her shirt out of her trousers.

She shivered with anticipation, and damn him if the devilish man didn't smile. She could feel the curve of his mouth against her throat, kissing her in that oh-so-sensitive hollow below her ear.

'Nikhil…' His name escaped her mouth before she could stop it.

But, if anything, it only made him haul her to him even tighter. As if the sound of his name on her lips drove him on all the more.

Sliding his hands beneath the fabric, he traced a series

of whorls higher—even higher—making her breath catch in her throat in her restlessness.

'Patience, *pyar*,' he told her.

But she didn't miss the tautness in his voice—all the evidence she needed that he barely held onto his own patience. She couldn't help it; she rolled her hips against him—then exulted when they both groaned softly.

And then, as he held her waist with one hand, he finally allowed the other to reach higher, nudging her breast aside and raking one thumb pad over her straining nipple.

Isla arched instinctively against him. She heard the low cry, but it took a moment to realise it was herself.

'I've missed these.' Nikhil's voice rumbled through her, as dark as the inky ocean, and just as deep.

As though it hadn't only been this morning that he'd left her bed.

As though it had been a whole eternity.

Part of her felt as though it must surely have been that long. And she didn't understand how, though her mind had replayed last night several times already—in spectacular detail—it had somehow failed to recapture quite the intensity of the effect Nikhil had on her.

Her mind had somehow played it down. That didn't seem possible. But it wasn't playing it down now; it was sending her wild and flooding her with a sense of lust that she could hardly believe she'd denied existed only twenty-four hours before.

Before she'd met Nikhil.

Now, she could do nothing but give into that fervour. More than that, she was practically racing towards it.

It was ludicrous the way her body reacted with memories and anticipation, and all she could do was press herself against him—hot steel against her softest part. Full of promise.

It was a noise outside the cabin door that finally broke into their fragile, fictitious little bubble. The voices of crew who could only be officers, talking confidently outside the room—reminding Isla and Nikhil exactly where they were. And what they were supposed to be doing.

Or perhaps, more the point, what they weren't supposed to be doing.

In one smooth movement, Nikhil swung her away from him and set her down, turning to stalk back to his desk whilst Isla scrambled to get her head together. And her clothing straight.

'This was a mistake.'

His words lashed through the air, and she was almost surprised when they didn't physically cut into her flesh.

'How very clichéd of you.' She barely recognised her own voice in her effort not to fold under his glower. 'Disappointingly so, in fact.'

'Is everything a joke to you, Dr Sinclair?'

'Dr Sinclair?' She was proud that her voice didn't waver too badly. 'Do you think that addressing each other formally can erase what just happened between us?'

'Clearly, we need some boundaries.'

'Boundaries?' She narrowed her eyes at him.

'I warned you that nothing more could happen between us again. And yet here we are.'

Isla busied herself tucking her shirt in, not quite trusting herself to answer straight away.

How had it come to this? She'd been so careful all her life, and then last night she'd met Nikhil and she'd decided that one night—just for once—she could throw caution to the wind.

And now she was standing in her boss's office—technically her boss's boss's office—her clothes in disarray, a low, molten ache deep within and her legs threatening to buckle beneath her at any moment. And now Nikhil seemed to be laying it all at her feet.

It was too much to bear.

'You say it like you think this is entirely *my* fault,' she managed at last. Then lifted her eyes to his with as much defiance as she could muster. 'Or have I misunderstood?'

He'd called her *pyar*.

My love.

Nikhil glowered across the room, torn between contemplating the madness of having sent her away from him just now and the lunacy of having brought her to his office in the first instance.

He had no idea how he'd managed to tear himself away from her. He had even less idea how he managed to stand in place, around the other side of the desk from her, as though it could provide some barrier between them.

As though it made her any less of a siren, and him any less the mariner drawn inexorably to her.

Although that would suggest that he was powerless and she was deliberately luring him, when the truth was that they were equal victims to this all-consuming attraction that crackled between them.

Not that his current state of fury at himself would allow him to admit that much aloud.

'You're a distraction, Isla,' he ground out instead. 'And I don't do *distractions*.'

He knew the moment he spoke the words that they were a mistake. They revealed far too many things that he would much rather have kept to himself.

He watched as Isla's eyes widened then crinkled, seeing his unexpected weakness for herself.

It was galling.

'Is that so?' She arched her eyebrows. 'How flattering that I'm a distraction. I wouldn't have thought that the savagely determined Nikhil Dara would have allowed anything to sway him.'

'I didn't say that I intended to allow anything to *sway* me,' he bit back.

'And yet here we are. With you taking time to drag me to your office just to kiss me and then tell me…what? That you don't intend to waste time being distracted by me?'

She had a point, but that wasn't the worst of it. No, the worst of it was that he—who had prided himself on control and restraint all these years—was now fighting the considerable urge to silence her with his mouth—*again*—whilst he stripped them both and worshipped her body the way he'd been dreaming about doing since he'd walked away from her hotel room.

It certainly didn't help that she wanted him every bit as badly. He knew women well enough to see it in the lines of her body. He could read it in every dark flash of her eyes, every deep breath she inhaled, every time she flicked her tongue out over her lips.

And every single one of her reactions only served to stoke that fire even higher, making it burn hotter and brighter until he feared his entire body might burst into flame.

It was ludicrous.

They'd had sex, just as he'd had sex with women before. Not an obscene amount of women—not like some of the officers he knew, who seemed incapable of preventing their trousers from ruling their heads, on practically a daily basis—but still, he didn't do repeat performances. It wasn't worth the hassle.

Which only made it all the more infuriating that he couldn't seem to shake this woman from his head. He wanted her.

His body *needed* her. And that simply wouldn't do.

He would stay away from Dr Isla Sinclair if it killed him.

CHAPTER SEVEN

THE BANANA PLANTATION was vast and dense, bustling with people. Isla followed the local tour guide with fascination, watching as men chopped down enormous clusters of bananas, already wrapped in plastic bagging.

'Did you know it isn't really a banana tree but a banana plant?'

She turned slowly to face Nikhil, her heart hammering so loudly in her chest that it was surely impossible that he couldn't hear it.

One moment she'd been rather enjoying her tour of one of Ecuador's—and apparently the world's—biggest producer of organic bananas, learning about hands and fingers and tiers, and watching as the workers loaded enormous bagged bunches onto a rail system, and the next she found herself face to face with the person she'd been trying so hard to shove out of her head.

It had been almost a week since their encounter in Nikhil's office, and she'd been congratulating herself on having managed to keep her distance from him.

Or at least she'd told herself that she *ought* to be congratulating herself.

She'd told herself that she didn't feel anything remotely akin to regret that things had turned out the way they had. Turning something that had been so electrifying and fun that night in Chile into something infinitely uglier. And sombre.

With such thoughts whirling around her brain, Isla wasn't sure how she managed to tug her expression into something she hoped was a light, airy expression.

'Mr Dara, what a surprise. I thought we were keeping our distance from each other. Or, more accurately, that I was to keep my distance from *you*.' Her voice sounded remarkably even. 'According to you, I'm too much of a distraction.'

She had no idea how she managed to infuse her words with condemnation, but she found she was rather proud of herself. Still, if she could have bound her erratic heart down with ropes and chains, she would have done.

'You are a distraction,' he replied easily. 'How else do you explain the fact that, instead of concentrating on the tour, I'm talking to you?'

'Perhaps you have a childlike attention span?' she quipped. 'I've inherited all the tours and duties of the doctor who I've replaced, and I'm here as the medical liaison in the event of any accident. Why are you here?'

'So you had no choice in this day-trip?'

'None at all. I'm sorry if it bruises your evidently swollen ego.' She made sure not to sound remotely sorry.

It was galling, but he didn't bite as she'd anticipated. Instead, something she might have taken to be amusement—had she not already known that Nikhil didn't have an amused bone in his body—tugged at his lips.

'No doubt I can get my fragile ego massaged back into shape, if need be,' he drawled.

Isla batted away a sharp stab of some emotion that she told herself couldn't possibly have been jealousy.

'No doubt you can,' she muttered darkly. 'Though you might watch what you pick up. I've just had to treat a rather nasty outbreak of genital warts and gonorrhoea that's ripping through a good proportion of the crew.'

'I'm aware, since all your reports ultimately come to me. But thank you for your concern.'

'It isn't concern.' Isla narrowed her eyes.

'Really? It sounded like concern.'

'Well, it wasn't.'

So much for trying to rile him; he was enjoying this far too much. But didn't that beg the question, *Why was she trying so hard to rile him?*

'I also happen to know that you've treated two heart attacks, a sprained ankle, a honeymooner's unexpected pregnancy and multiple passengers with known allergies who happened to decide that the food in question looked just that bit too tempting to pass up. And that's just amongst the passengers.'

'Right… Well, then… I guess that's you up to speed.'

Isla faltered, not sure what to say next, or even where to go. But then a shriek from the main excursion party a hundred metres or so ahead drew everyone's attention as Isla and Nikhil raced to the passenger.

'I've been bitten, I've been bitten…' The man was already beginning to panic. 'Is it a spider? I think I killed it, but it's still in my shirt. Get it out. You've got to get it out.'

As Isla began dealing with the man, a couple of the locals came running over. There was no obvious sign of a bite but, sure enough, in the man's shirt was a dead spider. As the two plantation workers peered at it, the passenger began to hyperventilate.

'Oh, God, I'm going to die out here.'

'No.' One of the workers lifted his head with a smile. 'Is not problem. Not bad spider.'

'Irritado,' the other added, making an itching action with his hands. *'No es venenoso.'*

A collective sigh went around the group. Most of them were clearly relieved, but a couple looked a little disappointed not to be treated to a more exciting show. Isla wasn't surprised when Nikhil took charge, reclaiming all the passengers' attention and getting the tour back on track as their guide moved them a little further from the action.

Isla crouched down carefully by her patient.

'Are you known to be allergic, Mr…?'

'Camberwell.' He didn't look convinced. 'You're sure it isn't venomous? I feel sick. I think I'm going to die.'

'Can we get him to shelter?' Isla asked as Nikhil materialised by her side. 'And maybe a chair, and some ice?'

He barely seemed to lift his hand before a couple of plantation workers hurried over, listening intently as he rattled off a few commands to them in Spanish. Firm, yet not imperious—*typically Nikhil*, as she was beginning to understand.

'Sí, sí.' The men made a chair with their hands and proceeded to carry the still overwrought Mr Camberwell from the plantation area to the processing plant.

Isla and Nikhil followed quickly.

'I still want him checked over properly,' Nikhil murmured.

'Of course,' she confirmed as the workers settled her patient onto a rickety chair.

She shot them a smile. *'Gracias.'*

'De nada.'

She turned her focus to her patient, not surprised when Nikhil launched into his own conversation with the men. But Mr Camberwell was her priority. She swung her little daysack off her bag, complete with some emergency medical supplies.

'All right, sir, let's check you over. I'm just going to take your pulse.'

Methodically, Isla checked her patient's pulse, breathing and reactions, applying an ice pack as soon as it arrived from the workers.

His blood pressure seemed fine, and the initial shock of the bite seemed to be wearing off now. Carefully she lifted the ice pack up and checked the area. There was perhaps the beginning of a little redness and swelling.

'It itches,' Mr Camberwell grumbled, trying to push her hand away to scratch it.

'Of course, sir—' Isla flashed her best smile '—but try not to scratch it, as that can make it worse. I'm going to clean it out for you now and apply a little antibiotic ointment, and then I think it's best to get you back to the ship and to the medical bay, just to check you over again.'

'Yes, yes.' Mr Camberwell nodded enthusiastically.

'Okay, so in the meantime I'm also going to give you an antihistamine to help with the itching.'

She began to quickly clean the area to prevent infection, keeping the man talking as she did so, more and more confident that it wasn't going to develop into something any more serious. Finally, she stood up and drew Nikhil to one side.

'Shall I return to the ship with Mr Camberwell?'

'What's the probability that his situation is going to develop?'

Isla wrinkled her nose. 'I can't say with absolute certainty, of course, but I'm confident that it's just a bite that's going to hurt and itch for a few days. I'd still like him kept under observation in the medical centre for twenty-four hours.'

'So you're better staying with this tour group, in the event of any other emergency,' Nikhil confirmed.

Isla nodded. 'Agreed, although Mr Camberwell should have someone to accompany him back to the ship.'

'Understood.'

Turning back to the party, Nikhil beckoned one of the shore excursion staff, who seemed only too eager to race over to him, her doe eyes growing wider as Nikhil began to instruct her.

One could only hope that she herself didn't look so besotted when talking to Nikhil, Isla thought irritably as she concentrated on the understandably still concerned Mr Camberwell. Not helped by the unwelcome thrill that she'd felt when she'd realised she would still get to spend another couple of hours of this excursion with Nikhil.

What was wrong with her that she couldn't push him into her past, the way he seemed to have done so easily with her? Was his appeal so great?

It had to be. Even now, she couldn't stop herself from admiring the way he was so effortlessly able to take control in any given situation. Calming yet authoritative.

And almost universally adored, of course. Men and women, passengers and crew. *That* certainly helped his appeal—and none of *them* had slept with him.

So what chance did *she* stand?

Especially when she couldn't shake the thought that, for all his words about never crossing that line between personal and professional, when he talked to her there was still an intensity in those dark, expressive eyes that she'd never, *ever* seen when he talked to anyone else.

Whatever Nikhil said, he hadn't quite pushed her into his past the way he would have her—and maybe even himself—believe.

Perhaps for him it was more about the physical, more about the sexual desire. Maybe he hadn't got quite that same kick of pleasure at the realisation that they would be spending the afternoon in each other's company. But neither was he entirely indifferent—and didn't they say that *indifference* was worse than anything?

Shaking her thoughts free, Isla busied herself tending to her patient and making a few notes, but it was no use. Her mind was filling with a slew of memories from that night. So vivid, and so real. That powerful body pressed against hers, making her *feel* things she'd never felt before. Her body shivered from the sheer memory of it, despite the heat.

'Right Mr Camberwell, let's get you back to the ship, shall we?' Nikhil's voice pierced her thoughts. Bright and firm enough to instil confidence into her worried patient, who looked up instantly, his watery eyes clearing as he took Nikhil's outstretched arm and allowed himself to be helped to his feet. Gathering up the last of her kit, Isla hurried after them as they headed for the vehicle.

A few more instructions, and the Jeep was heading off down the plantation path. But when Isla made herself turn around she realised the main excursion party had disappeared, around to some different area of the tightly packed banana stems. Now, she was alone with Nikhil, save for the processing staff who were all too busy concentrating on their production line to pay the two of them any attention.

'Well done,' he said quietly, turning to face her.

The full force of his gaze sent a primitive wave of heat crashing through her.

Isla forced herself to laugh. 'What for? Doing my job?'

'Doing it so quietly that none of the other guests have felt panicked enough to return to the ship along with Mr Camberwell. It happens,' he added when she frowned in surprise.

'Oh.'

It was all she could think of. Her mind had gone blank.

'You are always so discreet, Isla. It's a surprising quality, particularly on a cruise ship like ours, I find.'

The compliment was as unexpected as it was sincere, catching Isla off-guard. For a moment she flailed around for a response.

'Careful, Nikhil.' She swallowed at last. 'That almost sounded like a compliment.'

'Perhaps because it *was* a compliment. Though I'm glad to hear you've dispensed with the Mr Dara nonsense.'

Isla opened her mouth to object, but a gurgle of laughter came bubbling out instead. Unintended but, it turned out, the perfect way to break the tension.

'I could have called you *sir*; you are the First Officer, after all.'

He let out a low, deep chuckle of his own and before she could stop herself she seized it, filing it away somewhere special like the dragon hoarding its treasure. Or the chimera hiding the lost Inca gold, that Reginald had been telling them all about after his return from his day-trip to Peru.

'You wouldn't call me *sir* even if you had to,' he noted. Accurately, as it turned out.

'Not even if you commanded me,' she agreed.

But she wasn't prepared for the way his eyes suddenly grew hot. Hungry. Reflecting all the things she was trying to keep stuffed down, so deep inside.

'And what commands would you obey, Isla? If I uttered them?'

'None,' she retorted.

But her voice was hoarser than normal. A fact of which they were both aware.

She had no intention of adding any more, but then her mouth started talking all of its own accord.

'And what about you, Nikhil? What commands would you obey if *I* issued them?'

He took a step closer to her, and the whole world suddenly receded until it was just her and Nikhil. No one else existed for Isla. Not the plantation, not the workers, not even the tour group, only just out of sight around that corner.

'Do you really want to know?'

His tone was so heavy, so loaded, that it fired straight through Isla, pooling between her legs. Making her molten in an instant.

'Yes.' But it was barely more than a whisper.

It was odd, the way everything seemed so loud and yet so still. She could hear monkeys calling to each other, birds singing the most wondrous songs and insects chirping and squeaking. Yet at the same time she didn't think she could hear anything above the roaring in her ears.

She had no idea how long they stood there, staring at each other, some invisible thread binding them together, tighter and tighter, until she couldn't move.

Or didn't want to.

And still he didn't answer. He didn't speak at all. Yet she could hear his thoughts swirling through her. All the things he wanted to do to her, right there. All the things she wanted too.

Just when she'd begun to think he was never going to speak, he opened his mouth and murmured the words, only loud enough for her to hear.

'Why don't you try it and find out?'

And Isla didn't think twice. She lifted herself up onto her tiptoes, in her heavy, leather walking boots, and she kissed him, the way she'd been dreaming of doing all week.

And then he was kissing her. His lips slipping smoothly over hers, his tongue moving languorously as he tasted her, sampled her. Over and over again.

Unhurried and unfettered, as if they had hours. Days. Perhaps whole lifetimes. Another level again from the passion of that night they'd spent together, and somehow that made her tremble all the more.

His fingers traced her jaw, leaving her skin scorched in their wake. He made her feel infinitely precious, and utterly desired. No other man had ever made her feel so… *aware.* Aware of him. And aware of herself.

That night, he'd awakened something in her that she hadn't even known had been lying dormant. She'd told herself that she'd been in complete control of the passion of that night. She'd chosen to pursue the novelty of a one-night encounter with the clichéd tall, dark stranger, leading to her first ever one-night stand. At thirty-two, she'd decided to lose herself in a way she'd never done before.

But now, here, alone with Nikhil, she was finally forced to concede the truth. She hadn't been in control at all. It hadn't been about that night, or that place. It had been about *him*. Nikhil. She doubted any other tall, dark or handsome stranger would have made her lose herself the way that he had done. *He* made her feel things she'd never felt before. *He* made her discover more about herself. And the worst of it was that she wanted to learn more.

This was insanity, Nikhil thought as he knocked on the door to Isla's cabin.

He didn't realise he'd been holding his breath until she opened the door. And stared at him.

'Nikhil?'

'Can I come in? I'd rather not stand here in the hallway outside your room for longer than necessary.'

Her eyes gleamed at him then narrowed, echoes of their last encounter practically bouncing off the walls around them. And even though her stance was defiant, her voice was careful and low. Discreet.

'If you've come to insult me again, like the other day,

then I'd rather you didn't. I don't need you to come here to tell me that you regret kissing me earlier, and I'd rather you dealt with your guilt yourself. Quietly. In your own room.'

He didn't answer. Didn't tell her that the only thing he regretted was the fact that they'd had to stop, before the tour group walked back around the corner and spotted them. Or that he regretted that the excursion was so long that he'd been forced to carry on with the afternoon as though he was enjoying himself, when the only thing he'd wanted to do was get back here—and come right here, to her room.

But Nikhil didn't say any of that. It was hard enough to admit it to himself, without having to admit it to someone else. Even Isla.

Especially Isla.

'Can I come in?' he repeated simply.

She glowered at him a moment longer before sighing heavily. 'Apparently, I don't have a choice.'

He didn't answer. He merely followed her inside and closed the door.

'Why are you here, Nikhil?' she demanded, when he didn't speak. But he didn't miss the slight quake in her voice. 'To tell me that you regret what happened at the plantation? Because you've already made it clear we should stay away from each other, not give into distractions.'

And still he didn't answer. He had no idea what he *was* doing there, only that his legs seemed to have carried him along the corridors to her room, all of their own accord. The only thing he knew was that a week ago he'd sworn he'd stay away from this woman if it killed him.

He thought it damned near had.

How many times had he thought he'd seen her retreating around a corner just as he'd arrived? Or imagined he could smell that soft, lightly floral scent in the air as he walked down a corridor?

How many times had he found a reason to be near the medical centre when he could arguably have left it to another officer?

'Look, Nikhil—' she twisted her hands in mid-air in front of him '—I made a mistake earlier, and I'm sorry. I wouldn't want to distract you and mess up your head. Or your career. Or whatever.'

'It's already messed up,' he heard himself say, though he didn't clarify what, precisely, felt messed up.

Perhaps because he wasn't sure he knew the answer to that either. He only knew that, oddly, it felt like a good messed-up. As if he was messed up with Isla. How was it that the only time he ever really felt like himself—like the real Nikhil—was when he was with her?

It should be exactly the opposite. She made him act crazily, when he was all about control. How was that the *real him*?

He let out a low sound, not wanting to think about that right now. He just had to fight this impossibly overwhelming urge to put his hands on her shoulders and haul her to him, to claim that pink, perfect mouth with his, just like he had a lifetime ago.

He seemed to have no control where Isla Sinclair was concerned, and yet suddenly he couldn't bring himself to care. The rules he'd made for himself—rules that had worked flawlessly all these years—had been in disarray ever since she'd walked onto his ship.

Or even before that, when he'd been called to that damned bar brawl.

This wasn't how things were meant to be. His career wasn't supposed to merge with his personal life. It couldn't. Because each needed to be kept in its own box—one that he could pick up easily when it was time and put down just as easily when he needed to. But Isla didn't fit that black and white mould.

She didn't fit *any* mould.

She was too fluid, and vibrant, and…challenging. She was upturning all those carefully ordered boxes, spilling the contents of his life out onto the floor and mixing them up. And, for all his statements about not blurring the lines, he wasn't really preventing her.

Worse, he was *encouraging* her. *He* was the one who had kissed her back at the banana plantation, and *he* was the one who had come to her cabin now.

'I came to apologise,' he lied. Because that hadn't been in the forefront of his mind when he'd stalked the corridors to get here—though it should have been.

'To apologise?' Her eyebrows shot up, as if she didn't believe him either.

She already knew him too well, and what did it say that he liked the idea of that?

'You're right.' He dipped his head. 'It *was* me who called you a distraction, but kissed you today. It *is* me who is seeking you out now, to try to make things…less fraught between us. To make sure that, after this afternoon, I haven't given you false hope.'

'False hope?' she echoed again, this time in disbelief.

Though there was something else in her tone that made him feel he should tread warily. He just couldn't put his finger on what that *something* was.

'That there could be a repeat of what happened between us, in Chile.'

'I understood what you were referring to,' she managed stiffly. '*Sex.* You can use the word, Nikhil, I'm not prudish.'

No, she wasn't. A reel of X-rated images rolled through his head, from the unabashed way she'd come apart in his arms to the wild way she'd shattered under his tongue. All of which threatened to break his resolve.

His body was heating at the mere memory, his heart

beginning to drum out a beat in his chest. Low, and deep, and carnal. A call to action.

She was so close that he could smell the fresh scent of her shampoo, stirring his memories and telling him that she'd only recently emerged from the shower. Giving him a whole new set of images to contend with. Testing his apparently already fragile resolve.

'Sex then,' he growled, fascinated at the way she fought not to react.

'Sex,' she managed, and it was all he could do not to bend his head and lick the promise-laden word from her lips. 'We had it. And it was…fine.'

'Fine?' The exclamation was out before he could stop it.

'*Good*, then,' she amended. 'But you're mistaken if you think that I spend my days dreaming of more.'

'Indeed?'

Without really knowing what he was doing, Nikhil edged closer to her, ignoring the voice in his head shouting that this was the perfect way out. It allowed Isla to save face whilst giving him what he wanted—what he *said* he wanted—*distance.* It wasn't a challenge; he shouldn't take it as one.

'You don't think of it at all?' His voice sounded odd. Not himself.

'No.' Her voice was insubstantial. 'Never.'

Before he could think better of it, he dipped his head to her ear.

'Liar,' he murmured. 'You want a lot more.'

'No.' She jerked her head a little, as though trying to shake it. 'You're not the only one with no-go rules about colleagues.'

'I'm not talking about other colleagues, Isla. I'm talking about you and me.'

'There is no you and me.' She didn't even sound as if she believed her own words. 'And I don't want there to be.'

'Is that so?'

It took Nikhil all of his willpower not to throw her over his shoulder, carry her to her bed and prove to them both just how weak that declaration was. But he couldn't. He *wouldn't.*

He should never have come here.

He should have gone to the gym and gone several rounds with the punchbag, or run a decent half marathon on the treadmill, or even swum a couple of miles in one of the ship's special lap pools.

Anything to expend energy—and frustration—and to stop himself from coming here.

He should leave now—only he didn't. He stayed rooted to the spot, pretending that he didn't sense his renowned self-control starting to slip away.

The roar grew in Nikhil's head the longer he stood, looking at Isla. Watching the way her pulse jumped in her elegant neck, belying the calm exterior she was so desperately trying to present. That telling, hungry darkening in her glorious eyes. The way her breathing grew as choppy as the seas could around here.

She wanted him. Every bit as much as he wanted her.

Blood pooled in his sex, telling him what it wanted in no uncertain terms. His body at war with his brain. And there was nothing more to it than sex. There couldn't be.

He wouldn't *allow* there to be.

'What do you want from me, Nikhil?' she cried out suddenly.

'Nothing,' he rasped. 'And too much.'

Then, before either of them could analyse that any further, he pressed her up against the wall of her cabin and claimed her mouth with his. And, even as she emitted a weak moan of protest, her arms came up to loop around his neck and press her soft, warm breasts against his chest, their peaks already hard, making his palms itch.

Making every inch of him itch. And ache. And *need.*

She was driving him crazy.

He lifted his hands to her head, taking it gently in his palms and tilting it so that he could better kiss her. He revelled in the way her lips parted when he slicked his tongue over them, inviting him inside, making them both want more.

He kissed her thoroughly, completely, the way he'd wanted to since…for ever. He finally permitted his hands to trail over her body, reacquainting himself with all those mouth-watering curves that haunted him each and every night.

It was sheer bliss to finally give into this dark need to reach around the back of his neck and take her hands, intertwining her fingers with his as he held them against the wall above her head, making her arch into him all the more.

Then, as he encircled both her wrists with one of his hands, he moved his other hand down to relearn the lines of her face, the long sweep of her back and the indent of her waist. All so strangely familiar, as though he'd caressed them a thousand times instead of just that one night.

Or as though he knew them by instinct.

The same instinct that made him lift his hand to the underside of her breast, the sublimity of her heart as it thundered wildly beneath his palm. Betraying her. Confirming everything that he already knew.

Walking his fingers slowly higher, Nikhil allowed his thumb to graze the hard peak, evident even through the material of her uniform. Her harsh intake of breath only fuelling the fires that much more as she let her head tip back to allow his mouth access to her neck, and that sensitive hollow at her throat. And he took full advantage.

It was impossible to resist any longer. He could feel the monster inside him rattling to be let out. To take what he wanted, when what he wanted was Isla. To hell with all his rules and boundaries; she'd been breaking them all from the moment they'd met, anyway.

Sliding his hand down her belly to her abdomen, and lower, Nikhil deftly unbuttoned her crisp white trousers and slid the zip down with a shocking, thrilling sound.

'What…are you doing?' Each word caught deliciously.

But Nikhil didn't have time to dwell. He felt raw, and edgy. Primal. Even as he grazed his teeth over the smooth white of her throat, his fingers buried themselves in her heat. He could barely trust himself to think, let alone speak.

'Giving you what you want,' he managed to grate out.

She gasped softly. 'What about you?'

'Definitely what I want,' he confessed harshly.

And then he set about proving it.

CHAPTER EIGHT

It was an explosion of sensation, tearing through her like the hottest, most blinding light. Everything in her pulled taut. Perfect.

'So wet,' Nikhil muttered, his voice almost reverent.

And Isla let the dark, greedy heat close around them both, like a fist. Her sex flooded with need as he stroked her, slowly at first, taking time to build the pace, making her mindless. The more she bucked against his hand, the lower that growl of laughter, so deep in his throat. But he didn't stop, he didn't even react, his fingers just kept moving exactly where she needed him most, that lazy, leisurely pace that she found so ridiculously addictive.

Yet it wasn't the physical act that affected Isla the most. More, it was the knowledge that Nikhil, with his reputation for being so in control amongst his staff, seemed to consistently show her a different side to himself.

And surely it wasn't too arrogant to think that it could only be *because* it was her?

But there was no time to voice it, or even consider it. His fingers were sliding over her, sending her off into spirals of pleasure. In ten years together, Bradley had never once made her feel this incredible, this on the edge, this desired.

Perhaps worse than that, however, was the fact that she didn't think she'd ever cared. Yet right now, with Nikhil, it was all she could think about. The feel of his fingers playing with her, toying with her. And that incredible wave of sensation, swelling deep inside her, bigger, and higher, like a tsunami of lust until suddenly she realised that it was curling back around—so powerful and so fast—that she barely had time to cling hold of Nikhil before it began to crash over her.

And all she could hear were her own greedy sounds, as she was caught up in the most perfect wipe-out she thought she had ever known.

Isla had no idea how long it took her to resurface. She didn't particularly care. All she knew was that Nikhil was still there, holding her. And that she was desperate for him to feel a fraction of the fervour that he'd just rained down upon her.

She wanted to hear him call out her name, the way he always made her cry out his. And maybe that realisation should scare her more than it did. But, right in that moment, Isla couldn't bring herself to care.

'Now me,' she whispered shakily, one hand still clinging to his shoulder for support, as the other hand slid down his uniform to cup him where he was hard, and ready.

Just for her.

The knock at the door could hardly have been timed much worse.

The atmosphere in the room flipped in a heartbeat as Nikhil wrenched himself away from her, leaving her fighting to stay standing on her still-weak legs. But not before she'd seen the expression in his eyes harden, and she knew he'd shut her out—just as she'd been prising away those defences that he kept around him, like armour.

'Dr Sinclair?'

Another sharp rap seemed to echo through her room.

'Answer them,' Nikhil commanded quietly, his fury barely restrained.

But she knew it was directed more at himself than anyone else. Not that it made the situation any less awkward.

'And say what?' she hissed, relieved her voice didn't quake the way she had feared it might.

'Buy yourself enough time to sort your uniform out, then open the door,' and then he turned and stalked across her room towards the little seated area with the couch.

'I...' She faltered uncertainly, then lifted her voice as confidently as she dared. 'One moment, please.'

Hastily, she fixed her uniform, hoping that Nikhil couldn't see just how badly her hands were shaking. Nonsense, really, when she thought of the way he'd just made her shatter around his mere fingers.

But it didn't matter anyway, because he still had his back to her, apparently searching for something. Her brain couldn't even begin to deal with him right now.

Taking a step forward, she opened the door and a crew member she didn't recognise stared back at her.

'I'm Dr Sinclair,' Isla offered when the girl didn't speak.

'I...is my friend,' she managed at last in broken English. 'He is...ill.'

'If he's ill, then you should call the medical centre.' Isla smiled gently.

The girl looked unexpectedly horrified. 'No...no medical centre...please.'

'I see,' Isla said, frowning.

Alarm bells were going off in her head. If they didn't want the medical centre alerted, the chances were it was drug-related and they were hoping that, as the new doc on board, she was the weak link.

'Step in, please,' Nikhil's voice commanded evenly,

making them both jump. 'Let's not have this conversation in the corridor.'

Isla felt for the young girl as her face paled, and they both looked around the door to where Nikhil was sitting on her couch with a pile of papers on the coffee table in front of him, looking for all the world as though they had been conducting a meeting.

It seemed the crew member wasn't to know that professional meetings didn't generally take place in cabins. Or perhaps she was just too distracted with her own medical emergency to think. Either way, she began backing away from the door.

'No…no, no doctor emergency. Mistake,' she repeated rapidly.

Nikhil was by the door in a flash. 'No mistake,' he told her firmly. 'If someone is sick, whatever the circumstances, he needs to be treated. Dr Sinclair is coming now. You will take us straight to him.'

'No… I…'

'Ready, Dr Sinclair?'

Grabbing her medical bag, Isla pulled the door closed behind them.

'Ready,' she confirmed, waiting for the now terrified girl to turn around before mouthing to Nikhil to alert the medical centre.

They both knew that if drugs were involved then he, and the ship's security, would need to know. However, Isla couldn't help thinking that Nikhil turning up initially would be counter-productive. With a First Officer there, the other crew members—if any of them had hung around long enough—would be more likely to clam up, and Isla feared not learning what the patient had taken.

Besides, the faster someone got to him with a full medical kit, the better. Her bag didn't have that much in it.

She was grateful that Nikhil appeared to realise this, turning down a different corridor to head in another direction, leaving the crewmember visibly sighing with relief.

It took several minutes for Isla to reach her patient, even hurrying down the main motorway corridor of the crew decks. But then, finally, they rounded a corner and she saw a cluster of crew around the door to one of the tiny cabins, her fear heightening as they all scattered the moment they saw her.

'There...' The crew member pointed, redundantly.

Pushing her way into the tiny space, Isla finally saw her patient. He was lying on his side, his breathing extremely shallow, his body twitching now and then but otherwise unconscious. A quick measure of his pulse confirmed it was reduced, whilst a check of his eyes confirmed the pupils were constricted. At least someone had had the sense to put him into the recovery position.

Briefly, she checked his airway. Clear—that was good.

'What did he take?'

She didn't really need to hear it, but she asked all the same. Still, it wasn't really a surprise when no one answered.

'The more information I have, the better I am able to treat your friend,' she continued conversationally, biting back her frustration. 'Your loyalty won't count for much if he dies.'

'Skag,' a male voice bit out suddenly. 'Just a bit of Skag.'

Just a bit said it all really, Isla thought, swallowing down a sudden wave of anger. Still, at least it meant she knew the best way to treat him.

'You can treat...yes?' someone asked, their accent so strong that it took Isla a moment to work out the words.

'I need more kit. You have to alert the medical centre.'

This time no one argued. Though no one moved to do anything either.

'I'm not here to play judge and jury; I just want to help your friend.'

'Fine…' Another voice spoke, and Isla thought it was the same man. 'I'll go.'

'Just call them.' Isla fought to keep her voice even.

'No need.' There was a sudden flurry of activity by the door as Jordanna pushed her way through. 'I'm here.'

Isla eyed the med bag, oxygen cannister and mask with relief.

'That was fast,' she noted.

'Was it? Good, I felt like I went round in circles for a while, asking about a hundred people if they knew anything.'

Isla grunted. 'No one ever wants to be seen to be associated with it. Did you bring Naloxone?'

'Ah, that's what it is, is it? Yeah. I have that.'

'Great.' Isla concentrated on getting in a cannula whilst Jordanna dealt with the oxygen mask. They would need to support respiration with a bag-valve mask before she began to administer the opioid receptor antagonist.

'I thought it was Naltrexone?' a male crewman asked suddenly. Tellingly, Isla thought.

'No—' she lifted her head '—Naltrexone is used to treat drug addiction by blocking opioid cravings, and alcohol cravings for that matter, but it can't treat overdoses. Naloxone can treat the overdose but not the craving.'

The two might sound alike, but their different half-lives really made the distinction. Not that she thought the crewmen wanted that much information.

'Okay, let's start with nought point nought four milligrams—' Isla prepped the syringe '—and see how that goes. Be ready for them.' As soon as the medication hit the brain and began to reverse the effects of the overdose, Isla knew the patient could lash out.

Carefully, she administered the drug.

'What happened to you?' Gerd demanded as he walked into the medical centre a few hours later to see Jordanna on the couch with an ice pack on her eye.

'She got belted by an ungrateful patient.'

'Ah—' the senior nurse nodded '—I heard about that.'

'Already?' Jordanna lifted the pack up and winced.

'You know how news travels fast,' Isla noted, carefully taking her colleague's hand and placing the pack back down over the eye. 'And that kind of news travels even faster.'

'Yeah, well, he'll be escorted off the ship as soon as we get into port, and he'll never work for Port-Star again.' Gerd blew out with satisfaction. 'The security staff will be here any minute to take a statement.'

'Ah, speak of the devil,' Jordanna added, as they heard voices heading up the corridor.

All too familiar voices, Isla realised, as Nikhil's rich tones infiltrated the room. She froze, part of her wanting to flee, the other part knowing she would need to give her report.

She didn't dare look at either Jordanna or Gerd; nonetheless she waited, her heart jumping in her chest, but neither of them said anything more. Apparently, the grapevine hadn't included anything about Nikhil having been in her cabin, and for that she was eternally grateful.

And then Nikhil and the security guard were heading through the surgery doors, and she just about had time to plaster a cheery smile on her face.

'How's the eye, Nurse?' Nikhil asked at once, and Isla

couldn't help smiling as Jordanna practically glowed at the concern.

'I'll survive.'

'Glad to hear it. Are you up to giving your statement?'

'Sure.' The ravishing American flashed a killer smile despite the black eye, but Nikhil had already turned away, leaving her with the equally tall, equally dark, but not quite as handsome security guy.

Jordanna's smile faded for a second and Isla almost felt sorry for her. *Almost.*

But then Nikhil's razor gaze turned on her, and she had to concentrate on radiating a nonchalance she simply didn't feel.

'Doctor—' his tone was courteous, strictly business, and still it sent goosebumps through her '—I appreciate surgery has overrun, but I just need a brief word, please.'

'Of course.' Dipping her head slightly, Isla stood.

'Is your consultation room free?'

Nodding, Isla paced across the reception and into her space, closing the door as Nikhil followed her.

'How many of them were taking it?' he demanded without preamble.

'I don't know.'

'No other medical incidents?'

'Only that one crewman,' Isla confirmed. 'Though I assumed you'd be running a random drugs test.'

'The security team are doing it as we speak, though I'd be grateful for any further information you can provide.'

'I can't,' she apologised. 'I don't know who the other crewmen were; I've never seen them before. In any case, I was too focused on trying to keep my patient alive.'

'I appreciate that.'

'Do you?' she challenged quietly. 'Only it sounds to me as though you're hacked off that I can't give you names.'

For a moment he watched her.

'Where drugs are concerned, we operate a zero-tolerance policy on board our ships. I just don't like people flouting the rules.'

'I'm a doctor, Nikhil, I've seen what this stuff can do to a person. Trust me, I'm the last person you need to lecture on *zero tolerance*.'

He eyed her a moment longer and she resisted the urge to lift her hand to smooth her hair. Or her shirt. Or anything.

'You're right,' he acknowledged at last. 'You're a good doctor, Isla. You should find it easy to get a transfer.'

'Sorry, what did you say?' Taking an inadvertent step back, Isla stared at him in shock.

'You must see that we can't both be on this ship.'

'Why?' Her laugh was too high, too harsh. 'Because I can't tell you who else was involved in whatever happened down on deck five today?'

'Of course not.' He blew out a deep breath and raked his hand through his hair. It was a gesture Isla had never seen from him before, and it threw her for a moment.

'Then what?'

'We got caught, Isla. Right now, that crew member is in shock about her friend. But soon enough she'll put two and two together.'

'I don't agree.' Isla fought back the wave of fear that was beginning to flood her. 'You handled it well, Nikhil. You made it look like it was a genuine work meeting.'

'*This* time,' he emphasised. 'But what happens next time? Or the time after? When do too many coincidences add up?'

And it would only be later—much later—that Isla would consider the hidden relevance to Nikhil's words.

The truth that he no doubt hadn't intended for her to see, that he craved more of her, just as she did of him.

But in that moment she wasn't thinking straight.

'So what do you expect me to do?' Isla let out a sharp laugh. 'Put in for a transfer?'

The silence swirled around them, as shocking as it was unbelievable. In the end it was Nikhil who spoke first.

'You must see that we can't stay on this ship together without risking both our reputations?'

'You expect *me* to transfer,' she breathed quietly.

'You were never meant to be on this ship in the first place,' bit out Nikhil. 'You were supposed to be on the *Jewel of Hestia*. That night would never have happened if I'd known you would end up here.'

Isla didn't know what made her stand up taller and pull her shoulders back. Some belated sense of self-preservation, perhaps.

'It wouldn't have happened if *I* had known we would end up being on the same ship,' she declared. 'But here I am. And I'm not going anywhere.'

'I came here to offer a solution, not to argue.'

He actually looked as though he believed it, and Isla almost laughed. Instead, she fought to bite back her frustration.

'Then don't say stupid things.'

He cast her a disapproving look, and she hated the way it made her feel inferior. Wanting.

'I would rather do this with civility, Isla.'

A lesser person might have trembled at the lethal quality to his tone, despite the silkiness, or the actual words used. But Isla refused to be that *lesser person.* Not any more.

'Or what?' she asked, cocking her head to one side. 'Are you going to threaten me?'

'No threat.' How did he manage to smile in such a way

that she could practically feel his teeth, sharp against her skin? 'Just forewarning you.'

'Forewarning me?'

'If you don't put in for a transfer, then I shall have to request one for you. As your senior officer.'

'On what grounds?' Isla demanded incredulously. 'I've done nothing wrong.'

He couldn't do that, surely? He *wouldn't.*

'I wouldn't suggest that you had.'

'But the very fact that you ask for me to be transferred will raise suspicion.' Isla threw her hands into the air, her composure beginning to fray.

'Which is why I suggest that *you* put in for the transfer. Tell them you want to go back to a smaller ship. Tell them you aren't ready for a ship like the *Cassiopiea.*'

'You wouldn't dare,' she replied, fury slamming through her. 'That will sit on my record. It would affect my chances of promotion in the future.'

'I'll write you a glowing reference.'

'Dr Turner would write me a glowing reference. He is, after all, my direct boss. But it's irrelevant, because I'm not doing it.' She folded her arms over her chest.

Fury was beginning to override everything else right now, and for that she was grateful.

'There's nothing you can say, Nikhil. Sleeping with the First Officer might be frowned upon, but it happened off-ship, before we even knew that we would be colleagues.'

'What happened this afternoon wasn't *off-ship.*'

'No, but it was also after *you* came to *my* cabin,' Isla bit out. 'And if you insist on trying to get me transferred and interfering in my career then I'll have no choice than to tell people.'

'You're threatening me?' He glared at her in disbelief, something black and deadly crossing his features. Enough to make her skin prickle with awareness. 'To tell people I… What? Coerced you?'

'Of course not.' Isla was horrified. 'But the fact is, it wouldn't have happened if you hadn't come to my cabin. So, I'm not torpedoing my career just because this…attraction between us is so strong that you gave into temptation once and let your ridiculous high standards for yourself slip.'

'Twice.'

'What?'

'I let my personal boundaries slip twice,' he grated out. And suddenly Isla realised that Nikhil's battle was more with himself than with her. 'The first time was the other day when I kissed you in the damned corridor.'

'No one even saw.'

'But they could have,' he growled.

'But they didn't,' she repeated. But it was too late.

She could feel the rage and the hurt swirling inside her, and they made for a lethal combination.

'I'll tell you what, Nikhil Dara,' she threw at him, 'you stay away from me, and I'll stay the hell away from you.'

Then, before either of them could say anything further, she yanked open the door and stalked outside on legs she was sure would buckle under her at any moment. If only staying away from Nikhil was that easy.

If only her need for him didn't pump through her veins like a drug. Turning her into something all too close to that idiot patient in the crew rooms earlier.

Only Nikhil wanted her too. Just as badly. And if what had just happened was his attempt at intimidation then it had done exactly the opposite of everything he'd intended, because it didn't tell her that he regretted what had happened between them that first night in Chile.

It told her that he couldn't trust himself not to be tempted to do the same again. And being that desired by Nikhil Dara was a heady experience indeed.

CHAPTER NINE

THE KNOCK ON her door several hours later made Isla's heart lurch violently in her chest. Enough to leave a mark.

Nikhil.

It was all she could do not to race across the room and yank it open. She would *not* be the infatuated girl who fell all over him just because he'd changed his mind and chosen to bestow his time and attention on her.

With deliberate care, she walked to the door, placed her fingers over the handle and drew in a deep breath. She'd barely unlocked it when it was pushed open and a figure was sweeping past her, inside.

'Good grief, this hovel can't possibly be your cabin!'

Isla stared for a moment, horrified. 'What are you doing here, Mother?'

Marianna spun around dramatically, her arms outstretched. 'I came to see you, my darling. To make sure you were all right. I missed you that last night in Chile. We were going to have such a good evening together, but you had to go and get yourself transferred onto an earlier ship.'

Hardly how it had been, but Isla knew better than to argue with her mother over trivial things. She'd long since learned to save her energy for the bigger issues. Like how her mother was *here.*

'So you booked yourself a last-minute cabin on my ship?'

No need to ask her mother how much that had cost. It wasn't as though money was an issue to Marianna. No doubt she'd flown in from Chile by helicopter, with the top concierge standing out there on the landing pad to greet her. Her mother was a master at making an entrance.

Especially when Marianna was grinning at her like that. That was to say that a lesser woman might have *grinned.* Her mother *dazzled.*

'It occurred to me that it might be fun, my flower. Don't tell me you aren't pleased to see me?'

Isla opened her mouth, then closed it again as a smile tugged at the corners of her lips. No matter how frustrating her mother was, it was impossible not to be drawn to such a wild, charismatic personality. If nothing else, her mother was never predictable.

'Besides, you know I always enjoy a good cruise. Now, come and give me a hug.'

Dutifully, Isla stepped over to her mother and allowed herself to be enveloped in a tight embrace. Familiar, and somehow oddly comforting.

'Of course it's good to see you.' She pulled her head back and shot Marianna a warning look. 'Just don't interfere in my job.'

'Of course not!' Her mother had long since perfected the butter-wouldn't-melt look, not that Isla bought it for a moment.

'I mean it, Mother,' Isla reiterated. For all the good that would do.

Marianna had always been headstrong, wanting the best for herself, and for Isla.

'It's like talking to a metal bulkhead.' Isla rolled her eyes. 'Where's Leo, anyway?'

'Forgive a mother for wanting a moment to catch up with her other beautiful girl.' Marianna rolled her eyes, but they twinkled all the same. 'If only you'd been quite so delighted to see me.'

'I am,' Isla argued. 'You know I am.'

Her mother waved her hand dismissively.

'Anyway, Leo isn't here. She met someone.'

'*Leo* met someone? Wait—you seem remarkably smug about it. You set her up, didn't you? Oh, *Mother*.'

'It was purely fortuitous, I can assure you.'

Realisation walloped Isla. Clear and unequivocal.

'You've come to set *me* up with someone, haven't you?'

'Of course not.' For the second time in as many moments, Marianna flashed her an innocent look.

And for the second time in as many moments, Isla refused to be fooled; she'd seen her mother wield it as both a shield and a weapon for years.

'Mother, I am here to find myself as a doctor, the way I always wanted to do. Not to find myself a husband, the way *you* always wanted me to do.'

'You're here to lick your wounds after Bradley,' her mother corrected. 'But he simply isn't worth the upset.'

'I can assure you, Mother, I don't care in the least about Brad-the-Cad.'

'Well, of course, darling. Glad to hear it.'

But at least Marianna had the grace to look sheepish.

'Right.' Isla eyed her mother cautiously. 'Just as long as you understand that.'

'Oh, I do.'

It was all too suspiciously easy. Warily, Isla closed the door behind them. She might have known it was too good to be true.

'Although, if the opportunity with some eligible male should present itself, grab it by the…horns, I always say.'

'Mother…' Isla chastised.

'It's come to my attention that you have a very nice First

Officer on board, by the name of Nikhil Dara,' Marianna noted, her expression too casual.

'What do you know about Nikhil?' Isla breathed, realising her mistake too late.

Her mother eyed her shrewdly. 'How very interesting.'

Isla kicked herself. She knew her mother well enough to have known not to react. Marianna was too sharp by half.

'Mother…'

'I know that Leo is off with Daksh Dara. Not that she thinks I know it.'

'*Daksh* Dara?'

'He calls himself Dax, and he is Nikhil's older brother.'

'Nikhil's brother is still alive??' Isla exclaimed.

'Very much so?',' Marianna noted, and it took a moment for Isla to realise that her mother was watching her a little too closely. 'Why? Did he tell you otherwise?'

'Yes,' Isla managed. Then she stopped, and shook her head. 'Actually, no. He told me that he lost his brother a long time ago. I just…assumed.'

'I see.' Her mother arched her perfect eyebrows. 'Well, Nikhil's brother was certainly alive and well the last time we met. But they "are" estranged, from what I've been able to work out.'

'From what you can work out?'

'She met him when you two were in Chile together. In fact, he was the one I was trying to set you up with, that last night.'

Isla shook her head, utterly confused. *In Chile? When she had met Nikhil?*

'He never said. He never… I didn't even know his brother was alive.' She glanced up at her mother. 'So that's why you're really here? To find out about Nikhil and… this Daksh?'

Her mother hesitated a beat, then shrugged. 'You and

Leo are precious to me.' She offered a soft smile. 'You know how I think of her as much my daughter as you are.'

'I know.' Isla returned the smile instantly. 'It just… She met this Daksh in Chile, when Nikhil was there?'

'I understood that the two men were meant to be meeting. Something about a birthday?'

'Nikhil said it was his birthday…' Isla snapped her head up sharply. 'He took me for a meal at Te Tinca, but he never mentioned anything about meeting anyone.'

Clamping her mouth shut, Isla hoped her mother didn't probe her further on that point. Which meant she was surprised when Marianna closed the gap between them and, placing her hands gently on either side of Isla's face, upturned it so that she could look into her daughter's eyes.

'My eyes don't deceive me, Isla. You're blushing, and you never blush.'

Isla opened her mouth to object, but abruptly shut it again. There was little point in pretending to her mother. Not where men were concerned.

'It isn't what you think,' Isla offered at length. 'Can we just leave it at that?'

'If that's what you want.'

Isla chewed on her lip for a moment.

'It's…complicated.'

'Then let me just say three things. One, tonight I'm invited to the Captain's invitation-only gala ball, and you are my guest. Two, this man Nikhil makes you blush and I never, not once, saw you blush with that idiot Bradley. And three, never forget that beneath the Sinclair you're also a Raleigh, which gives you an impressive armoury of practically perfect genes at your fingertips. And the ability to use them.'

Then she dropped her hands and swept towards the door without a backward glance.

* * *

Nikhil wasn't entirely certain that he'd manage to stay standing when he looked up from his conversation with the Captain to see Isla standing at the gala entrance, a vision in the deepest, most glorious red. Her golden-brown hair tumbled down over her shoulders like a glossy curtain, caressing her skin in a way that made his body ache to do the same.

And that was without taking into account the way the gown hung from one shoulder, making love to her curves as it dropped, until it fell in a cascade of reds to another pair of killer heels.

Judging by the expressions on a fair few of his colleagues' faces, they were thinking the same, and yet when she looked into the room, her eyes colliding with his—and holding—he felt the most forceful punch of triumph.

It was impossible to tear his glance away. A point which was made clear when he heard the Captain coughing pointedly in his ear.

'I take it the rumours are true, Nikhil.'

It took Nikhil every bit of willpower he had to drag his gaze from Isla.

'Say again, sir?'

'I didn't believe them. Not until now. But there really is something going on between you and the doctor, isn't there?'

'You know me, sir.' Nikhil gritted his teeth. 'All work, no play.'

'It's served you well,' the Captain agreed. 'But a word of advice. The last time I saw someone wear that expression was when I looked in the mirror the first time I realised I was in love with my wife.'

'I am certainly not in love with Dr Sinclair.'

'That was thirty years ago,' the older man continued,

as if Nikhil hadn't even spoken. 'And she is still the only woman I have ever looked at that way. Even since she died there has been no one else. So if you care about that woman over there, Nikhil, I suggest you do something about it. Before one of these other blokes around here decides she's fair game.'

Nikhil clamped his jaws together so hard that it was almost painful. But he refused to let anyone see how his old mentor's words got to him. He refused to show any weakness. And these...*feelings* he had for Isla Sinclair were surely a weakness.

'And, you know, it couldn't have come at a more fortuitous time, actually,' the Captain confided suddenly.

'Is that so?'

Nikhil didn't really want to know. He didn't care. He just wanted to end the conversation so that he could go over and wrap her arm through his—staking his claim on her in front of all these would-be suitors, like a damned dog marking its territory.

'One of the other fleet Captains is retiring at the end of the year. We've all been asked to put forward potential candidates for promotion. I wanted to put you forward.'

'You *wanted* to?' Nikhil frowned, his mind struggling to keep up, when all it really wanted to do was snap straight back to the woman across the room.

'I have no doubt that you're the best officer for the role, Nikhil, but Head Office prefer their Captains to be married, or widowed. They don't like single, even one as dedicated and professional as you.'

Finally, Nikhil's gaze stopped trying to fight its way back to Isla. He stared at the Captain. 'You're saying that they wouldn't consider me for promotion without a wife?'

'Archaic, isn't it?' The older man shrugged. 'The one thing you've avoided all this time is going to be the thing that gets you the promotion you've been working for, your entire career.'

Nikhil watched her move. Her lithe body rippling under the sequinned fabric, arresting heads—and other, more carnal parts of the male anatomy. She was magnificent. Incomparable and, apparently, the key to getting everything he'd ever wanted.

His own ship.

So why did he know, without even thinking about it, that there was no way he could use her like that? He'd been fighting their attraction because he'd always prided himself on his professionalism, yet it seemed that resisting temptation would be his downfall, not his success.

So why not give in to it? Why not give in to Isla, and gain two things in the process?

Because she deserves better than that, a voice insinuated itself into his head. And he didn't exactly try to silence it.

Instead, he watched as she circled the room, apparently doing all she could to avoid moving to the point where he stood, still with the Captain. Now she was with the woman who declared herself to be Isla's mother.

He could certainly see the resemblance. The high, fine bone structure, the delicate nose and those oh-so-expressive eyes. But Marianna had a worldliness to her that Isla didn't possess. And though they both had an intelligent sharpness in their gaze, he could read the honed intellect in Isla's expression that simply wasn't present in that of her mother.

For over an hour he watched her move between guests, charming people and laughing with them, and he told himself that he didn't feel jealous, or possessive, or indeed anything at all.

He wasn't sure that he fell for it, for a moment.

And then, suddenly, she was right in front of him and every cell in his body *zinged* with awareness.

'Nikhil, I want to introduce you to my mother, Marianna Sinclair-Raleigh-Burton. Mother, this is Nikhil Dara.'

'Nikhil Dara.' Isla's mother held her hand out for him to take as he smiled politely, wholly unprepared for the blow he was about to suffer. 'Surely no relation to the delightful Daksh Dara of DXD Industries?'

Isla had no idea why she was standing there, unable to breathe, as Nikhil and her mother stood face to face, each weighing up the other in their different ways.

Her mother on one side, as glittery and charming as ever on the outside, but with the lethal blade of a smile that only Isla knew was being wielded as a weapon. And Nikhil on the other, a hard edge to his body that she'd never seen before, an expression she couldn't read playing across his harsh features.

There was no reason for her to have wished so fervently that things would go well between the two of them during these introductions, and yet that was exactly how she'd felt.

It had been like some insane torture, watching Nikhil from across the room and not being able to talk to him for fear of betraying every one of these bizarre, hectic feelings that swirled inside her. Despite everything she'd said about staying away from each other.

It didn't matter where she went, or where *he* went for that matter, she seemed to be constantly aware of him. Helpless to stop herself from tracking his movements around the room. Telling herself that she was just imagining the fact that he was deliberately avoiding her. She probably didn't even factor into his consideration at all, as he moved from group to group, playing the eligible yet professional First Officer to perfection.

But *he* factored into *her* consideration.

She felt perpetually on edge. On fire. As if there was a burning in her chest that roared louder the nearer he came. It thrummed through her veins, humming along her entire body, leaving her aching…right *there.*

Wanting him with a hunger she'd never experienced before. Ever. And it didn't seem to matter how many times she told herself that she was acting crazily, she couldn't seem to stop herself. It was as if a maelstrom of emotions was raging inside her and Nikhil was at the very centre of it.

Her only saving grace was the fact that no one knew her well enough to see that. And she couldn't work out if that was particularly lucky, or particularly sad.

Yet now here she was, at a Captain's gala with her mother and the man she couldn't stop thinking about—fantasising about—and they were eyeing each other like sworn enemies. Surely the last couple of minutes couldn't have gone any worse? Like some kind of terrible nightmare.

'You're not at all like your brother, are you?' Marianna spoke.

'I am not.' Nikhil's voice scraped over Isla, though she couldn't have said why. 'One of us is the exemplary, irreproachable Dara brother; the other is the Dara brother whose moral standing lies in tatters on the ground. We are not to be confused with each other.'

Isla tried to speak, to somehow shatter the tension of the moment, but all she could do was watch the scene unfold with increasing horror. This car crash of an introduction that she couldn't seem to avert; that shouldn't even matter to her. Finally, she watched her mother slip her arm through the Captain's—who had come to the rescue like some kind of perfect white knight in his ship's uniform—and the two of them wandered off.

She waited until they were out of earshot.

'What the hell was that all about?'

Nikhil turned to face her and she was sure she saw a brief flash of regret in his eyes before he switched up a blank expression.

'I believe your mother observed how dissimilar my brother and I are. I merely agreed.'

She wasn't sure why, but she had never felt so much like crying. Not even when she'd discovered how Brad had been using her. Using her connections, and her money, to get to where he wanted to be. Some might argue that was just the way her mother had behaved, with her series of husbands. The difference was that her mother had never feigned love.

Bradley had. And she'd been the damned fool who had believed him.

Which only made it all the more laughable that she'd actually heeded her mother's advice for once and dressed tonight with Nikhil in mind.

Not *for* him, she had told herself as she'd stood in front of the mirror, eyeing her reflection critically. But with him in mind, all the same. Going against the last thing she'd flung at him, about staying away from each other—because she'd thought that she'd begun to understood a little more of what made him tick.

And now she might as well be looking at a stranger.

'You deliberately made yourself sound like…like…someone else. Someone I don't recognise.'

'No.' His voice was harsh. Much too harsh, Isla thought faintly. 'I didn't make myself sound like anyone else. This is who I am, Isla. You just don't know me at all.'

'I know that wasn't you.' She held her ground.

'You know no such thing.'

'Is this because she asked about your brother?' Isla had no idea why that popped into her brain, but suddenly there it was.

And even though Nikhil didn't respond, the sudden set of his jaw and coldness in his eyes was answer enough. Also, oddly, there was a bleakness to his expression which made her heart twist for him, even as she didn't understand why.

Before she could say another word, Nikhil had taken her by the elbow and was manoeuvring her out of the ballroom and into an anteroom.

'What the hell do you know about Daksh?' Nikhil rasped. 'Did your socially climbing mother think I was her route to him? *Your* route to him?'

'I didn't even know he existed until tonight,' Isla managed, valiantly holding back the tremors that threatened to roll through her body like its own version of seismic activity.

'I told you I had a brother,' Nikhil cut her off.

'You made him sound like he was dead,' she cried.

His stony expression seemed to harden even further beneath her gaze. His voice all the more implaccable.

'Is that what you're going to claim?'

'It's the truth. And anyway, my mother didn't know I had met you back in Chile, least of all that I spent that night with you.'

'And I am to believe that?'

And finally—*finally*—she felt that hint of steel inside her that she'd begun to think had deserted her. Grabbing hold of it, she made herself face Nikhil.

'I can't say that I care what you believe,' she heard herself say, although she barely recognised her own voice.

Every sweep of his eyes over her made Isla feel as

though she didn't fit her own skin any more. Everything was shifting around her and she couldn't seem to make sense of it. And still she wished, more than anything, that she could read what was going on in Nikhil's head *right now.*

'You were right earlier, Isla,' he growled, out of the blue. 'We should stay the hell away from each other.'

CHAPTER TEN

THE GONDOLA RIDE up through the rainforest canopy had to be one of the most incredible experiences Isla thought she'd ever had. Sloths could be seen, hanging from the higher limbs of stunning towering trees. Bats and brightly coloured birds clung to the enormous leaves and, a few moments earlier, she'd even seen a monkey leaping from tree to tree, as if keeping up with the gondola's ascent.

'…such is the neotropical diversity of this rainforest.'

Isla tuned back in to their tour guide, trying to chastise herself for missing what he was saying. But surely it was impossible not to get caught up in the magical beauty of this place.

'Even to date we are still finding new species in the rainforest,' he continued. 'Especially insects. And now it's time for your aerial zip wire.'

'Not for me—' she laughed '—I'm here as the excursion doctor. That's all.'

'Surely you aren't going to be so disappointing as to bottle it, Dr Sinclair?'

Emotion rushed through her, devastating her. Her heart started pounding, though not in her chest. More like in the vicinity of her throat. And she despaired of herself.

Carefully, Isla steeled herself for the first sight of Nikhil in over a week—ever since that awful night at the Captain's gala. She'd also spent the past week avoiding her mother—not too difficult, since Marianna and the Captain appeared to have hit it off entirely too well that night and, as far as she could tell, her mother had barely been back to her palatial stateroom since.

Taking a deep breath, she slowly—so slowly—turned around…and promptly despaired of herself. How could it be that she *still* wasn't ready for the way her breath whooshed out of her lungs as her eyes seemed to drink in the sight of him?

Worse, when he inclined his head in a wordless instruction for her to move away from the crowd, to the far end of the summit station, she instructed herself that the ludicrous thrill that chased through her right at this moment was revulsion, not some sick kind of pleasure at seeing him again.

And she certainly didn't notice the dark rings around his eyes, or the taut lines by his mouth, as though he hadn't been sleeping much better than she had this last week.

'I'm on duty,' she managed, forcing herself to hold her position and smile. Though most of the group had already descended on the zip wire, there were still a few passengers awaiting their turn and she had absolutely no intention of alerting them to the fact that there was any tension between their doctor and the First Officer. 'I can't stray far from this group.'

'If there's a medical emergency, then the senior tour guide will be alerted on his radio and we'll soon know about it.'

Reluctantly, Isla forced herself to move off to the side with Nikhil, enough that they couldn't be overheard.

'I didn't request this excursion, before you ask. It was another…'

'Another one of your predecessor's choices. Yes, I am

aware of that fact. I had the good doctor's trip schedule emailed to me after Ecuador.'

'Of course you did.' She shouldn't be surprised. 'I don't know why I'm surprised.'

'I didn't come here to fight with you, Isla.'

'Did you not?' She raised an eyebrow, safe in the knowledge that the rest of the party couldn't see her. 'I'm agog to know why you did come, then.'

'I came to apologise.'

Isla's heart stopped. She must have misheard.

'Sorry?'

'This is your career too. I should never have asked you to transfer.'

'Then why did you?' She couldn't seem to help herself.

There was a beat of silence, but it felt like a lifetime.

'Perhaps it was an excuse to be with you again,' Nikhil bit out suddenly.

There was no way his words should be able to worm their way inside her so easily.

'Your excuse?'

'I think I probably convinced myself that if you were going to the *Hestia,* the way you'd been intended to do, then we would no longer be immediate colleagues. We could indulge this…attraction between us.'

'There's bed-hopping going on every night. From the lowliest crewman right up to the senior officers. And yet you're worried about us indulging with each other, and only each other?'

She could see the internal battle going on in Nikhil's head. She could read it in every tautened sinew of his impossibly perfect body. But she refused to let her head go there. Not now.

'I never indulge, *Doctor.* You know that.'

'Actually, I don't know that,' she heard herself snap out

abruptly. More because his use of *Doctor* made her feel things she didn't want to be feeling. 'I don't know that at all. I've heard rumours, but that's all they are. I don't know the first thing about you, Nikhil.'

'You know me probably better than anyone else on this ship.'

'Then I find that profoundly sad. Not least because I didn't even realise that your brother was still alive. Let alone that you'd been scheduled to meet him in Chile, the day that we met.'

Nikhil stiffened. A lesser woman might have quaked at the incandescent expression on his face. Isla had no idea how she managed to hold her ground.

'How do you know about that?'

'More to the point—' she refused to answer, though it took all she had '—how is it that in all our conversations about my family, you never once offered anything more about yours?'

'It wasn't…isn't your business,' he gritted out. 'It's nobody's business.'

'It's a detail. A minor, insignificant detail perhaps.' She carefully ignored the fact that her mother had told her the brothers were estranged. 'But a detail nonetheless.'

Let Nikhil tell her that. Let him at least acknowledge the fact that Dax existed. And again, he hesitated. So long, this time, that Isla feared he wasn't going to answer her at all.

'Perhaps it's self-preservation,' he growled at last.

'It isn't self-preservation,' she made herself reply. 'It's control. You set up these little parameters around yourself every day. That particular, irrelevant scrap of information was withheld purely because you get some kind of kick about no one knowing the slightest thing about you.'

'And yet I told you it was my birthday,' he reminded her.

Isla faltered. He *had* told her that, hadn't he? And yet she'd assumed he was making it up.

Nikhil was quick to exploit his advantage. 'I didn't tell you about my *brother*—' she was fairly certain he fought to keep his tone even, yet that hint of acrid rage slid through all the same '—because he is irrelevant to me. That is all. No great secret.'

'It's hardly usual,' Isla snorted.

'Many families part ways. Your close relationship with your former stepsister is more unusual than any fallout I may or may not have had with mine.'

'Which, I feel obliged to point out, is you deflecting—' she couldn't decide whether to feel smug or sad '—the way you always do.'

'I disagree.'

'It's *exactly* what you do.' She refused to be swayed. 'In fact, you turn the conversation back on the other person, or you simply dismiss them.'

'You're mistaken,' he began, but whatever else he was going to say was cut off by the low, insistent ring of a mobile. Nikhil's mobile.

As he stepped away to answer, Isla took the opportunity to slip past him and back to the group.

Or, more accurately, she forced her shaking legs to carry her away from him—every step feeling heavier than the last—as she tagged onto the end of the last few passengers waiting to enjoy the thrill of their zip wire experience.

'That was the team back at the hotel base. There's a problem with one of the guests who took the Orchid and Butterfly House tour. They want you back immediately.'

'Understood.' Swinging around, she began to head back to the embarkation point for the gondolas heading back down to the low station.

He caught her as she started to pass him, and it was

harder than ever to pretend that the contact didn't do anything to her.

'Where are you going?'

'Back down.' She frowned at him.

'Yes, but not that way.' He turned her around to the zip wire. 'We'll go this way instead. It will be faster.'

'Fine.' She gritted her teeth, telling herself that the jolt that ran through her was solely about the ride. 'Let's go.'

They were just coming into the rainforest hotel when the call came through to say that the patient was fine after all. It had turned out that their broken ankle had healed remarkably fast once they'd been offered an upgrade.

'A few weeks ago, I'd have been shocked,' Isla commented as they slowed down to walk up the beautiful tropical-tree lined driveway.

Sweat was trickling down her back, and her shirt felt heavy with moisture. The place was hot and humid enough, but they'd been practically jogging through dense forest to get back to the hotel.

'Let me guess,' Nikhil said dryly. 'The first few days aboard, you had several new arrivals coming to your surgery crying about being claustrophobic?'

'Only an upgrade to a cabin with a balcony would cure them.' Isla nodded. 'Yes. I truly didn't believe people would do that.'

His only answer was a grunt of disapproval. She supposed he'd got used to it after so many years, and so many cruises. What kind of a fool did it make her that she still, even now, longed to hear him tell her something more personal about himself?

'There are many more nice passengers, though,' she heard herself add.

Beside her, he seemed to stalk up the drive, but he didn't utter a word.

'And there's a lot to be said for waking up in a new place every morning. I mean, it's a stunning way to get to see the world.'

'Go in the back way,' he gritted out suddenly. 'Those lovely passengers you mentioned will descend on us the moment we walk through the door, and I'd like to at least get a shower and clean up first.'

She didn't dare to look at him. It seemed impossible, but even drenched in sweat he looked like a study in perfect masculinity. Perhaps more so. Moisture glistened on his skin, bronzed and healthy, making him look all the more like some billboard model. Only a more interesting, real version.

Oh, she was in serious trouble.

Following Nikhil as he skirted the main entrance to the hotel, an odd, short, instantly muffled sound made them stop simultaneously. For a protracted second, Isla struggled to work it out—and then her stomach turned. She set off at a run, but Nikhil was already ahead of her.

Rounding the corner of a store house, they saw that a lad, tall and muscled, had a maid pinned to the grubby wooden framework and was tugging her skirt up, despite her futile attempts to push him off.

Before Isla could say anything, Nikhil had placed both his hands on the young man's shoulders and was hauling him off the sobbing girl and swinging him around.

The girl began to scream, and Isla hurried to stop her. The last thing they needed now was for a load of hotel guests to come spilling out to see what was going on.

Turning back to Nikhil and the attacker, she saw the punch coming as if in slow motion, but it was only at the last minute that she saw a glint of metal and then the blood as the lad slashed Nikhil's shoulder.

In an instant the expression on Nikhil's face changed—a flash of a stricken expression, enough to make her blood run cold. It was gone in an instant, but even that fraction of a moment had been long enough to hurl images into Isla's mind—the scars she'd seen on his body that night in Chile. In particular, the one on his shoulder—the one he'd told her had been an accident. Suddenly, she wasn't so sure.

But there was no time to dwell on that now. Her attention was pulled back to Nikhil, who had already reacted, landing a few smart punches to send the blade skittering. He'd swiftly got his opponent against the wall, despite the lad's muscled form, his forearm to the lad's throat to stop him from escaping.

He growled to her, 'Go inside and get a member of security. Be discreet. And take the girl with you.'

She only hesitated for half a second. Then, wordlessly, she obeyed.

However she'd anticipated this day going, it couldn't have been like this. But that moment of barely controlled rage she'd seen on Nikhil's face kept tugging at her thoughts. Years as a doctor had honed her intuition, and right now it was telling her that the knife had triggered something in him, if only for less than a minute.

Her thoughts were still whirring, even as she escorted the trembling, sobbing maid in through the staff-only doors, soothing her as best she could in her broken Spanish.

'I need to clean the wound; it's going to sting,' Isla warned an hour or so later when, statements given, they were in his room, where she could tend to Nikhil without fear of any of the passengers seeing them.

Judging by the laughter and music coming from the

main ballroom as she and Nikhil had left the security office, the shore excursions staff were doing their usual sterling job of looking after the ship's passengers.

If they hadn't been happy, no doubt Nikhil would have rushed to clean up and get back to the party, when what he really needed was for his wound to be dealt with—butterfly stitches at least—and a bit of rest. With the canopy tour done and the tour group content, however, neither of them should be needed until the return journey to ship after lunchtime the next day, unless there was a problem.

Instead, the main problem was focusing on the task in hand when Nikhil was sitting in front of her, stripped to the waist, his chiselled body as mouth-watering as ever, and sending every inch of her body into a fever that had nothing to do with the soaring temperature outside.

She really was woeful.

'At least you've had all your tetanus shots, coming out here. Quite a barrage of injections, wasn't it?'

He grunted, but didn't speak.

'It will leave a scar,' Isla heard herself say. 'Though nothing like the one on your shoulder, of course.'

And she didn't know why she carried on—pushing that little bit harder.

'Will you tell people that it's the result of another accident?'

She might as well have struck him herself. Perhaps that was what she'd intended her words to do. Either way, Nikhil stiffened where he sat, and the silence in the room grew heavier in an instant. All she could do was continue to clean the wound and wait.

'I won't tell people anything,' he managed grimly at last. 'No one else will see it.'

She should stop talking. Now. But she couldn't seem to stop herself.

'I saw it.'

Something cracked through the quiet, like a thunderclap, though one glance at the window assured her the sun was still as sweltering out there as before.

'Most women I sleep with are less distracted by any…blemishes—especially those that are perceived. Clearly, I was remiss if some inconsequential childhood scar is what you remember most from our night together. I shall be more…dedicated in future.'

Isla swallowed, heat pouring straight down through her, right to the apex of her legs. Logically, she knew he didn't mean *in the future with her*, and yet it hung there, unspoken, all the same. Her heart faltered and swelled.

'What happened back in your past, Nikhil?' She paused but he didn't answer. Taking a steadying breath, she continued. 'I saw your face when you first caught a glimpse of that lad's knife. Your expression…'

'Leave it be, Isla.' The dark warning in his tone couldn't have been clearer.

And yet she couldn't seem to make her runaway mouth comply.

'Was it Daksh? Is that why you and your brother no longer speak? Why you claim that one of you is irreproachable, whilst the other has been left with no morals? Which one of you is which, Nikhil? Or is that the point?'

She waited for a moment, her agitation increasing as his jaw locked tighter. Angrier. 'I need to know, Nikhil. My stepsister is allegedly with him. If he's dangerous, then I want to know.'

His head snapped around to hers instantaneously, his voice rolling through her like black fury.

'Say that again?'

'Leo—I told you about her—is supposedly with him.'

'How?' The word was like a whip, lashing against Isla's skin. His gaze was boring into her, pinning her to the spot.

'They met in Chile. The day after you and I…' She tailed off awkwardly.

A myriad expressions chased through Nikhil's rich eyes and, to Isla's chagrin, none of them seemed good. But the one she recognised most of all was fury—with *her*.

'And you've known all this time?'

'No.' Isla shook her head. 'I only found out last week—from my mother. Please, Nikhil. Leo means everything to me. If she's in danger, then you have to tell me.'

He glowered at her for another long moment and everything in her was sounding an alarm. And then, finally, he spoke—as though through gritted teeth.

'Daksh was not the one who wielded that knife. Your stepsister is in no danger from him. At least, not physically.'

Relief coursed through her, but she still had to understand.

'What's that supposed to mean? *At least, not physically?*'

He looked as if he wasn't going to answer again, and then he opened his mouth.

'It means he would not physically hurt her. But he is no more capable of an emotional connection than I am. My brother is certainly not to be relied upon.'

And there was no mistaking the bitter tone to Nikhil's voice. But there was something else too. Something less easy to recognise.

Isla nudged at it, as if with her toe.

Hurt. That was what she thought she could see.

Whatever had happened between Nikhil and his brother had left Nikhil bitter, and hurt. Yet surely there was no reason for her to find that as interesting as she did? There was no reason for her to cling onto it as though it was another rare find, another precious piece of the Nikhil puzzle.

'So Leo isn't at risk of any harm with Daksh?'

'No,' he bit out. 'You need have no fear over her physical well-being.'

'Well, she's a big girl. In terms of her emotional well-being, she can look out for herself.'

And Isla didn't know if they were still talking about her stepsister.

For another few moments they lapsed back into the same heavy silence. Nikhil's face was set as she made her shaking fingers get back to their work of tending to the laceration on his arm.

She wondered if the cuts on his heart—the deep wounds he pretended didn't exist—could ever be treated as easily. But she didn't dare push him further. She'd clearly already probed too much, and he'd made it perfectly clear that it wasn't any of her business.

As much as that stung, she needed to respect that. For her own sake as much as anything.

Working quickly and efficiently, Isla finished tending to the wound, applying the strips and dressing it so that it didn't risk opening up under the white shirt of his uniform. Finally, satisfied it was done, she stepped back.

'Okay, you're all clear.'

It was harder than it should have been to sound cheerful. And harder still when he stood and turned to face her.

She fought to keep her eyes from travelling down from his chin.

'And thank you for telling me about Daksh. You…didn't have to, but I am grateful.'

He watched her wordlessly until she found herself shifting her weight from one foot to the other.

'Nikhil…'

'You're concerned for someone you care about.' He spoke suddenly. 'You shouldn't feel the need to apologise for that. It must be…nice.'

It was a closed statement. He certainly wasn't inviting a response. Yet, even though the voice in her head was screaming at her to bite her tongue, Isla couldn't help herself from responding.

'Are you sure you don't have someone like that either?'

'I do not.'

'What about your brother? Are you so sure he doesn't care?'

'He does not.'

'So why was he there, in Chile?'

'Careful.' Nikhil's eyes glittered, but she couldn't be careful. She needed to know.

Or maybe she needed *him* to know. To face up to whatever ghosts seemed to haunt him.

'Are you going to claim it was pure coincidence that he was there when you were, Nikhil?'

'Perhaps it was.'

He looked furious. Again. But, whether he liked what she had to say or not, he was still answering her. That had to stand for something. She couldn't stop now.

'On your birthday?' she countered. 'I think not. I think he cares more than you are willing to admit.'

'You're wrong.'

'Maybe I am,' she acknowledged, 'because how would I know? You said you'd "lost" him a long time ago but you made it sound like he had died. And don't pretend it was my interpretation, because we both know the truth. So, whatever happened between you, the fact is that he was there in Chile, on your birthday, waiting to see you. So is it at all possible, if you stop being defensive and just *think* for a moment, that maybe I'm seeing something you aren't?'

Isla had no idea how, or why, she had the courage to argue with him. It was as though that moment—that expression when he'd first seen the knife—had been her first glimpse of Nikhil. A flash of the real man who lay behind that front he so artfully presented to the world.

And now she'd seen that brief glimpse she couldn't let it go. She wanted more of it. More of him.

'You don't understand,' he growled.

'I'm sure that's true.' It was incredible how her voice sounded so even, betraying none of the churning, swirling emotions she felt inside.

Not even a tremor.

'You push and push, Isla.' He spoke so quietly then, it was almost dangerous. 'What is it that you hope to gain?'

And even though her skin goosebumped in response, even though her heart suddenly accelerated and galloped, thundering as loudly and as heavily as hoofbeats, she held her ground.

Surely it should terrify her that it mattered so much to her?'

'I want to understand you better, Nikhil.'

'Why?' he demanded, his voice harsh, uncompromising.

And still it didn't deter her.

She tilted her head to one side, her stomach feeling as though it had crept up her windpipe and was now lodged somewhere in her throat. She would never know how she managed to sound so calm.

'Why not? Tell me, Nikhil, or so help me, I'll walk out of that door.'

CHAPTER ELEVEN

He should let her go, of course. It would solve all of his problems.

Except for the biggest one of all, that was. Namely, that he couldn't bear the thought of her actually leaving. What was it about this woman that got under his skin? There she was, creeping around his head—no, *striding* around it—and kicking open doors he'd long thought locked and barred.

Even now she stared at him, her head cocked as though she had every right to ask the questions she was asking.

The worrying part was that, as much as he resented the intrusion, he couldn't bring himself to walk away from her. As though a part of him *wanted* to hear what she had to say. Worse, as though a part of him wanted to answer those questions that were falling from her lips.

So why not? What better way to show her the monster that you are?

The voice was almost insidious, and even as Nikhil tried to silence it, he couldn't. It taunted him, telling him that if she knew the truth about him then she'd surely run as fast and as far as she could in the opposite direction.

And wasn't that what he claimed to want?

'Fine.' He gritted his teeth at last. 'You want to know me, then don't say that I didn't warn you.'

But, instead of looking apprehensive, as he'd expected, she cast him an almost scornful look.

'Is this you playing the role of *Big Bad Nikhil*? Only I have to tell you I've seen it before, and it doesn't convince me.'

'It should.' He resisted the urge to step closer to her. *Barely.* 'But if you really need more convincing, then allow me to indulge you.'

With a supreme effort he made himself step back. Away.

'The day Daksh was in Chile, he *was* there to see me. Though the fact that it was my birthday is almost certainly pure coincidence. Either way, it would have been the first time we'd seen each other since I was fifteen. Since the day of our father's funeral.'

Almost two decades later—it still rankled. More than rankled, if he were to be honest. Good thing he'd learned to be so adept at lying to himself, then.

'What did he want?' Isla asked, when he didn't continue.

'I don't know,' he answered. 'Neither do I care.'

'I think that's a lie.'

Her voice was soft, so soft that it almost felt like a caress, and yet it was almost his undoing that she seemed to read him as easily as she did.

'That I know, or that I care?' he demanded, more to buy himself time than anything else.

'I think you care more than you want to admit.'

He chose not to answer. Instead he clung onto that old, familiar rage that had started to recede from him ever since she'd walked into his life. But he wasn't fooled. He wouldn't be stupid enough to think that it had suddenly disappeared after all these years.

All that anger, and resentment, and grief. All that debilitating guilt. This unique, incredible woman might have unwittingly chased it off for a moment, but it had to have gone somewhere.

It would only stay away for so long—until the novelty of someone as different as her wore off. Then it would be back, as dark, and winding, and bleak as ever.

Which was why he couldn't let her get close to him. He couldn't risk taking her down with him, when he eventually fell.

However hard it was—however much he'd kept this story inside and not told a single soul for almost twenty years—he had to say it now. He had to find a way to say all those ugly, twisted, damning words.

And the easiest way was to do it quickly. Like ripping off a plaster.

'My brother left me to rot in the home of our drunk, violent, abusive father.'

'Your father hurt you?'

She looked shocked for a split second, and then caught herself, slipping back that doctor's mask of hers.

He told himself there was no need to hate it.

'To be fair, our mother bore the brunt of his alcohol-induced temper when Daksh and I were growing up. But when she died, he found a new punchbag in Daksh.'

'Did he…hit you both?'

'Daksh protected me. He was twelve and I was ten. I guess he thought it was his duty as the big brother.' Nikhil lifted his shoulders, forcing down that bubbling thing inside him that he feared was too much like emotion.

'For four years, he took the beatings when the old man didn't have enough money for his boozing—which went from near the end of the month, to halfway through the month, to every day by the end. Daksh was earning money by then—we both were, but he was bringing in the main money for the house—and our father took every penny of it he could get his hands on.'

'For his drinking.' Isla spoke quietly, her way of encouraging him on, he knew.

Nikhil tilted his head, the bitterness tasting acrid in his throat.

'Then one day Daksh got offered a couple of months on a fishing vessel. It was a way out, and he took it.'

'Leaving you behind to face your father alone?'

'And the loss of the main source of income,' he ground out. 'He was furious. I was battered black and blue, hit with his leather belt—usually the buckle end—and knocked out more times than I can remember that first month. Then he realised I could take over my errant brother's old job and bring in more money, so he laid off me for a while.'

'The night I turned fifteen, I went out for a celebratory drink with some of the other fishermen—as far as they were concerned I was a working man not a kid, so they gave me little choice. It was just the one drink, and they bought it for me, but my father was in there, and to him I was spending *his* drinking money.'

'He beat you, didn't he?'

She tried not to react, but he heard it nonetheless, and it was oddly soothing, the fact that this beautiful, vivacious woman had had stepfather after stepfather and never once suffered anything like it.

It also said more for Isla's mother than he cared to acknowledge. Perhaps it wouldn't have hurt him to have been a little less abrasive towards her.

'The old man didn't say anything in the pub, but that night he rolled in, barely able to stand he was so blind drunk, and the belt came off.'

'Didn't you stop him?'

'No, I took it. It was easier to take it. It would be over

quicker that way. But that night he didn't stop.' Nikhil blocked out the memory, forcing himself to just say the words, not to actually *feel* them. 'The next thing I knew, he'd stumbled to the kitchen and grabbed a knife.'

Her hand moved to her throat and he heard the stifled sound. And what did it mean that a huge part of him wanted to cross that floor and comfort her?

'Your scar…' The anguish in her voice made him feel far too good. Not because of her pain, of course. More at the fact that she evidently cared.

When was the last time anyone had ever cared for him like that? Daksh, before he'd left all those years ago. His mother before that. But otherwise…there was no one.

'He was standing there, waving it around, swaying,' Nikhil remembered. 'I thought he didn't have the strength—or the ability to move in a straight line—to actually do anything about it.'

He let out a bark of laughter that didn't hold a hint of humour in it.

'Suddenly, he rushed me. I couldn't get out of the way fast enough, and the next thing I knew I was flying backwards and he had me pinned to the wall. Then he lifted the knife and drove it through my shoulder.'

He remembered that look on his father's face. The hateful, smug look of triumph as he'd laughed at Nikhil, pinned to the wall with the knife, unable to move. The threat to leave him there whilst he went to pick up his belt. The fear that once his father started he wouldn't stop, and Nikhil wouldn't be able to move, or run. Not that he was about to tell Isla that. It was too brutal, and he didn't want to subject her to it.

'I grabbed the knife, I don't know how, and I somehow yanked it out.'

He stopped as her expression changed. And he hated the

way she looked at him in that moment. The horror, the anguish, but also, far worse than any of that, the flash of fear.

'Nikhil…you said the last time you saw your brother was at your father's funeral…when you were fifteen?'

'You wanted to know what kind of a man I am.' He threw his hands up. 'Now you know. I'm not a man at all. I'm the monster people talk about, write about.'

'Nikhil, what happened?'

'You don't need me to say the words, *pyar*.' He laughed again, but this sound was even worse. He'd called her *pyar*. *My love.* Where had that come from? 'You already know.'

'I don't.' She shook her head. 'I can't believe that. You're…*you*.'

'And I'm a monster. And that's all you need to know. You asked for the truth. I gave it to you. You can't change it now just because you don't like it.'

And even though he'd known what he was all these years, it sounded so horrific falling from his lips in this room, with Isla standing across from him.

He suddenly realised he'd have done anything not to be the kind of man who'd put that expression on her beautiful face.

She stared at him a moment longer, then shook her head.

'It was self-defence, surely? How did it happen? Nikhil, please talk to me.'

'To what end?' He felt as though the words were being torn from his lips. 'What more do you want me to tell you?'

'I want you to talk me through it.'

'No.'

'Please, Nikhil,' she cried. 'You've told me this much. What have you got to lose?'

'It was the worst night of my life. You think I want to relive it?'

'I think you're afraid to.'

And it was the way she stared at him, unblinking, and so confident in him, that was his undoing. It made him wish for things that could never be. And that was the most hollow, scraping feeling of all. He stared at her, his mind in tumult.

'Even if I wanted to, I don't remember anything after pulling the knife out of my shoulder,' he ground out at last. 'It's all hazy.'

'What about the police? Surely they were called?'

'Yes.'

'Then what did they say?'

She clearly wasn't going to let it go. He could tell her what she wanted to hear—so easily—but that didn't mean he believed it. A fresh shame threatened to overwhelm him.

'The police exonerated me,' he offered flatly. 'Apparently there was a neighbour who told them what my father was. She'd seen it over the years, but she'd been too afraid to ever say anything. When she knew he was dead, she confessed every fight and every beating she'd heard over the years.'

Isla made a sound that was half a cry and half a shout. He made himself continue.

'When the police wrote their report they simply stated that I had passed out through blood loss, that I would have lacked the strength and so my father must have rushed me, and impaled himself on the knife.'

'So then, you did nothing,' she exclaimed.

'I don't believe it.' He shook his head. 'If I did nothing, then why can't I remember it? Why have I blocked it out?'

He didn't realise she'd closed the gap between them until he felt her hands cupping his face tightly, her expression fierce.

'Because you were suffering from blood loss. You said it yourself.'

'It just feels too…convenient,' he growled. 'I'm a monster, *pyar*.'

There was that word again. That term of endearment. Suggesting things that could never be his. He wanted her far too much, even now. *Especially now.* It had to stop.

'I'm a savage, Little Doc. An animal. I always was. He didn't just rush me; it doesn't make sense. I remember that final expression on his face. It was me, Isla. It had to be me. Everything else is just too…easy.'

Her heart felt as though it was breaking inside her very chest. For Nikhil.

She could have just taken him into her arms and made it all okay, Isla realised in that instant. He wanted it—*her*—she could tell. She could read that hunger in his eyes, and it echoed within her.

But that was just sex. He might want it, but he didn't need that. Not just yet. He needed something else entirely.

Shoving aside her own desire for him, as well as every shred of grief she felt on his behalf, she steeled her voice and glowered at him.

'You're an idiot, Nikhil Dara.'

His head jerked up, but she couldn't relent now. She had to stand her ground.

'This isn't about what you remember; this is about the fact that you always have to be in control.'

He frowned. 'I'm second in command of a floating city. It's my job to be in control.'

'And you always do that too,' she made herself snap out.

His voice might as well have been laden with ice. It was so cold. And hard.

'I beg your pardon?'

'You use your job, your career, as a convenient excuse.' Still, she had to remain unmoved. 'But I don't just mean in control of your professional life. I mean in control of *everything.* Even the night we slept together, you still had that hint of restraint. It has just taken me until now to recognise it for what it was.'

'You're reading too much into too little,' he ground out.

But this time she refused to be deterred.

'I don't think that I am. That's what you do, Nikhil. You're taking on the guilt of killing your father because a part of you would rather that than admit that you had no control in that situation. Everything with you is about control. You hold it around you like a shroud. Like armour.'

There was a beat of silence. Long. Promising.

'You're wrong.' Abruptly, Nikhil jerked his head out of her hands and took a step away. 'I'm going for a shower. I suggest that, when I come out, you aren't here.'

She watched him stalk across the room; every long, edgy line of his magnificent body was taut with suppressed emotion.

Her mind turned over for several long minutes after he'd closed that bathroom door behind him. But, far from feeling pushed aside, his actions had only underscored how right she was about him.

She could hear the sound of the shower running, a sign of Nikhil trying to claw his way back to normality. But Isla knew, even if he himself didn't realise it, it was too late for him to regain control. She'd already read the maelstrom of emotions in those rich cocoa depths of his eyes. She was so, so close to reaching the real Nikhil.

Slowly at first, then gaining confidence with every step, she crossed the room and slipped into the bathroom, letting the door click loudly behind her.

'What are you doing, Little Doc?' Raw emotion sliced through his words, his eyes darkening as he watched her.

'I'm not wrong,' she said. Softly this time. 'You wear so much armour that it's practically suffocating you, and you don't even know it.'

And if she wanted to pierce it—if she wanted to reach him—then she was going to have to create a weak spot.

Slowly, she unbuttoned her shirt and let it fall to the floor, and he swallowed but didn't speak. His jaw locked, a tiny pulse betraying his otherwise still appearance.

The rest of her clothing followed. Then she stepped into the large cubicle with him.

'I'll ask again.' His ragged breathing bolstered her confidence all the more. 'What are you doing? Is it that you won't answer, Little Doc? Or that you *can't*?'

She cocked her head on one side, her eyes meeting his boldly.

'I thought you used to call me that nickname to be sweet. Now I realise it's your way of reminding yourself of my job; reminding yourself to keep your distance; reminding yourself to stay in control.'

'I don't need nicknames to stay in control.'

She didn't answer. Not at first. She merely took a pace forward, as if silently matching him. And now they were so close that if he'd lifted his arm up he could have touched her. He *wanted* to touch her; she knew him well enough by now to tell.

'Getting you to relinquish control. Just for once,' she told him at last.

'Is that so?' he demanded through gritted teeth.

Isla made herself smile. 'It is.'

Then, reaching up onto her tiptoes, as the waterfall shower cascaded over them both, she pressed her lips to his.

CHAPTER TWELVE

HAD HE BEEN waiting a whole lifetime just to kiss her again?

It felt like it. And that mere realisation should have made him take stock. Instead it walloped into him, winding him, before turning infinitely softer and moving like a caress over him. It was a smile that made him take another—possibly perilous—step closer.

As though he was compelled.

He struggled, trying to pull together some semblance of discipline. Though whether for her or for himself he couldn't be sure. He'd spent his whole adult life feeling as though there was a monster prowling deep inside him, lurking in the dark, stalking around the edges. He'd thought of himself as some kind of ringmaster, trying to keep that monster in check.

Now, abruptly, he felt as though he wasn't the one with the power at all. She was—*Isla was*—and she was leading him by the nose.

Or something rather further down.

As if she was weaving some kind of magic around him, binding him. Worse, he *liked* it.

'Whatever game you think you're playing, Isla,' he ground out, only just able to pull his mouth from hers, 'it won't work.'

'And if I'm not playing a game?'

The suggestiveness in her words licked over him, blood pooling in the very hardest part of him. It was too much to think she wouldn't notice, when her eyes slid lower and widened that fraction.

Aside from the running water, the silence was hot, and heavy. Pulling around him, closing in until he felt it pressing on his lungs and stopping him from breathing properly.

And then, *God help him*, she licked her lips.

Nikhil didn't remember reaching out. He didn't remember hauling her to him. But suddenly she was there, in his arms, and he was kissing her as though he was a suffocating man and she was the oxygen he needed to survive.

Perhaps she was.

He'd certainly never felt so desperate, so ferocious, so feral before. He slid his tongue against hers, revelling in the way she met him stroke for stroke. The way she took his lip in her teeth and grazed it with just enough pressure.

Need fired through him. Raw. Unrestrained. It made the beast inside him roar. He would have her screaming his name again, as she had that first night.

Even the memory of it was intensified, now that he had her in his arms. It took everything he had not to simply lift her in his arms, carry her to the bed and rip her clothes off so he could indulge in every last erotic fantasy he'd had about her.

'I told you.' She drew back unexpectedly, as if reading his mind. 'Tonight isn't about me losing control.'

He wasn't prepared for the sense of loss, especially when desire was still unmistakable in her tone, her dark, lust-filled eyes never leaving his.

He wanted to pull her back to him. He didn't know how he resisted. Maybe because that male part of him still wanted to make her come back to him. To beg him.

'Then what?' he bit out; for the first time in a couple of decades he wasn't sure he trusted himself.

Every second of silence wrapped tighter around him. He felt more and more wired. And somehow Isla knew it. More than knew it—she was relishing it.

And just when he thought she wasn't going to speak, she stretched her hand out and ran it straight down the length of his body. Over his chest, his belly, her eyes never leaving his. Then, slowly and deliberately, she wrapped her hand around him, one long, elegant finger at a time, sliding from root to tip, leaving him forgetting to even breathe.

'Isla…' he warned. Weakly, if he was to be truthful.

'Like I said, I didn't come here to lose control.' He drew in a sharp breath at the sudden wicked glint in her eyes as, without warning, she sank elegantly to her knees in front of him. 'I came here this time so *you* would lose control.'

In that instant Nikhil knew he needed to stop her. He'd had countless women pleasure him this way, over the years, and he'd welcomed it. Encouraged it. Sometimes downright instigated it. But this was the first time he had ever, *ever,* felt like this. As though she was asking him to surrender to her. And he couldn't do that.

Then, that devilish gaze still locked with his, she leaned forward and took him straight into her mouth. And as his legs turned to water right there and then, Nikhil found he was powerless to do anything but let her do what she willed, whilst he thought he was about to die from need.

Pleasuring Nikhil was possibly the most sensuous thing she'd ever done in her life, Isla thought. Oh, she'd performed the act before, but it had never, *ever* felt so heady. So right. It had never made her feel as powerful as she did right now, with him.

As though she had all the control and he was simply at her mercy.

With every stroke of her tongue, every tightening of her fist, every graze of her teeth, she could hear his breathing grow all the more ragged and those hewn stone thighs of his tremble that little bit harder.

She drew him out to let her tongue swirl around his velvet-steel tip, then angled her head to take him in deeper. Her mouth, her tongue, her hands, all working in harmony, united in the same goal of making Nikhil give himself up to her completely.

And his taste. It was intoxicating. Stirring. It made her want to indulge all the more. Indulge for ever.

She was in so much trouble and she couldn't seem to care.

The realisation dragged a low moan from deep in her throat, rumbling down Nikhil's length and eliciting a curse from him as he speared his fingers deeper into her hair. As if he couldn't help himself. Another shiver of excitement jolted through Isla.

Gripping him tighter, she let her fingers apply pressure at his root whilst her mouth worked some kind of spell she hadn't even known she possessed. Until Nikhil's breath came harsher, his legs less stable than ever. She was driving him closer and closer to the edge and the taste of victory, of power, was almost too delicious.

And still she wasn't surprised when he found that last shred of strength to pull away from her.

'Not like this.' His voice was so thick, so gravelly, that it was almost unrecognisable.

It gave her an immense sense of satisfaction—almost making up for the sense of loss.

Then he was slamming off the shower, gathering her

into his arms and carrying her back into the bedroom as if he couldn't contain himself any longer.

He threw her down on the bed, stared at her for a long moment before offering a guttural sound of approval that juddered straight through her, and threw her legs over his shoulders. Then he licked into her greedily, urgently, without a single word spoken.

Bright and hot, like the sunlight bouncing off the waves outside her window every morning.

Better.

Isla wasn't sure how she didn't shatter in an instant. Because he didn't merely lick her, he feasted on her. As if she was the last meal of his life and he was hell-bent on sampling every last morsel. And she was helpless to do anything but spread herself out for him, every sweep of his tongue making her shake that little bit more uncontrollably, her hands thrust into his hair, her hips bucking up to meet him.

She felt utterly wanton. And somehow she knew that only fired Nikhil up all the more. She was hurtling to the edge and there was no way she could apply the brakes, especially when he cupped her backside with his large hands, pressed down on her sex with his mouth and then sucked. Hard.

Isla fractured apart, his name tumbling from her lips—a song and an incantation. She splintered, and still he kept going, relentlessly pushing her from one high to the next. She arched her back, her fingers grasping his hair, his shoulders, the sheets, for some kind of purchase, and his low rumble of laughter shuddered through her like a new form of exquisite, magnificent torture.

And this time she didn't simply hit another high; this time she hurtled off into space. And she could only hope that Nikhil would be her safety net when she fell back down to earth.

Isla had no idea how long it took her to come back to herself, but when she did she glanced around the room to check where she was. To make sure that it hadn't just been a dream.

But it hadn't. She was still here, in his room, and in his bed. She just didn't understand how he could upend her world like this—so easily—and yet the room wasn't equally torn apart.

Then he was moving up her body to cover it with his own as she reached for him, nestling him between her legs. A low gasp escaped her lips as she rolled her hips against him, revelling in the way his breath caught, the way they affected each other with barely a brush of heat against steel.

But wasn't this supposed to be about her being in control? She had almost forgotten. Lifting her hands to his shoulders, Isla made a supreme effort and pushed him off her, onto his back on the bed, straddling him before he could move.

Nikhil's expression flip-flopped between lust and amusement. 'Like that, is it?'

'Like that,' she whispered, leaning forward to brush her mouth to his, her tongue teasing at the seam of his lips.

Her chest pressed to his, her nipples chafing deliciously against the fine layer of hair scattered across his chest. She was so close. Again. How could that be?

His hands splayed around her hips. Lightly. As if he was trying to resist taking the reins—but only just. She liked that he even tried. Her gaze caught his and, for another moment, she couldn't breathe. Placing her hands on his shoulders, Isla levered herself slightly upright and, her eyes still locked with his, she slipped slowly—so slowly—down his length, taking him inside her.

Deep, and sure.

It was possibly the most provocative thing she'd ever done. And Nikhil seemed to think so too. His jaw was so tight she was half afraid he might break it.

'See what happens when you give up control?' she whispered, her eyes still held by his. 'Even for this tiny moment.'

'I only know that you're killing me, *pyar*,' he ground out.

And suddenly his perpetually dark expression cleared, if only for a moment, and she saw something in those depths that she had never anticipated. Something that called to her so loudly, and so clearly. A jagged puzzle piece, like those pieces of jewellery that were two halves of a whole. And, not that she'd ever realised it before, the matching piece lay—just as deeply buried—inside her.

It called to her, clawed at her and, even if she couldn't bring herself to answer, there was no way she could stop her heart from swelling in her chest. Insane, and dangerous, and just as undeniable.

And then she wasn't in control any longer. Nikhil's hands tightened around her hips and he began to set the pace. Slow yet inexorable, beating in her chest, her belly, and through her very veins. Building deliciously and carrying her higher still as her fingers bit into his shoulders as she matched him, thrust for thrust.

'Nikhil…'

'Forget about control, *pyar*,' he muttered, his voice gratifyingly strained. 'Forget about everything and just let go.'

'You first,' she murmured, scarcely recognising her own voice.

Her entire body was fizzing as she began to move again,

riding them both towards the edge. And suddenly it didn't matter who had fallen first as they toppled together, over the edge and into the gloriously endless abyss beyond.

It was an hour or so later when Isla swung her legs heavily over the side of the bed as Nikhil lay sleeping. She ached everywhere. A delicious bone-deep ache that reminded her of every last second of that glorious time together.

An ache that made her hesitate as her feet made contact with the wooden floor, wishing she didn't have to force herself to get up. To sneak out.

It was supposed to have been about quenching her thirst for Nikhil. How could it be that, instead, the more she had of this man, the more she seemed to crave?

Well, either way, it was too bad. They'd had their indulgence; he wasn't going to welcome her still being around when he woke. Nikhil would be about business, the way he was always about business. But this afternoon had been something special. Just between them. A moment where he had relaxed his control…and a memory she would have for ever…where Nikhil had been at her mercy—if only for a few hours.

She tucked it away as something precious.

Leaning forward a fraction, Isla placed her fists either side of her bottom, pushing into the mattress, and levered her reluctant body up.

'Going somewhere?'

She swung around quickly.

God, he still looked so impossibly beautiful. It wasn't fair, really.

'It's nearly dinnertime. I thought I should get changed for the evening.'

He frowned. 'You don't have to do that.'

Her heart faltered in her chest. Could he possibly want

her to stay? Her blood pumped harder in her veins and she tried to quell it. Even if he did want her to stay, she shouldn't. It was already starting to become too difficult to separate the sex from the emotion.

'I'm the scheduled doctor on call,' she offered instead, chewing on her lower lip, almost frightened of saying too much and spooking him.

'You have your pager?'

'Of course.' She looked around for her clothes, flushing when she saw them lying haphazardly on the floor, and remembering Nikhil's impatience at removing them.

The moment had been intoxicating. The memory still was, if she were to be honest. And yet she swept up the garments and held them to the front of her body, as though that provided her with any more dignity than standing here, completely naked, in front of him.

'Then they can reach you if they need to. You don't have to be down there with everyone else.'

'Right.' Isla swallowed.

She could barely breathe right now. Standing here, waiting—silently begging—for him to spell it out. But Nikhil just lay there, his hands locked behind his head, his bare muscled chest on display and the white sheet low over his abdomen, just concealing himself from her.

Teasing her.

Was he daring her to crawl back onto the bed and repeat what had happened earlier?

Her mouth actually watered, even as insecurity gripped her.

'So… I should stay?'

His eyes changed, something flashing through them that she couldn't quite identify, and then they darkened, looking more sensuous than ever.

'Are you waiting for an invitation?'

What was it about his tone that made her suddenly so bold?

'I wasn't presuming,' she teased. 'I've learned that can be a mistake where you are concerned.'

'And I've learned that no matter how much I try to resist you, *pyar*, I cannot. But there is a lesson to be learned there, I think.'

'What lesson?' Isla asked, trying to hold herself together. Trying not to read too much into the fact that he'd called her *pyar*. Again. Which, if she wasn't very much mistaken, was a term of endearment.

It was both terrifying and stirring that she should react so viscerally to the term. No matter how much she kept trying to remind herself that this was casual, that it didn't mean anything, that she didn't *want* it to mean anything, Isla was very much afraid her head and her heart weren't quite singing the same song.

Perhaps reading that all over her face, Nikhil suddenly took hold of her upper arms. Not roughly, but enough to make sure she was listening to him.

'Isla, you understand that I can't offer you anything more than this?' His voice was gruff.

'I don't want anything more.' The words slipped out easily enough. Yet she was still suspicious of her own traitorous heart. 'You forget, I don't believe in love. Or relationships.'

'So you said,' he confirmed.

But he didn't look entirely convinced and she knew how he felt.

'The point is, this isn't dating. It's just…'

'Enjoying each other's company,' Isla jumped in, though whether she was trying to convince Nikhil or herself wasn't entirely determinable.

Still, the words were the right ones. And, whether he believed her or not, it was enough to allow him to continue.

'Enjoying each other's company,' he muttered, already pulling her back to him and claiming her mouth with his own. As if he couldn't help himself any longer.

And didn't that say something all of its own?

CHAPTER THIRTEEN

WHAT WAS IT about an all-you-can-eat cruise ship buffet that induced a passenger with a known allergy to decide to sample the very food that could kill them? In this case, a newly married fifty-year-old gentleman with a shellfish allergy who had nonetheless decided to sample the aphrodisiac qualities of oysters with his new wife.

In a way, she could almost understand it. The past few weeks with Nikhil—ever since that night back at the hotel in the rainforest—had been incredible. Special. How many times had he reached for her that night? After that thrilling moment when she'd been about to sneak out of his room, when he'd told her that he couldn't offer her anything more than enjoying each other's company.

It had been more of a promise than she'd ever imagined she would hear from his lips. And he'd made good on it, giving her the key to his cabin every night they happened to be off together. Trusting her.

Because, as discreet as she'd tried to be, she knew that even if only one person spotted them, it would ruin the reputation he'd spent a decade building. He was risking it for her. It was more of a declaration to her than all the words he'd avoided saying. And one day, when she had the courage, maybe she could point that out to him and prove that he was wrong for thinking that he wasn't the kind of person who could love, or be loved.

Maybe. One day.

And Nikhil wasn't the only one who had changed this past month. How many times had she caught herself thinking and feeling differently? How many times had she felt wild, and daring, just because of the way this one, wonderful man affected her?

She was growing; she could sense it. She just wasn't quite sure what it meant yet.

But, either way, perhaps it wasn't such a shock that the new marriage made her latest patient feel as though he was invincible—even where shellfish were concerned. Taking the stairs two at a time, she raced to the main restaurant. Hopefully, he would have his allergy pen on him and his new wife would have administered it.

She might have known it wouldn't happen. Even by the time she'd elbowed her way through the rubber-necking crowd, the patient was deteriorating rapidly. His face had swollen up at least twice its usual size, contorted and red, and threatening his airway with every passing second. His breathing was already shallow and rasping, and even the guy's hands were swollen where he'd picked up the offending item.

His wife was evidently so distraught that it took Isla several moments to calm her down enough to discover that her husband's name was Stewart.

Clearing a space around her patient, Isla picked out an epinephrine injector from her bag and prepared to administer the medication, talking to where the eyes should have been on Stewart's distorted face. She was only glad that it was a lunchtime and the man was wearing shorts.

It was fortunate that, just as she finished, Lisa arrived

with antihistamines and an oxygen mask, the mobile gurney not far behind.

'Let's get you to the medical centre, Stewart.' Isla smiled at her patient, wondering if he could even see her. He seemed to be able to, but it was still too hard to tell. This was always the worst part, trying to deal with a frightened patient and equally frightened loved one when a hundred or more people were crowding around, trying to get a good view of the action.

It was several hours before Isla finally finished up the last of her paperwork, handed it to Gerd, who was on duty for the night, and slipped out of the medical centre.

Quickly and quietly, she hurried through the ship, grateful for the late hour if only because it made it easier to sneak to Nikhil's room without being seen. Not that the past couple of weeks hadn't been just a little bit thrilling, sneaking around the ship, snatching as many precious nights together as they could without anyone realising what was going on.

Not that they got that many between his work and hers, but in a way that only made them feel that much more delicious.

Some feat on a ship like this, and for Isla, who'd never done anything remotely illicit like this before, it was impossible not to get a bit of a kick from it.

No doubt it helped that the only two people who might possibly notice that something was amiss were either in some secret location with the other Dara brother…or holed up with the Captain on his downtime.

Ironic, really. Isla stifled a gurgle of laughter.

She had slipped inside Nikhil's cabin when he was there, and he was drawing her into his arms and to him.

'I wasn't sure if you'd still be on the bridge,' she breathed between scorching, devilish kisses.

'I got back here a few minutes before you did,' he muttered. 'I heard about the drama with the seafood roulette player. He's okay?'

'He's okay,' she confirmed, her fingers making their way to his waist to tug his already half-undone shirt out of the trouser band.

'Anything I need to know?'

'Nothing that can't wait for the report in the morning,' she said, shaking her head.

'Good,' he approved, pulling her up to wrap her legs around his waist and carry her across the room to drop her—both of them laughing like intoxicated teens on their first night out—onto the bed.

Isla was just finishing in the shower an hour or so later when she heard a soft knock on Nikhil's cabin door and the low exchange of voices. She paused, trying to stay quiet and discreet and not really trying to listen. Not that it mattered; the voices were too low for her to hear what was being said.

Waiting for the sound of the door closing, Isla wrapped the towel around herself and stepped out of the bathroom. She schooled herself to stay silent, torn between the fact that this was Nikhil's cabin and it was therefore likely to be ship's business, and sheer curiosity over what such a late-night call had been about.

But when she rounded the corner to see Nikhil standing, his face a shade of white to match the towel slung loosely around his hips, she didn't stop to think.

'What's wrong, Nikhil? What's happened?'

His eyes slid to her, but she had the strangest impression that he wasn't really seeing her. A moment later, he seemed to refocus.

'It's nothing.'.

'It doesn't look like nothing,' she pressed softly. In truth, he looked tormented. Defeated. And she could feel her insides twist themselves in knots as she fought the urge to go to him and try to make everything all right. Because she knew she couldn't.

She wasn't his girlfriend; she was…little more than a booty call. A supposedly mutually agreeable booty call, but suddenly she wondered if her mother had truly been right all these years.

Had her marriages always been mutually advantageous, or was it possible that they had been more one-sided than Marianna had ever realised? Or indeed admitted. Could it be that the husbands Marianna had selected had each fallen a little bit in love with her, in their own way?

Nikhil had warned her that he couldn't offer her anything more than *enjoying each other's company,* and she had agreed on the premise that she'd never wanted to get hurt again after Bradley.

But really, deep down, Isla was beginning to finally admit a truth she suspected she'd known all along. She had never loved Bradley; she'd barely felt much for him at all, so how could he ever have hurt her?

Had the emotions she'd held up as evidence of her hurt really been more about humiliation? Because she'd felt more for Nikhil in the last few weeks than she ever had for her ex-fiancé. Which made her fear that her affair with Nikhil wasn't quite so emotion-free as she'd imagined.

Certainly not as emotion-free as Nikhil.

But then, instead of shutting her out as she'd expected him to do, Nikhil suddenly picked up an exquisitely written note and passed it to her.

'That was Roberto at the door,' he told her woodenly, referring to the concierge. 'He just delivered this.'

It was such an unexpected invitation into his personal

life, yet Isla wasn't about to back away now. Her fingers shaking, she read the message. It was short and to the point and as she came to the end it was impossible to name what skittered through her.

'Your brother wants to meet again?' she stated redundantly.

'At any of the next ports of call.' Nikhil didn't even sound like himself. 'If I name it, he claims he'll be there.'

'Maybe you should,' she offered tentatively. 'Maybe it's time to find out what he wants.'

'Maybe I don't care what he wants,' Nikhil threw back, but she knew he wasn't angry at her.

'Then think about what you want,' she tried instead. 'Or, more pertinently, what you need.'

'I don't need him,' Nikhil bit out flatly, staring at her so hard that she felt his gaze was actually imprinting itself on her skin. 'I might have, a few decades ago. But I don't any more.'

'What happened, Nikhil?'

He shook his head. 'It's long-buried history. I see no benefit in resurrecting it.'

'And yet you chose to tell me about this, when you could have ignored it, as you did the last time he was in touch.'

Nikhil didn't answer, yet she could feel his emotions circling the room. Snaking around them, ready to strike. She knew she ought to keep out of it, but she couldn't. He needed her, whether he recognised it or not.

'What's your history with your brother, Nikhil?'

That pulse ticked harder, faster in his jaw, but he still didn't answer. And then, just as she was about to give up, he opened his mouth.

'He betrayed me, Isla. He was my big brother, and he left me at the very moment that I needed him most. That's all you need to know.'

'Really, Nikhil?' The words spilled from her lips before she could stop them. 'You think you're the only one to have been betrayed by someone? People do that. It's one of the uglier sides to human nature. But you want to know what one of our better qualities is?'

'I'm sure you're going to enlighten me.'

'We pick ourselves up—' she didn't let his wry tone derail her '—dust ourselves off, and we start again.'

'And who, might I ask, betrayed you? Your loving mother? Your idolising stepsister?'

And she didn't know what made her say it; she only knew she wanted to make a point to Nikhil.

'Try my lying ex-fiancé.'

Nikhil bit back whatever response he might have made. He'd spent the better part of a month trying to deny it, but the question of Isla's ex-fiancé had plagued him ever since he'd seen that light band around her ring finger.

From that very first day it had begged the question of what kind of man let a woman like Isla Sinclair slip through his fingers. And that was why, from that very first day, he'd realised quite how much trouble he was in when it came to this remarkable, bewitching woman.

'I met Bradley at med school, and I was with him for ten years. The last three of those years we were engaged.'

'Let me guess; he cheated on you.'

'He did.' She nodded. 'Many times, I discovered that final week before we broke up. But do you want to know the sickest part? That wasn't even the thing that hurt me the most.'

'Is that so?' he managed, fighting not to let her see the unexpected anger which had begun to swell inside him at her admission.

Indignation on Isla's behalf. A desire to find this idiot

Bradley and show him how duplicitous cowards like him deserved to be treated. But, more than that, Nikhil had to fight a sense that Isla deserved more, *better,* than to be cheated on.

Just as she deserves more than being used as a booty call? a voice demanded in his head.

'The worst part…' She licked her lips as though she was finding this harder than she'd expected. 'The worst part was that I let him dictate my life. I let him tell me that once we were married I was going to give up my medical career and become the kind of wife that could support *his* career.'

Nikhil blinked. Of all the admissions he'd expected from her, this was not one of them.

Isla was born to be a doctor; she clearly loved her work and she was good at it. It would be like throwing him off a ship and telling him to find a new career on land legs.

'And you agreed to this?'

She tilted her head to one side thoughtfully. 'I didn't disagree. At least, not at first. He was saying all the things that my mother had always wanted, so for a short while I lost myself.'

'I can't imagine that of you.'

'I was, frankly, an idiot. But I thought I loved him. And I thought that he loved me. It turned out he just loved my mother's social contacts. I was little more than a means to an end. Albeit one who also looked good on his arm.'

'I still can't see you being the kind of person who would agree to that.' Nikhil shook his head as Isla squeezed her eyes shut.

'That's the point. I was a different person back then. That moment was the catalyst for me to try to turn my life around. To become a ship's doctor, to tour the world, and to have the career I'd always wanted. I didn't bank on meeting someone like you.'

And though he warned himself not to react, that he shouldn't like the way that sounded, Nikhil found himself carried away by her words.

'I've changed, Nikhil. I'm not the girl I was a month ago. I might not have quite noticed it, but my mother has. And she put it down to you, that night at the gala.'

And God help him, but he wanted to believe every word that she was saying. He just knew that he shouldn't.

He had his own demons. And, unlike Isla, he didn't have the strength to confront them.

'That wasn't the agreement,' he balked. 'We said *no dating*, just enjoying time together. We agreed *no commitments*.'

'And now it has developed,' Isla pointed out evenly.

He might have believed her, had it not been for the slight shake in her hands. He gritted his teeth as he fought to harden his heart—whatever heart he had—against her.

'Not for me.'

He certainly didn't expect her soft, almost regretful response.

'You're lying.'

'Say again?'

'I don't know if you're just lying to me or if you're also lying to yourself, but you've felt something blossoming between us, just as I have.'

'You're mistaken.'

'No, I'm not. And you can growl at me all you want to, Nikhil, but it won't change the facts,' she pressed on, inching her way further and further inside the hollow cavern that was his chest.

Only he had the oddest sensation that she was shining light and warmth into the corners of it as she went.

'I don't do intimacy. Or commitment.'

'You didn't, no,' she agreed. 'But you can't pretend that

things haven't changed between us over the last few weeks. You're more open, and compassionate. It isn't a weakness.'

He had a terrible, wonderful feeling that she was right.

But she couldn't be right. Because even if what she said was true, even if he'd started to try to become a different person, the truth was that he couldn't. He was who he was. His past had made sure of that. Pretending to be someone different—the kind of man who deserved a woman like Isla—wasn't going to *make* him different.

It would be like papering over the cracks. His flaws would still be there, hidden temporarily beneath. And when they finally began to show again, when they finally broke through the surface, they would be all the uglier.

But the worst part of it was that he *wanted* to believe her. So damned much.

A part of him thought this might be love—or the closest thing he could ever get to it.

It felt like giving a kid a detonation device and then stepping back to see what happened. It couldn't end well. If he cared for Isla at all, he wouldn't put them in that position. And if that wasn't a reason to keep his distance…

'You're seeing what you want to see,' he practically snarled at her, as if to remind her—remind them both—of the monster that he truly was.

Instead of cowering, however, his beautiful, powerful Isla merely smiled, making everything inside him begin to shatter.

'I'm acknowledging what you pretend isn't there. I see you for who you really are, Nikhil, and, no matter what you try to tell yourself, I know you're a good man.'

'You haven't listened to anything I've told you,' he roared. 'I'm not a good man, Isla, and, no matter that you want to pretend differently, it won't make it true.'

'You're wrong, Nikhil. You have this one awful image

of yourself locked in your brain, I suspect because you think that's what your brother saw when he was at that funeral. But the Nikhil you hold onto isn't the man I have ever seen. Not once. You need to meet Daksh and listen to what he has to say.'

And in that moment he realised he would give anything to be the man that Isla thought he was.

But that wasn't him. She was wrong. And so the only thing he could do was protect her from himself. The only way he knew how.

Snatching up his uniform, he stalked out of the room. He had to go and speak to the Captain now, before he thought better of what he was about to do.

'Lock the door when you leave, Isla,' he managed. 'And don't return.'

CHAPTER FOURTEEN

IT WAS ALMOST a week later, when Isla was in the middle of tending to her latest patient, that she was summoned by the Captain.

'Thank you, Gerd.' She pasted on a bright smile, turning back to her rather glamorously dressed patient, who Isla had initially guessed to be in her mid-to-late sixties, but who had turned out to be a sprightly seventy-four.

Mrs Berridge-Jones had tripped down the last steps of the staircase in the Grand Lobby and been brought to the surgery because she'd been unable to put any weight on her ankle.

'I'm not disembarking,' the woman had declared imperiously. 'I've been waiting two years for this cruise. I refuse to be sent home just because I caught my heel in the hem of my wretched dress on the last step of your perfectly easy-to-see staircase. It would just ruin the entire cruise.'

She'd rolled the *r* of *ruin*, and Isla had seen flashes of her mother in Mrs Berridge-Jones.

Now, Isla helped the older woman swing around on the examination table, taking note of the wince of pain.

'Good news, Mrs Berridge-Jones.' Isla grinned as she presented the images to her patient. 'Your X-ray doesn't show any fractures; I'm confident that you've got a sprained ankle rather than a break, so I can say that I have absolutely no intention of ruining your cruise.'

'Jolly glad to hear it. So you'll patch me up in a jiffy and I can get back to my welcome drink? I'd just ordered a rather decent port.'

'As close to a jiffy as I can,' Isla answered wryly, checking over the foot. 'But it's still swollen and clearly painful, even though the painkillers I have given you are doing their job. There are also clear signs of a reduction of movement, so perhaps you won't be back upstairs in time to enjoy your port this evening.'

Mrs Berridge-Jones cast her a distinctly disdainful glance. 'Oh, just give me a few more pain pills to get me through the next couple of days and I shall be as right as rain.'

'Before you go racing back up there to your port, Mrs Berridge-Jones, I have to tell you that sprains still require care and can be very painful. It involves tearing or stretching the ligaments that help hold your ankle bones together and stabilise your ankle joint.'

'I'm not having a splint for a sprained ankle,' the woman scoffed.

Isla smothered another smile as she adopted her best disapproving doctor voice. 'Self-care is vital, Mrs Berridge-Jones. If you don't look after a sprained ankle you could end up with chronic ankle pain, ankle joint instability, or even arthritis in the ankle joint.'

'Piffle.'

'I want to see it elevated and wrapped before I let you leave here, Mrs Berridge-Jones.'

And although the woman blustered, Isla noted she nonetheless obeyed.

Now, an hour later, Isla found herself hammering on Nikhil's door and practically shouldering him out of the way to step inside, without waiting to be invited, the moment he opened it.

'I've just been summoned by the Captain,' she bit out. 'He offered me a new job.'

It was useless pretending that she wasn't nervous. That her heart wasn't suddenly pounding, or her mouth dust-dry.

'Right.'

She hated that he didn't look surprised. Or concerned. Or anything at all, really.

'The doctor who was originally on this ship wants to resume his post when the new cruise begins.'

'Yes, he retains that right.'

She didn't know what she wanted him to say, but it was more than that.

'So they've offered me a post on another ship. Better than the *Hestia,* but not quite the *Cassiopeia* either.'

'It's a good career move.'

Emotions bubbled up in her chest. She'd told herself she was being paranoid, suspecting Nikhil of being somehow involved. But now, given his reaction, she was beginning to suspect worse.

That perhaps he'd been more than just *involved.* That perhaps he'd been the one to actually instigate it.

'You knew,' she accused, her chest feeling as though it was about to crack.

'The Captain asked my opinion. It seems you've made quite an impression on Dr Turner. He wanted to keep you in favour of the original doctor.'

The truth walloped her hard, winding her.

'So you said I was better to move ships.'

'I merely pointed out that not letting the previous doctor resume his post might open us up to legal challenges. And your role here was only ever stated as temporary.'

'You didn't want me here.' Nausea rose in Isla but she

quashed it. 'You told me to transfer, and when I refused you found some other way to get rid of me.'

'You got a promotion,' he corrected. 'To a more prestigious ship than you were meant to have been on in the first instance.'

She supposed she should be grateful at least, that he wasn't choosing to lie to her. At least he had the integrity to tell her the truth. But it didn't make it hurt any less.

'This isn't about my career, Nikhil. At least have the decency to admit that. This is about you not wanting to open up to anyone. And my arrival messing up all your little rules that you have for yourself.'

'I considered what was best for the company. That's my job.'

'And thank God it fits with your personal leanings. You've been trying to push me away ever since I came on board. And you've been hating yourself because you couldn't do it.'

'It has nothing to do with *getting rid* of anybody. It has to do with supporting your transfer to another ship when the doctor you were replacing is returning here anyway.'

'No.' She refused to accept it. 'That's a convenient excuse—because it also happens to fit. But it's a side-effect; it isn't the main reason. It isn't your primary motivator. You endorsed that transfer because it also got me away from you. You have feelings for me; you just aren't prepared to admit them.

'But I won't transfer,' Isla stated flatly. 'What are you so afraid of, Nikhil?'

He blinked. It was fleeting, but it was there nonetheless, and it told her that her hunch—this odd, alien sense—about him had been right.

Isla felt as though she was splitting in two. One part of

her celebrated the fact that she knew this incredible, enigmatic man better than he even knew himself.

And the other part of her… That was terrified at the notion. Because she didn't want to be connected with him—with anyone—again. Not after Bradley.

And yet you never felt you knew Bradley a fraction of the way you feel you know Nikhil, whispered a voice inside her head. *You never* wanted *to.*

'You misunderstand.' His cold voice dragged her back to the moment. 'I'm not afraid. I'm never afraid.'

He knew it wasn't true even as the defiant words left his lips.

He was more afraid than he'd ever been in his life. And not least because the way Isla looked at him right at that moment made him feel as though she could read every last dark thought engraved on the cold, hard stone that sat in place of his heart.

'You were afraid the moment that message arrived at your cabin the other night, and instead of keeping it from me, as you would have done a week ago, you handed it to me to read.'

'It was just a message, Isla.'

'We both know it wasn't. You let me into your life and now you're regretting it. This is your way of pushing me away.'

'It's for your own good,' he ground out.

'Because you're a monster?' she asked scornfully, and he loved the way she sounded so fierce. *For him.*

'Because in your head it's somehow your fault that your stupid brother left you to suffer everything alone, and never came back?'

He wanted so much to believe her. He almost did—even though, unlike her, he knew the truth.

'I told you that he came to the funeral?' The words might as well have come out independently of his mouth. Certainly, independently of his brain.

'Your father's funeral, yes.' She dipped her head carefully, after a moment.

'He didn't come to the grave, but he stood by a tree and watched. I saw the disgust in his eyes. Like he thought I should have done better for the old man. The bastard was lucky I even gave him that much.'

'You didn't talk to Daksh?' Isla asked softly.

'No more that he talked to me.' Nikhil inclined his head curtly. 'I looked up one moment and he was there, then when I looked up again he was gone.'

'And that's why you think you are this…monster?'

'It's what I am. Even he could see it.'

'You're not. You're a man. And a good man, at that. But the sad part is that you will never take my word for it. I don't matter enough to you.'

And he wanted to refute it, so fervently. But he couldn't.

'So speak to your brother, Nikhil,' she continued, and he would have given so much to erase that desolation from her voice. 'Whatever he has to say, it can't be any worse than this hell that you've put yourself in.'

Then she kissed him and walked out of the door. Out of his life.

And he tried not to wonder what the hell he'd just done.

So this was what the most exclusive hotel in Rotterdam looked like, Nikhil thought as he glanced around the elegant lobby that practically oozed money.

He could pretend that he wasn't looking for answers that would make him the man Isla deserved. Maybe he should tell himself that he was here because the Captain had pulled him in less than twenty-four hours earlier to tell Nikhil that the promotion he'd been working towards for the better part of a decade was now his for the taking. Captain of his own ship.

But, on both counts, Nikhil knew he'd be lying to himself.

Moreover, he didn't deserve a promotion any more than he deserved her. *Isla.*

These past ten days without her had been hell. His entire ten-week cruise had been a rollercoaster—like being on the swell, far out at sea—but the fun part had only started in that third week when he'd walked into that bar in Chile.

And as he'd walked out of the Captain's office he'd found himself heading to the medical centre—instinctively wanting to share his news with Isla.

Nikhil still wasn't sure how he'd stopped himself. He only remembered standing on the deck, on a mercifully cold, rainy sea day, which meant that only a handful of other, waterproof-clad souls had been out there, braving the bracing air. And he'd finally admitted that Isla had been right that his shattered relationship with his brother had been eating him up inside all these years.

In that instant he'd wondered what he had to lose.

Before he could talk himself out it, he'd hurried back to his cabin, conducted an internet search for DXD Industries and picked up his phone.

And then, suddenly, his brother had been at the end of the phone, and Nikhil knew he'd have recognised that voice in an instant.

He'd even imagined he'd heard Isla's voice in his head, encouraging him, as he'd told his brother that their next port of call was going to be Rotterdam. And now here he was, sitting in the plush hotel lobby and waiting for the man he hadn't seen since they'd both been kids.

And then Nikhil saw him.

There was no doubt that Daksh Dara had money. More than that—wealth. It was in every long line of his body, every expensive stitch of his tailored suit.

The two brothers eyed each other for several long moments—perhaps a lifetime—each on their own side of the room. And Nikhil could practically feel the storm of recrimination at the centre of it, cracking and sparking, as the two of them held their ground. As if neither wanted to be the first to make a move.

Eventually, however, to Nikhil's shock, it was Daksh who began the approach—every long, powerful stride seeming to strike the ground with force—making Nikhil wonder which one of them was actually the stronger, after all.

'Nikhil.' Daksh spoke at last.

'Brother,' he replied, infusing each syllable with as much insult as he possibly could.

'It's been a long time.'

'Since we last talked? Or since we last saw each other?' Nikhil asked icily.

The last thing he expected was a flash of something that looked suspiciously like remorse in Daksh's eyes. It knocked him off-guard.

'I was a coward for not talking to you at…*his* funeral.'

Nikhil couldn't answer. He was too caught up in the way his brother had not only refused to call it *our father's funeral*, but also the hit of repulsion in the way he'd said *his*. As though he couldn't stand the old man any more than Nikhil could.

'I thought it was because you felt he deserved better than I gave him,' he managed stiffly.

And there it was, the look of disgust on his brother's face that Nikhil had seen at the funeral. Nikhil braced himself as Daksh opened his mouth to speak again.

'I didn't think he deserved anything even that good.'

It was about as far from anything Nikhil had been expecting as it could be.

'Say again?'

'He was a monster. I didn't think he even deserved the dignity of a funeral.'

Something coursed through Nikhil at that moment. Thick, and intense, though he couldn't have said what it was.

'Then why the hell didn't you even say one word to me?'

For a long moment Daksh didn't speak, and when he did it wasn't to answer.

'Shall we order a drink?' he asked, though it wasn't really a question.

Then he simply lifted his hand and a suited man moved instantly, one of several discreetly dotted around the room that Nikhil now realised were part of his brother's entourage.

Daksh had an entourage?

They sat in a heavy silence, each silently evaluating the other, until a waiter materialised with two tumblers of rich amber liquid. Its peppery tobacco heat pervaded his nostrils, telling him this was a quality not even seen at the Captain's table.

They both took a pull simultaneously, sending heat and spice across Nikhil's palate, followed by a creaminess that ended in rich, spicy fruits. It was impressive, though he wasn't about to tell Daksh so.

'I was ashamed.' His brother spoke suddenly. 'And full of guilt. That's why I didn't talk to you that day. I couldn't.'

It was such an unexpected confession that Nikhil didn't know what to say. He simply sat, every muscle in his body taut and still, unable to move.

His brain conjured up an image of Isla, and somehow that seemed to soothe his soul.

'I should never have left you to deal with him alone,' his brother continued, every word measured and heavy, as though he found it the hardest thing to say, as though he'd spent years rehearsing it. 'I knew what he was capable of. Most of the time he managed to keep it to just a beating, with a black eye or bruises that took weeks to heal. But there were a number of times I ended up in hospital because of him. Once with a broken leg, twice with a broken arm, twice with broken ribs.'

'Broken ribs. A knife wound. And once he sliced the bottom of my feet.'

Daksh cursed, a hollow, rasping sound loaded with hatred and suppressed fury. Somehow, it made Nikhil feel better.

'I thought he wouldn't touch you,' Daksh bit out. 'Or at least that was what I told myself. I thought that he targeted me because I looked more like our mother. I guess I wanted to believe that so that when I got out I could justify not going back. The one time I did, when he'd come out of rehab, you never mentioned anything. But I should have come back. I should have known he'd turn on you once I was gone.'

'He didn't at first,' Nikhil heard himself say. 'That first time you came back, he hadn't done anything. He went into rehab, and kept it going for a few months. I thought he had changed, but with hindsight I think he was just scared in case the authorities cottoned on. Not that they were any good back then.'

'I should have said something but…'

'You were embarrassed,' Nikhil finished when his brother trailed off. 'A grown-up kid getting beaten by his father. I know that feeling only too well.'

'You never should have had to. I was the older brother; I should have taken care of you.'

'Eighteen months older.' Nikhil shook his head. 'I don't think I'd have come back either, in your position. Though I've blamed you for it, all these years.'

It was odd how things could change in a heartbeat. Decades of censure and bitterness, gone in the space of half a conversation.

Because of Isla, a voice whispered. But Nikhil shut it down. She deserved better than him. She deserved a man who was good and true, who didn't have a black heart. At last Daksh had owned up to his mistakes, whilst he still hadn't faced up to his.

Maybe now was the time—there would be no other.

'I killed him, you know.' The confession scraped inside him, cutting and twisting as it left his body. And yet, even with the words out there, he felt something inside him begin to stir to life.

'No,' Daksh bit out instantly. Harshly. 'No, you didn't.'

'I had a knife.' For the first time in forever, Nikhil let his mind go back to that night, the silhouettes beginning to take better shape as the fog finally, finally began to lift. 'I stuck it in him.'

'No, you didn't.' Daksh recoiled, and Nikhil suddenly hated the horrified expression on his face.

It was extraordinary to find that after all these years he still sought his big brother's approval. He still felt lacking when Daksh looked at him with anything other than love. And still Nikhil forced himself to continue.

'I did. He was raging, and he had a knife. We wrestled and I managed to take it from him, I remember that. But then I felt suddenly angry, so angry, and he was still coming at me, and…then he wasn't.' Nikhil swallowed.

'I looked down, and there was blood, so much blood, and then his body was slumping on top of mine and I knew.'

'Christ, Nikhil…' His immaculate brother raked his hand through his hair, looking dazed. As if the two of them had just gone ten rounds.

'He was a monster, yes,' Nikhil ground out. 'But he didn't deserve to die. Not by his own son's hand.'

'You didn't kill him, Nik.' The unexpected nickname fired a salvo of memories at him, bombarding his head and bursting in his chest. 'Have you believed that all these years?'

'I remember it,' Nikhil managed harshly.

'You remember it wrong.'

Daksh sounded so certain, so angry, that Nikhil hesitated. It was as though he was standing right on the edge of some black, bottomless precipice—he wanted to back away; he just didn't know how to.

'You weren't there, Daksh.' He shook his head.

'But I read the police report.'

Snapping his head up, Nikhil could only stare at his brother.

'Not that I would care if you *had* killed him. He deserved it. But did you never wonder why, if you had killed him, you'd never been arrested?'

Nikhil felt as though his brain was swimming through treacle.

'I thought it was because I was fifteen, and there were no witnesses.'

'No, Nik, it's because you never did it. A neighbour heard the noise and they called the police. By the time they broke the door down, you were still in the position you'd been. Slumped on the floor with your back to the wall, and Dad on top of you.'

'But the knife was in my hand. It was in him.'

'The knife was there, in him, yes. But you didn't go for him. He put that knife right through your shoulder, didn't he? Pinning you to the wall? Your blood was on the knife, and the wall—it all fitted.'

'Yes…' Nikhil heard the voice but it took a moment to realise it was his own.

He'd never told anyone any of this—except for Isla—there was no way Daksh could have known it unless he had, indeed, read the report.

'The blood mark from your shoulder travelled down the wall, where you'd slid. There was no break, which means your body never left the wall.'

'No break?'

'None,' Daksh confirmed. 'Which means that if you didn't move off the wall, you couldn't have lunged for him. He had to have been the one to come at you again. And you were in the process of collapsing to the floor, Nikhil, so the only possible explanation is that he came at you too hard, maybe he stumbled, but, either way, he impaled himself.'

'No…?' Nikhil choked out.

Could it really have been that simple? Had he been carrying around a guilt, all these years, which had never been his to bear?

'Yes, Nikhil.' Daksh gritted his teeth. 'The angle of your hand, the force, it just wasn't there. You didn't do anything, little brother. I would say you were just at the wrong place at the wrong time.'

'No.' Nikhil shook his head again.

Was he really not the monster he'd believed himself to be? Had he sent Isla away from him, to protect her from him, for no good reason?

'I killed my father,' he repeated dully. 'I'm a monster.'

He watched, almost in slow motion, as Daksh threw himself up from his seat and came to crouch in front of him, his hand grabbing the back of Nikhil's head and pulling until they were forehead to forehead. The way they used to do as kids.

'You're no monster, little brother,' he bit out hoarsely. '*He* was the monster. Always him. And me, for leaving you there to suffer at his hands.'

'You were never a monster,' Nikhil managed, lifting his own hand to grab the back of his brother's head too. Like the biggest, most important of all the pacts they'd ever made. 'Though if you were I'd forgive you. I'd always forgive you.'

And despite the fact that he knew one conversation couldn't undo decades of self-loathing and recrimination, it somehow felt as though they'd made that first crucial step. The one that was always the hardest to make.

As if some healing process had begun—just as Isla had predicted. And it never would have happened without her. She'd already begun to change him. To help him take that step out of his past.

How had he failed to see that before? Or had he just been denying it to himself?

He was an idiot.

'I spent years thinking I had left it too long for us to ever stand a chance of healing the rift between us. I'm glad it wasn't too late.'

'It's going to take time.' The words were out before Nikhil had time to think about them. 'But it isn't too late after all.'

Was there such a thing as *too late*? he wondered suddenly.

What about Isla? Was it too late with her?

CHAPTER FIFTEEN

‘WHAT ARE YOU doing here, Nikhil?’

Her heart was hammering so loudly, so wildly, inside her ribcage. But she couldn’t allow him to see it. She *wouldn’t.*

‘I owe you an apology, Isla.’

Isla. Not Little Doc. She should feel triumphant.

She didn’t. She just felt shaky. Edgy. Her eyes were drinking him in greedily, when she shouldn’t have cared at all. It was galling the way she noticed the fit of his clothing, black jeans and a rock band tee, far more casual than the uniform he had practically lived in—unless they’d been naked in each other’s beds, of course.

She swallowed hard and his eyes caught hers immediately. They darkened, and in that moment she hated herself for her weakness, and hated him for noticing.

Except that this thing humming and coursing through her wasn’t *hate*, not even close. It took her all the way back to that beachside bar, when she’d sat with Leo and they’d argued good-naturedly about whether the honeymoon couple frolicking in the waves had really been in love.

Even now, she could hear her stepsister asking if that would ever be her, and she could hear herself scoffing, *No chance.*

But she didn’t feel like scoffing any more.

It took everything Isla had to shake her head and get back to her paperwork.

As if he didn't matter to her.

'That isn't necessary,' she managed.

'On the contrary,' he gritted out. 'It's long overdue.'

'I don't care. I don't want to hear it.'

'I went to speak with Dax,' he shocked her by saying suddenly. 'Just as you told me that I should.'

Isla wasn't sure what hit her hardest, the fact that he'd been to see his brother, or the fact that he'd said it was because *she* had told him to do so. Was it foolish to believe that she really had that much influence on him?

As much as her head was screaming at her not to turn back to him, she couldn't pretend she didn't want to hear it any longer.

Swinging around, almost in slow motion, she perched her bottom on the edge of the desk. Her arms dropped straight down each side, surreptitiously clutching the edge of the wood. Gripping it white-knuckle-tight, until she feared her fingernails would be damaged beyond all recognition.

But what was that compared to the way he'd damaged her heart?

And whose fault was that? a little voice whispered snidely in her head. She thrust it aside roughly.

'All right. I'm listening.'

'I should have told you what the Captain had advised me. I should have mentioned that appearing to be in a stable relationship with someone like you—an officer, a ship's doctor—would have enhanced my chances of promotion.'

'Yes,' she managed. 'You should have. But you didn't. Because you wanted it to look convincing, you wanted to make sure everyone was fooled, and what better way to achieve that than by ensuring that even *I* was fooled?'

'Yes,' he ground out, and her heart stalled. It faltered.

And in that moment Isla realised there was a part of herself that had hoped he would say something different. Something more palatable.

She'd been used. Lesson learned. She sucked in a breath and tried to make herself stand. Her very soul felt as though it was splintering, tearing apart, and if she was going to shatter into pieces then the least she wanted was to do it in private. Where he couldn't see her.

But her legs felt like jelly and all she could do was grip the desk tighter.

'Well…' She had no idea how she managed to sound so crisp. So cool. 'Thank you for finally being honest, if nothing else.'

'That's what I initially told myself I was doing, anyway,' Nikhil continued, taking a step closer to her, making every inch of her skin prickle with awareness. 'Yet who else knows about us? If I had honestly wanted to do that, then what was the point in us being so discreet?'

'You were playing the game,' she choked out.

'Only there was no game, not really. What we had felt too precious, too private, too *significant* to feed to the rumour mill. So maybe I initially told myself that getting into a relationship with you would be excusable if I could pretend to myself that it was a strategic career move, but I'm not sure the truth is that simple.'

The roaring sound in her ears was almost deafening. She didn't want to believe him. She didn't want to *hope.*

And yet…hope poured through her.

Nikhil sounded as though he was rolling the words around his head before he spoke them. Testing them out, seeing how they fitted. As though this wasn't easy for him. As though this was a truth with which even Nikhil himself was only just coming to terms.

'I don't have relationships with colleagues.'

'I'm know that.' She tried not to sound so bitter. Or hurt. 'You're too dedicated. Too career-driven to be distracted.'

'I never wanted to be in maritime,' Nikhil countered unexpectedly, and it wasn't so much an answer, Isla felt, as a tangent. 'In fact, it was the last thing I ever wanted to do. My father was a sailor; he worked in the boiler room, and I never wanted to do anything, *be* anything, remotely like him. For obvious reasons.'

No, she could understand that. Why would anyone want to follow in the footsteps of a violent, abusive drunkard who had caused so much pain? Mentally and physically.

'Then why join?' Isla asked, unable to help herself.

'Because there were scant other opportunities where I came from.' He shrugged. 'And so I decided that even if I had no other real option but to follow in his footsteps to join the profession, then at least I could make myself into the kind of man, the kind of sailor, that he'd never been. I could be the one thing he could never have even dreamed of—an officer.'

Which explained why he was dedicated, Isla supposed. Along with the way he had seemed to blame himself for how his father had died. Her mind raced. What had his brother said to him? Whatever it was, it must have been significant to bring Nikhil back here now.

Back to her.

'You never escaped him though, did you?' she asked quietly. 'You say you wanted to make yourself into an officer—something that your father could never have been—and yet you still let him haunt you all these years.'

'I did, but not because of him. More because of Dax.'

She wanted to speak, to answer, but she found she couldn't. Her mouth felt too dry, her tongue too thick. Even her body felt too tight in her own skin.

'I could say that I went to meet with him because of you, *pyar*. And perhaps I did. But I also went to meet with him because I needed to. I've needed to for probably twenty years, but I never had the courage before.'

'Before?' she croaked, as he nodded slowly and took a step closer to her.

'I didn't have it in me before you, Isla. But you have changed everything. You've changed me. And I don't want to go back to the man I was before you came along.'

The kick in her chest was ferocious. And savage. And yet it was more breathtaking than brutal.

He *loved* her. He might not be able to say the word itself, yet the admission was there in everything he was describing. Still, she needed to hear more.

To be sure.

'What did he say? Your brother?'

'The day of that demon's funeral—when I saw the blame and loathing on Dax's face—my life changed. I thought I really was that monster that I saw whenever I looked in the mirror. But today I met with my brother…'

He tailed off, shaking his head as though he still couldn't believe it, and Isla couldn't hold herself back any more. She closed the remaining space between them, placing her hand on Nikhil's chest and feeling the pounding of his heart. It slammed into her palm, the beat fusing with the one drumming through her own body.

Almost as one.

'He didn't blame you, did he?' she asked, almost breathless.

'No.' Nikhil's eyes shone with a light she didn't think she'd ever seen before. 'He blamed himself. He thought he should never have left me alone with that man.'

'He was little more than a kid himself,' Isla countered softly. 'Seventeen, I think you said.'

The corners of Nikhil's mouth pulled upwards as he reached out one hand to cup her cheek.

And, God help her, she couldn't bring herself to pull away.

'I know that, *pyar.* Do not fear, I do not blame him—at least, not any more. There have been enough recriminations and blame going around for too long. When the only one really to blame for it all has been long gone.'

'So, you and Dax have made your peace?' she asked hesitantly.

'We...are on our way to something like peace,' corrected Nikhil. 'Let us start with that, for now.'

Isla opened her mouth to answer, but the words didn't come. They were locked in some chaotic mess. As relieved as a part of her was for Nikhil, another part of her was still trying to work out how all that came together to bring him to her door.

'And this is your simple truth?' she managed after what felt like an eternity, lifting her own hand to cover his.

Though whether to cup his hand or to remove it, she couldn't quite be certain.

'No.' He shook his head, taking a final step to her and lifting his hand until he was cupping her jaw.

It was all she could do not to melt into it.

'No, the simple truth, *pyar,* is that I love you.'

The words walloped through her, leaving her winded. Any response was impossible; too many emotions were swooping and tumbling through her.

Nikhil loved her.

Just as she loved him. It was so obvious to her now.

'In fact,' he continued, as if oblivious, 'I think I've been falling in love with you ever since that first day on the quayside.'

Isla flushed instinctively. 'Maybe not that *first* moment,' she muttered awkwardly, but then Nikhil caught her upper arms, holding her tight and making her look at him.

'Yes. That first moment.' He nodded soberly. 'When you told me to *wind your neck in*. I think a part of me knew, right there, that you were the one for me.'

Isla tried to answer. She opened her mouth to speak, but nothing came out. She *loved* him. It should be terrifying, but Nikhil was taking all her fears and turning them on their head. And she liked it.

Maybe too much.

Because there were still so many other hurdles they hadn't even begun to overcome. How could she just pretend they didn't exist? However much she wished that to be the case.

'I want to be with you,' he told her. 'I want to share the rest of my life with you. Waking up to you. Going to bed with you. And everything in between.'

Her heart wanted to soar. She could feel it, pulling frantically at the tethers she'd used to ground it. To suppress it.

She didn't know how she found the strength to curl her fingers around his hand and pull it away from her face.

And then to drop the contact.

'I am pleased for you and your brother.' Her voice was more clipped than she would have preferred, but that couldn't be helped.

It was that or crumble completely.

'More pleased than you can imagine. But I'm confused at what you're saying. I have a posting as a doctor on a new ship, and you're getting your own ship to captain.'

His eyes gleamed but he didn't speak.

'So I fail to see how the two things are compatible,' she pressed on. 'Or is that the point? Now that you are secure in the knowledge that our lives are back on different courses, you realised that you felt safe enough to say the things you were too afraid to acknowledge before?'

'No. But I did realise something else.'

'What's that?' Her tongue spoke all by itself. And they both knew he had her where he wanted her. She despaired of herself.

'That was the moment I realised that I should walk away from you. And the moment I realised that I couldn't. And it had nothing to do with being secure in the knowledge that our lives were on different courses. I told you, it was to do with the fact that I am in love with you.'

And she wanted to argue. Or, more to the point, she didn't want to fall for words she'd been so desperate to hear. But she was finding it harder and harder to resist.

Then something else struck her.

'What do you mean, *our lives* were *on different courses?*'

He smiled. The most genuine, open smile she'd ever seen him give. And the tethers on her heart ripped and failed at that moment.

'I spoke to Head Office this morning.'

'If you changed my job again…'

'I never mentioned your job, Isla.' He silenced her with a look. 'I discussed my own career path alone. And I suggested that I might prefer to run one more cruise as First Officer before I take up a post as captain. But this time I want to run it aboard the *Star of Hermione*.'

'That's my ship,' Isla gasped, her head spinning wildly, like a kid's paper windmill in a beach breeze.

She fought to cling onto reality. It wasn't right. It couldn't be. She had to be hearing things. Conjuring up the words that part of her so desperately wanted to hear.

'Yes, your ship,' he echoed, as though reading her doubts.

And allaying them one by one, as if he really did care. As if he really did *love* her.

Her whole world was exploding—going up like the most spectacular New Year's firework celebration. Almost too perfect to be true.

She shook her head, trying to think straight.

'You would turn down captaincy of a ship, and move from a flagship vessel like the *Cassiopeia*, just to be on the same ship as me? Meeting up in the shadows like we did for those two weeks?'

And God help her if she couldn't pretend to herself that they hadn't been two almost perfect weeks.

'You misunderstand.' Nikhil cut across her thoughts. 'I don't want to hide in the shadows any more. I want this above board, if you'll excuse the pun, and I want us to be a proper couple.'

'A proper couple?' she echoed in disbelief.

'We would declare our relationship to Head Office and have them allocate us a cabin together. You are mine, just as I am yours. There will never be anybody else for me but you. And I no longer care who knows it.'

'You don't have to do that, Nikhil…'

'I love you, Isla,' he cut in. 'It's that simple. And maybe one day you'll be able to tell me that you love me too.'

'I already love you.' The words tripped off her tongue. That easily.

'Isla…'

And this time it was her who cut him off.

'I love you, Nikhil,' she repeated, and wasn't it incredible how each time she said it something feverish, and glorious, filled her from the inside out?

'You are mine,' she echoed softly. 'And I am yours.'

Isla had no idea who moved first; she didn't particularly care. She only knew that one moment they were standing apart, where an entire continent might have divided them and it wouldn't have made her feel any more distant from him than she already felt—and the next she was back in his arms, her body moulded to his.

As if it had always been meant to be there.

'The more people who know it, the better, I think,' she murmured, moments before tilting her head up and pressing her lips to his.

'The world?' he muttered against her mouth.

'It's a start.'

The most magnificent start she could ever have imagined.

EPILOGUE

STANDING AT THE prow of the *Star of Hermione*, the sun setting behind her, Isla reflected that the past seven months with Nikhil, and two consecutive voyages as a proper couple, had possibly been the best of her life.

But now she was waiting, her heart once again pounding in her chest, as Nikhil had been summoned to the Captain's cabin. A part of her celebrated the fact that it could only mean he had already been offered a new captaincy, whilst another part of her was terrified.

She'd already been unofficially approached about joining the *Hestia*, the ship she'd been intended to join almost a year ago now, that first day back in Chile. But it was surely too much to hope that Nikhil had been offered captaincy.

Whichever ship they offered him, he couldn't turn it down a second time, she knew that, but it would mean the end of their perfect little bubble.

She turned as she heard the sound of his soft footfall across the deck.

'Which ship?' she asked without preamble, forcing herself to inject a note of excitement into her tone.

He eyed her speculatively, but there was no mistaking that hint of shock in his expression that could only mean it was better than either of them had anticipated for him.

As much as she was proud on his behalf, a little corner

of her heart seemed to crumble a little. They had been so happy together on the *Hermione.* How was their relationship to survive such a move? Not that she didn't trust him. Unlike Brad, she had no fears that Nikhil would ever betray her; it simply wasn't who he was. But that distance just made things that much…duller.

Still, Isla was determined to betray none of those qualms as she forced herself to smile at him.

'Which ship, Nikhil?' she repeated.

'It is scarcely to be believed,' he managed, and there was an edge to his tone that was as unsettling as it was unfamiliar.

Her brain spun. 'Not the *Hestia*?'

'Not the *Hestia*,' he confirmed.

'Then which?'

'The *Cassiopeia*.'

Disbelief swirled around her and, despite the fact that her heart still felt as though it was under arrest, she was incredibly proud of Nikhil.

Her Nikhil.

'That's amazing.' She threw her arms around his neck and embraced him as fiercely as she could. 'Really, I'm so pleased for you.'

'Well, there is something more.' He caught her face between his hands, holding her still so that he could talk to her. 'Dr Turner has been champing at the bit to get you back ever since you left.'

'Sorry?' She froze, scarcely believing it.

'The Captain asked me if I thought you'd be interested. I told him you probably wouldn't, but that I'd ask you just in case.'

'You said what?' she cried, disbelief flooding through her, moments before she realised he was teasing her.

'Nikhil, that isn't funny.'

'It is from where I am standing, *pyar.*'

The nausea began to lift. 'So that isn't what you really said?'

'Of course not.' He looked amused. 'I told him I would pass the message on and you would find him when you had an answer.'

'You didn't accept?' she cried, appalled.

Did Nikhil not want her to join him on the *Cassiopeia*?

'Of course I didn't accept, *pyar.* I have long since learned my lesson regarding interfering in your career.'

'But you want me to join you?' She tried not to feel anxious, but it was impossible. Nikhil still had that odd edge about him, and it was disconcerting her more and more. 'Nikhil, what is it?'

He paused, and her stomach rolled.

'I was going to wait but…' He didn't quite shrug, but it was close.

'Nikhil?'

He swept his hand around and, whatever Isla had been expecting—or fearing—it certainly hadn't been to see a box in his hand. A small leather box with the finest gold filigree, that could surely only be one thing…

'Nikhil…' she echoed.

'I was going to give you this when we reached Hamburg tomorrow. But I don't think I can wait to hear your answer any longer.'

He opened the case, and Isla couldn't help gasping as a stunning pear-shaped ruby set in a cluster of shimmering diamonds winked up at her, so glorious that they seemed to reflect the very beauty of the sunrise itself.

'You saved my life, Dr Sinclair. I could never have imagined my life as full and as wonderful as it is without you in it,' he told her soberly. 'I love you more with each passing day, and I don't want to spend a single one of them without you in it. You chased away all of my nightmares, so marry me, *pyar*, and make the rest of my life a series of dreams instead?'

'You aren't the only one to have been saved when we met,' Isla choked out. 'My life would never have been so complete if I hadn't met you that day in Chile. I love you, Nikhil. Of course I'll marry you. I can't imagine my life without you.'

Slipping the ring on her finger, he finally kissed her—a kiss full of unspoken promises—and then he turned her around again. Her back nestled against his reassuringly solid chest and, his arms enveloping her, they stared towards the glorious sunrise on the horizon ahead.

It felt as if it wasn't just a new day. It was a whole new life. And it was going to be a glorious one.

Together.

* * * * *

REUNITED WITH HER SECRET PRINCE

SUSANNE HAMPTON

MILLS & BOON

To my amazing family and friends, who have supported and encouraged my writing journey… and unknowingly given me the most wonderful inspiration for my characters.

PROLOGUE

IT WAS THE twelfth of June, a perfect summer's day in the northern hemisphere, and one that nurse Libby McDonald would never forget.

It was the day her life changed for ever. Perched precariously on the edge of her bed, she struggled to fill her lungs with air as her emotions threatened to overwhelm her. Her life was suddenly spinning out of control and Libby was powerless to change anything, which was completely at odds with her character. She was, without exception, calm even in the most stressful times but this was not Cardiology or the ER and she was not triaging patients; she was suddenly trying to triage her escalating fears. And failing miserably.

Her emerald green eyes darted from the test results to the floor and back again as her fingers nervously tapped on the side of her bed, making a sound barely audible above the beating of her heart. It was as though if she didn't stare too long in the direction of the test strip, it wouldn't be real. But it was real. There were no faint lines. There was no ambiguity about it. Libby was going to have the baby of the man who had exited her life as mysteriously as he had entered it.

The boldness of the two lines on the pregnancy test were almost screaming the result at her.

And reminding her of her poor judgement when she fell

in love so quickly and realised in hindsight that while she had thought he was everything she was looking for and more, she had fallen in love with a man she really didn't know at all.

Her life would most definitely be nothing close to the 'white picket fence' perfect one that she had imagined. The one where she was happily married to the man of her dreams, living in a rustic cottage by the ocean with a baby on the way. In reality, while Libby had a baby on the way, she was renting a condo in Oakland, about 20 minutes from San Francisco and not not too far from her retired parents. And she was still paying off her student loan while trying to save for a car to replace the ageing one in the driveway.

There was nothing perfect about her life in her mind, at least not any more. Less than two months earlier she had thought it was as perfect as any woman could dream possible when she'd unexpectedly found herself falling in love. He was a six-foot-two dark-haired, handsome and charismatic doctor and they had been working together at the hospital for almost a month when she had taken a leap of faith and changed their relationship status from colleagues to lovers by inviting him home late one night. While it had been out of character for Libby since they hadn't been actually dating, it had felt right.

They had spent many hours working together in ER and they had been sharing lunch whenever possible and having lengthy discussions about their mutual love of medicine over late-night coffee when ER was quiet and they could steal away to the twenty-four-hour cafeteria. He had encouraged Libby to consider specialising in Cardiology when she'd told him how much she enjoyed rotations in that department and he had gone so far as to find out the next study intake for her.

She had tried to hide her growing feelings for him but

at times that had been almost impossible. Observing him with patients, many seen under extreme duress, Libby's admiration had grown by the day. He had been equally as kind and caring as he was thorough and responsive, and she had watched as his knowledge and experience had changed the outcomes for many critically ill patients. Her professional respect had blossomed into something so much more.

Libby could not help but notice that his demeanour had seemed a little sombre and distant at times, but his mood had always seemed to lift when he'd seen her and she'd felt like she was floating whenever he was around.

She had only dated two men before him, one just out of college for a year before they'd both realised they were better off as friends and then there had been another six-month relationship with a medical student that had been set up by their mothers. When it had ended it had broken their respective mothers' hearts but not their own. And neither relationship had been overly passionate, closer to lukewarm, so she had decided to concentrate on her studies and her career.

But that fateful night when she had acted on her growing feelings, he had made her believe she was the only woman in the world. The way he'd held her and made love to her had made her naively trust that he was the man who would love her for ever. As she'd lain in the warmth of his tender embrace, with the dappled moonlight shining through the open drapes, listening to him gently sleeping, she'd hoped that since they had crossed over from colleagues to lovers, she would learn more about his life outside the hospital and over time something of his family, his past and his dreams for the future.

Libby had thought in her heart she had found *the one.*

But the opportunity to learn anything about him outside medicine had never come as the next morning she had awoken to find him gone. His side of her bed had been cold and empty and she'd soon learned the devastating truth that he had left town. He had given notice at the hospital that morning via email and disappeared. Very quickly she'd discovered he was not *the one*.

Almost eight weeks later she was facing the biggest challenge of her twenty-nine years and the fact that the one night they had shared had changed her life from nurse to single mother despite them taking precautions. There would be no better half to help her. No partner to share the joy and the pain.

Libby no longer cared to know anything about the man, his life or his past. What she did know was that she would have to face this alone and she also knew that she could never again allow her emotions to cloud her judgement. And never let her heart rule her head.

Collapsing back across the bed and staring at the ceiling fan as it slowly made circles in the warm air, Libby couldn't pretend, even to herself, to be surprised by the confirmation of her pregnancy. Her hands instinctively covered her stomach. There was no physical sign but in her heart she was already protective of her baby. Even in the pharmacy as she'd purchased the test that afternoon, she'd thought her action was redundant.

She had been feeling nauseous for almost six weeks and she had eaten more olives, fish and bread than she cared to remember in the preceding days. Which for anyone else might not be odd, except Libby detested olives. But, like a woman possessed, she had driven to the late-night supermarket close to midnight in search of black olives. They had to be Kalamata olives. And artisan bread. And that week she had started visiting the fish market and she ordinarily hated the smell of fresh fish.

Her cravings were Mediterranean, just like the father of her unborn child. The man who had shattered her heart and her trust.

Suddenly, there was a knock on the front door, breaking through the jumbled thoughts that were threatening to send her mad.

'Hello…anyone gorgeous at home? Other than me, I mean?' the voice chirped loudly.

She recognised the voice of her best friend, Bradley. The rock in her life since nursing school. She had been expecting him but was clueless as to how he would react as he hadn't known she had even been interested in someone and Libby had never kept secrets from Bradley. Slowly she sat up and then climbed to her feet. Her legs were still shaking and her mind racing.

'The door's unlocked and I'm in my room, Bradley… There's something I need to tell you.'

Thirty minutes later, they both sat staring in silence at their empty iced tea glasses. Bradley had moved Libby into the kitchen and insisted that she have a cool drink and something to eat. He had brought home two cupcakes from the local bakery and there were now only crumbs on their plates. She suspected that he needed something to calm his nerves as much as her. Learning about her pregnancy had come out of left field for him.

'He's a lying, deceitful bastard on every level.'

'I feel so stupid. I mean, I didn't really know him, not outside work, but we just clicked. We talked for hours literally and it seemed right. But it was so wrong. And I don't have that much dating experience, not in last few years anyway. I guess I read too much into it.'

'He clearly wanted you to read into it. He's a dreadful excuse for a man.'

'I'm an idiot.'

Bradley patted her hand with his. 'You're not an idiot. Love just makes us do crazy things. Heaven knows, I've fallen for the wrong man more times than I care to recall.'

Libby nodded. She was done with talking about the man who had broken her heart. And there would be no more tears either. She had shed enough in the weeks since he'd left to last her a lifetime and now she needed to focus on herself. And her baby.

'I know it's a lot but *we've* got this,' he said with his chin definitely jutted and his hands on his hips. 'I'm in this with you, all the way.'

'That's so sweet, Bradley, but I made a mess of everything. Not you. You've got a whole wide world out there. You don't have to tie yourself down to me and…' Libby paused as her gaze dropped to her stomach. 'And my baby.'

'What sort of gay best friend walks away from his best friend for ever and her baby? Not me, that's for sure,' he retorted, standing and reaching for both cups. He walked to the dishwasher, put them both inside then spun on his heel to face her with a look of determination. 'You will be the most amazing mommy ever and I will be the most awesome, stylish uncle that any little poppet ever had. Ooh, I wonder if the baby will have your stunning red hair? Here's hoping as I can see the tiny wardrobe already, hues of green and copper and, of course, yellow. Goodness, there're so many choices ahead of us…'

'What would I do without you?' Libby cut in.

'You'll never know 'cos I'm not going anywhere. This baby will be loved and cherished. And my adorable niece or nephew will have anything in life that he or she wants.'

Everything except a father, Libby thought, but said nothing as she swallowed the lump in her throat and blinked away the last of the tears stinging the corners of her eyes.

'And we will throw the best birthday parties ever!' Bradley continued, his face animated with excitement and his hands moving around wildly. 'I can see them now. Like tiny carnivals with rides and cotton candy and a petting zoo.'

Libby's lips began to curl upwards as her spirits lifted just a little. 'You're spoiling the baby and we still have seven months to meet him or her.'

'Of course it's my responsibility as Uncle Bradley. I'm in your baby's life for ever.'

Libby felt a stab in her heart, wishing the father of her baby would be in their lives for ever too, but that would never be. She had no clue where he had gone. The hospital could not give Libby a forwarding address and he had not mentioned leaving to anyone other than his short, and apparently sudden, resignation email.

Clearly, she meant nothing to him. Neither had their time together been as special as she had imagined. It had all been in her head. She had romanticised the entire affair. She feared he might feel the same about the child they had created but she would never know because there was no way for her to tell him.

As he sat staring out across the brilliant blue water Dr Daniel Dimosa's thoughts unexpectedly returned to the gorgeous redheaded nurse who, only months earlier, had unknowingly made him forget about the uncertainty of his future, if only for a few short weeks. She was sweet and kind and the woman he'd wanted but knew he couldn't have. Not for ever, at least.

Daniel had fought the attraction over the time they had spent together while he had been Acting Head of ER. He had valiantly attempted to keep their relationship professional. But he had failed. Her nursing skills, genuine empathy with patients and wonderfully warm, kind manner was nothing he had witnessed before. She would work past her shift to allay the fears of patients and their families, go the extra mile to transfer her knowledge to inexperienced medical students, and make all the medical team around her feel included and important. And against everything he had promised himself, he had begun to fear he was close to falling in love.

No matter how much he'd tried, Daniel couldn't ignore his feelings for her. He would look for excuses to spend time with her even over a coffee in the early hours of the morning at the twenty-four-hour cafeteria, but he'd still kept the conversation about their mutual love of medicine. Nothing about the past and nothing about the future.

He couldn't allow himself to make promises he couldn't keep. Daniel had known it was only a matter of time until he would need to leave. He had long known he could not in any good conscience promise a future to any woman and for that reason he had kept his love life to flings with women who wanted nothing more.

And for that reason Daniel had left that night without saying goodbye or offering an explanation. It wasn't his to offer. Instead, he had climbed from the warmth of the bed they had shared and disappeared into the night. He had left without waking the woman who was beginning to steal his heart. He thought back to the moment he had gently moved the strand of red hair resting on her forehead and tenderly kissed her one last time as she'd lain sleeping like an angel. His heart had ached with every step he'd taken away from her. Knowing he would never see her again. Never make love to her again. Never hold her again.

He knew it had been a mistake to take their relationship from that of colleagues to lovers but the passion had overtaken them and he had given in to his desire to have her in his arms, if only for one night.

Before he'd closed the door he'd silently mouthed, *I will never forget you, Libby.*

Then he had walked away, knowing there was no choice.

He had done it to protect her…and now he had to do everything he could to forget her. And he hoped she would do the same.

CHAPTER ONE

'I LOVE YOU, BILLY.'

'I luff you, Mommy.'

'You need to be a very good boy for Grandma while I'm gone,' Libby said, blinking back tears as she squatted down to the little boy's eye level and ran her fingers through his thick black hair. 'I'll only be away for a few days, and I'll miss you very much.'

'I'll be good. I promith,' he said, and threw his little arms around her neck.

'Grandpa's waiting in the car to take me to the airport. I need to go now but I'll be back soon.'

'Grandma told me seven sleeps.'

'That's right,' Libby replied, then kissed his chubby cheek. 'I love you to the moon and back.'

'I luff you this much,' he said, stretching his arms as far as he could.

Libby stood up, ruffled his hair gently and redirected her attention to her mother. 'Please call me if you need me, anytime, day or night. My cell phone will always be on. I'll call every night but if Billy gets a sniffle or a tummy ache or just needs to talk to me during the day or night, please call me.'

'I will, I promise. Billy will be fine with us. Now go or you'll miss your plane,' her mother told her as they all walked to the car, which was idling in the driveway with her father at the wheel and her luggage already in the trunk. Libby climbed into the front passenger seat and as the car drove away she watched her son holding his grandmother's hand and waving goodbye. She felt empty already and the car hadn't left the street.

'Now, don't you go worrying while you're away, poppet,' her father said as they merged into the freeway traffic. 'We'll take good care of our grandson.'

'I know you will, Dad,' she said, trying to blink away the tears threatening to spill onto her cheeks. 'It's just I've never been away from Billy and it's…it's…'

'I know it's hard, Libby, but, believe me, it's probably going to be a lot tougher on you than him. Worrying and missing your child is all part of being a parent,' he said with a wink and a brief nod in Libby's direction. 'But we'll keep him busy and your mother has an itinerary to rival a royal visit. I swear you get your organisational skills from her. We're off to the zoo tomorrow and the playground the next day, and on Thursday Bradley's heading over to take him out for ice cream and a walk on the beach, and he's got a play date with the neighbours' grandchildren on Saturday… Oh, I almost missed out a day. Your mother booked tickets for that new animated car movie at the cinema on Friday. I tell you we will all sleep well this week from sheer exhaustion.'

Libby McDonald listened to all her father was saying. She appreciated everything her parents had planned for Billy so much but it didn't help as her heart was being torn a little with each mile they travelled. She was thirty-three years of age, mother of the world's most adorable little three-year-old boy, single by choice, and she loved her son more than life itself and didn't want to be away from him.

'You might have fun in the Caribbean. It's not every day you get asked to fly to the other side of the country to tend to a wealthy patient for a week on a luxury yacht. What was his name again?'

'Sir Walter Lansbury,' Libby replied as she looked out of the car window, feeling no excitement at the prospect.

'That's right.' Her father nodded as he flicked the indicator to change lanes. 'He's quite a philanthropist and a generous benefactor to the Northern Bay General Hospital. Even had a wing named after him, your mother told me.'

'Yes, he's very generous and that's why the hospital board agreed to his request to have me as his post-operative nurse while he cruises through the Caribbean for seven days and nights. It's quite ridiculous really. He should be at home, recovering, at seventy-nine years of age, not gallivanting on the open seas five weeks after a triple coronary artery bypass graft.'

'Sounds like he's a bit of an adventurer.'

'Or a risk-taker and a little silly.'

'A risk taker without doubt,' her father remarked. 'But he wouldn't have amassed a fortune if he was silly.'

Libby didn't answer because she was completely averse to risk-taking and Sir Walter taking one with his health made him silly in her opinion. She had taken a risk falling in love and that had all but ensured she would never take another unnecessary risk. She planned everything about her life and she liked it that way. Libby McDonald hated surprises and risks in equal amounts. Her life was settled and organised and was almost perfect, except for the occasional night when she couldn't fall asleep and her thoughts turned to Billy's father. But they were becoming fewer and fewer and she hoped in time she would all but forget him.

'We never know what the universe has in store for us. This trip might be a life-changing experience for you,' her father continued as he checked his rear-view mirror and took the next exit from the freeway. 'All I do know is that Sir Walter has secured himself the finest cardiac nurse in the whole country.'

Libby smiled at her father's compliment but she was far from convinced he was right. She felt certain there had to be other nurses who would jump at the opportunity but the hospital board had insisted she go. And there was no get-out-of-jail-free card attached to an order from the board. It was signed and sealed and in less than a week she had been packed and on her way to nurse the generous benefactor she had cared for after his heart surgery. How she wished at that moment that she had been in ER and not in his recovery team.

Later that day, Libby's flight finally landed in Miami and she caught a cab to the Four Seasons Hotel where a room had been booked for her by Sir Walter's assistant. Being a few hours ahead of the west coast it was getting late in Miami and the sun had set so she ordered room service, called home and said goodnight to Billy and, after eating dinner, she ran a hot bath. Surprisingly she had managed to doze just a little on the five-hour flight. Business class, courtesy of her temporary employer, was as luxurious as she had heard. But with no sleep the night before as she'd tossed about in her bed at home, she was close to exhaustion when she finally climbed into her king-size hotel bed and drifted off to sleep.

The next morning Libby woke, went for a brisk walk before she ate breakfast in her room, checked out of the hotel, and caught a cab to the marina. She was due there at eleven. Her stomach began to churn as the cab drew closer. The previous day's uneasy feeling was returning and while it was in its infancy, she feared it could gain momentum quickly.

She lowered her oversized sunglasses and looked through the cab window at the busy road leading to the wharf and prayed that the week would pass quickly and there would be no surprises. None at all. Pushing her glasses back up the bridge of her nose, Libby collapsed back into the seat, second-guessing herself.

Suddenly her thoughts began to overwhelm her. The sensible, well-organised life she had created felt a little upside down and it weighed heavily on her. Her throat suddenly became a little dry and her palms a little clammy. The air-conditioner in the car suddenly didn't seem enough and she wished she hadn't agreed to the week-long assignment on the open seas.

She knew she would miss Billy terribly. He was her world and her reason for getting up each day, the reason she kept going, determined to create a life for the two of them.

Suddenly her cab driver made a U-turn and her hand luggage fell onto her lap and she heard a thud as her suitcase toppled over in the trunk. She rolled her eyes, quite certain that Bradley had packed more than she would need. But she hadn't argued as she'd had no idea what she would need. She had no clue since she had never done anything like it before.

Libby McDonald had been playing it safe, very safe, and now she felt at risk of becoming a little…lost at sea.

'We're about two minutes away, miss,' the driver said. 'I'm taking a shortcut through the back streets as the traffic jam ahead would make it fifteen.'

'Thank you,' she said, smiling back at him in the rear-view mirror. His voice had brought her back to the present. It was not the time or the place for doubting herself.

She had to quash her rising doubts because there was no turning back.

The cab was weaving around a few narrow streets until finally Libby could see the ocean and rows of yachts of all shapes and sizes.

'I think this is your stop,' he announced, finally coming to a halt.

Once again, she dropped her glasses to rest on the bridge of her nose and, in an almost teenage manner, peered out of the cab window again. She spied the yacht—gleaming, magnificent and standing tall and pristine in the perfectly still blue water. It was the most magnificent ship she had ever seen. Not that she'd seen any up close and personal. Her experience was from travel shows on cable television but she had not expected it to be so grand and beautiful in reality. Regal was the word that came to mind as her gaze roamed the structure and her eyes fell on the name emblazoned across the bow, *Coral Contessa.* That was definitely the one. She had been told that Sir Walter Lansbury had named it after his beloved late wife, Lady Contessa.

Libby's stomach knotted with trepidation. The yacht was going to be both her workplace and temporary home for the next seven days. Suddenly motion sickness, or something like it, came over her even though she was still on dry land.

While she had worked in both Emergency and Cardiology at the hospital for over seven years, she knew nothing of nursing on a ship. And that bothered her. Libby had consulted with the cardiologist a few days before she'd left for her trip and had been reminded that their patient had had a post-operative elevated blood pressure and a BMI that indicated he needed to lose at least twenty pounds. To the frustration of his specialist, Sir Walter loved bad food, cigars and strong liquor and he didn't take his health as seriously as he did the stock market.

Initially, Libby had also been concerned about the number of passengers and crew and whether she would be responsible for everyone, and how many that would be in total. She had been reassured by the hospital that there would be no more than twelve to fourteen other passengers and eleven crew members, including the two-person medical team. They felt confident most of the passengers would come on board in good health and remain that way for the duration of the cruise.

She would be focused on her client and occasionally managing passengers' nausea, the effects of too much sun or too much alcohol, the odd strained muscle or twisted ankle. There was always the risk of more serious conditions but Libby hoped her cruise on the *Coral Contessa* would be uneventful, busy enough to keep her mind occupied but not overwhelming. Nothing would go wrong, she reminded herself, if the number one patient followed their advice.

Everyone agreed Sir Walter would be better off not going to sea five weeks after heart surgery and instead resting at home but, being headstrong, he clearly wasn't accepting that. She hoped the ship's doctor was equally headstrong and together they could manage their patient.

Libby wasn't entirely sure if the impetus for her decision to accept the job offer had been Bradley's contagious excitement or another one of her parents' well-meaning heart-to-heart talks about her taking chances and moving on with her life.

She was still young, they constantly reminded her, and she had so much to experience and a whole world to see. And Billy needed to grow up knowing she was not only the best mother he could wish for but also a strong independent woman who had a career and a life. Just thinking about him, her fingers reached for the antique locket hanging on a fine silver chain around her neck and she held it in the warmth of her palm. Inside was a photograph of the beautiful dark-haired, blue-eyed boy. He was the image of the father he would never know.

Libby stilled her nerves and blinked away the unexpected threat of tears she was feeling at the thought of being away from her little boy. It was only a week at sea, she reminded herself firmly, and her parents wanted so much to spend quality time with their beloved grandson. But she and Billy had never been apart for more than a day in three years. He was the light in her life and she wasn't sure how she would cope.

True to his word, Bradley had thrown a birthday party for Billy every year and had hosted his third birthday two days before Libby had left. Their family and friends had come and showered Billy with presents as they always did, and those with small children had brought them along to enjoy the celebrations, including a face painter. Bradley had enthusiastically dressed as a giant sailor bear. He thought he'd looked like a furry member of the Village People—Libby wasn't sure but the image still made her smile.

There had been way too much cake, far too many sweets and more balloons than Libby had ever seen, courtesy of her mother. Everyone had had a wonderful day but Libby had been preoccupied at times throughout the afternoon with doubts about her impending trip, although it had been pointless to fight the inevitable. The trip was going to happen. And everyone except Libby seemed very happy about that fact.

That night Bradley had insisted on helping her pack.

He'd included a swimsuit and a light denim playsuit and a stunning silk dress that skimmed her ankles. It was deep emerald-green silk with a plunging neckline and nothing close to the practical clothes she generally wore, a going-away present from Bradley.

'Take a risk for once!' Bradley had told her when she'd unwrapped his parting gift. 'You have the body for it, so flaunt it!'

Libby had frowned at him.

'It's perfect for you and what's the point in having a stylish BFF if you don't listen to me? Besides, it matches your gorgeous eyes so you have to take it.'

Libby had laughed and given Bradley a big hug. At six feet four he was almost a foot taller than her and she always felt secure in his hug, if not always secure in his choice of clothes for her. The outfit was very far removed from her usual conservative style. She wasn't sure she would wear it, because even if she was brave enough, she felt quite sure she wouldn't have the occasion to do so, but Bradley had insisted. He had released his arms from around her tiny waist, ignored her concerns, packed all of his choices in her luggage and had returned to her closet to find some sandals to complete the look.

'Let's face it, *all* of your cute outfits and shoes have been Christmas and birthday gifts from me,' he had said, with a pair of unworn gold high heels he had given her for Christmas the year before balanced in one hand while he pulled another dress from a hanger, along with a sarong and a wide-brimmed straw hat. He placed all of it neatly into her open suitcase. 'Anything conservative is staying home. I refuse to let my absolute best friend in the world morph into a soccer mom. You're too young for that. At least wait until Billy's actually old enough to play soccer.'

Libby smiled as she remembered his remark and silently

admitted that what he'd said wasn't too far from the truth. She knew she would never wear most of the outfits Bradley had packed but she didn't argue. There would apparently be two ports of call, which meant that if Sir Walter wanted to go ashore she would visit the islands with him, and if not she would remain on board.

Bradley had done his research and had told her that golden sandy beaches, translucent underwater caves and exclusive private isles were awaiting her. He told her to go ashore whenever she had the chance and not to be a party pooper by staying in her cabin. As he'd held up the travel brochures, he'd insisted she should do everything she could. Clearly, he was going to live the next week vicariously through her.

Libby wasn't fussed about any of it and, to be honest, wanted to get the trip over and done with so she could get back to her real life, but she didn't tell him that. He was excited for her so she let him tell her all about the sightseeing. At least one of them was excited.

Together they'd continued to pack and had selected shorts, T-shirts, jeans, lightweight jackets and a summer dress that Libby thought were far more her style. It became a compromise, with Bradley less than enthusiastic about some of Libby's clothing choices but agreeing if it didn't mean his choices were sacrificed to make room for them. At the end of the packing, she'd looked at her bursting luggage, convinced it would be way too much since she was working on the ship not socialising, but again Bradley had insisted.

Through social media, he had found out that the luxury, multi-million-dollar yacht had a pool, an intimate movie theatre and even a rock-climbing wall, and he reminded her that while Billy would be well taken care of by his doting grandparents and his fabulous fashionista Uncle Bradley, she needed to have some fun.

'She's a beauty,' the cab driver told her, breaking into Libby's reverie as he climbed from the cab and popped the trunk.

'Yes, she is,' Libby agreed, as she collected her belongings from the back seat and met him at the rear of the car.

'I'm sorry I'm a bit awkward with bags,' he began as he reached into the trunk. 'My fingers are a bit twisted. I think it might be arthritis.'

Libby looked down at the hands of the driver as he took hold of her bag. 'May I take a look?' she asked softly.

'Sure, why not? Are you a doctor?'

'No, I'm a nurse,' she replied as she reached for his hands.

He held both hands quite still for Libby to examine. Immediately she could see quite clearly there was a thickening and tightening of tissue under the skin of both hands. It was affecting the ring and little fingers. Both fingers on the right hand were almost completely closed into his palm. She recognised the problem immediately.

'How long have you had this condition?'

'A few years now but it's been getting worse lately,' he told her with a voice that signalled acceptance of his fate. 'I'm worried if both hands close I might not be able to drive and that would make life tough for the family. I'm fifty-two years old and I'd like to drive for another ten years if I can. My daughter's getting married next year and she wants the big wedding with all the bells and whistles so I can't be out of work.'

Libby said nothing as she continued to examine his hands. 'I'm not an expert but you may have a condition called Dupuytren's contracture.'

'Is there a treatment for it?'

'If it is what I think, it can be managed,' she told him. 'And it's definitely worth your while seeing someone. You would need to be referred to a specialist. My father had the condition and that's why I'm aware of it.'

'My ma told me it was arthritis and there was no hope. It's in my genes, she told me. My pa had it, but he died nearly twenty years ago 'cos of his diabetes.'

'Again, I am not an expert but if you make an appointment with your regular doctor…'

"I haven't seen a doctor in over ten years,' he cut in. 'I've been healthy as an ox and haven't needed one.'

Libby was well aware that there was a genetic predisposition to the condition but Dupuytren's contracture could be aggravated by cirrhosis of the liver and the presence of certain other diseases, including diabetes, which she was now aware was in his family along with thyroid problems so a visit to the doctor was well overdue. It could uncover a hidden condition that needed to be managed. The man's hands might be a sign that something even more serious was happening out of sight.

'I would make a time and get a general check-up and blood work while you're there. We should all do that every year. I'm sure you want to be heathy and happy and dance with your daughter at her wedding.'

'I do,' he said. 'I'll make a time next week to see a doctor. Honest, I will.'

Libby smiled and paid the fare, including a generous gratuity, and then reached down for her belongings.

'Thank you for taking the time to talk to me. Not many people do that nowadays. Everyone's in a rush. It was real nice of you,' the driver continued as he slipped the cash into his shirt pocket. 'You're a princess and I think you're a real good nurse.'

Libby smiled again and then reached for the suitcase

that he had managed to pull from the trunk and place on the kerb. 'You take care of yourself.'

'And you have a great trip. Hope you meet a prince on that yacht,' the man said before he climbed into the cab.

Libby suddenly felt a little flustered with the thought as she struggled to manage her belongings. She didn't want to meet a prince—or any man for that matter. She just wanted to get the next week over and done with and return to the only man who mattered to her: her son. With a bag across her chest and a laptop case slipping from her shoulder, she reached for her large suitcase sitting on the pavement where the driver had placed it and tried to calm her nerves. It's only a week, she reminded herself. *Only a week.*

Accepting her fate, she drew in a deep breath, put a smile on her face and hoisted the slowly slipping laptop bag back up onto her shoulder and made her way to the walkway onto the yacht. The sun was shining down and she could feel the warmth through her thin T-shirt. As she climbed aboard, she could see the shining deck, perfectly arranged with black wicker outdoor seating, scattered with oversized striped cushions in striking colours. Everything about it was stunning, even the sky and sea matched perfectly.

Under different conditions she might have enjoyed herself. But Libby had a job to do and then get home. She had no intention of socialising. She had no intention of doing anything other than tending to the medical needs of Sir Walter.

Brushing away wisps of red hair that had escaped her ponytail, Libby hoped that the days ahead would pass quickly.

Dr Daniel Dimosa stood at the bow of the *Coral Contessa*, looking out across the perfectly still blue water. His mood was reflective, borderline sombre. It was the first day of his final ocean placement, then it was time to return to his family. The time had come. He looked down at his phone and reread the last message from his mother.

My darling son,

Thank you so much for agreeing to return to your home and your rightful place.

Your father's condition has deteriorated further since the last time we spoke. He has not made any public appearances in the last week and he must abdicate very soon. There are days that he struggles to remember his advisors' names. Thankfully, he is still very aware of who I am, and my prayer is that our love for each other is strong enough to help us through the most difficult times ahead.

I know the people of Chezlovinka will be elated to see you take up your role as Crown Prince, just as your father and his father before him. Without you, my darling, I know there would be unrest and instability and I fear what may become of our land and the future of the people who so rely upon us.

Your loving mother xxxx

Daniel knew he had no choice but to stop running from his past and stop wondering what might have been. There were still question marks over the future, but he would deal with those in time. His own time. In his heart, he knew that he was destined to follow in his father's footsteps, perhaps in more ways than one. Early onset dementia was a genetic disease and he was not certain that it had eluded him.

He knew he would miss the spray of salt water on his face, the sounds of the gulls whenever they drew closer to shore, and the serenity of the endless blue horizon. And most of all the freedom to practise medicine. He drew a deep bitter-sweet breath of warm, humid air. Sadly, his love affairs with both the sea and medicine were drawing to an end at the same time.

Daniel knew he had to face the fact that his current way of life was over and no matter how much he wished it could be different, it couldn't. He was a realist. His path and his fate had been chosen the day he was born and now he had no choice but to return to his homeland. He had seven more days as Dr Daniel Dimosa before he turned his back on his life as a doctor and returned to his life as Crown Prince Daniel Edwardo Dimosa.

The breeze picked up and Daniel felt a familiar emptiness in his heart. He had grown accustomed to a life with no ties but it didn't stop him wishing for more and wanting to feel again how he had felt in San Francisco all those years ago. But he would never put a woman he cared so deeply for through what his mother had faced since his father's diagnosis five years earlier. The worry of not knowing when her husband and the man she had loved her entire life would look at her as if she was a stranger.

His expression fell further as he admitted to himself that this would be the last time he was on US soil for a very long time. It would make this trip even more poignant.

While the day was warm and calm at that moment, weather at sea was more unpredictable and prone to drastic change. Not unlike some of the women Daniel had bedded over the last four years while he'd been trying to forget the sweet, loving redhead who had so unexpectedly captured his heart. Wherever the ship docked there were women who were happy to share one night of pleasure with no strings attached. It was enjoyable, and both parties were happy to walk away knowing it would never be more than that. He forgot them as quickly as he met them and he felt sure they did the same.

A tic in Daniel's jaw began on cue, the way it always did when he thought back to the woman he had loved so briefly. With all of his being, he wished he had handled it differently or, better yet, never become involved. He wished he had been in a place where he could have explained everything and told her the truth but he hadn't been. He had been sworn to secrecy and he couldn't break that promise.

Daniel was a man of his word—both as a doctor and as Crown Prince Daniel Edwardo Dimosa.

Travelling had been all he had known for so long and he was reluctant to leave that way of life, but he was needed at home so his choices were limited. Daniel's father had carried the burden of royal responsibilities for a long time. Now, at only sixty years of age, his condition had worsened and Daniel would not turn his back on the man he both loved and admired and who was slowly being trapped inside his own deteriorating mind.

By taking over the throne, it would allow his father to retain his dignity and see out his final days away from the scrutiny of the public eye. And keeping that secret was paramount to the economic security of the principality. There was really no debate. Daniel needed to be there for his father and for the small European principality of Chezlovinka.

Over the years there were times late at night when his thoughts sometimes wandered back to the woman he had left behind. He hoped she had forgotten him, married and had a family. She deserved that and more…even if it wasn't with him.

'Dr Dimosa,' the young concierge began, 'I thought I'd let you know the ship's nurse has just boarded and has headed to her cabin. You asked me to notify you.'

'Thank you,' Daniel replied, turning momentarily to

acknowledge the young man then just as quickly turning back to the view.

His life was to be one of duty to the principality he was destined to rule. It would be a life without freedom.

And one without love.

CHAPTER TWO

LIBBY STOPPED OUTSIDE her allocated cabin and reached into her bag for the door swipe card she had been given by one of the three stewards. They had offered to take her bags to the cabin but she'd wanted a few moments alone to take in her surroundings, to be alone with her thoughts and steady her unsettled nerves.

She was huffing and puffing, as well as flustered and anxious again by the time she reached her cabin and felt quite silly having a bag large enough for a month-long vacation. What was she doing? Why hadn't she fought the board's decision? And why had she allowed Bradley to pack so many outfits into such a large suitcase?

Everything was suddenly a little overwhelming again.

She should be home with her son instead of on the other side of the country, and sailing even further away. It was like the other side of the world to Libby, and her world was her boy. She didn't want to be anywhere without him.

'Hello, there.'

Libby turned quickly to find a young woman with a mop of blonde curls and a wide smile approaching her.

'Oh, my goodness, it can't be,' the woman began, then took a step backwards and faltered momentarily. 'Libby McDonald? Is that you?'

Libby realised instantly that she knew the woman. Standing before her was one of her closest friends from junior high.

'Georgie? Georgie Longbottom? I can't believe it's you.'

Without hesitation, the two embraced with wide grins and genuine elation.

'How long has it been?' Libby began as she released her hold and stepped back a little. Her previous apprehension and nerves were temporarily replaced with a much-needed feeling of comfort and familiarity as their eyes scanned each other with their smiles still broad and their shared joy palpable. 'It must be…almost twelve years?'

'Thirteen actually. I remember because I returned to London at the end of my sophomore year. Our crazy fun year at Seaview High was the best year of my school life,' Georgie confessed, then paused for a moment as a wistful smile washed over her pretty face. 'To be brutally honest, it was probably one of the best years my life, full stop. We were fancy free and had no idea just how tough the real world can be.'

Libby nodded, silently admitting the carefree days of the final years of senior school had been some of the best for her too. The reality of Georgie's words brought her back to reality. They were not seventeen, wide eyed and looking for an adventure any more. The Caribbean adventure that Libby was facing now was not one about which she was feeling any real level of excitement.

Life had certainly not turned out as Libby had expected…in so many ways. And it sounded as if life had not been perfect for Georgie either but Libby didn't want to dwell or complain or ask too many questions, at least not immediately, of the friend she had not seen in for ever. She wanted to live at least for a little while in the unexpected joy that seeing Georgie had brought to her.

'That was a wonderfully happy year, wasn't it?'

'Absolutely,' Georgie replied as she reached for Libby's laptop bag that was slipping from her shoulder. 'What's your role on board?'

'Sir Walter's nurse. What about you, what brings you on board?'

'I'm Walter's chef again for this trip,' she replied. 'He's a lovely man and easy to work for. I've done the Caribbean trip a few times for him. I've also catered some of his large, exclusive parties in his UK residence. He has a place in Miami, another in San Fran and one in London, and I own a restaurant not far from his London home. He tells me often enough to boost my ego that my restaurant is his favourite in the world. Anyway, he invited me to have a working holiday in the Caribbean, overseeing the galley crew and making some fabulous desserts, and I couldn't say no.'

'That's so exciting and what a compliment. I never knew you wanted to be a chef,' Libby confessed. 'I never even knew you cooked.'

'It's a long story, but I found my passion in life after I left school. But enough about me. I want to hear all about your life and since your cabin is right next to mine, I'm sure we'll have lots of time to catch up. I saw your name on the room register half an hour ago. I knew you always wanted to be a nurse so I wondered if it could possibly be you, but I didn't want to get my hopes up because there's more than one Elizabeth McDonald in the world.'

'Yes, it's not an exotic or exciting name…'

'And you think Georgina Longbottom sounds like a rock star?'

Both girls laughed.

'Hey,' Georgie continued as she took Libby's laptop bag

and put it on her own shoulder. 'Let's get you unpacked before the staff meeting.'

'I think I've over-packed.'

Georgie smiled again. 'I would have to agree with you on that…and from memory that's not like you. I was always the one with too many bags when we'd take off down the coast for a few days to one of those music festivals. You were always the sensible one with everything packed neatly into a backpack. Quite the minimalist. Clearly things have changed in regard to that.'

'My friend Bradley made me pack…'

'Bradley,' Georgia cut in, looking her friend in the eyes with a cheeky smile and her head tilted. 'Is he your other half?'

'No, Bradley's other half is Tom and he's super nice. I'll tell you all about him when we get inside, if I can fit all of this in the cabin.'

'We'll manage. The cabin's quite tiny but we can put the suitcase under the bunk.'

'Bunk?'

'Yes, bunk, but you have the cabin to yourself as there aren't too many staff on board so you have the choice of top or bottom bunk. It's not a stateroom like the guests have but it's quite nice in there.'

Libby smiled as she tried to recall the last time she had slept in a bunk. Then it came to her. 'Like at Big Bear camp?'

'Maybe a little, but this cabin has a porthole. It moves with the motion of the waves but you'll get used to it,' Georgie remarked with a half-grin.

Libby nodded as she retrieved her swipe card from the unlocked cabin door and they stepped inside. She was definitely older and she prayed wiser but the fact that she was on a luxury yacht so far from home had her doubting her wisdom. Seeing Georgie made her feel a lot better about the situation but it also brought back a time that had been uncomplicated and for the longest moment she wished she was that innocent again. A time when everything was exactly what it seemed. A time when she could trust people's intentions.

Libby drew a deep breath. 'I think the next seven days are going to be a lot better with you on board,' Libby said, feeling a little more relaxed than she had thirty minutes earlier.

'Have you been on many ships other than this one?' Libby asked, pushing unwanted thoughts of romance from her mind as she quickly checked out the cabin and found a small bathroom with a toilet, wash basin and shower. It was clean and compact like the rest of the accommodation and with Georgie's help she was quickly becoming more comfortable in her surroundings. She was gaining control in small ways and it was making her relax just a little.

'No, just Walter's. I'm busy running the restaurant so I can't afford the time to do it for anyone else.'

'You're back so I guess you must have enjoyed it.'

Georgie nodded. 'Yes, I did. It's stressful at times but so much fun and you end up becoming good friends with the other team members. Or even more sometimes.'

'Romance at sea. That sounds like a dreadful idea,' Libby said with a look of disdain. She couldn't think of anything worse at that moment.

'It's happened before and the doctor on this trip is ridiculously handsome—tall, dark and single—but he's too aloof for me. The crew all say he's a nice guy but he's way too mysterious. I'm over that type but maybe you...'

'Absolutely not. I'm definitely not looking for romance,' Libby cut in, shaking her head and feeling shivers run over her body. Tall, dark and mysterious was everything in a man she never wanted again.

'Never say never.'

'No, I can say never. Believe me, I'm not interested in anything other than looking after my patient, seeing some sights and then heading home to my…' Libby stopped, pulling herself up again from mentioning Billy. She decided to leave that conversation for later. She was already too emotional and she didn't want to talk about Billy and risk crying.

'Your…?'

'My…um…family. It's the first time I've been away in for ever.'

'Sometimes being thrown into new situations out of your comfort zone is the best way.'

'I'm not sure about that but I guess I'm going to find out.'

Daniel was waiting to meet the nurse who he had been told had boarded and was settling into her cabin. While there were still thirty minutes until the scheduled briefing with the captain, the rest of the ship's staff had already made their way to the deck. He wasn't sure why he was feeling anxious, but he couldn't ignore the stirring in the pit of his stomach. It was almost a feeling of déjà vu and it made him feel less than his usual relaxed self. There was more than enough time to prepare for the dozen or so passengers and their host and the *Coral Countess* would not be setting sail for another two hours, so there was nothing he could put his finger on at that moment, yet he was still uneasy.

The cabin that had been converted into a makeshift hospital room was next to Sir Walter's suite. With only five weeks since the long heart surgery, Daniel had requested it be set up to resemble as closely as possible a hospital room with everything he and the cardiac nurse would require should Sir Walter have any post-operative complications. It was uncommon but not impossible to suffer issues a few weeks post-op and he wished that Sir Walter had delayed the trip a little longer.

Daniel's sense of unease wasn't abating and he put it down to the fact that this would be his last voyage. He ran his fingers through his dark hair, took another deep breath and began pacing the pristine deck overlooking the helipad again, his mind slowly filling with remorse, regret and more than a little melancholy as he thought back over his life at sea and how it was coming to an end. At forty-one years of age, he had spent ten years of his medical career consulting in different hospitals all over the world and almost four tending to the needs of passengers on both private yachts and larger cruise liners. And twice he had tended to the needs of their families when one of the passengers had died at sea.

Daniel sighed as he thought back over the good, the bad and then the sad moments in both his personal and professional life. It had certainly been a mixed bag but he did not regret his decision to leave Chezlovinka and taste freedom for the last decade. He was also very grateful to his mother for encouraging and supporting his desire to pursue a medical career and now he would repay her by returning to rule so his father could abdicate.

Daniel lifted his chin defiantly at the thought of the life that lay ahead for him. There was so much he didn't know about his future. All that was certain and all that he could control was the next seven days on the *Coral Contessa.*

Georgie looked down at her watch. 'We'd best be off, then. We don't want to be late.'

'Late for what?' Libby asked, her blue eyes widening suddenly.

'Our briefing with the rest of the ship's crew, including our hunky mysterious medic. I mentioned it a moment ago.'

Libby shook her head and climbed to her feet. 'Of course, I'm sorry, you did mention it. I'm just a bit distracted.' Meeting the ship's doctor was not her focus. She was still worried about Billy and how he would cope without her. And how she would cope without him.

The last thing she wanted was to appear unprofessional in front of the rest of the crew so she was grateful that it was only Georgie in the cabin. She nervously brushed her jeans with her hands. There was no dust but it helped her to regain her composure.

'Hey, you'll be fine. Once we set sail you'll realise this is a piece of cake.'

'I hope so,' Libby replied, and quickly pulled a comb from her purse and hastily redid her ponytail, catching all the unkempt red wisps.

'If Dr Dimosa is easygoing underneath his moody Mediterranean demeanour, the trip will be a joy for you.'

Libby froze on the spot. Her stomach fell. 'Dr Dimosa is the ship's doctor?' she said, forcing the words past the lump that was forming in her throat. It was made of tears and anger and complete disbelief.

'Yes, Daniel Dimosa. He's the one I was talking about. Do you know him?'

Libby's pulse began to race and her stomach sank further. Dr Daniel Dimosa? *Her* Daniel? The man who had broken her heart and left without a word.

Billy's father.

Libby felt the colour drain from her face. Suddenly the cabin began to spin and she grabbed the edge of the desk to steady herself. An onslaught of emotions rushed at her as the blood drained from her head to feed her pounding heart. Libby felt herself falling and she was powerless to stop herself from crashing to the floor.

CHAPTER THREE

'WHAT EXACTLY HAPPENED before she fainted?' Daniel called down the corridor as he walked quickly with his medical bag in his hand. Concern was colouring his voice as he neared the cabin where Georgie was waiting outside. 'Was there a critical incident, or any sign she wasn't well?'

'No, nothing. I just told her that we needed to head to the deck for the captain's briefing with you.'

'How is she now?'

'She's conscious but on the floor still.' She motioned with her hand as she opened the cabin door but paused outside. 'I placed a pillow under her head and called for you. I asked her to remain where she was until you arrived. The fall was very sudden and it doesn't make sense…unless she has an underlying health issue that she never mentioned during our conversation.'

Daniel moved past Georgie, stepped inside and looked over to the young woman lying on the floor. He was forced to steady himself on the frame of the doorway. His whole world changed in an instant. Nurse Elizabeth McDonald was Libby McDonald. The woman he had loved and left. The same woman who had never completely left his thoughts.

And the woman he had never thought he would see again.

* * *

Daniel stared in silence, so many conflicting thoughts running through his mind. Over the years since they had parted he would sometimes be reminded of her by the sight of a woman with long red hair in the crowd or hearing a laugh like hers. And he would wonder what would have happened between them if only his life had been different.

But it wasn't different and now more than ever he knew that.

He stilled his nerves, crossed the small cabin like a man possessed, and knelt down beside her. While her breathing was laboured, she was conscious and staring at the ceiling. He fought an unexpected but strangely natural desire to pull her into his arms.

'Will she be okay?' Georgie asked, breaking into his thoughts.

He had to remind himself that he was the ship's doctor, nothing more, although being this close to Libby again was suddenly making him wonder how easy that would be.

Placing his fingers on her neck, he took her pulse. It was racing but strong. Her eyes were open and looking towards the ceiling. And they were the most brilliant green, just as he had remembered. She was alert but saying nothing. Her pupils, he could see, were equal in size and not dilated.

'Libby, it's me. Daniel.'

Libby closed her eyes and turned her face away from his as he spoke. She said nothing to even acknowledge his presence in the cabin.

He knew he deserved her reaction. 'I had no idea you were the nurse on this trip. I guess I never thought of you as Elizabeth.'

Still nothing.

'I've always thought of you as Libby.'

She slowly turned back to face him. He saw her eyes

were as cold as ice, her lips a hard line on her beautiful face. 'I don't care how you thought of me,' she said coldly, before she rolled her face away from his again, and he watched as she wiped at a tear with the back of her hand. 'Just leave, Daniel. I don't need you here.'

'I'm not going anywhere,' Daniel said before he turned to Georgie. 'Please leave us alone. I can take it from here.'

From Georgie's expression he could see she was clearly perplexed but she did as he asked and walked from the cabin, pulling the cabin door closed behind her.

Using her elbows as support, Libby tried to ease herself into an upright position.

'Please don't move,' he told her, and placed his warm hand gently on her wrist.

'Don't…don't touch me,' she said, pulling her arm free. 'I need to leave, now.'

'I'm checking your vitals before you're going anywhere.'

'Take them if you must,' she said curtly. 'Give me a clean bill of health then I'm leaving the ship. There's no way on God's earth I'm spending the next seven days working with you.'

'Let's deal with that in a minute. First you have to remain still while I check your BP.' Swiftly and efficiently, Daniel removed the blood pressure cuff from his medical bag and wrapped it around the arm she had reluctantly given him. The result took only a few moments. 'Ninety-eight over fifty.'

'I have low blood pressure,' she spat back as she quickly unwrapped the pressure cuff and shoved it in Daniel's direction. 'It's nothing out of the normal range for me. I'm fine.'

Daniel looked at the cuff lying in his hands and then back

at Libby. There was so much he wanted to say but couldn't. And things he was feeling that scared his cold heart.

He had to stay focused and ignore his reaction to the woman who was so close to him he could smell the perfume resting delicately on her skin. What they had shared was in the past and had to remain there, he reminded himself. He had left her bed in the early hours of that morning for good reason.

Nothing had changed. In seven days he would leave the yacht and begin to transition to ruling the principality; he wasn't about to risk the distance he had purposefully put between Libby and himself when he had walked away.

It was not just about two people any more. He had to think of his father and the people of Chezlovinka.

'I understand why you're reacting the way you are,' he began, his voice low and controlled. 'It's justified and I deserve it but it was a long time ago.'

'You think you understand? Really? I don't think you could possibly understand,' she said in an almost breathless voice as she glared at him again.

'I understand more than you'll ever believe.' He was fighting his mind's desire to remember back to the wonderful weeks they shared and their last night together.

'I doubt it because if you truly did, then you wouldn't have left San Francisco without the decency of an explanation. It's been four years, Daniel. That's more than enough time to reach out.'

'I couldn't, Libby. It's complicated.' He moved back, creating distance between them. Distance she clearly wanted and he definitely needed.

'Complicated? That's the best you can come up with after all this time?' she responded, shaking her head. 'That's beyond pathetic but I don't care any more.'

'I don't know what else to say,' he began, knowing that

she wanted and deserved more but he was not ever going to be in a position to let her know the truth.

'Don't bother trying, Daniel. There's nothing you could say that would make a scrap of difference now. It could have once, but that was a very long time ago.'

Daniel took a deep breath. 'As I said, I had my reasons…'

Libby looked away, staring at nothing. 'We all have choices in life. You're just not telling me the reason why you made yours.'

Daniel chose to say nothing because there was nothing he could say. He couldn't admit that he had never meant to take their relationship as far as making love to her that night because he had not been free to become involved. He could not tell her about his family, his destiny to rule the principality, or the secret they were all forced to hide from the world to maintain the stability of the small principality. His hands were tied.

'Honestly, Daniel, I don't give a damn.' Libby's voice was cold and matter-of-fact. 'But you can do the right thing now by getting out of my way and letting me off this ship. Find yourself a new nurse and give my sincere apologies to Sir Walter.'

Daniel shook his head. 'I wish it was that simple but it's not. Unfortunately, you can't leave the yacht, Libby.'

'Just watch me.'

'No matter how angry you are with me, you can't just leave,' he replied as he ran his fingers through the black waves of his hair. 'I need to have a qualified cardiac nurse to assist with his care.'

'Are you serious? I'm expected to care what you need?'

'No, but you need to consider what Walter needs, and that's an experienced nurse. He's five weeks post-operative. I can't have just anyone on board.'

'Then get an experienced temp from an agency,' she cut in angrily. 'I'm not that special.'

Daniel disagreed silently. Libby was very special in many ways but he would never be able to tell her that. 'It can't happen, Libby. I'm sorry. It's just not possible.'

No matter how many nights he had ached to have her lying in his arms, to feel the warmth of her body next to his and taste the sweetness of her kiss again, Daniel knew now more than ever he had to keep her at arm's length. He had to keep their relationship the way it had begun all those years ago before he'd overstepped the mark.

'I need to have a competent nurse with your experience and qualifications,' he told her, quickly re-establishing the professionalism that was required.

Libby stared at him for a moment, her eyes roaming every inch of his face before turning her gaze back to the ceiling. Daniel felt even more confused. While she had every right to be angry and distant, it was as if there was something more behind her words. He wasn't sure if it was just more anger but there was something. Something she was holding back from saying.

'I'm sure there's a nurse who can fit the bill,' she said in a voice devoid of emotion.

'We need clearances and we're leaving in less than two hours. The process can't happen that quickly.'

'Call someone. Expedite it. I'm sure Sir Walter is well connected.'

Daniel shook his head. 'No one is that well connected, not even Walter. There's a process that can't be fast-tracked when you're sailing in international waters and that's removing the most obvious and pressing fact that we have a patient with specific needs. Walter's condition is precarious. He needs a highly skilled nurse and you agreed to travel with him. You have a duty of care and you signed a contract.'

'The board at the Northern Bay General Hospital signed that agreement…'

'On your behalf and, again, for good reason, they have put their reputations on the line. Walter is one of America's wealthiest men and I imagine he's also a very generous benefactor to the hospital. He's also in need of high-quality, specialised care. For all of these reasons, you have to stay on board. I'm sorry, Libby, there's really no option. The ship can't set sail without you and I don't think you want to have Walter and the board suing you for breach of contract.'

Libby slowly got to her feet as Daniel rose to his with his hand extended to her. She ignored his offer of assistance and used the bunk to steady herself.

'Then write me a sickness certificate and clear me to leave so they can't sue me. Tell them I have an unexpected medical condition.'

'But you don't have any condition, Libby. I can't lie.'

He watched as she took a deep breath and considered his words. Again, her demeanour was so different from that of the woman he had met all those years before; the hurt clearly still ran deep but there was something else. There was something less carefree about her. Something behind those beautiful eyes that he couldn't quite work out.

'You lied to me…'

'I didn't lie, Libby. I left without an explanation. I never lied.'

'Well, if you find that acceptable, how about I do the same now? I'll just leave without an explanation, if you believe that's acceptable behaviour,' she said in a controlled but clearly hostile voice. 'I deserve the right to walk away just like you did. The only difference is that you'll know why…and it's your choice whether to tell them or not.'

Daniel nodded, accepting the truth in her words. 'I deserve that.'

'Yes, you do and I deserve your help to get me off this yacht now.' She closed her eyes and shook her head.

Daniel wished he could help her but he couldn't. 'If I could I would but—'

'Write the certificate and I'll be gone. It won't matter if Walter delays setting sail for one day. They can all stay aboard here in the port and party into the early hours.'

'Unfortunately, even a delay of two hours let alone a day to secure a new nurse would cause Walter to miss his niece Sophia's engagement party.'

'Engagement party? What engagement party?' she demanded as she slumped back down on the lower bunk shaking her head. 'I thought this was just a week's cruise.'

'It is, with a small engagement party in San Lucia. He's brought his favourite chef from London to oversee the catering. Guests are coming in from all over the world to meet him there.'

'So, that's it, then. It's a fait accompli. I'm forced to stay.'

'I'm sorry, Libby.' Daniel's long fingers rested on his clenched jaw as he looked at the woman over whom he had lost countless nights of sleep—from both guilt and the realisation that he would never find a woman like her again.

Her face held a mix of anger and hopelessness. 'Trapped on this ship and expected to work with you? It's so unfair and you know it.'

'It is unfair, but I will find a compromise. I will make our working time together minimal. We can visit Walter at separate times and any incidents with the other passengers we will handle the same way unless there's an emergency…' he began, just as he received a pager alert. He looked down momentarily at his device, then moved towards the door. 'If you agree to those terms we can work this out for the next week.'

Libby chewed the inside of her cheek anxiously. For her there was more to think about than just not wanting to spend any time with Daniel. There was Billy to consider. Daniel had no idea he was father to her son. How would he react to knowing that? Would he even believe Billy was his child? And if he did believe her, would he actually care? It was a dilemma she'd never thought she would have to face. She tried to calm her breathing as Daniel left, closing the door behind him. She was stuck between a rock and a hard place and there was no choice but to agree to Daniel's terms. Being sued was not an option. She had lost her heart once to the man—and almost her mind—when he'd left, and she wasn't about to lose her home and her future because of him.

There was so much at risk by staying but even more by leaving. For nearly four years she had resigned herself to never seeing Daniel again, never having to think about telling him that he had a son. And now she was going to be at sea for seven days and seven nights with the father of her child. The father of the little boy who was so much like him. The deep blue eyes that looked up at her every night when she tucked him into bed were his father's eyes. The black hair that she smoothed with her hands in the morning when Billy ran to her, arms outstretched, for a cuddle was his father's hair. The skin that turned a beautiful golden hue in the summer sun, that too was his father's Mediterranean skin.

But when Daniel had disappeared, Libby had had neither the money nor the desire to hire someone to find him. To tell him that he had a son he might not even have wanted.

But now it was an option. Now there was the opportunity to tell him and she was confused, *terribly* confused about how he would react to the news. The man she had fallen in love with and who she had invited into her bed would care, but the man who had walked away might not care at all and that would break her heart all over again.

Libby watched as the door slowly opened again. Her heart picked up speed and she felt it pumping erratically. She dropped her gaze as Daniel stepped back inside the cabin. She didn't want to look at him. She was worried she would see her precious son in his eyes and consequently soften towards Daniel. She needed time to think. Time to work out in her mind what was best for her son. Not for her and not for Daniel. Her thoughts were only on what was best for Billy. He was the innocent one and needed to be considered above anyone else. Did she have the right to hide Daniel's son from him? Did his behaviour, leaving without an explanation or a forwarding address, take away his right to know he was a father? But if she told him, and he became a part of his son's life in some capacity, could he leave again without warning and the next time break Billy's heart?

She needed time and a clear head to sort it out. She wasn't going to rush into making a life-changing decision for Billy.

Libby wondered if time on the yacht would allow her to learn more about Daniel, get to know the real man and try her very best not to let their failed relationship influence her decision. Libby knew she had to make a truly informed choice, not just react emotionally. Perhaps that was what fate had planned—time for her to learn as much as she could about Daniel and allow her to make the very best choice for Billy.

'Your decision?'

Libby continued looking down at the cabin floor as she shifted her feet nervously. Little did he know that she had two decisions to make…

'Let's be honest, Daniel, I don't really have much of a choice. It's been made for me. I have to stay.'

'Thank you, Libby. It's best for everyone.'

'We'll see,' she told him. Her heart was still beating out of her chest. She had so much at risk. There was much to protect and consider for the next week.

'There's one more thing,' he said as he turned to leave. 'I'm sorry, Libby, but you'll still have to attend the briefing with the senior members of the crew on the stern deck in thirty minutes. It's a regulation procedure. After that I will do my best to ensure there's minimal contact between us.'

Libby nodded. She was still struggling to process it all.

'Fine, but I want minimal contact, Daniel. I don't care how you arrange that but you need to make it happen,' she said, her words short and her tone curt. 'And don't even try to change the terms of this arrangement. If you do, I swear I'm getting off this ship at the first port and you'll be the one explaining why.'

CHAPTER FOUR

'ARE YOU OKAY, LIBBY?' Georgie asked as she stepped back inside the cabin, her big brown eyes even larger than before. 'I was so shocked when you fainted.'

'I'm okay. I think I was just overwhelmed. Maybe I didn't drink enough water and my blood pressure fell.'

Georgie's expression changed and Libby watched as her old friend closed the cabin door slowly, and purposefully moved closer as if she was about to learn a secret that could bring down a nation. 'Libby, from the day we met all those years ago at school we connected and we could never hide anything from each other. Nothing's changed; it's like we were sisters in a previous life.'

'I know but…' Libby began, then stopped, knowing she couldn't lie to her friend.

'Is there something you want to share with me? The way he looked at you, and the way he spoke, it was more than a little bit obvious you two have chemistry and if it's old chemistry, then it just re-ignited in this cabin.'

'It's nothing.' Libby stiffened at the question and felt her pulse pick up again. But nothing had re-ignited, she reminded herself. It was just the shock of seeing him and the decisions that came with having him so close to her.

'Oh, really, nothing? One, he called you Libby and, two, he said, "It's me, Daniel." And if that wasn't enough, he asked me to leave the cabin. Why would he do that unless he wanted to have a private conversation with you? You two definitely have history. You can tell me to butt out but I know there's something there.'

Libby couldn't talk her way out of it. She respected Georgie too much. She had no choice but to tell her part of the story. Just not everything.

'We dated briefly, *very* briefly a few years back. It feels like a lifetime ago.'

'I knew it,' Georgie said crossing the room and sitting on the bed beside her friend. 'However brief, and however it ended, it's clear to me that it was rather an intense relationship. It's so obvious that it wasn't just a casual fling for either of you.'

Libby closed her eyes and drew a deep breath. Once again, she was feeling overwhelmed with the reality of it all. Georgie's questions, while well intentioned, were confrontational and almost too much to handle. 'It's complicated.'

'I'm sorry, Libby, I didn't mean to pry. You don't have to go into it. I overstepped good manners and I do apologise, truly. I mean, by the look of you now and the expression on his face, what you shared might be better left alone, at least for now.'

'I'm sorry, Georgie. I'm not up to talking about it. Maybe later.'

'Absolutely. Whenever you're ready,' she replied as she reached out and embraced Libby. 'Like they say in the Hollywood movies, "I have your back, girl."'

With the kindness of Georgie's embrace, Libby found a ray of hope amongst the rubble that had suddenly become her life. Trapped at sea with Billy's father, the man whom she had loved deeply but briefly, was a disaster she had not seen coming. 'Thank you.'

Georgie finally released her hold. 'Men…can't live with them and apparently you can't sail without them.'

Libby nodded. She was still on very shaky ground with her emotions but somehow she had to dig down and find the strength to get through the cruise and make what could be the single most important decision in her life. And in her son's life. Her stomach was churning as she battled with doubts about making the right decision for everyone. And her own feelings about Daniel. Were they truly dead and buried?

'I guess if I have to go to the briefing, I might as well get it over and done with,' she announced, getting to her feet and lifting her chin and making her way to the cabin door, her heart pounding with every step.

Moments later, Libby and Georgie arrived on the deck where they found the rest of the crew waiting. Libby looked around her but didn't take in too much. It was by far the biggest yacht at the dock—and the most luxurious—but Libby was oblivious to all of it. Nothing was registering with her. Her mind was racing in many directions, all of them leading back to Daniel.

'Hello, there, I'm Captain Mortimer but you can call me Eric.' The captain acknowledged Libby and Georgie's arrival with a smile. He was a man in his late fifties, not particularly tall, with a kind face and short hair just beginning to grey at the temples. He was dressed in a white uniform, complete with epaulettes and a captain's cap, all with the *Coral Contessa* insignia.

Sir Walter really did like a very professional-looking crew; the younger, blond and slightly taller man next to Captain Mortimer wore the same uniform. There was nothing casual about this yacht. 'I have the pleasure of navigating this magnificent vessel for the next eight days and with any luck this weather will hold up and it will be quite lovely. We'll be setting sail this afternoon and cruising out across the Caribbean Sea for the next three days.

'On day four we'll be docking at Martinique. You can work out between yourselves who'd like to go ashore that day. We'll anchor there for about six hours to allow the guests to tour the island. At seventeen hundred hours we'll once again set sail with the intention of docking the next day around eleven-hundred hours in San Lucia.

'On this second and final stop we will remain in port for the day and the night so those who missed leave on Martinique can take some time in San Lucia. On the sixth day we hoist anchor at zero six hundred hours for the trip back across the Caribbean Sea to Miami. Any questions?'

Libby heard every word from the captain but didn't retain too much as she was distracted by Daniel's presence so close to her after so many years. It was like a nightmare and one she wished she could wake from to find herself in her bed, in her home, hearing the giggles of her son playing in his room.

She blinked, hoping to make this reality disappear, but it didn't. She tried not to look in Daniel's direction but was powerless to prevent herself. She was drawn to him like a moth to a flame that would undoubtedly burn her if she got too close. He cut a powerful silhouette dressed in the starched white uniform too, a stark contrast to the darkness of his tanned skin. She watched as he stood alone, resting his lean fingers on the railing and staring out to sea. His look was far away but he didn't appear cold or arrogant. She couldn't help but notice he looked like a man in pain.

She didn't want to stare at him; she wanted to be able to look away; she wanted to hate him—and part of her did, but there was something in his expression that confused her. The pain in his eyes looked real. It was coming from somewhere deep inside and for some inexplicable reason Libby suddenly cared. Her reaction didn't make sense.

She should have been happy to see him looking sad but she wasn't. She was seeing a man who looked like he was at war with himself. The cleft in his jaw was just as she remembered it. The blackness of his hair falling in soft waves, like the ocean, had not changed. In fact, everything about him was just the way she remembered, except for the almost overwhelming sadness. That was new. And somewhat perplexing for her.

For the first time in a long while Daniel was unsure how to behave, how to manage the situation and his own feelings. So he chose to remain silent and look out to sea. Look towards where they would be travelling for the next week and wish it to be over. He couldn't change the outcome so every moment would be difficult for him as he now knew it would be for Libby too. She had every right to be angry with him. His behaviour, without explanation, had been appalling. And he couldn't provide any explanation.

While he had imagined his last assignment at sea would be challenging, he could never had dreamt just how much.

He did not want to make it obvious to anyone else that he and Libby had once been as close as two people could ever be so he would make all communication minimal. Theirs had been a love affair that should never have happened. But he still wished with all his heart that it had never had to end.

'Let's go around the group and introduce ourselves and since we'll be working and living closely together for the next week perhaps tell us something interesting about you,' Captain Mortimer began, bringing Daniel back to the task at hand. Meeting everyone. 'Well, you know me so let's begin with our First Mate, Steve.'

'Thanks Eric, I'll keep it brief since I don't want to bore you all with stories of my perfect childhood, college sporting prowess or my new golden retrievers. I'm Steve Waterford. I've been First Mate for about five years now, and it's my second stint on the *Coral Contessa*. I was raised in Boston and still live there with said dogs when I'm not at sea. Boris is six months old and Molly's three months old and into everything, including my boxers drawer.' Steve smiled and then looked towards the casually attired man at his left, who was rolling his eyes but smiling. His head was clean shaven and he had a beard and wore heavy black glasses.

'Probably too much information, Steve. I'm Laurence Mitchell and I'm the Chief Engineer and I've been working on various yachts and cruise ships for just over six years. I've worked three stints with Eric and Steve. I'm a native New Yorker and also still live there when I'm not on the high seas.'

'I'm Stacey Langridge, the *Contessa's* purser,' the tall blonde woman began. She too was in uniform. 'This is my second cruise with Eric and I think I've worked with Steve more times than I can remember but I'm new to this ship. I grew up in SoCal near Venice Beach but now I live in Miami. I made the move over here about a year ago with my husband. No dogs in my life…although I've dated a few over the years.' She laughed then followed suit and looked to her left.

'I'm Daniel Dimosa, I'm half of the medical team.' Daniel kept his words brief. He had no desire to socialise or to mention anything about his personal life so he looked over in Georgie's direction, willing her to step up next.

'Georgie Longbottom. I'm from the UK, although I'm

quite certain my accent gave that away. I'm the owner of a restaurant in London and, at Walter's request, the ship's chef for the second time on this yacht and, as fate would have it, my best friend from sophomore year in San Francisco when I was on an exchange is standing next to me. We haven't seen each other in for ever, so there's a lot of catching up to do.'

The group all then looked at Libby. Daniel could not avoid doing the same. He could not help but notice she nervously but purposely made eye contact with them all but not with him. He could also not help but notice that she was as beautiful as he remembered, perhaps even more so. Her stunning red hair was tied away from her face in a ponytail. He recalled it flowing across the white pillowcase as she lay naked beside him in the warmth of her bed.

He dug his fingers into his palms, trying to keep his mind from wandering back to that time. He couldn't let the memories overtake him. He had to stay on task. Thinking even for the briefest moment of the way it had been would be pointless. He could not change what had happened or make amends. She was angry and hurt even after all the time that had passed and she had every right to feel that way, although he thought she would have moved on by now and not reacted the way she had when she'd seen him. Perhaps—and understandably—she would have been cold and distant but her reaction was more than that. He had never made contact, never written or called so he had given her no reason to think of him.

'Elizabeth McDonald, but I prefer to be called Libby, and I'm from Oakland, which is about twenty minutes outside of San Francisco. I have nursing experience in both A&E and Cardiology and recently I was one of Sir Walter's nurses pre- and post-operatively. And, this is my first time on a ship.'

The group all smiled back. All except Daniel. His look was sombre and he didn't take his eyes off Libby. He couldn't. He was momentarily caught up in thoughts of the past. Daniel knew he had to get a grip on his feelings. Something tugged at his heart as he stood watching her from across the room and it scared him to the core.

Daniel Dimosa had a battle with his feelings on his hands.

'Okay, I guess now we know a little about each other and too much about Boris and… I've forgotten the other one's name already,' Eric said in a light-hearted manner.

'Molly,' Steve interjected. 'And to think I was going to give you one of their pups.'

'No, please, that's not necessary. In fact, my wife would be mortified by the thought,' Eric said, shaking his head. 'So, let's get down to the briefing. You know most of it but it's regulation to go over it so I will, particularly as a few of you are new to this particular ship. The previous voyages of the *Coral Contessa* have been without incident and I hope this trip will be the same.

'We're on a US-owned ship sailing in international waters. In keeping with guidelines, all staff are on call twenty-four hours a day. You will be assigned eight-hour shifts but you will have a pager in case you're needed twenty-four hours a day. It is not to be switched off at any time and I expect that you report here immediately if called. Neither Steve nor I will call unless it's an emergency. There's always the chance we could find ourselves in a situation where we need additional support or we may need your assistance to help seriously sick or injured patients to disembark so I need to know I can always reach you.

'Georgie is fluent in French and Italian, Stacey in Spanish, and I also speak a little Greek so we should be able to assist Sir Walter's international guests according to the information I was provided. Oh, and Steve is fluent in golden retriever but we won't be needing that on this trip.'

The team laughed, except for Libby. She stood staring into space, not capable of reacting, and Daniel understood why. She was feeling trapped and, while it wasn't his fault, Daniel felt guilty. Her distaste at being in the same space as him was understandable.

He watched as Georgie leaned over and gave her a hug. There was a very real bond between Libby and Georgie and one that, it appeared, had not diminished despite their years apart. He was not surprised because Libby was hard to forget. She was genuine and compassionate and so much more he didn't want to remember, but all of it was coming back to him at lightning speed.

CHAPTER FIVE

'Sir Walter and his remaining guests are due to arrive shortly. His grandson and guest arrived early and have already boarded and are in their stateroom. We are scheduled to set sail at fifteen hundred hours,' the Captain announced. 'So please take this time to get to know your way around your home away from home and meet the rest of the crew who have been on board for quite a few hours, some since yesterday, in preparation for the voyage.'

Daniel was still coming to terms with the situation. It was surreal seeing Libby and he had to keep reminding himself that after this week he would never see her again. Their paths would never cross. There was nothing to bind them together and everything to keep them apart. He had to make sure he did not let old feelings creep into the present. He could not truly make amends and he did not want to lie or hurt her further. She had made it clear she wanted their time together to pass quickly and she was only here because she had no other option. How he wanted it to be different but that wasn't in the stars for them.

The senior crew were dispersing but Daniel needed to speak with Libby about Walter's condition and in general about her role on the yacht, and after that he would keep his word and restrict all interactions to a professional minimum.

'Libby, can you please stay back?' Daniel asked. 'I would like to clarify a few things as this is your first time as a ship's nurse.'

Libby paused in mid-step and turned back. Daniel could see by her expression her distaste of the idea.

'Do you want me to stay too?' Georgie asked in a lowered voice.

'I'm good, Georgie, thank you,' she said softly. 'I'm sure this won't take long and then I'll head back to my cabin.'

'Five minutes, tops,' Daniel responded, making it clear he had heard both of them.

Georgie walked away, leaving Daniel and Libby alone for the second time that day. Libby crossed her arms and glared in silence at him. Her hostile body language told him everything he already knew.

'Libby,' he began. 'I will keep this very brief, but I do need to explain what we do and don't have access to on the yacht in regard to providing treatment to Walter and any other passengers.'

'I'm quite happy to go and find that out for myself,' she retorted as she paced the deck.

'I'm sure you could do that but it might be more efficient if I was to give you a brief overview because we don't know what the next few days might hold in terms of Walter's health. What we do know is that we have an almost eighty-year-old man who has undergone a triple coronary artery bypass graft and insists on behaving as if he has never seen the inside of an operating theatre. You and I are both aware that he is not fully recovered and he is as stubborn as the next billionaire and believes he knows best in every aspect of his life…' Daniel's words were cut short by the arrival of a uniformed young man.

'I'm Stan, one of the stewards, and I need you to come quickly. There's a young woman on the top deck. She gashed her head and one of the stewardesses is sitting with her. There's a load of blood.'

'Let's go,' Daniel said, immediately following the young man.

'I'm coming too,' Libby answered.

Within moments, the three of them climbed the circular staircase leading to the top deck to find a young woman dressed in shorts and a bikini top sitting in a deck chair. A stewardess stood beside her, holding a blood-soaked white hand-towel against the young woman's forehead. She had visible injuries, including grazes and cuts to the exposed skin on her shoulders, upper arms and face. There was a first-aid kit lying nearby.

'Do you know what happened… Rose?' Daniel asked as scanned the stewardess's name tag.

'Natalie had a tumble on the top deck,' Rose replied matter-of-factly. 'One of the engineers found her. It looks like she fell from the climbing wall, which had been cordoned off as it was unattended, and she had been on it without a harness. I asked her not to move; I thought she might have neck injuries. I've done first aid and knew she should remain still and wait for you as she might need a neck brace but she ignored my instructions.

'She climbed to her feet and then collapsed back down in the chair. I brought the first-aid kit up with me when I was called.'

'Do you know if she was conscious when she was found?'

'No, they said she was unresponsive. The engineer initially thought she had hit her head and been killed in the fall,' Rose told him. 'Poor man, he was quite shaken up by it.'

Daniel took a pair of disposable gloves from the open

first-aid kit and Libby followed suit, slipping on a pair and moving closer to the young woman.

'I can take over and give your hand a rest,' she told Rose as her gloved hand replaced the stewardess's and held the bloodied towel in place.

'Natalie,' Daniel began, looking directly at the young patient. 'I'm a doctor, my name is Daniel and this is Libby, the ship's nurse. We need to take a closer look at your injuries.'

'It's not that bad,' the young woman mumbled. 'I just need to wash up and have some painkillers for my head… and I'll be fine. Honest I will.'

'I think you'll need a bit more than that, Natalie,' Daniel said firmly before turning to the stewardess. 'Thank you, Rose. Libby and I have got this. We can take it from here.'

Her reaction to hearing the words from Daniel took Libby by surprise. They reminded her of how Daniel would say that in ER. 'Libby and I have got this,' he'd said more times than she could remember…or cared to remember at this time. They had been such a great team. Everyone had recognised how well they'd meshed on the job. They thought the same way, Libby pre-empting what Daniel would need. There had been an unspoken trust. They had worked like a hand and glove… Libby just wished it had been the same in their personal lives.

'We haven't even set sail yet, so it's not a good omen for the rest of the trip,' Rose commented before leaving the area. The young woman was still sitting upright but swaying a little. On closer inspection, Libby could see there were deep grazes to her elbows and knees with trickles of blood on her left leg. Her right slip-on-style shoe was missing but as Libby's eyes darted around, there was no sign of it close by.

'I'm going to carefully take the towel away from your

head so we can look at the wound,' Libby told her softly to allay any fear. Libby had stepped into medical mode and made a conscious decision to leave their personal issues behind.

The young woman remained very still as Libby released the towel. She knew immediately it was a deep wound and would require stitches or else there would be an unattractive scar running across the victim's forehead above her left eye. Some of Natalie's blonde hair was matted into the bloodied area. The length of time between the fall and being found might have been more than first thought.

'It appears the bleeding has ceased for the time being at least,' Daniel told Libby as he leaned in and examined the wound very closely. The scent of his musky cologne filled her senses and her immediate reaction was to pull away but she couldn't. She was still supporting the young woman so she had to stay closer to Daniel than she'd ever thought she would again. She swallowed and tried to calm her racing heart. It wasn't anger surging through her veins. It was something she had forgotten how to feel.

'She will need stitches,' Libby remarked in a tone that gave away nothing of how she was feeling.

'I agree,' Daniel responded. 'However, I would suggest that since it's in a prominent place on your face, a plastic surgeon would be your best option.'

The young woman nodded but appeared unperturbed with the news about her face.

'I'm just going to check your pulse,' Libby cut in.

'I need to ask you some questions while Nurse McDonald takes your observations.

'What is your name and date of birth?' Daniel went on.

'Natalie.' The young woman paused and looked up, her eyes darting about as if searching for the words. 'Natalie, Natalie… Martin.'

'And how old are you?' Daniel asked, not taking his eyes away from his young patient as he observed her reactions.

'I'm eighteen…no, no, I'm nineteen,' she told him as she reached up to the wound area with her blood-stained fingers.

Gently but firmly Daniel directed her hand away from the wound. 'Your hands are contaminated. You need to refrain from touching the wound until it's dressed.'

'Can you please tell me today's date and the day of the week?' Libby asked.

'Monday, June tenth.'

Libby looked at Daniel. It was Sunday, June eleventh. The woman was lucid but still a little disoriented.

'Natalie, are you in significant pain anywhere other than your forehead and the scratches on your legs?' Daniel asked as he reached for a stethoscope.

'It kind of hurts all over but if you can clean me up and give me some strong painkillers I'll be okay.'

'Pulse is seventy,' Libby announced.

'Is that good or bad?'

'Your observations are good, Natalie, but it's not as simple as a strong pulse and a few painkillers. I need to better understand how you're feeling as there can be underlying issues from a significant fall. Is there any significant targeted pain or generally a battered and bruised feeling?' Daniel continued the line of questioning. Libby was aware he was not convinced that the injuries from the fall were as clear cut as they could see.

Natalie's loss of consciousness for a still undetermined period of time and a fall from a height were concerning him. He was a thorough doctor and not one to compromise a patient's health care so he was taking his time and remaining calm. He always had.

'The back of my head is the worst,' she said very slowly, purposely rolling her head in a circular motion. 'But a shot or two tonight and I'll be fine.'

'Best not to move your head that way, and I might remind you that at nineteen you're underage and would not be served alcohol on this ship. Please stay as still as possible and let me look at the back of your head,' Daniel said as he walked to the other side of the examination table and carefully checked the posterior skull region.

'As I suspected, there is an area of your skull that is somewhat depressed. For a conclusive prognosis we will need to do X-rays and you're going to need to be in hospital under observation.'

'For how long?'

'Overnight at least. I'm not sure how far you fell and for how long you were unconscious. Both are concerning me.'

Libby began to clean the wound. Careful not to dislodge the blood clot, she freed some of the matted hair and applied an antiseptic solution and sterile gauze dressing. Daniel reached over and his hand brushed hers lightly as he held the dressing in place while she reached for a soft wrap bandage.

'I'll wrap the wound,' she began, trying to steady her breathing. Even through the gloves she had felt the warmth of his hand on hers and she was surprised at her reaction. 'I don't want to use anything adhesive on her skin.'

'Good call,' Daniel replied.

The young woman was agitated but staying still enough to allow Libby to dress the wound.

'Can the plastic surgeon come on board to see me?'

'No, Natalie, the only course of action now is to clean up the wound, give you a temporary dressing and then arrange for you to disembark and transfer immediately to the local hospital. I would prefer that you are transported in an ambulance so I will make a call now and arrange for that. They may have a plastic surgeon on staff at the hospital or refer you to one. I'm not conversant with the local hospital's scope.'

'I'm not leaving,' she announced loudly. 'I'm going to the engagement party with my boyfriend, Ernest. You know, Walter's his great-uncle and he owns this yacht. You can't force me to leave.'

'I'm sorry, Natalie, but that's exactly what I'm doing and I can guarantee you that Sir Walter will not argue the point,' Daniel responded. His voice was firm but not at the volume of hers. 'It's not in your best interest to remain on board with your injuries. You need to get to the nearest hospital as soon as possible for a complete assessment... and I mean as soon as possible.

'Head injuries are not to be taken lightly—the extent of your injuries from the fall may not become obvious immediately and the damage to your skull is concerning me. There's a risk of internal bleeding. You need a CAT scan and may be admitted to the intensive care unit dependent upon the results. While you feel fine now, don't be cavalier about the seriousness of the fall.'

'Cava what?'

'Cavalier. It means don't dismiss how serious the injury could be,' Libby explained.

'But Ernest can watch me and tell you if there's anything wrong.'

Daniel reached for the ship's phone. 'We might well be out at sea when either of you notice a problem. And that would be too late.'

'There's a helipad. I can get taken back to shore anytime.'

'While there is a helipad, there's not a helicopter on board. You could lapse into a coma without warning and it would be too late to call for the coastguard and I'm not prepared to take that chance with your life.'

'Are you serious? A coma?'

'Yes, there's always a risk, however slight, with a severe blow to the head of what we call extradural blueing from the middle meningeal artery or one of its branches and as a result a haemorrhage inside your skull. I understand it's all medical jargon to you, but I'm letting you know that it has the potential to be serious. Your well-being is my priority, Natalie, not your social life. Take another trip with Ernest, but next time don't climb an unattended rock wall.'

Ten minutes later Libby watched as paramedics arrived and secured Natalie on the barouche in preparation for the ambulance trip to the Western Miami General Hospital. Daniel provided them with the background and a copy of the medical notes that Libby had taken during the examination.

Ernest had come to say goodbye but he had chosen to remain on board. He told her not to worry and that she would be fine. He'd have shots in her honour at the party and send selfies to her. Libby could see the young woman's disappointment and anxiety about being transported to hospital was heightened by the sadness of doing it alone. Her boyfriend had chosen partying with his family over her and that had to hurt. Particularly at nineteen.

'Thank you for your assistance, Libby.'

Libby nodded to Daniel and turned to leave. Her work was done. Now she knew she needed distance more than ever.

'I will be suggesting tighter controls over the management of the climbing wall. I might suggest it's closed altogether unless there's someone experienced managing it twenty-four seven. Perhaps I'll speak to the chief stewardess and ascertain the number of young people on board who may be tempted to do something similar. I don't think there're any others but I'd rather be safe than sorry.'

'That's a sensible idea,' she said, not wanting to remain near him even a moment longer. She admired him immensely as a doctor and she worried that might somehow influence how she felt about him as a man. It had once before. From the first day Daniel had stepped into the Northern Bay General Hospital A&E where Libby had been nursing, she had been drawn to him, and history was at risk of repeating itself.

He was a skilled and knowledgeable doctor and she had adored working with him as she'd felt that every moment she did so she learned more and became a better nurse. He had taken the time to explain procedures and the reason for his diagnoses, prognoses and treatment plans, however unconventional or, at times, unpopular they might have seemed. He was thorough and methodical, leaving nothing to chance. He was also very handsome and charismatic and none of that had changed.

An empathetic bedside manner was not at the forefront on this occasion but it was understandable. Daniel wanted what was best for the young woman, and wasn't about to be swayed by her pleas. He didn't mind being the bad guy in her opinion if it meant saving her life—or at the very least keeping her pretty face from being disfigured by ugly scarring.

But Libby had to save herself from being drawn back in. She had to get away as quickly as she could because she could not afford to be swept away by her feelings.

Forgetting the past was not an option and she could not let his professional abilities overshadow the ruin he had left in his wake and the decision that still weighed heavily on her mind. She walked away from Daniel without another word.

Libby arrived back at the cabin and found Georgie waiting outside her door. She gave her the abbreviated version of the events with the climbing incident as they stepped inside.

'I wondered what took you so long. I thought it might have been a heart-to-heart with Daniel,' Georgie said as she leaned against the bathroom door.

Libby was in the tiny space, washing her hands, and shook her head. 'Not interested. That time has passed. He's had years to reach out and explain what happened and he didn't. I'm done wanting to know.'

'Good for you. There's plenty of fish in the sea and the Caribbean is the perfect place to go fishing. Speaking of that, how about we step out and have a quick look around the yacht? I've done all the prep in the galley for tonight's dinner, which is a seafood buffet, and I've left it with the other two crew members who can manage for the next hour or so. I'll head back and put the finishing touches to it and make the dessert later. We can find somewhere to sit and enjoy a little sun. Walter wouldn't mind at all. Believe me, if he's fed well—and he will be—then all will be well in the world.'

'I'm not really in the mood, but you go,' Libby replied, deep in thought as she made her way to her still unpacked suitcase for a clean top. She had noticed a few tiny spots of blood on the one she was wearing. 'I don't want to ruin your fun.'

Socialising was the last thing on her mind. She felt like a prisoner in a glamorous floating penitentiary and wondered how she would stay sane for the next few days. No matter what she'd said to Georgie, in her heart it wasn't over and she found her mind wandering to thoughts of him and their time together…and to the son they shared.

The brief time tending to Natalie together had made it all so real again. Everything that she had struggled to forget was returning as vividly as the day it had happened. The good, the wonderful, the exciting, all of it, along with the heartache and the confusion. It was overwhelming her.

Without thinking, she reached for her pendant. Her every reason for living was her son and she was not yet ready to share that secret with Daniel. He was a man who could sweep her off her feet, make her feel like she was so special and then disappear overnight without an explanation. Daniel was a brilliant doctor but Billy deserved more than that. He deserved stability and a loving father who would not disappear on an unexplained whim.

There was also the niggling question of whether, upon learning he was a father, Daniel might demand shared custody and Libby had no idea where Daniel lived. That was something that Libby had neither the funds nor the emotional strength to fight. She just needed time to decide whether Billy would be better off with Daniel in his life and, if so, when she would tell him.

There was much that Daniel would have to explain and prove for her to make such a huge decision and she worried that seven days and nights might not be a long enough time. Libby felt certain that if it wasn't for them being on the ship together, he would not have given her another thought.

She just wished she felt the same.

'You can't turn into a hermit because of Daniel,' Georgie said firmly. 'We've known each other since we were sixteen and you haven't changed. You're so sweet and lovely and I don't want to see you lock yourself away because of him.'

'That's not the reason...'

'Libby.' Georgie looked at her friend. 'That's a porky pie and we both know it.'

Libby frowned in Georgie's direction with no clue what her friend was talking about.

'A porky pie is a lie,' she continued, without Libby responding. It was a lie. Daniel was the reason for her simmering anxiety and her lack of enthusiasm about everything, except getting off the ship. Disembarking the *Coral Contessa* was the one thing she was looking forward to very much but she knew something had to be resolved one way or the other before she did.

'Libby, I didn't mean to be rude or forward in any way. I just meant that you're making up an excuse not to get out and about because of whatever happened between you and Daniel. But locking yourself in the cabin won't change anything. All it will do is waste the experience of your first time on a yacht.'

'Maybe I'm making an excuse but it's complicated, Georgie, and...to be honest, I guess I'm still in shock. I never thought I'd see him again in my life.'

'Your fainting made it very clear that even hearing his name was a huge surprise and not a pleasant one. It's always complicated when men are involved. They generally manage to make a complete mess of things most of the time.'

'More than you know.'

'I guessed it didn't end well and, again, I'm not prying. You can share as much or as little as you want with me, but I'm going to share some things I know about the man.'

'Things you know about him? What things?'

'Daniel is handsome and could have pretty much any woman he wanted within ten miles of the ship but from what I've heard from the other crew members he's single and has never become involved with anyone he works with and that's not because there haven't been offers. Passengers and crew alike literally throw themselves at him, but he keeps his distance.'

'How do you know this?'

'Ships' doctors don't exist in huge numbers, and Stacey and one of my galley crew have worked with him before on larger cruise ships. It's a tight-knit community and someone as handsome and eligible as Daniel is fodder for gossip. Only there isn't any about him. He's the ultimate elusive bachelor and a gentleman. His liaisons, and there will be some, no doubt, must be fleeting and kept ashore and discreet with no drama. He's never married and he's quite private about his personal life and his family, if he has any, but he's an amazing doctor and a good and fair colleague. That's it.'

'That's a lot of background,' Libby said, still uneasy about how quickly the crew of the *Coral Contessa* had updated Georgie about Daniel. All the more reason to keep her secret safe. That would no doubt spread like wildfire and she didn't need that. Her anxiety was suddenly on the rise again.

'He's squeaky clean and that makes him even more desirable...and almost a celebrity. There are a lot of Latin lovers at sea, but he's not one of them.'

'No offence, Georgie, but I don't think I want to hear any more. I'm not ready to hear wonderful character references about my ex,' Libby said as she sat down on the bunk and slumped back against her pillows.

'I don't know how to make you feel better about the situation, Libby. I told you what I know so you can feel better about yourself. By your reaction you were clearly in love with the man and I wanted you to know, whatever happened, he's a decent man so your instincts when you fell for him were right.'

Libby closed her eyes and wished she could open them and find herself in her own bed in her own house and not staring at the lower deck of a yacht about to sail through the Caribbean. She should have paid more attention to her initial doubts about the trip and fought harder not to be sent on an adventure at sea. The reality was closer to a disaster.

'I know your intentions are good and I appreciate what you're trying to do but I don't trust my instincts about much right now.'

'Then trust mine,' Georgie said as she stepped closer again. 'You can't change anything except yourself into a swimsuit. Let's get some sun while we can. There's another few hours before Sir Walter's guests claim the sundecks for their own.'

'Like I said, you go. I'd rather stay here and call home.'

'Call home while I slip into my swimsuit and then we'll go for a walk at least. Wallowing inside your cabin won't change anything. The sun at least has a chance to change your mood and lift your spirits, so let's give it a chance. We need to relax with a fruit cocktail, non-alcoholic of course since we're working, but maybe later tonight we can switch it up for a champagne. It's not often you find yourself at sea with your absolute best friend who you haven't seen in over a decade.'

CHAPTER SIX

'ISN'T THE SUN GLORIOUS?' Georgie asked her reluctant companion. 'The view's stunning and we haven't even set sail yet. I think we're going to have a lovely time.'

'Mmm,' Libby responded, staring straight ahead as the two strolled around the deck. She had called home and spoken to Billy and her mother and everything was fine. Billy was about to have lunch and then help his grandfather build a big red racing-car bed. Her parents were spoiling their grandson and he was clearly so excited about sleeping in a racing car that night that he didn't have too much time to talk to her. Knowing that Billy was happy and not missing her was a relief.

She had changed into white shorts and a navy striped T-shirt. Georgie was in a pink and green floral bathing suit but Libby had no intention of baring that much skin. Knowing that Daniel was on board was making her self-conscious, not to mention that Bradley had packed the skimpiest of bikinis in her suitcase.

The crew were busily preparing for the final passengers yet to arrive and tending to the needs of those already on board. Sir Walter was the most important passenger and he was yet to arrive. Libby had not seen him since he had been discharged from hospital a week after his surgery and she was genuinely looking forward to seeing him again. If only it were under different circumstances.

'I'll take "mmm" for the moment but by tomorrow I'll be looking for a smidgen more enthusiasm.'

'That might be my limit, I'm sorry,' Libby said as she drew breath, unable to forget for even an instant that Daniel was at any time only a deck away from her. The thought of him was making her heart and her body react in ways that made her very uneasy. It was the most confused she had been in four years.

Georgie returned a half-smile and Libby suddenly felt pangs of guilt. Her behaviour was less than gracious after Georgie's earlier excitement to see her and the support she had shown when she'd needed it most. Libby knew she needed to lighten up. She had agreed, albeit reluctantly and under duress, to be on board for the next seven days...or six and a half, she told herself as the first day was almost half-gone.

'I'm sorry, let's walk around and find a seat in the sun. You're right, it will be lovely.'

After just over an hour of Miami sunshine, incessant chatter and a delicious pineapple smoothie each, Georgie excused herself to return to galley duties. Libby was returning to her cabin to change into her uniform when a steward caught up with her.

'Sir Walter has just boarded and wants to see you.'

'He's early. I didn't think we would see him for another hour and I haven't changed into my uniform.'

'He won't mind, I'm sure,' he told her as he led the way to their host, who was making himself comfortable on a sun lounger on the deck at the bow of the yacht. He had an entourage of people with him but, as Libby quickly and thankfully noticed, no Daniel.

'Hello, Nurse Elizabeth. It's lovely to see you again, my dear. I hope you're not upset that I kidnapped you for a few days?'

'Hello, Sir Walter. I'm happy to be here,' she lied. While lying was not a habit of hers, it was not Sir Walter's fault that his yacht was the last place on earth she wanted to be. She wanted to appear gracious and not dampen his excitement about the cruise and his daughter's engagement party. 'I just want to keep you on your path to a full recovery on this cruise.' That was not a lie. That was Libby's sole focus. Daniel was not a focus of hers. Although avoiding him was.

'We'll see about that.' He laughed. 'You see, I'm going to enjoy what time I have left on earth and not fuss too much with healthy hoo-ha. If I want a beef Wellington with gravy then I shall have one, and I do not like exercise. At all.'

Libby knew she would have her hands full with Sir Walter. It appeared that both men of significance on the *Coral Contessa* were going to challenge her reserves.

She just needed to dig deep and rise to the occasion.

'So now we've caught up, why don't you take a look around my little yacht, make sure you know where everything is and I can sit here and catch up with my friends. I'm feeling as fit as a bull and I don't need you...'

'Are you sure?'

'Couldn't be more sure,' he told her. 'And I know you have one of those pager things, so someone will find you, or the doc, if I my ticker starts acting up.'

Libby left Walter and his group, and took an unaccompanied tour of the yacht. It was magnificent on every one of the four decks, all of which were serviced by a glass elevator. The decor was like that of an Italian hotel from a magazine, with white marble floors, ornate gilded furnishings and a ceiling in the formal dining area that was reminiscent of the Sistine Chapel.

As she passed one of the two oversized columns near the bar, a steward pushed on a small panel and to Libby's surprise the entire column opened and she saw it was filled with shelves of polished crystal glasses and decanters. Opulence was the word that came to mind everywhere she looked. She'd had no idea what a yacht of that much splendour would be worth but she knew she couldn't earn enough in a million lifetimes to buy one. Libby looked around, knowing she had something far more valuable in her life. Something money could never buy. She had her son.

After roaming for a little while longer and stumbling across the room towards the bow of the yacht, which housed a speedboat and two jet-skis, Libby thought she had seen enough. A boat on a yacht was too much for her so she made her way to her cabin to shower and change into one of the uniforms that had been hanging in the wardrobe. She pulled her slightly damp hair into a low bun at the nape of her neck and checked her appearance in the mirror on the back of her cabin door. Libby was very conscious that she wanted to appear professional and there to do her job.

It was a message she wanted to send to everyone. Including Daniel.

Libby returned to find Walter with a lit cigar in one hand and a short crystal glass of what she felt certain was whiskey over ice in the other hand. She could not mask being upset to see him smoking and drinking. She was disappointed and angry in equal amounts and suspected that was why he had sent her on a sightseeing trip around the yacht. He was completely disregarding everything he had been told in hospital before and after his bypass surgery.

He had been warned that smoking could increase his

chance of blood clots and he risked a serious chest infection along with a slower healing process. It was behaviour far more dangerous than consuming a beef Wellington and she intended to tell him exactly what she thought.

'Sir Walter—' she began as she drew near, her voice not masking her distress at the situation.

'Walter, remember, I want you to call me Walter,' he returned with a laugh under the wide-brimmed hat he was now wearing.

'Fine, I will call you Walter and in return I want you to put that cigar and that drink down now. You cannot be smoking or drinking after your heart surgery.'

Walter stared back at her in silence. Libby didn't care if he fired her. In fact, that would be a blessing but it wasn't her motivation in telling him off. Keeping Walter alive and assisting him back to good health was all she cared about.

'I'm going to be blunt,' she said, staring into his eyes. 'What you're doing is reckless behaviour and you know it. You're barely five weeks out from major surgery that saved your life and you're sailing around the Caribbean, smoking and drinking and acting like a teenager. You've contracted me to be on board as your nurse and what I'm seeing is, well...silly behaviour on your part. I'm not going to stand around and pretend it's all right. I just won't. The walls of your arteries were lined with fatty plaque caused by a diet high in animal fats, refined sugar, smoking, inactivity and excessive alcohol. And you're indulging in all of that again!'

Libby lifted her chin defiantly as Walter looked back at her, taking his time to reply. It was as if each was staring the other down, not unlike the prelude to a gunfight.

'I am neither silly nor reckless in spending what time I have left sailing, young lady. This yacht and the Caribbean are the closest I get to being with my beloved late wife, Contessa. She was the love of my life and if I go, it will be while I feel close to her. I told her as much when I held her hand as she died and I know she will hold mine in the bow of this yacht if I die on it.'

Libby was taken aback at the emotion in his voice, the sentiment in his words and the tears forming in the corners of his weary eyes. She softened her tone but kept resolute in her message. 'I do understand what you're saying and how you're feeling, Walter, but you don't have to die anytime soon. You can sail as much as you like and feel close to your beloved wife for many years to come but you must stop smoking and drinking heavy liquor.'

'Well, maybe I don't want to live a great many years,' he retorted, turning away from her. 'Maybe I'm lonely and tired and I want to enjoy what little time I have left, and if I hasten the end, then so be it.'

'Please forgive me for saying this, but I think that's being quite disrespectful.'

'Disrespectful? And to whom am I being disrespectful?' His head turned back to Libby, his eyes wide and his lips cutting a thin line in his clearly irritated face.

'To the doctors and theatre nurses who saved your life.'

'They're paid to do that. It's their job, just like it's your job to take care of me for the next week so I make it to my niece's engagement. Not that I completely approve of her fiancé but nonetheless you and the doc will keep me alive to see that day.'

'And what about the day after?' Libby said, taking the empty seat beside him. One of the family entourage had quickly moved away when the polite but somewhat heated discussion had erupted. 'What about living to see her children, your great-nieces and-nephews? To bounce them on your knee and look into their gorgeous cherub faces. Don't you want to live to do that?'

'Using unborn children to get your point across,' he said butting his cigar on the ashtray nearby. 'Now, that's hitting below the belt.'

'I'll do whatever it takes, Walter, to make you see reason. You've survived a massive operation and now it's up to you to take care of yourself and since you're from the UK, if you do as your medical team say you may even make a hundred and receive a letter from the Queen. Wouldn't that make your day? You could frame the letter and hang it in your suite or perhaps behind the bar for everyone to see.'

'Using Her Majesty now. To what ends will you go? Have you no shame, Libby?'

'No shame at all when it comes to your health. I will do and say whatever I must to keep you healthy.'

'Well, the whole hundredth birthday and the Queen won't work,' he argued with a raised eyebrow. 'My hundredth birthday is twenty-one years away so I'm sure if I make it that far it won't be the Queen who'll be writing to me. She'll be in a better place by then.'

'The reigning monarch, then,' Libby cut in. 'Does it matter who signs the letter from Buckingham Palace? Let's just get you to the age to qualify first.'

'Lovely thought, but I'm painfully aware that while the survival rate for bypass patients who make it to five weeks after the operation is pretty darn good, everything changes after about seven or eight years. The chance of me falling off my perch jumps considerably so I'll be lucky to see my ninetieth birthday let alone my hundredth. Anyway, I've decided I'm going to damn well enjoy the next few years and leave the rest to fate. I'm most certainly not going to spend what years I have left sitting in an armchair, looking out of a bay window with a mohair rug on my knees… and a cup of Earl Grey tea in my hand.'

'With all due respect, Walter, there's quite a lot of space

between a nursing home and smoking cigars and drinking whiskey in this very ornate floating bar.'

Walter eyed Libby in silence again. His lips once again formed a hard line in his wrinkled face but he didn't look annoyed. She couldn't read his expression at all. Libby knew she should never play poker with him as he was giving nothing away. Her stomach suddenly dropped.

Had she gone too far? She really liked Walter but she couldn't sit by and watch him risk his health unnecessarily, but neither did she want to appear unprofessional and cross the line. Under his gruff exterior, he was a kind and generous man and, quite apart from her duty of care as a nurse, she had grown fond of him while he had been in her care in hospital. She wanted to see him live as many years as he could and not throw them away on cigars and alcohol.

His lips turned to a smirk as he grudgingly placed his glass on the table.

'I like you, young lady. You have what I think you Americans called *spunk* and what we British call unbridled determination. Some might even call it stubbornness, but a word of warning: I too have stubbornness in bucketloads. It's how I built my empire and I'm not going to roll over and play dead anytime soon. You'll have your hands full if you think I'm going to change my ways easily.'

Libby climbed to her feet. She'd been worried that she had overstepped the mark but by his tone and the fact he'd said he liked her, clearly she hadn't said too much.

'I'm up for the challenge, Walter.'

'And what challenge would that be?'

Libby turned to see Daniel standing far too close for her liking and quickly she turned her face back to her patient. Her heart had instantly picked up speed and she hated herself for the way she was reacting. She should be angry whenever she saw him. Furious, in fact. But she wasn't.

Her body had no shame, she realised. Immediately upon hearing the timbre of his voice or seeing his tall, dark silhouette or when the scent of his cologne overtook her senses, she lost all reason and self-respect. And Daniel's effect on her wasn't lessening in impact. She had already witnessed how handsome he looked in his crisp white uniform with its stark contrast to his tanned Mediterranean skin. She didn't need to look at him again and be reminded of that. Everything about him and the way he made her feel frightened her.

She was just grateful that all of what she was thinking and feeling was not obvious to anyone else.

'It appears, Daniel, that Libby thinks she can change my *reckless* ways and make me see a ripe old age so I can get a letter from Buckingham Palace,' Walter told him with a wink. 'But I'm trying to tell her that it's pointless to try to change a man. Once we're out of nappies, or diapers as the Americans call them, no woman can change us. It's really quite pointless to try, don't you agree?'

Libby closed her eyes. The words resonated in her heart. Daniel, she suspected, was a man who didn't want to change. He was a man who was happy with the way he lived his life. Loving and leaving women with no thought for the hurt he caused or the hearts he broke.

'I believe, Walter, that under the right circumstances and with the right incentive, a man can change.'

Libby was taken aback by Daniel's answer to Walter's question. *The right incentive?* Did that mean she hadn't been incentive enough for him to change his philandering ways all those years ago? And what did he mean by the right circumstances? She was terribly confused and she felt anger starting to brew deep inside. Strangely, she liked the feeling of anger. It gave her perspective and control over the situation.

'Codswallop!' Walter bellowed. 'That's all New Age, politically correct codswallop. I have no intention of changing my ways, no matter how sweet or how pretty the messenger may be.'

Libby shook her head at the backhanded compliment as she refused to look in Daniel's direction. She didn't want to see the reaction on his face.

'Let's not debate whether men can change,' Libby suddenly interjected to put the conversation, and her thoughts, back on a professional level. 'Let's get back to the issue at hand. Your health and the responsibility of your ship's medical team.'

'Let me see if I have this correctly. I'm paying you both very well—not to mention handsomely donating to a hospital in San Francisco—to have you accompany me on this trip with the sole purpose of preventing me from having fun and reprimanding me at every available opportunity?'

'No.' Daniel stepped closer as he spoke. 'Walter, Libby and I are here to ensure you have the best chance of a full recovery. You must understand that the surgery you underwent is not a cure for coronary heart disease. It's a second chance if you change your ways, but if you don't you will be right back to square one in a very short period of time and we don't want that.'

'Oh, dear, I have no chance here. You're both singing from the same hymn sheet,' he said with an expression of defeat crossing his face. 'Fine, I will refrain from my wicked ways for the next week but after that, when you two are out of my sight, all bets are off. I will do as you ask for the next week purely because I can't handle seven days of incessant nagging…in stereo.'

With that he stood up and stretched his back from side to side. 'I think I will have a nice shower and change for dinner. Georgie is preparing some of my favourite food and

I intend to enjoy it…without a cigar or whiskey, as ordered by my keepers, but I'll damn well have dessert if I fancy it. And if either of you try to stop me, I'll have you thrown overboard and you'll be swimming with the fish tonight.'

Daniel smirked and Libby's lips formed a half-smile as Walter left. Suddenly his entourage followed suit and dispersed, leaving Libby and Daniel standing together.

Libby looked out to sea for a moment before she began to walk away. Being alone with Daniel as the sun began to set was a recipe for disaster. The setting was far too romantic and she knew, despite all the unanswered questions and her simmering anger, there was the smallest chance that she might still be vulnerable to him.

And she could not afford to go down that path again. There was so much more at stake this time.

'Please don't go, Libby,' he began. 'I know I said I'd find a way to ensure we're not working together but perhaps we could sit and talk sometime. I do think fondly of the time we spent together.'

'Not fondly enough to get in touch any time over the last four years,' she spat back at him coldly.

CHAPTER SEVEN

'MR HUDSON.' LIBBY addressed the man she had directed to follow her inside the makeshift infirmary. She paused as she closed the door. 'Please come in.'

'It would be my pleasure,' he told her, then continued, 'But you can call me Maxwell.'

Libby drew a short breath. His response had been followed by a peculiar stare in her direction. Her intuition was telling her that Maxwell's gaze was not purely patient-nurse. His eyes seemed to hover on her lips, not meeting her eyes at all. It was odd but she shrugged it off. Maybe his hearing was compromised and he was lip reading. Some of the older patients she had cared for over the years did that, although Maxwell appeared to be in his late forties but she couldn't be sure. He was not particularly tall and quite stocky in build, with a receding hairline so his age was difficult to pinpoint.

'Please sit down,' she said, motioning towards the chair adjacent to the cabin desk as she stepped inside the en suite bathroom and washed her hands. 'The doctor is not available, but I can take some notes and see what the issue is and call for him if there's anything urgent. He isn't too far away.' Just far enough to allow her to feel more comfortable.

'He can't go too far—we're on a ship. Unless he jumps overboard and then it would just be you and me.'

His response was odd and made her feel uncomfortable. And the way he was looking at her when she reappeared with freshly scrubbed hands even more so.

'It was a joke,' he said with a snigger and a raised eyebrow. Still standing a little too close for Libby's liking, he continued, 'I'm sure he wouldn't jump off the ship—at least not while you're on here.'

Libby was not impressed but was determined to remain professional and move past the blatant flirting.

'What appears to be your problem today?' Libby asked in a monotone.

Maxwell stared at her in silence, his eyebrow still arched.

'Is everything all right, Mr Hudson?' Libby continued in the same professional but unemotional tone, only a little louder.

'Call me Maxwell. It's less formal,' he said with a smirk.

'Maxwell, as I said, please take a seat…' she motioned again to the chair '…and tell me what the problem appears to be.'

He sat down without taking his eyes off her. 'It's my back. I fell asleep in the sun and now I'm burnt.'

'I see. Please remove your shirt and I can take a look.'

Maxwell began unbuttoning his brightly coloured shirt, patterned with flamingos and palm trees. His eyes remained fixed on hers and he mimicked a male entertainer as he slowly undid each button, making Libby's discomfort grow by the second.

'I don't see a ring, pretty lady.'

Libby had a fairly good idea where the conversation was heading and she had no intention of helping it along. Quite the opposite, she was going to stop it dead in the water by ignoring it.

'It's such a lovely day and I'm sure you want to get back to the group so let's look at your sunburn.' Her tone was courteous and professional as she slipped on latex gloves. She trusted she was making it clear she was not interested in his line of questioning.

'I'd rather stay in the cabin with you.'

Libby drew a deep breath. The man had the faint smell of whiskey and a strong smell of suntan lotion and bad cologne. The combined scents were as unpleasant as his personality. 'Well, I have a lot to do, so let's get you seen to and back out there.'

'It must be a bit dreary not being able to join the party,' he continued, still not following Libby's clear line of conversation.

'I'm on board to work. That's the only reason I'm here and I'm happy about that. Looking after Sir Walter will keep me busy enough.'

'When you finish your shift, you should come up on deck and get some sunshine with me.'

'I don't have a shift, I'm on call all the time. Now please turn around so I can look at the sunburn.'

'It's not that bad actually.' The man's mouth curled into a grin that immediately turned Libby's stomach. She had feared the worst and very quickly her fears were being realised.

'I came here to see you.'

'Then we're finished here.'

'Not so fast,' the man said. Standing up and moving closer, he grabbed her wrist with his stubby fingers. 'I watched you sitting by the pool yesterday with your girlfriend, in your skimpy shorts, and I did some digging around to find out about you. It seems you're single… and available.'

Libby tried to pull free but the man moved even closer.

His breath was warm on her neck as he stared into her eyes. Suddenly, being in such close proximity to him, she noticed the stench of alcohol was not so faint.

'Let go of me now.' Her voice was raised and her tone cold as she pulled her arm free and moved to the other side of the room. A sense of panic was stirring inside. She was alone in the cabin with a drunken, lecherous man.

'Come on, don't play coy. The doctor's not here. It's just you and me. The rest of the group are up on deck, a long way from us, so let's make friendly.'

'Get away from me,' Libby yelled, trying to quell her anxiety. The situation had escalated from uncomfortable to dangerous very quickly. Her heart was picking up speed and she felt the heat rising from her core. Her fight-or-flight response was kicking in as she backed up to a wall-mounted telephone.

'Come on, you and I both know you signed up to have some fun. If you weren't the type to *party* you would've stayed on dry land,' he said as he reached for the zip on his shorts. 'And I'm the man who can give you a good time, right here, right now. I've got plenty of time to seal the deal.'

The door opened abruptly as the man reached for Libby. Seemingly unperturbed, he ignored the sound and continued to fumble with his shorts.

Daniel was standing in the doorway. With powerful strides he crossed the room, grabbed the man by the collar and spun him around. Libby could see the rage in Daniel's eyes. She had never seen him like that before. With her emotions on a roller-coaster, it both frightened and calmed her at the same time.

'Don't ever speak to a woman like that again,' Daniel roared. The volume and tone of voice commanded attention.

The man straightened up and looked Daniel up and

down. Ignoring the uniform, he continued to display a level of arrogance that Libby found appalling.

'Chill out, buddy. Go back on duty and do your steward thing. It's all good…the little lady's happy to chat with me.'

'Nurse McDonald is most definitely not happy to speak with you. She's made that clear. Now leave.' Daniel stood his ground and Libby felt very safe and protected by the man she had wanted to hate.

'Like I said, chill out. It's all good.'

'I said leave. Now.'

'Make me,' the now irate passenger said with a cocky expression on his alcohol-flushed face. He suddenly began shifting unsteadily from side to side on his feet as if he were in a boxing ring.

As Daniel stretched out his long arm to escort him outside, the man took a swing at him, his right hand clenched into a fist, trying to connect with Daniel's ribs.

'Daniel, be careful,' Libby called out with concern etching her voice. Concern for the man she had never wanted to see again in her life but was so relieved to see at that moment.

Daniel dodged the man's punch as it cut through the air. 'Don't be stupid,' Daniel told him. 'Just leave before you get hurt.'

'By who? You?' the passenger laughed scornfully as he tried yet again to punch Daniel but this time taking aim at his stomach.

Libby could see that Daniel had no choice but to act in self-defence. He deflected the man's punch with his forearm, then, grabbing the man's arm, twisted it behind his back and forced him to the floor in a secure hold, his knee resting firmly on the man's back.

'Please dial nine, Libby. It will put you through to the bridge. Ask the captain to send down the first mate and a steward to take care of this creep. I'm going to insist this excuse for a man is escorted off the ship when we arrive in port tomorrow morning.'

Without hesitation, Libby did as Daniel asked and explained the situation before turning back to see Maxwell restrained, red faced and unable to move as Daniel still had him pinned to the floor. Maxwell's eyes were darting about, his cheek pressed against the floor, and he was muttering inaudible comments to no one in particular. Perhaps his sober self was having regrets, she thought. She didn't care. He was a predator and she was relieved that Daniel was going to have him removed from the ship. Under the influence of alcohol or not, he was a risk that needed to be mitigated.

'You can't throw me off.'

'I can and I will,' Daniel said in a voice that continued to bring reassurance and calm to Libby. 'I'll speak with Walter immediately.'

'But I'm family,' Maxwell muttered. 'He won't throw me off. He'll throw you two off for treating me this way.'

'I don't think so, buddy. You're a risk to every woman on the ship and I'm not going to allow that risk to remain on board.'

The first mate and two stewards arrived within minutes to find Daniel still restraining Maxwell.

'There's always one who overdoes the alcohol and oversteps the mark,' the slightly taller of the well-built trio said. 'We can take it from here. I assume you'll be speaking with the captain or Sir Walter. This guy's probably family so it might be difficult to drop him off at the next port. If they keep him on board we'll just have him followed when he's out of his cabin.'

'I don't care who he is, he's getting off this vessel, no ifs, no buts about that. He's gone.'

Thwarted in his attempt to seduce Libby, and no doubt feeling humiliated by the ease with which Daniel had grappled him to the floor, the man had ceased struggling. He lay in a crumpled heap with Daniel clearly in control. But it was not lost on Libby that without Daniel it could have ended very differently.

It could have ended very badly.

As the door closed, leaving them alone, Daniel turned to Libby and looked at her for the longest moment before he spoke. His blue eyes were piercing her soul with the intensity of his gaze. It was as unnerving as it was comforting.

'Are you all right, Libby?' he finally asked in a voice that was strong and masculine but coloured with layers of warmth and tenderness.

His concern seemed genuine and his expression was serious but Libby could not answer for a moment. She was once again seeing Daniel and the man she had been so very close to, not the man she had wanted to forget. His eyes were drawing her in just as they had in the past. They were like two brilliant blue crystals but they were far from cold. And, against her will, their warmth was thawing her heart.

'I'm…fine,' she managed to say, with so many mixed emotions colouring every thought. His eyes looked so much like her precious son's that it caught her breath.

'I'm not so sure,' he replied and crossed the room, gently pulling her into his arms.

Libby wanted to fight him, she wanted to pull away but she couldn't. She fell into his embrace. Into the warmth of his chest and the strength of his arms around her. It was everything she needed at that moment. The past was gone and the future didn't matter. Libby just wanted to remain in the comfort of Daniel's arms for as long as she could.

* * *

There was a knock on the open door and they both turned to see Walter standing there with the chief stewardess beside him. Daniel dropped his arms and Libby stepped back, immediately creating space between them.

'I heard what happened, Libby,' Walter began. 'I'm so sorry, my dear. Are you all right?'

'I'm… I'm fine, thank you.' Her voice quavered from the reality of what had almost happened with Maxwell… and the embrace she had shared with Daniel.

'It appears you're fine because of our doctor.'

'Yes.' Libby nodded and looked fleetingly at Daniel. He was staring back at her, his concern for her evident in his expression. Her heart was torn with so many emotions. He had come to her rescue despite the way she had spoken to him the day before. Despite the way she had pushed him away.

'You're a strong woman, Libby,' Walter continued. 'I know that first hand but what you just faced is not something to brush off lightly. Maxwell is leaving the yacht tomorrow morning. The captain has called the coastguard and they're picking him up first thing and what they do with him, frankly, I don't care. For what he just did, I'd drop him in the middle of the ocean, to be honest, if I could get away with it. I've never liked him but he married his way into the family years ago and we've never been able to shake him. Well, we have now. And for good.'

'Thank you, Walter.'

'Don't thank me, Libby, thank Daniel. He was your knight in shining armour, rushing to your rescue, and it's a good thing he did,' Walter interjected. 'Now, you need to have a good rest in your cabin or on deck. You do not have to fuss over me for the rest of the day. I've told the steward to lock Maxwell in his cabin and if he tries to leave they can find a broom closet. I don't care where they damn well put him. They could strap him to a jet-ski for all I care.

'We'll let him sleep off the booze in preparation for his exit from the yacht, and the family, tomorrow. I'll be glad to see the back of him. He's been a leach for years but now he's crossed the line. I'm just so very sorry he stayed long enough to do this to you.'

'It wasn't your fault; no one could have known.'

'While that may be true, my dear, I'm going to try to make it up to you by having your belongings brought up to one of the empty suites on this deck.'

'There's no need, really.'

'Yes, there absolutely is a need,' Walter argued. 'That excuse for a man tried to assault you and would have succeeded if it wasn't for Daniel. The suite is adjacent to Daniel's and I think it might be reassuring for you to have him close by.'

With that, Walter and the chief stewardess left the cabin.

The suite next to Daniel's cabin? Libby wasn't sure that was such a good idea. For anyone.

'I'm truly sorry that happened…' Daniel began.

'You have nothing to apologise for,' Libby cut in, never having expected to say those words to him. 'I… I don't know what I would have done if you hadn't arrived.'

'Don't think about it, Libby. It's over and he's gone. For good, so you can relax for the rest of the journey knowing you don't have to look over your shoulder.'

Libby drew in a deep breath in an effort to still her nerves—about the attack and about being in the arms of her saviour. Both were playing on her mind.

'But how did you get here so quickly?' she asked with a curious expression on her face.

'I was just outside the cabin.'

'From when he arrived?'

'A minute or two afterwards,' Daniel told her, nodding his head and running his fingers through his hair. 'I know how you feel about me, Libby, and your determination not to spend time with me, and I don't blame you. I do understand. But I'd previously seen the jerk being incredibly disrespectful to the female crew members. He looked like potential trouble.

'I know the type too well. Too much sun and too much alcohol. I was going to raise the matter with Walter and the captain tonight but when I heard he was heading to see you with a medical condition I followed him and waited nearby. It's not that I don't trust in your ability to manage a situation as a nurse, Libby. Believe me, I've witnessed how you handle the most volatile situations in the ER but this was different. You were alone in a cabin and I feared it could go very wrong.'

Libby said nothing. Her anxiety was abating by the moment and, against her better judgement, her desire to once again be in Daniel's strong arms was growing by the second.

'When you raised your voice, I knew that, despite your rules, I had no choice but to step in.'

Libby looked at him sheepishly and in a way she had not expected to ever again. He was not the man who had broken her heart, he was her handsome protector.

'I'm glad you did,' she said softly.

Daniel looked at her in silence for the longest time and she felt her heart melting. All the feelings she had buried were starting to resurface and she wasn't sure how to fight them. Or if she even wanted to try. The urge to feel his strong arms around her again was overwhelming. And unexpected. Libby suddenly saw Daniel for the man she had fallen in love with all those years ago. She was looking at the man who had captured her heart. And the way he was looking at her at that moment made her wonder if perhaps he had not forgotten what they had shared either. There were questions that needed answering…but did she want to know the answers now? They had a week to unpack the past. It was a silly way to think but her heart was leading her thoughts.

She was so confused at that moment. Adrenalin was still surging through her body, along with something else. A warm feeling. A feeling of safety. A feeling of something she couldn't define.

But she liked it and realised she'd missed that feeling.

And she'd missed him.

CHAPTER EIGHT

DANIEL STOOD LOOKING at Libby. He wanted her with every fibre of his being. He wanted to pull her back into his arms and carry her to his bed. He wanted to make love to her more than anything he had ever wanted. But he couldn't. It wasn't right for so many reasons. She was vulnerable. And he knew whatever they would share would only be for a few days. It couldn't be for ever. And Libby deserved better than that.

Libby deserved a forever man. And he could never be that. He had to step back. He had to walk away again but this time in the light of day and before he lost the ability to do it a second time.

'As long as you're okay, I should go,' Daniel said abruptly, pulling them both back to reality.

As he stepped away he fought the need to taste the sweetness of her mouth. It was a battle he had to win against his own desire for the woman so close to him he could smell the soft scent of her skin. He would recognise that scent anywhere. It was Libby's scent. It had been in his memory for the longest time.

But they could never be that close again.

No matter how much he wanted to be with Libby, Daniel knew he couldn't. That would be taking advantage of the situation. Taking advantage of her need to feel comforted after what she had just faced. Daniel knew that walking away all those years ago had been cruel but he believed his reasons had made it justified. Doing it again would be unforgivable.

He had to accept that being together wasn't in the stars for them. Fate had very different ideas for his future and he knew he cared for Libby too much to put her through what lay ahead for him. He wished with all his heart that the life ahead for him was a simple one that could include the most beautiful, kind, wonderful redhead he had ever met, but it couldn't.

His life would play out very differently from the one she deserved.

As he made his way to the door, he turned back to her. 'I'm sorry for what happened today, Libby. And, trust me, he will be gone in the morning. You'll never see his face again.'

Libby was taken aback. Daniel had just pushed her away. It was just as she had asked but that had been before she had fallen into his arms again. Before she had realised that she loved that feeling.

And wanted more.

Her heart sank a little. Her knight in shining armour was just passing through. Yet again. She felt so stupid for getting her hopes up and letting her heart be tempted, if only for a moment, toward the path that had broken it so completely all those years ago.

Biting the inside of her cheek, Libby watched Daniel leave the cabin and close the door behind him. And close the door on any chance for them, she told herself.

She would never be that stupid again. Clearly, she meant nothing to him or he would not have behaved so dismissively. He would not have walked away, leaving her standing there like a stranger he had rescued. Like any other colleague, not a woman who had fallen in love with him. Who had slept with him, no matter how long ago it might have been.

Libby couldn't help but wonder why the universe had brought Daniel back into her life for only a few days. Perhaps it was to let her know he was not the right man for her. To remind her of what he had done and could do again.

To remind her that she was a strong woman, a mother and a nurse, and that was all she needed to be. She didn't need Daniel Dimosa and now she had five days to prove that to herself.

And to work out exactly what sort of man he really was. And if there would be a place in her son's life for him.

Daniel had no choice but to put distance between them. He was close to losing the ability to see reason and surrendering to his desire to pull Libby to him and tell her everything. Tell her that he hadn't wanted to leave her all those years ago. Tell her why he'd had to go but how much he wished he'd never left. But he couldn't do any of that so keeping her at bay was his only defence.

Sombrely he walked back to his cabin and shut the door. He needed to shut his heart on Libby. He went into the bathroom and washed his face with cold water. Staring into the mirror as he patted his skin dry with a hand towel, he knew he was in trouble. Libby McDonald was still in his heart and now she was within reach. And tonight she would be even closer. Her cabin would be right next to his. She would be lying in her bed with only a thin wall between them. A wall he would gladly break down, if only he could.

Stepping away from the mirror, he crossed to the open

doors of his balcony. Looking out across the still blue water, all he could see was Libby's beautiful face.

He was struggling to understand why the world had brought them together, only to tear them apart.

That night, as he lay awake in his bed, Daniel thought back to the day he had first laid eyes on Libby at the Northern Bay General Hospital in San Francisco. With a short-term contract as head of ER, Daniel had instantly been taken by the beauty of the redheaded nurse who had efficiently organised everyone and everything in sight. As she'd rushed from one bay to the next, directing paramedics and nurses alike, he'd also seen the sweetness of her face and, as he'd drawn closer, the kindness in her eyes. The way she had engaged with the anxious patients and their loved ones was nothing quite like he had witnessed before.

The days had become weeks and as he'd spent more time working closely with Libby in ER, the more and more he'd come to appreciate her extraordinary ability as a nurse. She'd managed the younger nurses as if she had been doing it for decades yet he'd felt sure she was only in her late twenties. And the desire to impart knowledge and give guidance along the way to the young nurses and the medical students had had her staying back some days long after her shift had ended. She'd swept them up on a journey with her in the love she had for nursing.

Libby was born to have a career in medicine, he'd soon realised. She was a natural and, against his better judgement, and everything he had told himself and the rules he had lived by, he'd soon felt himself falling for her. When they'd worked the same shift in ER she had pre-empted his needs and together they'd managed the most difficult cases, some with wonderful outcomes, others ending in tragedy, but they had done it in a way he had never experienced before. And she'd brought comfort to every situation.

Daniel rolled over in bed and stared at the ceiling as his mind travelled back to the night they had crossed the line. The night he had reached out for her not as a colleague but as a lover.

It had been the most wonderful evening, a hospital fundraiser with an Easter theme. There had been oversized glitter-covered eggs in floral arrangements on every one of the one hundred and fifty tables, and six-foot stuffed rabbits placed at the entrance dressed in waistcoats and top hats. Daniel had worn a tuxedo as it had been a black-tie affair. The women had worn glamorous floor-length gowns, adorned with jewels, some real and some costume, and the men were a sea of black suits.

But Daniel had seen none of it once Libby had arrived. His breath had been taken away as she'd walked into the room wearing the most stunning white sequined gown. As she'd turned to greet another guest, his eyes had roamed the bare curve of her back. Her red hair had been swept to one side and as she'd caught him staring at her, she'd smiled the most beautiful smile back at him. Immediately, he'd realised she was not only the most gorgeous woman in the world, and without doubt the most amazing nurse, she was dangerously close to being the love of his life.

He'd noticed they were seated on opposite sides of the same table so he had politely, and with the other guests' approval, rearranged the seating to be next to her. They'd chatted all night about everything and anything. And then Daniel had asked her to dance.

It had been a dance like no other. As he'd taken Libby in his arms, her body had moulded to his, the softness of her perfume filling his senses. Her hair had brushed against his face and when she'd laughed and rested her head ever so lightly on his shoulder, he'd never wanted the night to end.

It had been after midnight when the band finished and their last dance had come to an end. Daniel had offered to drive Libby home and she'd accepted, with a smile that had lit up the room and his heart. When he'd walked her to the door, he leaned in to kiss her goodnight on the cheek but his lips had moved to find hers in the porchlight. Passion had overtaken them both and she'd invited him inside.

It had been the most wonderful night. He would never forget it but he would always regret it too. He should not have crossed the line.

With only a sheet covering his body, Daniel turned and stared out to sea. The curtains were open as they always were and the moonlight was dancing on the gently rolling black waves, painting them silver. Daniel had seen it many times before but tonight was different. Tonight he knew that Libby could be looking at the same darkened horizon from the window in the suite next to his.

The next morning, he woke with a resolve to keep his promise to himself and his family, no matter how difficult it might be. He was returning to Chezlovinka in four days. He could not complicate it further, neither would he ever hurt Libby again. There was a divide between them that he could never again cross. This time he could not afford to get swept up in his feelings.

Libby had finished breakfast when he arrived on deck, looking for her. He had taken a call from the chief stewardess when he'd stepped from the shower about a crew member who was unwell.

'Good morning, Libby.'

She turned and smiled a half-smile in his direction. 'Good morning, Daniel.'

He wanted to ask if she had slept well but decided to stay away from any personal conversation and keep it about work only. 'I hope you can put yesterday behind you. The coastguard picked up Maxwell early this morning.'

Libby nodded. 'Good to hear.' Her reply was without emotion and it made Daniel wonder what she might be thinking, but he knew he had no right to ask.

'If it's okay with you, we need to make a crew cabin call.'

'Why do you need me?' she asked curtly as she placed her plate back on the end of the buffet with others that had been used by guests.

'It's a young woman. She sounds a little distressed and is complaining of gastro symptoms. I hope to hell it's not, because we know that can spread through the ship very quickly. Her symptoms do sound vague but I'm also hoping it's not appendicitis. I would ordinarily go alone, as it's nothing I can't manage, but she asked for a female doctor. When we explained that wasn't possible, she asked for you to attend with me.'

'That's fine. Whatever she wants,' Libby replied matter-of-factly.

He suspected it was not her ideal situation, but she was showing him professional courtesy and he appreciated that.

'Thank you, Libby. I've got my bag with extra gloves, masks and a couple of disposable gowns just in case it is gastroenteritis,' he told her as he began walking in the direction of the glass elevator.

'If it is, how do you plan on controlling that on board?' Libby asked as she followed him.

'If I consider it a risk, I'll take away her swipe card and secure the cabin. If she has a cabin buddy we will keep an eye on them too and quarantine her in another cabin if possible. I don't like to do it but sometimes it's necessary even on a yacht this size. There's still four days' cruising to go and it would be unfair to the other passengers and particularly nasty for Walter.'

'Let me take that,' she said, reaching for the small bag. Her soft skin brushed against his as her fingers took the handle. His heart unexpectedly began racing as he had not been expecting her touch.

Libby suddenly released hold of the bag and stepped away from the elevator door. Neither made eye contact but each automatically created a distance between them. Daniel's reaction reaffirmed to him that it was going to be the most challenging four days of his life. He was still unsure how Libby felt but he realised it was best he didn't know.

They reached the cabin within a few minutes and Daniel checked his pager.

'The young woman's name is Alexandra and she just confirmed that she's been vomiting for two days now.'

Libby pulled from her bag the two disposable gowns, masks and a pair of gloves for each of them, which they immediately donned before knocking. Daniel had a swipe card that opened every one of the ship's cabins in case of an emergency.

'Come in,' a very drained and weary female voice called out.

Daniel and Libby stepped inside the tiny cabin with no windows. It was on the lowest deck and not too far from Libby's original cabin. Alexandra, still dressed in pink pyjamas, was sitting on a chair with her head resting in her hands. Her complexion was drained of any hint of colour.

'Hello, I'm Dr Dimosa and this is Nurse McDonald but please call us Daniel and Libby,' Daniel said, then looked at Libby for approval.

It was after the fact, but Libby nodded her agreement; she was happy to use her less formal first name and with what they were facing she wasn't overly fussed whatever they called her.

'I'm Alex,' the woman said in a strained voice and little energy behind her words. 'I've seen you both around but I didn't know what you did. I'm a cleaner. I do some galley work now and then but mainly clean the suites.'

'Please tell us what's happening and how you're feeling now,' Daniel said.

'I've been throwing up for two days and I'm not sure if it's something I ate or sea sickness but whatever it is I feel dreadful.'

'When did this start? And what were your initial symptoms?' Daniel continued, as he reached back to find Libby was already holding the digital thermometer he wanted. He couldn't help but smile to himself. Naturally she had known what he would be needing next; she always had.

'It was about two days ago, when I woke up. I thought it was something I ate because I felt a bit queasy,' the woman began.

Daniel rested the thermometer gently inside the woman's ear and it quickly beeped the reading. 'Thirty-six point five,' he reported to Libby, who was already taking notes. 'You don't have a temperature. Not even a low-grade fever.'

'Is that good? What does it mean?'

'It means your body's not fighting a bacterium or virus so there must be another reason for the nausea,' he said as he turned to find Libby reaching for the thermometer, discarding the disposable cap, wiping the handle clean with antibacterial wipes and returning it to the medical bag. She was her ever efficient self.

'But what can you give me to make it stop? I've been

vomiting for hours and my stomach hurts,' the woman asked. 'And I want to get back to work.'

'Before I give you anything, I would like to know what we are dealing with.'

'I feel like death warmed up again, but…' she paused as she made her way to the bunk and lay down, pulling the covers up to her chin protectively '…it did improve both days after lunch.'

'So the nausea stopped completely after lunchtime?'

'Yes, I had some dry toast and then by dinnertime I was fine and then it started again the next morning. Last night I was fine again and I ate a good dinner and could work but now today it's back,' she said with her eyes starting to close. 'I'm exhausted with all of this throwing up. Is it seasickness? I've never worked on a boat before.'

'No, Alexandra, I don't think so.'

'Then what is it?' she mumbled wearily, her blue eyes as pale and drawn as her skin.

'Your lack of fever and the transient nausea are leading me to believe it might be a case of morning sickness…'

'Morning sickness?' The young woman almost yelled her response as she sat bolt upright. 'Are you telling me I'm pregnant?'

Libby silently agreed with Daniel's diagnosis. While it wasn't how she had felt when she'd been pregnant, it was a common symptom during the first trimester of pregnancy. For her entire pregnancy she had been overtaken by cravings for food she couldn't ordinarily stomach and, once she had given birth, never ate again.

'I'm putting it forward as a possibility,' he said calmly. 'We would need to confirm with a pregnancy test and then bloodwork.'

'I can't be pregnant. It's not possible,' she said, shaking her head as she slumped back against the pillows.

'You haven't had sex in the last month?'

Alexandra looked down at her hands, they were trembling slightly in her lap.

'Or months,' Daniel added. 'If you are pregnant, you may have conceived a few months ago and be further along in the pregnancy.'

'This is a mess,' she said, turning back to face Daniel and Libby with tears welling in her eyes. 'I haven't had a period in over eight weeks but I thought it was the stress of the separation. I left my husband six weeks ago.'

'I'm sorry,' Daniel and Libby said simultaneously.

Libby leaned in and instinctively put her arm around the young woman to comfort her.

'We were told we couldn't have children naturally—' Alexandra continued.

'Again,' Daniel cut in as he looked at the woman with compassion, 'I'm not saying that you are pregnant but it's something we need to consider as the symptoms do align.'

'I can't believe it,' she returned, as she began shaking her head again. 'If it's true, the timing couldn't be worse. I just secured the job with Sir Walter and I really need to keep it. I'm employed to clean the yacht when he cruises and look after his house in Miami the rest of the time. He's a good boss and I need the money to pay rent now that I'm not living with my husband.'

Daniel nodded. 'Walter is a good man, Alex, and I can have a word with him once we know if you're pregnant and see what sort of arrangement can be made for maternity leave. Do you have any other support at home?'

Libby pulled her arm away slowly and turned her attention to the medical bag nearby. She wondered if there was a pregnancy test inside. It was a long shot but if there was one on board it would either confirm or negate the pregnancy diagnosis and ensure any decisions made by Alexandra were based on fact.

'No, my mother and father passed away in an accident in Mexico three years ago. It was just my husband and me and now…now it's just me.'

Libby was surprised to find a two-window pregnancy test. While it was what she wanted, it wasn't what was normally in a medical bag—but, then, she surmised that a medical bag on a cruise ship was not a regular medical bag. She checked the date then held it up for Daniel, her eyes signalling her intention to suggest Alex take the test. He nodded his response.

'There's a pregnancy test here,' Libby announced in a low and equally calm voice. 'Would you like to go to the bathroom and find out one way or another? As Daniel said, you'll need bloods when you return to shore but these over-the-counter pregnancy tests become more accurate all the time.'

'How does it work?'

'It will detect the hormone chorionic gonadotropin. When an egg's fertilised and attaches to your uterine wall, the placenta begins to form and produces this hormone, and it appears in your bloodstream and your urine. As you get further along in pregnancy, the hormone levels rise more rapidly, doubling every couple of days. That's why if the test is positive, you'll need to see your obstetrician in the next week or so to gauge how far along you are in your pregnancy.'

The young woman reached in silence to take the test kit from Libby and then swung her feet around and slowly moved to stand up. She was still visibly weak so Libby held her arm as she made her way to the bathroom.

'Do you know what to do?' Libby asked. 'It's a two-window test so two lines indicate positive and a single line is negative. But, remember, while the positive result is generally accurate, the negative may not be definite and if the symptoms continue you may want to visit your GP for bloodwork.'

'I've done this too many times before and each time it's been negative and that never changed with a blood test,' she said as she stepped inside the tiny bathroom.

'We're nearby, if you need us,' Libby said without making any further comment as she closed the bathroom door.

Libby was distracted thinking about the anxiety surging through Alex behind the small bathroom door. She knew and understood it first-hand. For Libby it was a lived experience, and one she would never forget. She reached for her locket and held it in her gloved hand, wondering if in the not-too-distant future Alex would be holding a much-loved child in her arms.

She looked over at Daniel and felt a pang of guilt. He had no idea what she'd been through on her own. Part of her was still angry and part of her felt sad for him that he had not been able to share the joy of the little boy who was his son.

If he had known, perhaps he still would have stayed away. Perhaps he would have returned, not for her but for his son.

'If she's pregnant,' Daniel suddenly said, breaking her thoughts and completely unaware of the enormous decision weighing heavily on her mind, 'Alexandra's nausea might be temporary with any luck, and she might be a mother-to-be who has cravings more than sickness. My mother was apparently like that when she was pregnant with me. Lived on olives, grilled fish and homemade bread for months.'

Libby's eyes grew wide. She couldn't believe what Daniel was telling her. He was describing exactly her pregnancy diet with Billy.

The door opened tentatively and Alex stood there crying, her body visibly shaking, with the test in her hand.

'There are two lines. I'm pregnant. I'm actually going to be a mother,' she said through tears. 'I'm so happy and so sad and so confused. It's all I ever wanted and now I'm not sure I can do it. Not alone.'

Libby, still reeling a little from Daniel's story, crossed to Alexandra and took her arm to lead her back to the chair. 'Sit down and catch your breath. It's a lot to take in. Particularly when it's unexpected.'

'I'm… I'm happy. I'm actually so happy but I'm not sure what to do. It's all so surreal to me and part of me still can't believe it. We went through three rounds of IVF and three negative pregnancy tests and my husband said he couldn't go through it again.

'It wasn't just the cost. The devastation of the last negative test made me go a little crazy. I wanted a baby so much and my husband shut the door on the idea. He said the hormones I had to take made me so sick and he didn't want me to go through that again. He said he loved me too much to do that but his decision ripped us apart. I wanted to try just one more time. I knew he would be the best father and we would be so happy. With no parents, a family of our own meant the world to me. But he wouldn't. He said it wasn't meant to be.'

'I understand, and I might be out of line here,' Libby began, 'but your husband sounds like a very caring man who made that decision from concern for you.'

'I know. I still love him, I always will, but…we did nothing but argue and then I went into my shell and shut him out because I wanted a baby so badly.'

'And now that's become a reality,' Daniel said, rubbing his chin. 'While it's unexpected, I'd say it's a great outcome.'

'But what if I lose the baby? What would happen? I

would go completely crazy and I can't put him through that,' she said as she moved to the bed and curled up into a foetal position, pulling the covers over her. 'I can't do that to him, I can't.'

'It looks like we're both at risk of being out of line,' Daniel started, 'but I think you might be selling your husband short on this one. There's no indication that you'll miscarry, so if you don't tell your husband he will have missed the joy of these months. The joy of finding out he's going to be a father. That would be a very special time for him. Don't take that away from him. My advice, both professionally and as a man, would be to let him know.'

'But what if something goes wrong with the pregnancy?'

'You're jumping to the worst-case scenario,' Daniel said as he drew closer and looked intently at Alexandra. 'As I said, unless the obstetrician has identified an issue and told you there would be a risk, you should not be overly concerned. You're young and appear otherwise healthy so make sure you see your GP and obstetrician and start an antenatal plan, and seriously take this time to consider bringing your husband up to speed with the fact he's going to be a father. Give him the chance to step up. I'm not a counsellor, but you said you still love him so at least give him the chance to tell you and your baby the same thing.'

Libby felt a lump rising in her throat with every word that slipped from Daniel's lips. The previous pang of guilt threatened to become a tsunami of regret.

Her mind was spinning and her stomach churning in a way they never had before.

She and Alex each had a huge decision to make.

But Libby had only five more days before the opportunity might be gone for ever.

CHAPTER NINE

LIBBY SPENT THE following days concentrating on Walter. He didn't like any fuss, so she caught up with him after he had enjoyed his breakfast on the deck, after lunch and then just before he retired to his luxurious cabin for the night, checking his blood pressure and his wound. Despite the less than healthy diet, her patient was progressing very well. The wound was healing nicely and his blood pressure was back within normal limits. The sea air certainly agreed with him.

When she wasn't with Walter, she returned to the quiet of her suite to call home and check in with Billy and her parents—and more importantly avoid seeing Daniel. She had done some soul searching after hearing Daniel speak openly and honestly to Alex about her need to tell her husband about her pregnancy. It wasn't a decision she was making in haste, the way she had done the night Daniel had driven her home. She was going to tell Daniel that he had a son.

Her decision was born from thinking hard about the words Daniel had imparted to Alex, both as a doctor and as a man, and knowing in her heart they were true. Libby didn't want to keep Daniel from his son to punish him. With hand on heart, she knew her immediate reaction had been to protect Billy but she had to trust that in letting

Daniel know, whatever the outcome she had not prevented Billy from having the opportunity to know his father.

Now it would be up to Daniel whether he wanted to take on that role. And what that role in Billy's life might look like in the coming years.

The time alone in her cabin was giving Libby the space she needed to think about everything.

She could not be sure that Daniel would not leave Billy the way he had left her four years ago, without an explanation and with no way to contact him, but it was a chance she had to take. She just had to get the timing right. If he reacted badly and they still had a few days at sea, it would not be fair on Walter and the rest of the passengers. Libby decided she would tell him the night before they docked. It would give her sufficient time to tell him everything, answer his questions, and then he could process his feelings about it alone, not trapped on the yacht surrounded by a group of strangers.

Libby had no reason to socialise too much. Georgie was busy with preparations for the upcoming engagement party and the day-to-day running of the galley. It was busier than she had thought so they both caught up every evening for half an hour to chat and then head to bed early. That was the time when Libby called home because there was a time difference.

She missed Billy, Bradley and her parents. She had no intention of raising the fact that Daniel was on the yacht to either Bradley or her parents as she didn't want to be swayed by their bias. They would naturally want to protect both her and Billy and none of them had known Daniel. Not the man she'd fallen in love with, at least. They had only known him as the cad who had broken her heart. So their opinion no doubt would not favour Daniel.

Libby headed down to see Walter on the morning they

docked at Martinique. She needed to know if Walter intended to go ashore with his guests. If so, she would accompany him; if not, she would remain on the yacht and head to her cabin until his next medical check was due.

'Are you heading to the island today, Walter?'

'I've done it more times than I care to count,' he told Libby as she packed away the blood pressure monitor and stethoscope and sat down beside him. 'And between you and me, I could do with some peace and quiet with that lot gone for a few hours.'

Libby smiled, happy that she could just relax.

'How's my ticker doing anyway?' he asked. 'Is sacrificing my whisky and cigars paying dividends?'

'Absolutely. Your blood pressure is perfect and your scar is healing so well you'll hardly notice it when you're sunbathing on your next cruise.'

'My next cruise will be without those monkeys,' Walter scoffed as he looked in the direction of the guests disembarking the yacht. 'The extended family on Contessa's side are the worst. They're noisy, obnoxious and for the most part quite ungrateful…not to mention the clothing. I loved my wife; she was a beautiful, stylish woman, not unlike Grace Kelly, but her family are quite a different matter altogether. They have the most terrible dress sense. Abominable is more to the point. I know she wasn't adopted but I've always wondered where she fitted in. It's fortunate that I met Contessa first; if I'd met them I might have run in another direction.'

Libby bit the inside of her cheek so she didn't laugh as she watched the dozen or so family members heading ashore. She had to agree that their clothing was very loud and there were myriad patterns with a Hawaiian feel to them. She could only imagine what Bradley would have said.

'I do love my side of the family, of course,' he continued. 'My brother and his wife passed away a few years back now but they had the most gorgeous daughter, Sophia. She is the image of her mother and since Contessa and I were not blessed with children of our own, we unofficially adopted her when she was seventeen and she came to live with us for a little while until she went to college.

'As I said, she is the most perfect creature ever created and I love to spoil her whenever I can, which is why I'm throwing her this party. She's all grown up now—twenty-nine and an investment banker. She looks more like a model but she has a heart of gold and a mind like a steel trap. I think that's why we get on so well.'

'You modelled too?' Libby asked with a cheeky smile.

'I like you. You're funny. My side of the family will like you too; they're all flying in to San Lucia tomorrow. Should be a splendid night and I'm so excited to be seeing Sophia again. She did visit me in hospital but it was a whirlwind trip on her way to France to meet her fiancé's parents.'

'I'm sure she'll be excited to see you too.'

'You're very kind, Libby,' he said with a smile as he reached for his freshly squeezed juice. 'Tell me about your family. Do you have any shockers like the ones who just headed off to scare the locals?'

Libby laughed. 'My family is a little quieter. I adore them and I'm their only child,' she said, and without thinking she reached for her locket and held it in her hand as she spoke. 'My mother and father live quite close to my home in a suburb in San Francisco.'

'I think being close to your parents is lovely. It doesn't happen much nowadays. Everyone is on the go and travelling all over the world for work, never in one place for too long.'

'My parents are both retired and rarely travel, and being a single mother it's wonderful having them there to help out…' Libby stopped in mid-sentence. She hadn't meant the words to slip out and wished she could take them back. She'd been so careful not to mention Billy for five days and now she had just told him everything. Well, almost everything.

'Oh, you're a mother?'

She shifted in her seat uncomfortably but knew it was too late. Trying to hide the fact would only make it worse. 'Yes, I have a son.'

'Tell me more. How old is he and what's his name?'

'Billy…he's just turned three,' she managed to tell him, all the while wishing she had never opened up about her personal life.

'Just turned three… Hey, when was his birthday?'

'Last week, on the tenth of January.'

'That's three days after my birthday. He must be a lovely little chap.' He chuckled, then leaning in he whispered, 'You know, I was told by my mother that I was an Easter Bunny surprise. Of course, I worked out as I grew up that meant I was the result of a night of lovemaking in April after perhaps too many chocolates and champagne for my mother and more than likely a Guinness or two for my father.'

Libby froze. She couldn't laugh along with Walter. She swallowed as she remembered the Easter fundraiser the night Daniel had driven her home. There had been no chocolates or Guinness but there had definitely been a night of lovemaking that April. She felt heat rushing to her cheeks. She had tried to push the night from her memory but now it was coming back to her at lightning speed.

'It's lovely to know a little more about you, Libby,' he said, putting the glass down again, to her relief completely unaware of her reaction to the conversation. He reached for a scone. 'But I'm going to cut our chat short because you are too young to stay on board with an old man who you just confirmed is as fit as a Mallee bull…'

'A Mallee bull?' Libby asked with a quizzical look. Her mind was spinning with what she had confessed and now they were talking about bulls.

'It's Australian slang for healthy. Comes from the Mallee region in Victoria, where there are a lot of cattle and where I invested in a sheep station. They can be an odd bunch in the land Down Under, and they use funny terms like that. I've picked up one or two on my travels there.'

'I never heard it before. I've learned something today.'

'And you'll learn more by heading ashore and exploring the island. Georgie told me you haven't travelled much so don't waste this time sitting with me when you can enjoy life in the Caribbean.'

Libby was still trying to calm her nerves. She had never expected their conversation to be so revealing. It was unexpected and she hoped it would not complicate her plans to tell Daniel about Billy in a few days. 'Thank you, Walter, but I'm very happy to stay on board today.'

'Hogwash,' he retorted. 'I've arranged company for you for the day, so there's no point arguing.'

'You've asked Georgie to go with me?'

'No, my dear,' Walter replied. 'She's up to her neck making an engagement cake for tomorrow night's party, so I asked Daniel. He was quick off the mark to accept the invitation and he should be here any minute.'

Libby suddenly felt her heart pick up speed. She had hoped to avoid Daniel for the next few days until she was ready to confess everything.

'Goodness, you suddenly look flushed, my dear. Let me

pour you a glass of water,' Walter said as he reached for the pitcher of chilled water and filled a glass. 'Take this.'

Libby accepted the glass and drank the water quickly. 'Thank you. I'm sorry about that. I don't think I had enough fluids today,' she lied. She had no choice. She could not tell Walter that the thought of spending the day with Daniel was not what she wanted or needed.

'Make sure you take a bottle of water with you today, young lady. Can't have my nurse unwell on the island. Daniel might have to carry you back on board,' he said with a laugh.

Libby heard footsteps and turned her head slowly to see Daniel approaching from the other end of the deck. He was wearing a white T-shirt and beige shorts. His tanned feet were slipped inside dark-coloured espadrilles and he had a baseball cap covering his hair. He was dressed for a day on the island. And he looked so very handsome. Just as she knew Billy would one day.

Libby quickly climbed to her feet. She needed a few moments to calm her nerves. Her thoughts were racing and she felt emotionally dishevelled. Time alone together was definitely not in her plans.

'I'll go and change into something more suitable,' she told Walter, unsure of exactly what she intended to do but she knew if she could find an excuse not to go, she would. 'Please let Daniel know I'll be back as soon as I can.'

With that, Libby made her way to the glass elevator without passing Daniel. Ordinarily she would take the spiral staircase to the next deck but that would mean crossing paths with him.

As she stood waiting for the glass doors to open, she heard Walter call out cheerily, 'Good morning, Daniel. I can see you're all ready for your island date with Libby.'

* * *

Libby's hand began shaking as she pressed the call button again. *A date?* Was that just Walter's perception or was there any possibility that Daniel saw it that way too? She wished more than ever that she had never accepted the assignment to care for Walter. She would never have seen Daniel again and her life would not once again have been turned upside down by him. Her emotions were firmly strapped in on the roller-coaster and she couldn't escape.

The doors opened and she stepped inside and turned to see Daniel looking in her direction. Her heart began racing again. While she intended to go through with her decision to tell him about Billy, she was growing more concerned by the minute that her feelings for him were unfortunately still very real. The way her heart skipped a beat when his hand accidentally brushed against hers, how she'd felt so safe in his arms after the horrible situation with Maxwell, and finally seeing him appear on the deck ready for their *date*.

All of it was telling her that she was at risk of losing her heart to the man again if she didn't take control of her feelings and the reality of the situation. Her focus had to be on letting Daniel know about Billy in the right way and at the right time, and establishing a relationship with him that would allow him to be in Billy's life if he chose to do so. Full stop. Nothing more. Nothing romantic. No risk to her heart. None at all.

Trying her best to keep everything in perspective and on the task at hand, Libby changed into something more suitable for sightseeing. She chose a floral summer dress that skimmed her knees and flat white sandals. With a straw hat in her hand and a cross-body purse holding the few things she would need, she made her way to the door, knowing the day ahead would be challenging but an important part of telling him about Billy.

As she descended the highly polished oak staircase to the deck again, she decided the time she would be spending on the island with Daniel was purely an opportunity to find out more about him. Perhaps he had changed. Her stomach churned a little; she couldn't deny she was worried that he would raise the topic of their past and that it would hurt her to hear the truth. Or perhaps he would keep everything close to his chest and still stand behind the only explanation she had heard so far: *it was complicated*.

Had it just been a one-night stand that she had mistaken for more? Had Daniel been planning on leaving the hospital anyway and had assumed she knew? There were so many questions but she wasn't going there. The day was all about Billy. Libby needed to know enough about Daniel to know she was right in her decision to open up her life and that of her son to the man who had broken her heart. She had to make sure, as best she could, that he wouldn't break Billy's heart too.

'Ahh, there you are,' Walter said with a smile as Libby drew closer. 'You were quicker changing than my wife ever was. Must be the nurse in you. Always efficient and, I must say, looking very pretty.'

'Thank you, Walter,' Libby replied, not looking in Daniel's direction.

'I agree,' Daniel said, thinking that she looked far more than just pretty. He thought she looked stunningly beautiful. Just as she always had. Just as he had remembered her over the years.

'Then off you two go. Make the most of this beautiful weather and don't worry about me. You have your pager and I have the captain, the chief stewardess and a whole crew, so I'm well covered. And as a bonus I have a day of peace without those blessed, noisy folk who drive me to drink!'

Daniel nodded and Libby smiled a half-smile before they turned and made their way to the gangway. Libby held on tightly to the railing and Daniel suspected the rocking of the yacht in the shallower water made her a little nervous of falling into the marina. She didn't have to worry, he thought. He would be there to catch her for the next few days. In fact, if the world had been a different place, and he'd had any control of the future, he would always be there to catch her…in his arms.

'What would you like to do, Libby, shopping, sightseeing or an early lunch?'

Libby looked at her watch. 'Lunch sounds lovely.'

Daniel looked around. It wasn't his first time on the island and he had a favourite street market he wanted to show Libby that wasn't too far away so they could be back if there was any emergency on the yacht.

'This way,' he said, and began walking past the street vendors selling fresh fish and produce. He watched as Libby looked around, her eyes wide as she took in the sights and smells of the colourful French Caribbean island. 'It's not too far.'

It took all of Daniel's self-control not to reach for her and pull her close as they walked. He wished he could hold her hand and as lovers visit the island together for the first time. But he could not behave the way his heart was wanting. He had to allow his head to control every part of his behaviour. He just wanted to spend time with Libby and hopefully heal the hurt he had inflicted, although he wasn't sure how he could do that.

It didn't take long for them to reach the bustling street market.

'Martinique is a French Caribbean island so the food

is French with a Caribbean twist,' Daniel told her as they made their way to a stall where he could see the food he loved and hoped that Libby would also enjoy.

'What exactly does that mean? I've not eaten much French food and I have no idea what Caribbean cuisine would be like.'

'The two most popular dishes are Boudin Creole and Boudin Blanc. I think you'd like the Boudin Blanc. The Creole is made from pork, pig's blood, onion and other ingredients...' Daniel paused as he noticed Libby's nose wrinkling up as he spoke. 'Just as I thought. Blanc it is.'

'What's in the second one?' she asked, her face not masking her concern.

'It's a white sausage made from pork, without the blood, and includes prawns, crabs, sea snail or fish.'

'That sounds much nicer.'

Daniel ordered two portions of the Boudin Blanc in his best French and then stepped back to Libby.

'I didn't know you spoke French.'

'I suppose there was no need to use it when...' He paused, feeling awkward about how to frame that time. He'd wanted to say *when I fell for you*, but he knew he couldn't tread that path.

'When we worked together,' Libby cut in, to his relief, and then continued, 'I guess not. San Francisco probably doesn't have a large French population.'

The brightly dressed woman behind the counter called Daniel's name and he stepped up and collected two plates of food and they made their way to a table for two nearby. The chairs didn't match and the table was faded by the sun but he noticed that Libby didn't seem taken aback by it. Daniel sat the plates down and then pulled out her chair for her. She immediately leaned down towards the plate in front of her.

'It smells delicious.'

'It is, believe me,' he said. 'I'll just get us some drinks. What would you like?'

'Water would be lovely, if it's okay to drink the water on the island.'

'I'll get bottled water for you.'

Daniel bought two bottles of water and returned to find Libby looking around her. The sun was dancing on the red waves of her hair and kissing her bare shoulders the way he remembered. While he loved being with Libby, there was an ache in his heart for what he could not have.

After their lunch Daniel suggested a walk by the shore.

'That sounds lovely,' Libby told him as they left their table and began walking down towards the beach.

Their conversation was light and mostly about the island.

'You seem to know a lot about Martinique. It's very beautiful and serene,' Libby said as she looked out across the creamy white sand to the still, blue water.

'For the most part it's a very pretty island…'

'For the most part?' She repeated his words with a questioning inflection as she slipped her sandals off and walked barefoot on the soft sand.

'Like most places in the world today, there is a risk at times. It wouldn't be advisable to wander around the largely empty back streets of Fort-de-France after dark. It's an area best left alone after the sun sets.'

Libby nodded and continued looking around. 'The names of the places and the food just roll off your tongue. How many times exactly have you visited?' she asked as they walked a little further.

'I can't be sure. I've lost count over the years, to be honest, but I do love it. I've worked on the cruise ships that call in at Martinique with tourists for the last few years.'

Libby looked at him then looked away back out to sea. 'I'm sure you've seen many exotic places.'

'Yes, I've travelled all over the world. I've been the ship's doctor on trips through the Caribbean, the Bahamas, Alaska and even all the way over to Australia and New Zealand.'

Daniel noticed Libby's mood suddenly shift and she fell silent, appearing to be deep in thought. She looked up towards the cloudless sky then walked away towards the shade of a huge palm tree.

'That must have been a culture shock from ER in a major hospital?' Libby said as she sat down, smoothing her dress out on the sand and crossing her ankles. 'I mean, one day you're in an inner-city emergency room and the next you're travelling the world on a yacht or cruise liner.'

One day in your bed and the next on a plane to the other side of the country, Daniel thought. He suspected the question was not just about the culture shock but more about the shock of his hasty departure.

'Libby,' he began as he sat down beside her, 'everything about the time with you in San Francisco was unexpected. You have to believe me, I didn't plan for any of it to happen and I wanted to explain everything to you but as I told you before, my life is complicated.'

'Perhaps we should leave that alone, Daniel,' she cut in without turning to face him. 'But I do want you to know that I would never have slept with you if I thought it was going to be a casual one-night stand and that you'd be gone before the sun came up. That's not who I am.'

'It wasn't just a casual one-night stand.'

Libby looked out across the water, saying nothing.

'It meant so much more to me than that,' he told her.

'Let's not go there, Daniel. I really don't want to spend the day talking about the past,' she said, turning to face him. 'That was not my intention. We need to make peace with whatever it was that happened between us.'

'Libby, believe me when I say that I'm truly sorry I caused you pain. I swear that if I could take it back I would.'

'Which part, sleeping with me or leaving in the middle of the night?'

'Leaving,' he told her honestly, not sure if she had heard him. 'Until my dying day I will never regret making love to you.'

CHAPTER TEN

LIBBY WOKE UP THE next day remembering Daniel's words but not knowing whether to believe them.

'Until my dying day I will never regret making love to you, Libby.'

Goddamn it, why did he have to say that?

None of it made sense to her and now he was making her life even more complicated. Whatever he said, it didn't change anything. His life was apparently *complicated.*

Well, life *was* complicated, for so many people, including her. Daniel didn't have the monopoly on a complicated life.

And he had no clue just how complicated hers had become because of him.

They had returned to the yacht without saying anything else to each other. She had to find the right time to tell Daniel about Billy and at the same time ensure she set ground rules. Billy deserved that. She wished her son had a daddy who would kiss him goodnight every evening and hug him every morning. While Daniel clearly couldn't be that man, she hoped he would find a way to be a part of Billy's life. Not be someone who might show up every few years or who Billy might bump into occasionally on an exotic island in the Caribbean.

There was a hurried knock on the door and Libby jumped out of bed, threw on her robe and rushed to open it.

Georgie was standing there with a look of panic on her face. 'I'm so sorry to bother you this early but Alexandra's throwing up again and I can't have her near the food, particularly not the engagement cake.'

'Come in,' Libby said, opening the door wider. 'Of course, it's the engagement party tonight. I'll help you in any way I can. I just need to check on Walter…'

'Daniel's already doing that,' Georgie cut in as she closed the door. 'He said he'll look after Walter, get him dressed and to the party on time. The other guests can make their own way there and the lovebirds flew in last night. They're staying at the resort already with the rest of the UK guests who also flew in late yesterday. The party is on the beach near the resort and the event planner arrived two days ago and has a local team already setting up before we dock.'

Libby curled her unruly bed hair into a makeshift bun and reached for a hair tie on the nearby table to keep it in place. 'It sounds like it's all organised, a bit like a military exercise. Let me know what you need and I'm there.'

Georgie gave her the biggest hug. 'I knew I could count on you.'

'Always.'

'Okay, we dock in San Lucia in a few hours so perhaps have your shower, get ready and pack a dress for the party…'

'I'm not going to the party,' Libby corrected her friend. 'I'm going to help you so I can wear shorts and a T-shirt because I'll be out of sight.'

'That's just it. I only need you to help me with some dessert preparation in the galley as I'm such an annoying perfectionist and I have to have someone I trust to manage quality control. Alexandra is as fussy as me but, as I said, unfortunately she's out of the picture, so you're my go-to. I'll also need you to help me put the cake together when we get to the party. It's baked and decorated but I have to assemble it on the beach.'

'We can't do that on the yacht?'

Georgie laughed. 'Can you imagine what could go wrong carrying a five-tier cake across the sand?'

'Five tiers? How many guests are coming?'

'I think close to a hundred and fifty. Some are sailing in and others have flown in. It's quite the social event. There are whispers that a couple of Hollywood A-listers will be there too.'

'Goodness, it sounds like all the more reason for me to stay in the background and look after the last-minute bits and pieces for you.'

Georgie appeared to ignore Libby's remark and, making her way to the closet, she opened the doors where there were only uniforms. 'Where are all your clothes?'

'In my suitcase,' Libby replied matter-of-factly.

'But you have a huge space in this stateroom. Why on earth are you not using it?'

'Because I wear my uniform most days and the rest of my clothes I can pull out of my suitcase and throw on.'

'Do you have *anything* glamorous in said suitcase?'

'Glamorous? But it's an island party. Wouldn't shorts or a cotton dress be okay?'

Georgie shook her head. 'No, they wouldn't. There will be the most fabulously dressed people at the party and you are absolutely not going to look like Orphan Annie. You, my friend, have to look equally fabulous.'

Libby suddenly thought Georgie sounded decidedly like Bradley.

'Where's your suitcase?' Georgie asked as she looked around the room.

Libby pointed to the second closet on the other side of the dressing table. 'It's in that one.'

Without wasting a second, Georgie sprang into action, crossed the room and found the suitcase lying inside the closet. She dragged it out onto the carpeted floor, opened it and began looking through the clothes like a woman on a mission. Within seconds she came upon the emerald-green silk dress. 'This,' she announced, climbing to her feet with the dress in her hands like a triumphant explorer with a golden chalice, 'is perfect. Just perfect. Do you have any shoes?'

'There are some gold strappy sandals in there somewhere but honestly, Georgie, please just let me help out in the kitchen and leave the party to the guests. I won't know anyone anyway.'

Georgie ignored Libby's pleas and continued to rummage around until she found the gold shoes in a plastic bag at the bottom of the suitcase. She unzipped the bag and held them up. 'Gorgeous. Not too high for navigating the walkways that are being erected on the sand leading to the floating pontoon.'

'A floating pontoon?'

'Yes, a floating pontoon with a Caribbean band. I'm not sure if you're aware that Walter is one of the wealthiest men in the UK, if not the world and he doesn't do things by halves—neither does his niece Sophia, I've heard. That's why I have to get this cake to be just perfect and you will be responsible for ensuring no one, and I mean no one, including those strange family members sharing the yacht with us, goes near the cake before the lovebirds cut it. I don't want anyone hovering too close and being tempted to touch it. That's why you must be dressed up and looking your gorgeous self so you can blend in and still be on cake duty.

'There was a strict direction from the event planner that they did not want anyone snapped in photos not looking the part. Alexandra even brought a lovely dress with her but I can't risk her throwing up at the party. Can you imagine Walter's reaction to that? Not to mention the guests having a fit and jumping into the water to get away. Now, that would make the front page of the tabloids!'

Libby could see Georgie's point and agreed to help her friend out. 'Okay, I'll pack my things into…actually, I don't know what to pack them in but I'll find something and then I'll jump in the shower, get dressed and head down to the galley to help you.'

'You're the best friend ever,' Georgie said, hugging Libby again and then making her way to the door. 'Don't rush. We don't dock for a few hours so there's plenty of time to do the prep work on the desserts. And you will be my pseudo apprentice sous chef.'

Libby thought that sounded outside her skill set but she could definitely manage some simple prep work in the galley and guard the cake, but that was her limit. She had only been cooking for Billy and herself for the last few years so her repertoire consisted of simple healthy food with lots of vitamins but no fancy plating. She hoped Georgie wasn't going to expect too much.

About thirty minutes later there was another knock on the door and Libby, still dressed in a towel and drying the mop of her hair, rushed to open it. 'I won't be long, Georgie—' she began, and then, lifting her head, realised it wasn't Georgie. It was Daniel standing there with a suit bag in his hand.

'Georgie asked me to drop this off to you for your dress. The stewards are all busy.'

Libby wanted to slam the door shut, partly from embarrassment and lingering anger but mainly from feelings she wished she didn't have for the man. But she knew that would be bad manners considering he had brought her the suit bag to transport her dress to the party. Words had temporarily escaped her but suddenly she realised that if she reached for the bag, there was a very real possibility she might lose her towel. Libby had no choice but to invite Daniel into her stateroom.

'Um…er…please come in. You can leave the bag over there,' she said, motioning towards the chair beside the desk. 'I'll just finish getting ready so please let yourself out.' With that, Libby crossed the room, her heart racing and her head spinning again, and stepped inside the bathroom. She slipped on the large guest bathrobe behind the door to make her feel less exposed as she stepped back out, determined to send him on his way. She had to be firm and set boundaries—for her own good because she was scared by her reaction to him.

'I appreciate you bringing the suit bag, but I don't want to hold you up,' she told him, trying to hide how self-conscious she felt. 'Georgie told me you're tending to Walter today while I'm helping her so it looks like we'll both be busy.'

'Yes, we will,' he began. 'But it wasn't just the bag that brought me here. We need to talk.'

'I think we did that yesterday and nothing really changed. Lunch was lovely and I enjoyed your company, but you have a complicated life. And that makes two of us,' she said, closing her robe even tighter around her otherwise naked body. She felt vulnerable to her own feelings with Daniel so close. 'Let's leave it at that, Daniel, for the moment. There's something I want to talk to you about but now is not the time.'

'I agree. Yesterday proved to me that we need to talk about what happened so we can have closure.'

'Fine, whatever you think, Daniel. Please just go. We

can talk about it another day. I have to help Georgie prepare for the party and I'm running late.'

Libby shut the bathroom door on Daniel as her fingers reached for the locket around her neck. Her heart was racing as she accepted that all hope for them was gone in an instant. He wanted closure. Not that it should have come as a surprise since he had not reached out since leaving but it did sound very final. She held the locket tightly in her clasped hands, praying that she was doing the right thing for Billy's sake by telling Daniel he was a father. Perhaps that closure would include walking away from the son he had never met but if so it would be best to know now.

Disappointed he had not been able to speak with Libby, Daniel headed back to the bridge to check the arrival time with the captain. He needed to have Walter ready for the party and had offered to assist him to dress. Daniel had lain awake until the early hours of the morning, thinking about Libby. She was so close and yet so far from his reach. He wanted to step back in time and do everything differently but that wasn't possible. He had allowed himself to fall for her when he'd had no right to do so. And no right to let Libby believe he was free.

Each moment in such close proximity to her had been torture to him. Knowing she was in the suite next to his, breathing softly as she'd slept, had made his body ache to hold her. He'd ached to tell her how much she meant to him and that his feelings would never change, no matter how far apart they were, but that was unfair. She needed to be free to move on.

He'd tossed and turned in the huge lonely bed as he'd thought back to how natural it would have felt to reach for her hand as they'd strolled around Martinique. How easily he could have kissed her while waiting to order their food and how much he'd wanted to pull her into his arms as they'd walked barefoot across the warm sand. She was everything he wanted and couldn't have.

It had been three a.m., the yacht being tossed about in unruly waves, and Daniel had been no closer to sleep than when he'd climbed into bed four hours before. The Caribbean seas could be temperamental but that had never bothered him before. He had become accustomed to rough water and strong winds. Sleep had never evaded him in bad weather the way it had for the last five days in the calmest of waters. Thoughts of Libby had been keeping him awake. Thoughts of what he had done and how much he continued to hurt her by keeping the truth from her.

Daniel had decided, before finally succumbing to sleep, that he could not live with himself knowing he had caused the sadness and confusion so evident in Libby's beautiful eyes. It would be unfair to let that continue when he had the power to change it. Or at least temper it a little. He would let Libby know enough about his life so that she understood his feelings were real and that the reason he had left was just as real. He would explain his role in Chezlovinka and the need for him to return to take over from his father.

Just spending a few days with Libby had made Daniel realise he could trust her to keep the secret of his father's illness and that it was imperative he return to his homeland—a principality so obscure she would know nothing about it. But at least she would know he did care for her and that what they had shared had been real. It just couldn't be for ever. Her life was in San Francisco, his was a life of serving his people on another continent but the time they had spent together would always be in his heart. She deserved to know that much.

He just had to find the perfect time to tell her before that time ran out.

CHAPTER ELEVEN

LIBBY DRESSED QUICKLY in shorts and a T-shirt and hung her party dress in the suit bag behind the door with her gold sandals, a small gold evening clutch and some long emerald costume jewellery earrings that Bradley had packed. All the while, Libby was thinking about Daniel and wishing that anyone but him had been the ship's doctor.

Her life could have remained simple but at least there were a few days until she told Daniel everything…and he told her whatever it was he had kept from her.

Then they would both, according to him, have closure. Libby wasn't so sure.

As she zipped up the suit bag, she thought that Georgie and Bradley should have their own make-over show called 'How to save the poor nurse with zero styling ability and a million things on her mind'.

Georgie was already under way with the desserts when Libby arrived in the galley.

'How many tarts have you baked?' Libby asked, astonished at the sight of a galley stacked to the ceiling with handmade individual pastry cases.

'Two hundred.'

'For one hundred and fifty guests?'

'You never know, they may like a second and Walter

doesn't want anyone missing out on his favourite dessert—Persian custard tartlet with mango, papaya and guava.'

'That sounds exotic and delicious. What can I do to help?'

'It would be wonderful if you could cut up the fruit the way I have done as an example,' Georgie said as she began to make the custard filling with more cream and eggs being taken from the cool room than Libby had seen in her entire local supermarket.

Libby spied the cut fruit resting on a chopping board. It looked perfectly presented. Libby knew her work was cut out for her to ensure her fruit looked as lovely. She reached for an apron and began to peel the first of dozens of mangoes. 'What about the savoury food? Please tell me you're—or *we're*—not preparing that as well?'

'Good God no.' Georgie laughed. 'The chefs in the resort are preparing that part of the menu.'

'That's a relief,' Libby said as she put the first peeled mango in the huge bowl in front of her and tried to push away thoughts of Daniel and the conversation they would have before the end of the cruise.

The two women and a galley hand spent the next few hours preparing the different elements of the fruit tarts and packing them away in the cool room for transportation to the resort when they docked. Libby had seen the engagement cake resting in the cool room and it was magnificent. Once upon a time she had dreamed of an engagement party and a wedding, both with stunning cakes and all the trimmings, but now she didn't believe in happily ever after.

The chief stewardess arrived to alert them that the yacht would be docking in fifteen minutes. This gave the team time to pack everything ready to be transported to the cool rooms at the resort. It would be like another military operation with everything cut and carefully placed in containers along with three enormous pots of custard that had been chilling.

'When will you do all of the work putting two hundred desserts together?'

'Once we dock, I'll follow the crew to the resort and once mains are served I will begin final preparation. I don't like to chill the pastry so I keep the other ingredients cold and construct and plate the dessert at the last minute. It's so much nicer to bite through room-temperature pastry into a chilled filling. It just adds that bespoke touch at the end of the meal, and Walter loves it done that way.'

'You're such a fussy pants, aren't you?' Libby joked with her friend as they busily gathered everything and stacked it all safely on a trolley for collection by crew members. 'But so is Walter. He loves the whole regalia of uniformed crew and it does look lovely, I must admit.'

'It's the little touches that make the difference,' Georgie replied with an expression that showed she was ready for battle. The engagement cake had to be transported too and Libby could see that was weighing on Georgie's mind. This was a huge event and a lot of the focus would be on the work undertaken by Georgie.

'It will be the best engagement party that San Lucia has ever seen,' Libby said.

'I have a feeling that tonight will absolutely be a night to remember for everyone!' Georgie responded with a wink.

Daniel assisted Walter to dress for the party. The proud uncle was wearing a tuxedo and bow-tie and requested Daniel do the same.

'The invitation says black tie, so I will truss up like a turkey for the next few hours only because I'll never hear the end of it from Sophia if I don't…and because that is what Contessa would expect of me.'

Daniel noticed Walter turn away abruptly as he spoke and he suspected it was to hide a tear or two.

'It will be a wonderful night, Walter. Everyone will have the best time and you're looking very suave,' Daniel told him. 'Sophia will be proud and Contessa will without doubt be watching all of the celebrations with you.'

'Hmm, do you think so?'

'Absolutely.'

'All right, enough of the mushy stuff,' Walter said gruffly, and he brushed non-existent lint from his jacket sleeves and crossed to the door of the largest suite on the yacht. 'Let's get this show on the road. I think it will be a night to remember.'

The party had begun and Libby stood in the perfect, balmy night air, looking around in amazement at the most beautiful setting she had ever seen. Fairy lights were strung across four giant pontoons only a few metres from shore. Two of the pontoons had tables and chairs, one had a dance floor and there was one for the band, and all four were joined by arched bridges that were also lit by fairy lights and covered in an array of brightly coloured Caribbean flowers, including hundreds of enormous coral-coloured hibiscus flowers. It was a sudden splash of colour and a stark contrast to the predominantly white decor.

The pontoons were secured by large pylons driven through the water and deep into the sand so they didn't shift with the movement of the tide that gently lapped beneath. It was postcard perfect and Libby was standing guard in front of the most stunning engagement cake that she thought had ever been made by anyone anywhere in the world. It was divine in every aspect and Libby was still amazed that it had made it onto the floating pontoon without dislodging one piece of the delicate filigree flowers that cascaded down the five layers like a waterfall of pastel shades of coral tipped with gold leaf over a naked Belgian chocolate torte. It was a piece of art and Libby had watched Walter look over more than once or twice with a smile born of pride in Georgie's work.

Georgie had also been correct in saying that stray hands might be tempted to touch the cake and the potential perpetrators were just as she had expected—the extended family that had sailed in with Walter. Libby had to be firm in reminding them to keep their fingers away from it.

Sophia and her fiancé, Etienne, arrived and the party was soon in full swing. Sophia wore a striking coral-coloured dress that skimmed her shoulders and fell to the floor and her blonde hair was styled in a high ponytail secured with a silk hibiscus flower encrusted with diamonds. Her fiancé was wearing a tuxedo, as were all of the men at the event. Libby thought Walter's niece looked absolutely beautiful and she told him as much when he passed by.

'Thank you. I told you she's the spitting image of her mother.' Then, stepping back and running his gaze over Libby, he added, 'And you look very beautiful yourself.'

'Why, thank you, Walter.'

'But I'm still not completely sold on her fiancé,' Walter leaned in and whispered in her ear. 'He's an actor apparently but I've been told I don't get a choice in the matter.'

'He seems lovely and the way he looks at her shows he is a man in love, and that thought should bring you comfort.'

Walter nodded. 'I guess when you pare everything back, finding true love is all that really matters in life.'

'Yes, it is.'

Walter reached for Libby's hands in a fatherly way. 'Tell me, my dear, are you married? I know you have a little boy but you never mentioned a husband neither do you wear a ring.'

'No, I'm single.'

'Not met the right man yet?' he asked with an impish wink as he sipped on his lime and soda.

'I thought I'd met him but he had other ideas. It's complicated.'

'All matters of the heart are complicated but, just between you and me, if you're looking for a potential boyfriend, I think Dr Daniel is more than a bit keen on you. I've seen the way he looks at you when no one's watching. It's all happened quite quickly since you only met on my yacht, but that level of emotion can't be feigned. It was love at first sight for Contessa and myself so I never judge the speed at which Cupid's arrow hits,' he said with a wink.

'Anyway, I'm not sure how you feel about him, but his face lights up when anyone mentions your name. I've not raised it with him because it's not my place, and he's a bit of a closed book. I thought I'd test my theory yesterday so I asked him to accompany you to Martinique and, just as I thought, he jumped at the chance. I'm quite intuitive when it comes to people. You know, Libby, he's not a bad looking rooster and you'd have medicine as a common interest. You could do worse…if you're in the market for a husband, I mean.'

'I'm not in the market,' she snapped quickly.

'Well, maybe not now, but keep our Dr Daniel in mind for the future. Who knows, he might grow on you. It took me a while to win my gorgeous wife but eventually she fell in love with me. Anyway, enough of my matchmaking, I'd best be off and mingle with all the other guests… And by the way, you're doing a wonderful job keeping Contessa's relatives away from the cake. Georgie told me you were on duty. Excellent job, keep it up.'

Libby felt her back stiffen, her heart begin to race and her thoughts become airborne swirling above her, unable to be reined in. She was having a fight-or-flight response to what Walter had told her before he'd rushed off to mingle with the guests. It was fortunate he had left her alone because she was both stunned and speechless.

Just when Libby thought their conversation about Daniel was finished, Walter came back. 'By the way, he's looking your way from over at the bar. You've certainly got him mesmerised…and a man mesmerised is a man in love.'

Libby instantly turned to see Daniel standing at the bar with a drink in his hand. His smile widened and as much as she didn't want to smile back, her lips seemed to take on a mind of their own and curled upwards. He looked so handsome in his tuxedo. But Libby had to admit that Daniel looked handsome in anything he wore…and even more handsome when he wore nothing.

Suddenly, she was so angry at herself for having romantic thoughts about Daniel. In fact, any thoughts about him. He was a closed book—even Walter agreed about that part and the rest of what he'd said was disturbing. She turned her attention back to the cake and away from him. Guarding the cake was her job for the night until Sophia and her fiancé cut it, and then she could return to the yacht and close the door on the world.

It wasn't long before the happy couple made their way to the cake. Mains had finished and the Persian tartlets arrived and were quickly devoured by all the guests, with a number asking for seconds, including Walter. Libby took a few small steps backwards as the couple posed for the photographs by the professional photographer and guests alike. She hadn't realised how close she was to the edge of the pontoon but that soon became evident. Her stomach sank with the realisation that her left heel was off the pontoon and hovering over the water. Suddenly, she lost her balance and with her arms flapping ungraciously she fell backwards into the water. There were gasps from the guests and Walter signalled the band to stop playing. Daniel sprinted from the bar where he had been standing most of the night and dived into the water in his tuxedo. While it wasn't overly deep or cold, it was eerily dark and the moment Libby felt Daniel's strong arms around her, she felt safe. Humiliated but safe.

'Are you all right?' he asked as he gently swept away the damp curls clinging to her face.

'I'm fine thank you…' she began, trying to catch her breath. 'But I can't believe you did that. Your tuxedo is drenched now and we both look silly. You should've let me look silly on my own.'

Daniel smiled. 'You don't look silly, you look beautiful. I've wanted to tell you just how beautiful you looked all night. Now you look wet and beautiful.'

Libby looked back at him in silence and realised just why she had fallen in love with him. And why it had been impossible to forget him.

'Is everything okay?' Walter called out from the edge of the pontoon, where he stood surrounded by an army of concerned guests, including Sophia and Etienne.

'We're fine, just felt like a late-night swim,' Daniel said as he took Libby's hand and led her from the water to shore. 'We might head back to the yacht…for some dry clothes.'

Libby didn't remember much about the walk back to the marina and the yacht. With Daniel's hand still holding hers, she felt like she was home even though she was four thousand miles from San Francisco. She couldn't pull her hand free despite how much she knew she should. She was tired of doing everything alone and she loved feeling protected. Perhaps she was making another mistake, she wasn't sure, but at that moment it felt right. Her heart felt light and she couldn't remember ever feeling this happy.

Finally, they reached the *Coral Contessa* and one of the stewards, who must have seen them making their way towards the yacht, greeted them with two large white towels.

'Late-night dip?'

'Something like that,' Daniel said as he wrapped one of the towels around Libby and pulled her close.

The steward departed as quietly as he had arrived, leaving them alone on the deck. Daniel looked at Libby and knew it was time to tell her everything. He cared deeply for her and he knew in his heart he could trust her. She had given him no reason not to trust her. He wanted her to know everything. He knew it wouldn't change the outcome but she deserved to know it all.

His family was going to have him for the rest of his life so he deserved to give Libby what she needed to move on with hers. Daniel looked into the blackness of the star-filled sky. The dark canvas above them was dotted with tiny sparkling beacons of hope and, while there were none in Daniel's mind, he knew he was doing the right thing.

'You have to stop saving me,' Libby said softly. 'You're starting to make a habit of it. First rescuing me from Maxwell and now Caribbean sharks.'

Daniel smiled. He would willingly rescue Libby for the rest of his life if he could. But he couldn't.

'I want to tell you something, Libby.' He turned to her and began, 'It's something I've wanted to tell you for a very long time and I tried to tell you this morning.'

'That you actually still care for me and that's why you jumped into the water to save me?'

'That…and something else…'

'If it's true that you still care for me then the something

else can wait until tomorrow,' she told him as she stood up and looked into his eyes. 'Let's not talk any more… let's just have tonight and talk about the rest tomorrow.'

Daniel was surprised but he didn't want to argue. He felt the same way. He hadn't made any promises and he never would. Libby knew that, and yet she wanted to spend the night with him and he wanted her more than words could say. What he needed to tell her could wait until the morning.

His arms reached for her like a man possessed, his mouth hovering inches from hers. 'Are you sure?' he asked, his voice low and husky.

Libby nodded and with her head tilted upwards she stood on tiptoe to meet his lips. Unable to wait a moment longer, his mouth met hers with a tenderness and urgency that she returned. His hands gently roamed the curves of her still-damp body as their kisses become more passionate. Her back arched against the hardness of his body and his lips began to trail kisses down her neck. Within moments, Daniel scooped her into his arms and she buried her head against his chest as he carried her to his suite and to the bed that would be theirs for the night.

CHAPTER TWELVE

DANIEL WOKE IN the morning with Libby lying naked in his arms and he wished with all of his heart he could wake that way for ever. Gently she stirred and, turning to face him, she smiled the most angelic smile he had ever seen.

'Good morning,' he whispered, and kissed her tenderly.

'Good morning, yourself,' she said, and kissed him back.

Daniel rolled onto his back and looked towards the ceiling while Libby rested her head on his chest. 'Would you like some breakfast?'

'No,' she murmured. 'I'm fine right here. I don't want to leave bed, it means we have to face reality and I'm not ready yet.'

Daniel turned his face away and looked into the distance. He had to agree, but he also had to tell Libby the truth.

'Nor me,' he told her with a melancholy tone to his voice. 'It couldn't be more perfect but there's something I do need to tell you. I tried to last night…'

'I know,' she said. 'I'm sorry I stopped you.'

'I'm very glad you did,' he said, kissing her softly. 'But now we really do need to talk. It's important that you know everything.'

'I have something I need to tell you too, Daniel,' Libby began.

Daniel smiled a bitter-sweet smile, knowing he would love to spend his life learning everything there was about Libby, but instead he had to tell her the harsh realities of his so they truly could have closure.

'To understand why I did what I did four years ago, you need to know about my background, where I came from—'

'I'm not going to judge you by where you grew up,' Libby interrupted him, and stroked his arm. 'I don't believe in that whole "born on the wrong side of the tracks" idea. I think you are what you make of yourself; it's not where you came from.'

Daniel couldn't help but smile again at what Libby had said. She obviously thought he came from a disadvantaged background and was trying to make him feel better. Her heart was huge and accepting and she didn't have a judgmental bone in her gorgeous body. He couldn't have loved her more and that made it all so very sad. Libby deserved better than a life with him.

'No, Libby, I didn't struggle growing up. In fact, it was quite the opposite. I grew up with great privilege.'

'I see,' she said with a curious look on her face. 'What sort of privilege? An elite school and a nanny?'

'Yes…and some.'

'And some?'

'My family is the royal family of a small principality in Europe.'

'You're a member of a royal family?' she asked in an incredulous tone. 'An actual royal family?'

'Yes, but it's not a huge country. I doubt you've heard of it. My Father is the Crown Prince of Chezlovinka.'

'Chezlovinka? The principality that borders Greece.'

'You've heard of it?'

'Yes, I've heard of it,' she replied with curiosity on her face as she propped herself up on the pillow and looked into his eyes. 'I studied it in my final year of college.'

'You studied Chezlovinka?'

'Yes, it's a beautiful Mediterranean country…' Libby paused, her eyes wide with shock and a little disbelief. 'But I never saw any images of you.'

'My mother was very protective and she kept me from the scrutiny of the media so I could have a relatively normal childhood and early adult life. She was the one who encouraged me to pursue medicine. I studied in London.'

Libby was silent for a moment. 'Oh, my God, that means you're a prince.'

'Yes,' he nodded. 'Prince Daniel Dimosa.'

'So that's what this is all about. Now it makes sense,' she said, pulling the covers up around her and moving away. Her forehead wrinkled with a frown as she stared at Daniel. 'You're a prince and I'm a commoner. I get it. You need a princess and I'm a long way from that.'

'No, Libby, you're not a long way from that. You're kind and intelligent and empathetic and everything a princess needs to be, but there's a dark side to the story, as there always is in fairy tales. My life isn't about palaces and joy. It will be filled with sacrifice and duty and I don't want you to have to sacrifice anything in life. I want you to have everything you want and I can't give you that.'

'I understand, Daniel. You're letting me down gently,' she said softly as she closed her eyes.

'No,' Daniel said, reaching for her and pulling her close again. 'That's not it at all, Libby. You're far too good for the life I could give you.'

'That's sweet, Daniel, but it's not true. You will have a wonderful life there.'

'It is true, Libby.'

'You don't have to say anything else, Daniel. I wouldn't fit in to your royal lifestyle and you can't fit back into mine. My life is simple. I'm just a nurse from San Francisco.'

'Don't say that,' he cut in firmly. 'You're the most amazing woman I've ever met and I would fly to the end of the earth for you, but a life with me is not one I would wish on anyone. Least of all you.'

'You're a wonderful man, Daniel. I understand that you wanted to protect me from the scrutiny of a life that you are very accustomed to but one that's a very long way from mine,' she said as she moved away a little and looked at the ceiling fan gently circling above them. 'You need a woman who comes from the same place in society, not a woman who may be a liability. You don't need a woman clumsy enough to fall off a pontoon and embarrass you.'

'Libby, you could never embarrass me. And I would dive off a million pontoons for you but it's not about you. It's about my family.'

Libby reached for the towel on the floor and slipped from the bed and into the bathroom and returned in a bathrobe.

'Your family? What do you mean?' she asked as she began to collect her clothes from the floor.

'It's my father. He's not well and I need to return to take over the country. I knew it would happen one day and that's why I didn't want to become involved with you. I'm sorry I lost the ability to see reason and walk away. I was selfish to want one night with you. It was unfair and I had no right, but a part of me was in denial.'

'I guess I understand. It's sort of how I behaved last night… I just wanted one night with you and to hell with the consequences.'

'And, believe me, I'm glad you did, but one night is all it can be. I'm sorry.'

'I know it was just one night. You said upfront you wanted closure between us and I'm a big girl. I went into last night knowing that. You have nothing to be sorry about.' Her voice was still barely more than a whisper and filled with sadness.

'I told you yesterday when we were on Martinique that my life was not my own to live. It's not mine to make my own choices—many have been made for me by virtue of being a member of the royal family and some by virtue of being my father's son.'

'Isn't that one and the same?'

'Not quite, but I must return home. My father's condition will never improve. There's no medication or treatment that can change the prognosis.'

'Is your father's illness terminal?' she asked as she sat on the edge of the bed just out of his reach.

'Yes, but we have no idea how long he has left. My father's is a cruel fate because he has early onset familial Alzheimer's disease. He's wasting away inside his own body.'

Daniel suddenly felt relieved saying it aloud to Libby. He hadn't told anyone before and now he had it was as if half the weight of the world had been lifted from his shoulders. Nothing had changed, and nor would it, but he felt more at peace than ever before. He had never expected to feel that way. He'd thought he would feel tortured and racked with guilt for betraying the family, but it was as if he had been betraying Libby for the longest time by not letting her know.

Libby's expression fell into one of all-consuming sadness. 'Oh, Daniel, that is so very sad. I'm so sorry. I can only imagine how hard it must be on you and your mother and everyone around them.'

'It's been difficult but my father has been able to manage until now. It's been an early onset but also a slow onset. But the symptoms have worsened over the last month so my mother sent for me. I will be heading there next week. I can't delay my return any longer.'

'The people of Chezlovinka must also be saddened by the news of your father's illness.'

'That's just it,' Daniel said with a resoluteness to his voice. 'They can't know. I have to step up and take control so my father can quietly abdicate and keep his dignity. It would cause doubt in their minds about him and about me and about the future of the country. There's been too much unrest in the world lately to bring more uncertainty to them now.'

'I understand you don't want to upset them with news of your father but why do you say the same about yourself? It's a disease afflicting your father, not you.'

'That's just it, Libby. It could affect me. My father's condition is caused by a mutation in a single gene and a single copy of the mutant gene inherited from either parent will cause the disease in the child. There is every chance I have inherited the mutated gene and my life in a few years may be just like his.'

'But you don't know that for sure.'

'No, but I also have no guarantee it won't and the people of Chezlovinka are not naive. If they learn the nature of my father's illness, they will quickly work out that it's genetic and one day in the future I too may be affected. They need stability and that's why I will head back to my country and begin grooming my successor so that in the event I do succumb to the disease, he can ascend to the throne.

'I have looked into altering the constitution to allow my adopted paternal cousin, Edward, who is studying law at Cambridge, to reign over the principality. Because he was adopted at birth by my father's brother and his wife, there would be no risk of the disease continuing in the family but he would carry on the Dimosa name.'

'And you have to keep this secret to yourself.'

'Not entirely. I can't. My father has deteriorated to a point now that he has a loyal team of nurses who have all agreed to assist and say nothing outside the palace walls.'

'But what about you? You must know how I feel about you. I can be there for you, if you'll let me.'

'You're the most wonderful woman, Libby, and you know how I feel about you too, but I can't ask you to do that. I can't ask you to give up the life you have and risk spending your life caring for me. I don't want that life for you. I don't want you to have to look after me the way my mother has looked after my father and will continue to nurse a man who soon may not even recognise her.'

'But you may not have the condition, Daniel. And if you did it wouldn't change the way I feel about you.'

'It would change everything to me,' he said. 'I can't allow you to risk being trapped with a man who is trapped inside himself.'

Daniel wanted to add *And one who didn't want children*. Libby would be the most wonderful mother and he wasn't prepared to risk having a child who might also carry the gene. Daniel was adamant he wouldn't be tested until he showed symptoms. No good would come of learning his fate early. He felt certain that he would not have been spared the same destiny as his father and he didn't want his mother to have the worry of her only child being trapped like her husband. If he didn't have the test, he didn't have to lie to his mother about the prognosis.

Libby wiped the tears that were spilling down her cheeks. 'If you truly care for me, why don't you let me make that decision?'

'I'm giving you the chance to find a man who comes without the risk of a disease that will rob you of a long and happy life. I don't want you to be a care-giver. You should be a man's wife and lover for ever without the risks that being with me would carry.'

'It wouldn't change my feelings for you whatever the result but if it's forcing you to make this decision to shut me out, why won't you get tested? You would know what the future held and then be able to make rational decisions based on fact.'

Daniel drew a deep breath. 'I will be tested one day but not now. I need to be strong for my family and my country. I need to focus on them and not me. If it was confirmed now that I had the gene for early onset familial Alzheimer's disease, then every day I would live with that knowledge and I would not be able to hide that from my mother. It would not be fair to add further to her worries. She shouldn't lie awake concerned about both of the men in her life.'

'I do understand, but perhaps not knowing is also a worry for your mother…'

'Maybe I'm being selfish, Libby, but if I learn the truth, and it's as I suspect it will be, then I may not have a single moment of peace. I will live my life in fear of how it will play out.'

'But, Daniel,' she told him, 'that's how you're living your life now.'

Daniel looked at Libby in silence, considering her words…and wondering if she was right.

Libby reached for her locket as Daniel climbed from the warmth of the bed in silence and, slipping on a bathrobe, stood by the window, looking out to sea.

'There's something I need to share with you,' she said

as she followed suit and climbed from the bed. Pulling the sheet around her, she crossed to him. 'Something that may change the way you feel about everything. About your future…and even about being tested.'

Daniel turned back to her and held her tightly to him. 'There's nothing in the world that can change my future, no matter how much I wish it to be true. And I will not consider testing until it's absolutely necessary. I need to think of my mother and my country, not myself, at this time. I'm sorry, Libby, but there's nothing you could say that would change how I feel or what lies ahead for me.'

'I disagree. I know there is.' She began stepping back and started to open the locket that hung around her neck, the one that held the picture of Daniel's son, *their* son, who looked so very much like his father.

Suddenly the yacht was tossed by a wave with such force it sent Libby back into his arms. 'Are you all right?'

'I… I think so,' she stammered. 'I've never felt anything like that. Are we going to be all right? That was a huge wave. The water hit the window and we're on the top deck.'

'We're back out in the Atlantic Ocean, and I'm guessing there must be bad weather ahead. Please sit down. Don't leave the cabin,' he began as he grabbed some casual trousers and a shirt from the closet and dressed quickly, looking outside to see ominous dark clouds had overtaken the sky. 'I'll head to the bridge and check with the captain to see what's happening. I'll also call in to see Walter on the way. I shouldn't be long.'

'Please don't forget I need to speak with you,' Libby said as she sat down, still draped in a sheet. 'It's important.'

'We'll talk, I promise, as soon as I get back.'

CHAPTER THIRTEEN

DANIEL CHECKED HIS watch as he closed the door to his cabin where he had left Libby. It was seven o'clock and the scheduled time to give Walter his daily early morning medical check. He made his way to the master suite at the end of the corridor, all the while being tossed from side to side with the motion of the yacht in the waves. His arms were outstretched and he kept his balance with his hands firmly against the corridor walls.

Suddenly, he realised it had been the first day he hadn't checked the time upon waking. It was his habit to check and plan the day but that morning, with Libby so close, knowing the time had been the last thing on his mind. But everything he had told her weighed heavily on him—not that she would betray his trust but that she wouldn't accept his resolute position on setting her free.

He had a swipe card to open the door in an emergency and when there was no answer to his knocking, he did just that, but quietly. Walter, he found, was still sleeping and it appeared that the waves tossing the *Coral Contessa* about hadn't broken his slumber. Daniel let him be. He had heard the guests rowdily return in the early hours and had assumed Walter would have been one of them, so he was not surprised that his patient was still happily asleep under his covers.

Daniel guessed that most of the other guests would be doing the same, as they had both eaten and drunk themselves merry in San Lucia.

The captain had made mention the night before that they would be heading off at six in the morning for two days at sea on their way back to Miami, so they would be able to sleep off the effects of the party for forty-eight hours if necessary, but Daniel was concerned that with the rough weather he might need to check on the nausea medication supplies after he visited the bridge. Then he would return to Libby so they could continue their talk. While it wouldn't change anything, he wanted to spend every last minute of this time with her before they parted for ever. It felt good that there were no secrets any more. It was how it should be.

Daniel arrived at the bridge and received an update on the weather from the captain. They were in the tail end of a storm that was heading south and further out to sea, but they were still feeling the effects of the waves.

'We're on the clean side of the storm,' Eric told him, dividing his concentration between the navigation panel and the undulating horizon ahead. 'Unless there's a sudden change, we'll have the shallower waves and lower winds this side. We're surrounded by thirteen thousand tons of yacht so there's not much risk to us.'

'So we shouldn't be concerned about the waves hitting the top deck a little while ago,' Daniel said, remembering the force that had thrown Libby off balance.

'Before the storm shifted southerly, we were slammed by towering walls of water but they've subsided now and the skies should clear up soon. The seas will still be a little rough for another two hours but nothing as severe as we've just encountered. After that, it should be smooth sailing back to Miami. However, I've asked the stewards to inform guests not to go out onto their balconies for the next few hours until I give the all clear.'

'Do you think they would actually consider doing that in this weather?'

'You'd be surprised,' Eric said, rolling his eyes but still looking ahead.

A steward appeared at that moment to inform Daniel that a guest had been thrown from his bed in the last big wave, lacerating his head. He was bleeding profusely and another thought she had a sprained ankle after falling on the way to the bathroom. Concerned there might be more injuries over the next two hours in the rough seas, exacerbated by the effects of the too much alcohol at the party, Daniel needed Libby to assist him. He knew she had her pager, so he sent her a message and asked her if she could change and head to the infirmary as soon as she could while he left the bridge and headed to get his medical bag and then go to the head injury patient first.

Within minutes, Daniel was at the first patient call and knocked on the cabin door. A clearly distraught woman opened it and invited Daniel inside. 'There's so much blood. I think he'll need stitches,' she told him as she took a sip from her wine glass.

Daniel could see the injured man sitting on the bed slightly slouched over. He appeared to be in his late sixties and was holding a white hand towel on the area over his left eye. There didn't appear to be too much blood on the makeshift bandage.

Daniel opened his medical bag, donned gloves and with some sterile swabs crossed to the man.

'I'm Daniel and I'm the ship's doctor. You've no doubt seen me around the ship. What's your name?'

The man looked him up and down. 'I'm Stan and I've

not seen you on the yacht but I saw you dive into the water last night. That was an odd thing to do at a party.'

'It was very peculiar, I agree,' the woman chimed in.

Daniel chose to ignore their comments. 'Let's look at your injury, Stan. If you could drop your hand, I'd like to take a look at the cut.'

Slowly the man released the pressure he was applying to the towel and Daniel leaned in, prepared to see a deep wound, but instead found there was a slight abrasion. A graze of sorts. There was little sign of bleeding.

Daniel wiped the area with the swab. 'Would you like me to cover the skin with a dressing?'

'You're not stitching the wound?' the woman asked with the glass still in her hand. 'I think he needs stitches or he might start bleeding again. He could bleed all over the cabin.'

'Yeah, you should just stitch it and be done with it,' Stan agreed.

'There's nothing that requires stitches…'

'Are you sure?' the woman asked as she swayed with the movement of the yacht, though that wasn't the only reason for her inability to stand upright and perhaps for Stan falling out of bed. Daniel could see a small pile of minibar-size bottles of liquor on the dresser. It appeared that the party had continued in their room. He applied an adhesive dressing to the clean area and reassured them that the injury was not as serious as they had first thought. He left their cabin and called instructions through to the stewards to keep an eye on the pair and perhaps not refill the minibar that day.

Daniel arrived at the infirmary to find Libby inside with another guest.

'When did the nausea begin?' he heard Libby ask the man as she drew closer.

'When the big wave hit, we both started throwing up.'

Daniel looked around but there was no one else there. 'You said *we.* Is there someone else suffering from nausea?'

'Yes, my wife, but she didn't want to come down. She decided to go out on the balcony and get some fresh air. She thought it might help.'

'In this weather? She's out on her balcony? Which room?'

'The first deck, cabin nine.'

Daniel raced to the phone and called for a steward to head to the room immediately and he did the same, leaving Libby to attend to the man's nausea. Daniel needed to check on the man's wife. There was still another two hours of bad weather and rough seas ahead and Daniel didn't want anyone on their balcony, particularly if they'd spent the night drinking. The steward was already at cabin door nine, already knocking when Daniel arrived.

There was no answer so Daniel used his swipe card to open the door and, just as he had feared, the woman was leaning over the railing and vomiting. He crossed the room with long purposeful steps and pulled her inside just as a large wave slammed the yacht. It was low on the side but still powerful and Daniel and the steward shook their heads in unison, both aware that it could have ended very differently if they hadn't arrived in time.

'Can you knock on every cabin door and remind guests again that they are not to step outside under any circumstances? And don't refill any minibars until we dock in Miami.'

Daniel then headed to see his next patient with the suspected sprained ankle. He arrived to find Stella lying on the bed with her foot elevated. He looked around the room and was relieved to see no sign of empty bottles. Stella was in her early forties and travelling with her mother, who had headed off to bring her back some breakfast. Daniel remembered seeing them both dancing at the party. On close examination of her ankle, foot and lower leg, he could see it had been damaged in the fall. There were a number of points of tenderness and pain when she attempted even the slightest movement.

'It appears to be just a sprain, Stella, so I'd advise you to rest and avoid movement that causes discomfort. I'll order up some more ice and I'd like you to pack that around your ankle for about twenty minutes and repeat that every two or three hours during the day.'

'Better today than yesterday. I would have missed the party and the dancing…and seeing you dive into the water in your tuxedo to save your wife.'

Daniel said nothing. Libby was not his wife and never would be. Spending the night with her in his arms had made the thought of saying goodbye and never seeing her beautiful face again overwhelming but he had the next two days with her and he intended to make the most of that time.

'Should I see my doctor when I get back to New York?' Stella asked.

'If the pain's not subsiding after a day or so I would definitely make an appointment with your GP. He may need to arrange an X-ray or MRI. However, I'll return later to check on you and I may compress your ankle with an elastic bandage to manage any swelling and we will have a better idea if you have sustained a fracture, but at this time I believe it's just sprained.'

After ordering an ice pack for Stella, Daniel headed back to check on Walter. He was his most important patient and had been left alone in the rough weather. He apologised when he arrived at Walter's suite.

'I'm fine,' Walter told him. 'I'm an old sea dog. I quite like it when the sea gets angry and tosses us about. It's invigorating. Lets you know you're alive.'

Daniel wasn't convinced but didn't argue the point. He just checked Walter's blood pressure and was happy it was still within normal range and the wound was continuing to heal. Perhaps the trip to the Caribbean was just what the doctor should have ordered.

'So how did the pair of you dry out after your midnight swim?' Walter asked as Daniel closed his medical bag and slipped off the latex gloves. 'Quite heroic of you to dive in like that.'

'It was only a few feet of water…'

'That's not the point. Women love to be saved and I'm sure Libby appreciated your chivalry,' he said, smiling. 'I did notice you two didn't come back to the party. I assume you took the time to become better acquainted.'

'We decided to stay on the yacht and talk,' Daniel said, running his lean fingers along his chin.

'I hope you stepped up and finally kissed her,' Walter said with one eyebrow slightly raised.

'I'm not telling you—'

'You don't come across a young lady as lovely as Libby more than once in your life,' Walter cut in. 'And I'll take your lack of a denial as a yes. It's about time because I could see you had feelings for her from the moment you met and she'd be perfect for you. I suspected it was a case of love at first sight…'

'Actually, Walter, we knew each other before this cruise.'

'You knew each other? Libby never said a thing to me and I thought I knew everything about her.'

'You know everything about her? You must have spoken to her for longer than I did.'

'Well, I know she lives close to her parents.'

'In San Francisco. It's where we met.'

'She's never travelled much before this trip.'

'I think she's a bit of a homebody,' Daniel said with a smile as he crossed to the door to return to the woman about whom they were speaking.

'And she's the single mother of a three-year-old little boy.'

Daniel stopped in mid-step and his expression was suddenly no longer light-hearted as he turned back to face Walter. 'Libby has a son?'

'Yes. Billy's his name and his birthday's only a few days after mine.'

'Which is when, exactly?'

'January tenth. He had his birthday a few days before we sailed. I told Libby he was an Easter bunny conception like me.'

Daniel felt the blood drain from his face. An Easter conception?

'How old did you say her son was?' Daniel asked.

'Three, she told me.'

Surely not. It couldn't be. His mind was racing. They had slept together on the night of the Easter gala almost four years ago.

'But don't worry, there's no husband. Libby told me she's single. When I asked about the father of her child, she told me it didn't work out. She mentioned something about it being *complicated*.'

Complicated? Daniel rushed from the room without saying another word. He had to find Libby. He had to know if she had been keeping something from him. He'd told her everything about his life and she hadn't told him about her son. Why would she hide that unless it was deliberate? Unless there was a chance the little boy was his son.

Daniel knew she would not be in his suite so he headed to hers. He needed to know why she had been hiding her son from him. He suspected he knew the answer already. He knocked on her door like a man needing the oxygen inside the room to breathe.

After a few moments Libby opened the door and he stepped inside and slammed it closed behind him.

'I know you have a son. I need to know, is he my child?'

Libby was stunned by Daniel's question and the look of fury in his eyes. She had wanted to tell Daniel herself and not have him learn about their son from someone else.

Her heart began to pound inside her chest. Her chin was quivering, tears building by the moment as she nodded her reply.

'Walter told you, didn't he?'

'How I know doesn't matter. I just want to know, is he mine?'

'Yes, Daniel, he's yours. You have a son.'

Suddenly, her reasons for keeping her secret from him for all these days escaped her. She was searching for something that made sense. Something she could tell Daniel that would justify her actions. It all seemed wrong now. Very wrong. She'd had every opportunity to tell him for the last week and she had chosen silence. She told herself that she had been looking for the right time but was there ever going to be a right time? Or had she been looking for a reason not to tell him?

'Was it as simple as just wanting to punish me?' he asked with both anger and sadness colouring his voice.

'No, it wasn't that. I wasn't punishing you—'

'I disagree, Libby. I think you very much wanted to punish me for leaving you the way I did after we slept together.'

'I was eight weeks pregnant when I found out.'

'Why didn't you contact me then?'

Libby looked at him with her guilt quickly morphing into something closer to resentment. 'By that time you had long gone. As we both know, you'd slipped away before the sun came up the morning after we made love.'

'You could have found me if you wanted to,' he told her without taking his gaze from her.

'How dare you! I tried to find your contact details through the hospital HR records but they were closed. And it was well above my pay grade to request that they be opened. I guess a *prince* can have anything he wants but a commoner like me has to play by the rules.'

Libby was furious at the accusations Daniel was throwing at her. He had no right to put all of the responsibility back on her when he was the one who'd left without saying a word. Or leaving a forwarding address.

'After I left without an explanation, you had every right to be angry,' he replied, softening his tone slightly but still sounding cold and distant. Then just as quickly it grew in harshness as he spoke. 'But keeping me from knowing about a child, Libby, for all these years, that's more than just punishing me. You've been punishing *our* son too.'

Libby felt an ache in her heart as those words slipped from his lips. It was true what had happened, although it had not been deliberate. But the way he had called Billy *our son* brought a sting of tears to her eyes. Now that she knew why he had left, she knew Daniel was not the cold, callous man she had created in her own mind over the years but she couldn't change the past. Nor could he. They had both kept secrets that could tear them apart for ever.

She knew she should have told him after they'd left the

engagement party. She should have told him before they'd made love. Or that morning. There were so many times when she should have told him.

'Billy did not deserve to be denied knowing I was his father or I denied knowing I had a son,' he said, pacing the room with long purposeful steps that led nowhere.

'I tried to tell you this morning…'

'So you were only going to tell me because we spent the night together? If that hadn't happened were you going to leave the yacht and not look back? Why didn't you tell me the first day you saw me? Or on Martinique, or any of the other times we were alone? Did you want to cement us, rekindle what we had before telling me?'

'No. I didn't want to rekindle anything with you.'

'I think you did. That's what all of this was about. You wanted to know if we would reunite before you told me about my son. I remember you saying, "Let's have the night and to hell with tomorrow." And clearly to hell with me knowing I had a son if it didn't work out between us.'

Libby was furious again with the way he was speaking to her, accusing her of only telling him when she'd got what she wanted. It wasn't true.

'I never said to hell with tomorrow…'

'Maybe not the words but it was what you meant when you said, "Let's have the night."'

'How can you twist my words like that?' she asked, holding back the tears that were building as the accusations poured from his mouth.

'I'm not twisting anything, Libby. I'm telling you how I see it.'

'I wasn't sure you would even care…'

'You had no right to make such a sweeping assumption about me, Libby. You don't know me.'

'That's right, Daniel. I don't really know you because

you kept your real life a secret from me. And perhaps there's more you've kept from me.'

Daniel stopped in his tracks and stared across the room at Libby. 'I laid my life bare for you this morning, Libby. Everything was out for you to know. Nothing was hidden because I trusted you and in return you couldn't even tell me that I have a three-year-old son. Now I know my trust was misguided.'

'I was trying to tell you about Billy this morning…'

Daniel shook his head. 'I guess you didn't try hard enough, did you?'

CHAPTER FOURTEEN

DANIEL STAYED IN his cabin with his thoughts for as long as possible. The rough seas had abated and the captain had given the all clear for the passengers to venture onto their balconies again. Daniel spoke to him about the minibars being left unstocked, at least overnight, and they agreed it would be in the best interests of the few somewhat intoxicated passengers in order to ensure they were safe and not likely to do anything silly. They could have a drink with dinner in the dining area but not in their cabins.

Daniel's mind kept wandering back to Libby and her son. Their son. He wanted to know more about the little boy. What he liked to do. What he looked like. His favourite colour and favourite food. Daniel wanted to know everything. But most of all he wanted to know he was safe. Safe from the genetic disease that ran through the Dimosa family. But that was Daniel's responsibility. Not Libby's or anyone else's.

That lay squarely with him. He knew what he had to do.

Daniel ate his lunch and dinner in his cabin. He didn't want to see anyone. He had so much to think about now. More than he could have ever imagined when he'd set sail on the *Coral Contessa*.

* * *

Libby remained in her cabin too. Georgie had called by but Libby had told her friend she was tired and would rather stay inside and they would catch up the next day.

Libby couldn't stop thinking about the angst written all over Daniel's face when he had confronted her. She knew that while she'd had her reasons for keeping Billy a secret initially, she should have told Daniel before he'd discovered it from someone else. She had been the judge and jury and found him guilty three years before and she hadn't lifted that life sentence.

She lay on her bed thinking and rethinking everything from the day they had met until that morning. The tears flowed for what might have been but what was most apparent to Libby was Daniel not asking for proof of his son's paternity. He trusted Libby's word that he was the father. While he was angry and hurt, he had never doubted her the way she had doubted him.

She knew in her heart that Daniel had done the wrong thing for the right reason. He had wanted to protect her from a life in a country far from home, potentially nursing him, and she had repaid that chivalrous behaviour by denying him knowledge of his son, even when she'd had the chance.

Libby didn't expect that Daniel would want to see her again and she wasn't sure how they could move forward but she knew somehow that they would work out visitation for Daniel with Billy. Of that she was certain. Libby knew her first instincts about Daniel had been right all those years ago. He was a good man and she would make sure his son got to know that too.

But there was something else she wanted to do. Daniel deserved to share in Billy's life up to that day. She opened her computer and began the task of piecing together her son's life from the first ultrasound to his third birthday. Every precious moment—Billy's first steps, his first words and everything else that she thought would bring Daniel closer to knowing his son.

It took all night but finally, at seven the next morning, it was complete and saved to a USB that she slipped into an envelope with her number in San Francisco if Daniel wanted to make a time to meet his son. She quietly left it by his door.

It was night time before they docked in Miami and there was a knock on Libby's cabin door. She was almost packed, just leaving out shorts and a top to wear the next day.

She was expecting Georgie as they had arranged for drinks on the deck. While it wasn't something she was keen to do, Libby knew she owed it to her friend.

'One minute,' she called out.

'I will wait as long as it takes,' the deep voice replied.

Libby froze. It was Daniel's voice, not Georgie's. Taking a deep breath to steady her nerves, she tentatively crossed to the door. It took a moment longer for her to open it.

'I didn't expect to see you,' she said honestly.

'I guessed as much as you left your telephone number in the envelope,' he told her without taking his eyes away from hers.

'I thought if you were ever in the area you might like to call and make a time to meet Billy.'

'I want much more than that,' he said. 'We need to talk. May I come inside?'

Libby nodded and stepped back from the door. Her worst nightmare was about to be realised. Daniel, she surmised, wanted to talk to her about more than visiting his son. There was the very real risk that he might want joint custody. And she knew he had the right to ask for that.

'Every child has the right to know they are loved unconditionally by their parents, no matter how their parents feel about each other,' he began, confirming her suspicions as he crossed to the balcony doors. They were open and the cool evening breeze was softly moving the sheer curtains. Slowly, he turned to face Libby. 'I want our son to know that I will love him until I take my last breath.'

'I know you will, and I'm so sorry, Daniel,' Libby began. 'I know I should have told you but I stupidly thought I was protecting Billy from being hurt. He's my world. He's my everything.'

'Protect him from me? How could you think I would hurt him?'

Libby collapsed back onto the bed, her tears beginning to flow. 'Because you hurt me and I didn't want him to love you the way I did and have you walk away. I couldn't let him know you and love you, only to have you disappear. I thought it would be better for Billy to never have you than to lose you because that is an unbearable pain.'

Daniel looked at Libby in silence and she felt her heart breaking all over again.

'I'm sorry, Daniel, I'm so sorry.'

'You said you loved me. Do you still feel that way? Do you still love me, Libby?' he asked, staring deeply into her eyes as if he was searching her very soul for the answer.

She nodded as she wiped the tears away with her hands.

Without saying another word or asking another question, Daniel crossed to her and gently pulled her up and into his arms.

'Then I should be the one apologising, Libby. I'm sorry I left you that night. I'm sorry I stayed away and I'm sorry I let you down.'

'I know now you had your reasons—'

'None that were good enough to put you through what I did. I've made some calls and I'm taking the genetic test. Not for myself, I'm taking it for Billy and for you. And I swear, if you give me a second chance, I will never disappear again.'

Libby raised her face to him. 'You want a second chance with me?'

'More than anything I have ever wanted.' Daniel's lips hovered very close to hers as he whispered, 'I love you, Libby. I have since the day I met you and I will never stop loving you, if you let me.'

EPILOGUE

LIBBY GAZED THROUGH the lead-light window at the picturesque palace grounds. The pastel-hued roses were in full bloom, the immaculately trimmed deep green hedges were framing the flower beds, white pebbles along the meandering pathways glistening in the early morning sun. And the sky above was azure and cloudless. It truly was fairy-tale-perfect, and so much more than Libby could have dreamed possible for her Easter wedding day.

The test results had arrived the day before and they were negative for Daniel. He had not inherited the mutated gene from his father, which meant that Billy was not at risk either, but Libby had agreed to marry Daniel without knowing. When he had proposed, on the condition they wait for the test results, she had insisted the wedding was going ahead no matter what the report said. She would love him for better or worse and she meant it. Daniel and Billy had bonded almost immediately upon meeting. They were like two peas in a pod. Billy was his father's son in more ways than just good looks and Libby knew they would never spend another day apart.

'Only a few more buttons and I'll be finished,' her mother said softly as she poked her head around her daughter's waist and smiled at her reflection in the antique oval mirror. 'You truly look like a princess. Just beautiful. You do know it's almost guaranteed your father will cry when he sees you.'

'I don't think so. Dad's not like that. I've never seen him cry,' Libby replied, with a hint of disbelief creasing her forehead.

'He cries on the inside. You can't see it but he cries and today there will be tears of happiness that might just overflow,' her mother said, returning to her original position as she looped closed the last few pearl buttons that secured the back of the stunning silk wedding dress. It had been made by a team of local seamstresses and had taken three weeks to complete. It was a tradition for all the royal brides of Chezlovinka.

The ornate ivory gown skimmed her shoulders, with a band of antique lace from Daniel's mother's wedding dress. The sleeves were of the same lace and they had been cut to a point that framed her manicured hands. The bodice was cinched at the waist with a low back and a long train.

The door suddenly burst open.

'Oh, my Lord, you look like a princess!' Bradley pronounced as he came rushing to the bride. He was dressed in an emerald-green-and-black-striped silk suit with lapel embellishments. Libby thought momentarily it was a little more Broadway than Chezlovinka but that was Bradley. She smiled as he grew closer, his arms outstretched. He was never understated. He was loud and fun and she wouldn't change a thing about him. He was her best friend and that would never change.

'That's just what I told her,' Libby's mother said, and she spun around with her hand outstretched not unlike a traffic controller. 'But absolutely no hugging, you two. You'll crush the dress.'

Bradley stopped in mid-step. 'Of course. I wouldn't dream of crushing that divine creation.'

Libby laughed. 'A little hug would be fine.'

The two embraced cautiously before Bradley stepped back. 'Honestly, Libby, you look like a china doll, a red-haired china-doll bride. You couldn't look more beautiful. Or more perfect.'

'That's so sweet of you.'

'Honey, it's the truth and I hope Daniel knows just how lucky he is—'

'He does,' a little voice interrupted.

All three turned to see Billy standing in the doorway. 'Daddy did my bow-tie this morning and he told me that he is the luckiest man in the world because he's got Mommy and me for ever and ever.'

Libby felt her eyes begin to fill with tears.

'Oh, no, you don't,' Bradley cut in. 'You can't cry, you'll ruin your make-up. No smudgy bride on my watch.'

Libby laughed and Bradley pulled his crisp handkerchief from his top pocket and gently mopped the tears at risk of staining her cheeks.

'What would I do without you?'

'I have no clue and Tom and I will be visiting this quaint part of the world often so you won't have to find out,' he said with a smile. 'Plus, you have to come back to visit us at least twice a year. We can't have Billy losing his accent. I just won't allow him to grow up with some posh European way of talking that I can't understand.'

The door opened and an immaculately dressed woman with an earpiece entered. She smiled but it was a somewhat strained smile and her general demeanour, behind her chestnut chignon, midnight-blue suit and nude stilettos, was that of a woman on a mission.

'Bradley, this is our wedding planner, Simone,' Libby said.

'Lovely to meet you,' Bradley replied, after giving her

the once-over and approving of her outfit. 'I'm guessing it's time to get this show on the road.'

'The groom and the wedding party are in place, along with the rest of the royal family and international guests,' Simone announced with a heavy Western European accent. 'You are only a five-minute carriage ride to the church but you need to leave now.'

'This is it, and the last time I can call you Libby McDonald,' Bradley said, as he carefully lowered the antique lace veil. 'Next time we meet, you will be Your Royal Highness.'

Libby leaned in as the veil dropped over her face. 'You will always call me Libby, that won't change. Not ever.'

Moments later, after the short trip in the open carriage to the two-hundred-year-old church, Libby stepped down onto the red carpet and smiled at the crowd as the bridesmaids hurriedly smoothed her dress and straightened her veil and ten-foot train.

'You look stunning, Libby. You're a true princess,' Georgie whispered, then took her position as Maid of Honour.

There were gasps of joy and waves from the people who had gathered there, many of whom had been waiting since dawn to see their beautiful new princess. She waved and smiled back at them with genuine joy filling her heart. She should have been overwhelmed but knowing that Daniel would soon be her husband and finally they would be the family she had always wanted lessened her nerves.

Despite Simone's exemplary planning, protocol had been thrown to the wind when it came to Billy. He had travelled in the carriage with Libby and his grandfather but once they'd come to a stop he had jumped down, patted the large grey horse nearest to him then raced inside the church on his own. It had been planned that one of the groomsmen would walk Billy to Daniel, who was waiting at the altar, but Billy was far too excited to see his father.

Georgie and the other bridesmaids and flower girls did follow protocol and walked on cue to the church doors and as the organ music began they walked in step inside and out of Libby's view.

'Well, it looks like there's a whole lot of pretty important people who've travelled a long way to see you,' Libby's father said as he patted her hand. 'We'd better not keep them waiting. Not sure if they can still behead for such a thing in this part of the world, but let's not find out.'

Libby giggled from behind the veil and, taking her father's arm, walked inside the church. Organ music filled the church, the beautifully dressed guests were seated in pews decorated with white roses and lily of the valley, but Libby saw none of it. All she could see was the most handsome man in the world turn to see her. Her soul mate, the love of her life, and the father of Billy and their future children was waiting at the altar, dressed in his red military attire and a smile that spoke to her heart. It told her everything she needed to know. Prince Daniel Dimosa was the man of her dreams and she was about to become his wife.

As she took her first step down the aisle, she read his lips as he said, 'I love you, Libby.'

Libby's heart was bursting with happiness. She had found her prince and her happily ever after.

* * * * *

MILLS & BOON

Coming next month

RESCUING THE PARAMEDIC'S HEART
Emily Forbes

The lifeguard buggy pulled to a stop at the bottom of the metal stairs that led from the sand to the tower entrance and Poppy's jaw dropped as a lifeguard jumped out. Tall and muscular, tanned and fit.

Was that Ryder?

She managed to close her mouth as she watched him help his patient out of the buggy and up the stairs.

She hung back, out of the way, as Ryder got the man into the tower and onto the treatment plinth. Jet went to assist, instructing Bluey to keep an eye on the beach. Poppy stayed near the desk by the windows. The lifeguards had a job to do and she didn't want to be a nuisance but staying out of the way also gave her a chance to check Ryder out unobserved. She knew he hadn't noticed her, he was too focussed on his patient.

The last time she'd seen him there had been a hint of the man he would become, of the man waiting to emerge, but he'd still been a gangly teenager. He'd been tall but he'd yet to have a fast growth spurt or develop the muscle definition that would come with adulthood. But all traces of adolescence had disappeared now. Now there was no hiding the man. And no ignoring the feeling of warmth that was spreading through her belly and into her groin. Poppy leaned on the desk, taking the weight off her suddenly shaky legs.

Fortunately Ryder had his back to her and wouldn't be aware of her reaction but she was very aware of him.

He'd grown even taller and he'd definitely filled out. He'd developed muscles where he hadn't had them before. He wore only a pair of black boardshorts with 'Lifeguard' emblazoned across his hips and she had plenty of opportunity to admire the view of sculpted muscles and smooth, tanned skin. His shoulders were broad, his biceps bulging, his waist narrow. He looked fit. He looked healthy. He looked magnificent.

She ran her gaze up the length of his spine and up his neck. She could see where the knobs of his vertebrae disappeared into his hair. He'd always had amazing hair, dark blond and thick, and at almost twenty-nine years of age it seemed he'd lost none of it.

Her gaze traced the line of his jaw. It was strong and square. He looked good, even better than she remembered, and she felt another rush of blood to her cheeks as her heart skittered in her chest.

Her hands gripped the edge of the desk as she observed him, keeping her fixed in place, and she wondered at the involuntary response. Was she stopping herself from crossing the room? While her rational mind might tell her that Ryder's unexpected appearance was of no consequence, it seemed her body had other ideas. Her palms were clammy and her mouth was dry and she suddenly felt like the sixteen-year-old schoolgirl she'd been when she'd last seen him.

When she had kissed him.

And he had kissed her back.

She knew from talking to her girlfriends that first kisses often weren't anywhere near as fabulous as they'd dreamed about but the kiss she and Ryder had shared had been everything she'd hoped for and more. It had been the biggest moment of her young life. It had changed her life.

She'd fallen in love.

First love.

She had only been a teenager but that hadn't made it any less real, any less all-encompassing, any less all-consuming.

And it hadn't made it any less painful when he'd walked out of her life.